THE DARKNESS GREETED HER

THE DARKNESS GREETED HER

CHRISTINA FERKO

sourcebooks
fire

Copyright © 2026 by Christina Ferko, LLC
Cover and internal design © 2026 by Sourcebooks
Cover design by Lisa Marie Pompilio
Cover images © eva_mask/Shutterstock, JuliarStudio/Getty Images, Hania
Najla/Shutterstock, Ihnatovich Maryia/Shutterstock, Lisla/Shutterstock
Internal design by Tara Jaggers/Sourcebooks

Published by Sourcebooks Fire, an imprint of Sourcebooks
1935 Brookdale RD, Naperville, IL 60563–2773
(630) 961-3900
sourcebooks.com

Cataloging-in-Publication Data is on file with the Library of Congress.

Printed and bound in Canada.
MBP 10 9 8 7 6 5 4 3 2 1

For Greg,
the guardian of my solitude.
I love you forever.

A NOTE TO THE READER

This novel contains themes and/or mentions of Harm OCD and intrusive thoughts of violence, off-page suicide, alcoholism and domestic abuse, child abduction, home intrusion, and death (including cancer-related death).

If you feel these subjects are not for you, please consider choosing a different book.

ONE

There's a difference between dead and dead enough. My father is dead—but he's not dead enough. He's not dead *and* gone. He still finds a way to cling to me like tar, sticky and suffocating.

And I hate him even more for it.

I pick up my sketchbook, shoving away any thoughts of my father, and scan my list of everything I'll need this summer: shirts and bras, shorts and underwear and socks, toiletries. But no phone.

The last one is emphasized on my list with a little sketch of a sad-faced phone, frowning with tears trailing down the graphite-drawn screen. Thick, heavy lines mark an *X* over it. Not that I could forget.

No cell for the entire summer. Not at Camp Whitewood— well, not a *camp*, exactly, even if that's what they named it. More like a therapy program and wellness retreat wrapped up in the aesthetic of a normal summer spent in the mountains. At least, that's how the brochure made it look. I suppose calling it a camp does feel more welcoming than saying I'm signing my summer away to an intensive therapy center.

And while I'm not excited to give up my phone for the next few months, I need this. I chose it.

Besides, both Mom and my therapist think it'll be good for me too. And it's not like I have any friends left to text with anyway.

The sound of a creaking floorboard slips under my bedroom door. Mom's footsteps tap lightly in the hallway before pausing.

Hovering. That's what she's doing. What she's *been* doing for the last four months since my father died. Since his voice started whispering thoughts in my ear and telling me what to do.

To be like him.

Mom's footsteps scrape against the floor again until the sound crawls under my skin. I get it. She's worried. She's watched me get worse and worse these last few months while doing everything she could to help. She's worked long hours to have enough money to afford this camp, and she only watches me to make sure I'm all right because she cares—and also because of all the times she couldn't protect me from my father.

It's a mix of love and guilt that keeps her pacing outside my door. A combination that I understand too well. I love her too, but when she does this, I can't help the shame that crowds my chest. She'll never truly be free of my father when his voice is still in my head.

Sitting on my bed is my stuffed bunny, with faded purple fur and a yellow heart on its chest, which Mom made when I was a baby. I pick it up, gripping it to my own chest, heart-to-heart, like when I was little.

I repeat the mantra my therapist gave me: *My father can't hurt me anymore. My intrusive thoughts don't control me.*

But the words don't help, and Bunny doesn't comfort me the same anymore. I almost drop the stuffie onto my pillows but hesitate. My suitcase sits open on my mattress, overflowing with clothes and toiletries. There's not much room left, and I'm too old for toys, but I gently tuck Bunny into it anyway.

I scan my room for anything else I might need while waiting for Mom to finally knock on the door or move on. My gaze trails over the mural she let me paint on the wall two months ago. *After* we learned how to spackle the holes my father left behind. The paints bleed and blend into each other until it looks as if a giant paintbrush dragged strokes of abstract watercolor over the ivory walls, rosy pink and the palest buttercream yellow, the first hint of an indigo dusk and the softest lilac. Colors to brighten up the small space. To draw the eyes away from the splintered window-pane held together with tape. To distract from the stains that never fully scrubbed out of the tan carpet, spilled whiskey and speckles of blood.

Little by little, Mom and I were improving things. Fixing the house when fixing ourselves was too hard.

I slip my pencil out from behind my ear and scratch another check mark on the list. The tip of my pencil is rounded and dull, nearly worn down to the wood and leaving clumsy lines.

Sharpen it, a voice whispers in my head. *Until it can pierce flesh.*

I shudder. The voice is mine and not mine, the timbre and tone distorted. It is a melding of mine and my father's. A nightmare that won't leave me alone.

Mom finally knocks on bedroom door. "Penny?" she calls out.

Stab her. Watch her blood stain the wood.

My grip tightens on the pencil.

There are more in the desk. Sharp and dangerous.

Are there sharpened pencils in my drawer? My heart thumps heavily against my ribs. My face flushes with warmth. But Mom dulled them for me, scratching senseless lines on paper until the tips were blunted and less tempting to use for violence.

I take a deep breath, willing my heart to calm. There's nothing in my desk that I could turn into a weapon like that voice wants me to believe.

"Penny?" Mom says again. "Can I come in?"

Use it! Stab her! the voice screams as Mom twists the doorknob and peeks inside.

No, I tell the voice that is somehow both mine and my father's. *No.*

I drop my pencil, and it bounces silently against the carpet.

It would be so easy, it replies, softer. Gentler. Coaxingly.

And that's what scares me. What makes me want to run away

to the mountains for the entire summer. I thought his death would free me, but I'm still trapped by my father.

I can't keep going like this. Having Mom hide away any possible weapons: steak knives and scissors, candles and their lighters, the gardening spade and shears she bought to fix up the overgrown flower beds. Even the metal spatula from my own paint supplies.

Pick up the pencil. Here she comes, that voice says as Mom steps into the room, a hesitant smile on her wrinkle-worn face. She looks as if she's aged years these last few months, but the lines creasing her skin are so much prettier than the bruises she used to wear.

I toss my sketchbook into the open suitcase and shove my shaking hands into the pockets of my shorts. Mom comes closer, holding something half-hidden in one hand. I drop onto my bed and use the heel of my foot to kick the pencil under the bed frame so I can't hurt her with it like that voice wants me to.

"Are you almost ready?" Mom glances at the clock on my desk. "We should leave soon."

"Yeah." I stand and flip the top of the suitcase over. I grab the zipper, but Mom stops me.

"Wait, I have something for you." She bites her lower lip, worrying it between her teeth. Her free hand brushes the flyaways of her pin-straight hair, the brown now tinged with gray. "I know how you don't like the smell of that hair removal cream, plus it takes a while to work. And I don't know how long they'll give you for showers, so…" Her forehead creases. "I found these and thought they might help."

Mom holds out a plastic package. Inside are three shaving razors.

Shiny and sharp, the voice starts. *Perfect for slicing. Let it bleed and bleed and bleed.*

I step back and almost fall onto the bed. Fear fills every breath I take. I'll hurt her. "I can't," I say, and whether I'm talking to Mom or the voice, I'm not sure. Maybe both.

"No, they're safe. They're special." Mom points to the packaging, but the words printed on it are a blur. "They have these locks on the blades, and Whitewood said they were an approved item. They're designed to prevent self-harming, but I thought…I thought maybe they'd be good for you too," she finishes weakly when my breathing doesn't even out.

"Get them away." The backs of my legs slide against my bed as I move. Terror at what I could do with those razors—safe or not—makes my limbs shake. Images of blood and broken skin flash in my mind. My therapist says these intrusive thoughts are a result of my Harm OCD. She doesn't believe I'd do the terrible things it whispers. But with the way they've become more frequent—louder and more violent too—it's getting harder to believe her.

Which is why I need Whitewood and the programs they offer.

Mom already pulled me out of school halfway through the year when things started getting bad. If I can't get this *voice*—these fears and urges—under control, then I won't be able to go back for my senior year. Worse, I won't be able to attend art school if I can't even hold a sharpened pencil. Whitewood is my last hope.

"Breathe, baby," Mom says. She tosses the package of razors on the floor behind her—away from me—and takes my hands in hers, cradling them in front of us. "Do what Mrs. Ashley said when you're feeling like this." She nods at our joined hands before letting go.

I listen to Mom, remembering what my therapist taught me, and take a deep breath first. "One," I say and tap my thumbs to my pinkie fingers. "Two." Another tap to the ring fingers. "Three." I move down the line, touching my thumbs to each finger and counting. "Four."

But my attention snags on the razors thrown to the floor.

Take them. I shake my head as the voice dips lower, sounding even more like my father. *Use them.*

I touch my thumbs to my fingers, counting in my head this time. *Tap, tap, tap, tap. One, two, three, four.* I do it again and again, rushing through it when I should stay calm. *Slow and steady,* Mrs. Ashley would say, but my father's voice is still there, and I can't tear my gaze from those razors.

Watch her bleed, it says, and each word fills me with horror. With disgust at myself.

I take another deep breath, but it shudders. The constant worry that one day this voice will be stronger than me makes my hands shake—until I can't even do my tapping anymore. It doesn't help enough anyway.

"I'm sorry," I tell Mom, guilt churning within my chest. I wish I could be a better daughter for her, but it doesn't seem possible. I stumble away, as if I can outrun the voice that's within me.

Mom reaches out, but I slip by her, my feet stumbling as I race past the abandoned razors. I don't want to hurt her—or anyone else—like *he* did.

The bedroom door slams behind me, and I flinch. I *can't* become him. I'll throw myself into a hospital's white padded room if Camp Whitewood doesn't help.

But I am my father's daughter—and maybe that's something no one can fix.

TWO

The bus taking me to Whitewood pulls off the asphalt road and bumps along a rough dirt path. After a tear-filled hug goodbye from Mom and half a day on a charter bus, I was picked up, with seven other girls, by one of the staff. And now, after another two-hour drive on a repurposed school bus, we're finally close to camp. They weren't kidding with the whole remote location; easier to *disconnect from distractions*, the brochure said.

The air conditioner hums down the aisle and pushes the scent of gasoline and sweet coolant through the air in a nauseating combination. Besides that and the engine's rumbling, the bus is relatively quiet. There are only a handful of girls, so few of us that no one has to share a seat, but two girls moved to sit together during the drive anyway. Their soft conversation filled the last hour but has been too quiet to catch from where I sit in the back.

The rest of us have mostly stayed to ourselves, except for a few quick hellos when we accidentally made eye contact. We'll be together all summer; plenty of time to meet. But for now, I need this solitude. The voice in my head has been whispering to me all morning, and I don't want to tempt it—to give in. I sit alone instead and do my finger tapping when those thoughts become too much.

It isn't long before Whitewood appears before us like a mirage. The forest of silver birch trees surrounding our bus splits apart to show off the camp in all its glory. A carved wooden sign with the name arches over the entrance as we drive under it. Little triangle cabins dot the space ahead, quaint and cute with colorfully painted numbers and doors. In the distance a blue lake glitters under the summer sun.

The bus screeches to a stop, and we all jerk forward in our seats before the door hisses open and a woman climbs inside, clipboard in hand. She wears a long, flowing tie-dyed skirt with a pale blue shirt, knotted at her hip. Wire-framed glasses slip down her nose while frizzy brown curls fight to cover her face. She looks like she'd be more at home in an art class than secluded out in the middle of the northern Appalachian wilderness.

"Hello, girls," she says, smiling brightly. "I'm Ms. Peterson, and I'll be one of your camp counselors and therapists for the summer. I'm also in charge of all things admin, so you might remember my name from the intake papers and emails. Aaaaand," she says, drawing the word out with a flourish of her clipboard, "I lead the art and yoga sessions that we'll be doing too!" She adds a little shimmy, and I can't help but be half-horrified and half-amused at her excitement.

A round of mumbled hellos passes through our group. Ms. Peterson smiles wider before nodding toward the bus driver, a blond girl who can't be more than a few years older than me, maybe nineteen or twenty.

Ms. Peterson introduces her. "This is Delaney. She's our resident kitchen staff."

"And bus driver and maintenance person and canoe instructor," Delaney adds. "Oh, and don't forget, I build the best bonfires."

"We appreciate everything you do, Delaney," Ms. Peterson says. She points out of the open bus door. "And waiting there is our last staff member, Ms. Evans. She's our other counselor and lead therapist. Ms. Evans is the one who went through your applications and picked each of you lovely girls to be here with us."

Ms. Evans stands on a grassy lawn next to the dirt road we're parked on and waves. Her brown hair is wrapped up in a messy bun, and she wears cargo shorts and hiking boots and actually looks like she belongs in a cabin in the mountains.

"Now," Ms. Peterson says, tapping a pen on her clipboard, "let's make sure everyone is here."

I glance around. There are only eight of us on the bus. Five A-frame cabins sit outside, and across from them is a larger building that the brochure showed has a dining area and kitchen, admin offices, and rooms for various therapy sessions. Past the campgrounds is a large lake and wooden pier. And surrounding it all are gray birch trees that spread out as far as I can see, their canopy of leaves a vivid green this time of year.

All in all, Camp Whitewood is small—*specialized, intimate, and focused on individual needs* is how the website described it, but *tiny* is more accurate.

As Ms. Peterson calls out names, each girl grabs her backpack or purse and files out of the bus.

"Penelope Davidson?"

"Penny," I correct and raise my hand.

If I'm spending my entire summer here, where I'll be expected to talk about my father and try to get past…everything, then I can't do it while being called that name—the one *he* spoke with disgust curling around the syllables.

Penelope died with my father. And without him, without that name, I can be someone new.

I can be *just* Penny.

I hope.

"Penny, then," Ms. Peterson says as I swing my backpack onto my shoulder before following the girl in front of me, her red curls bouncing as she walks ahead of me.

Push her, that voice whispers within my head. The words hiss and sear. *Watch her skin split open. Watch her bleed.*

Fear crawls up my throat, and I swallow hard. I close my eyes.

My fingers start tapping as I silently count—until images flash across my mind and stop me. *Hands thrown out. Pushing? Grabbing? A shout and a cry. A crash.*

As quickly as they came, the images—intrusive thoughts?— fade into blackness like wisps of smoke. When I open my eyes, I find my free hand hovering in the air where the redheaded girl was. I quickly drop it.

I take a deep breath, let the air out of my lungs slowly, and relax my hands. *Fear is a liar*, I repeat, another mantra my therapist taught me. *I'm in control of my thoughts. They're not in control of me.*

Except, why did those images feel so different from the voice I normally hear?

"Is everything all right?" Ms. Peterson waits at the front of the bus and stares at where I've stopped in the aisle.

"Yeah, of course," I say, embarrassment warming my cheeks. A couple girls shuffle their feet behind me. "Sorry, I'm going."

I rush down the aisle but pause when Ms. Peterson smiles and says, "If you need anything, you can come to me or Ms. Evans anytime."

A mixture of relief and anxiety swarms in my chest. Ms. Peterson really seems to care. Maybe she can actually help.

When the last girl climbs off the bus, Delaney grabs our luggage from the back and stacks it in a row. She's sweating in seconds from the heat but waves me off when I offer to help. I hesitate, feeling like I should still grab a bag, but end up stepping back, worried I'd only be in the way.

A light breeze washes over our group, and I relish the cool air as it brings the scent of lake water and fresh earth. The trees sway and creak in the breeze, their leaves rustling. The buzzing cicadas and a splash from the lake reminds me just how far away from civilization we are.

"Hello, ladies," Ms. Evans says, pulling my attention back to the group, "and welcome to Whitewood. We're so glad to have you here with us. If you need anything, please let me, Ms. Peterson, or Delaney know, and we'll be happy to help."

"Is…is this it?" one girl asks. She brushes her long hair off her shoulder and the strands are so silky they look like an ebony water-fall. She wears a fitted pink T-shirt and wide jeans that hug the generous curves of her hips. When she catches me looking at her, she smiles softly.

Heat flushes my cheeks, and I turn my attention back to Ms. Evans like I should have been doing anyway.

"What do you mean?" Ms. Evans asks the girl.

"I mean," she says before glancing around at the rest of us, "is it just us? This is everyone?"

"Yes," Ms. Evans says. "At Whitewood, our focus is on individual needs. And with only Ms. Peterson and me to lead the different sessions, we can only take on a few—"

"How can you afford to run this whole place with only eight… patients?" another girl interrupts.

"As a wellness camp, we prefer saying *campers*, not *patients*."

Ms. Evans gives a small, if not awkward, laugh. "But thankfully we have sponsors who really believe in the work we're doing here. You don't want to be bored with how running this place works, though. So"—she claps her hands—"let me officially welcome you, and let's get our cabin assignments. We'll have a bit of time to rest and unpack. Dinner will be served at six, and after we'll have a 'Welcome to Whitewood' meeting for all of the information and schedules you'll need to know."

She motions for Ms. Peterson, who steps forward and flips the page on her clipboard.

Ms. Peterson calls out names and pairs girls off, giving them their cabin numbers, as Ms. Evans splits from our group and heads into the main building.

"Cabin three for Emma and Penel—Penny," she corrects, and something warm and happy spreads within my chest. That easily, that quickly, Ms. Peterson listened. It's such a small thing, but to me…it's everything.

"Hey, roomie!" a girl calls out. She skips to my side with a wide smile on her face and immediately loops an arm through mine like we're old friends. Her eyes are a deep brown that swim with sweetness as she bounces on her toes, filled with the excitement and energy of a small puppy. "I'm Emma. And you're Penny, right?" She has a long ponytail that swishes behind her back as she continues to bob up and down with that happy, chaotic energy.

"Um…yeah," I tell Emma. She hears the hesitance in my voice and slowly draws her arm back, untangling us.

"Sorry, I come on a bit too strong sometimes." Pink flushes her cheeks, and she pulls her dark ponytail forward, running her hands down her hair in a nervous gesture.

"No." I shake my head. "You're fine. It's fine."

"You're sure?" She smiles, her teeth a bright white against her brown skin, and there's something about her that reminds me of my old best friend, Beth. They share that same contagious happiness, offering it to me as well. At least, Beth used to. Until my father died and my problems got worse. Until she found new friends when *I* became too much for her.

I don't want to make Emma feel like that.

"Yeah." I nod, and her smile stretches wider.

"Well, come on, roomie." She flicks her ponytail over her shoulder. "Or *matey*? Cabinmates?" She laughs and the sound is so light, so airy, it's almost infectious. "I'm gonna stick with *roomie*. Or Penny?"

"Penny's good," I say, giving her a small smile back.

I look from Emma to the other girls already heading toward their cabins. Some look as happy and comfortable as Emma, while others are a little more withdrawn like me. We're all so different and yet alike. They were brought here to work through whatever trauma they've been dealt. I don't know their stories, and they don't know mine, but at least there are others that understand. I sneak a peek at Emma, this girl that knows I'm here for therapy also but doesn't shy away from me like Beth did. For the first time in months, hope unfurls within me like a new spring bud. Because maybe, here at Camp Whitewood, I don't have to sit in the dark alone.

THREE

The rest of the day passed in a busy blur. I unpacked in the cabin with Emma, unable to stop myself from scanning everything she brought and worrying which of her things could turn dangerous in my hands. We had a buffet-style group dinner where I pushed away my butter knife and repeated my mantras in my head.

And then we had the welcome meeting that really should have just been called "the Dos and Don'ts of Camp Whitewood" with a weekly schedule thrown in. I spent the meeting sitting on my own hands and trying to drown out the voice in my head that told me to yank another girl's chair out from under her.

By the time I'm walking back to my cabin with Emma, I'm ready to sleep for a week straight. The day is catching up, not to mention the exhaustion of being on high alert.

My eyes burn with each blink, and my feet stumble over the dirt path. Thankfully, Ms. Peterson handed out flashlights. Even with a couple lampposts by the main building, the closer we get to the cabins across the lawn, the darker the path gets. Each A-frame has a mounted outdoor light, but they only shine as far as the three wooden steps on the little porches.

Around us, girls veer off in pairs into their cabins. I get to the third one, identical to the others except for the green door with its number stenciled in black.

Emma climbs up the steps first and flicks the interior light on before holding the door open for me.

"Thanks," I say and scoot past.

She closes the door, dimming the cries of the crickets outside.

I flop down onto my bed, making Bunny bounce where I set her next to my pillow. I almost kept her hidden in my suitcase until Emma pulled out her own stuffie, a bright aqua cat, all rounded and squishable—and not as old or worn as Bunny.

I sit up, the vinyl-wrapped mattress crinkling as I try to find a comfortable position. The cabin is one open room that's filled with the scent of cedar and the mustiness that comes with aging wood and hot air. It's not huge, but not small either. Two beds are on opposite sides with matching nightstands, and in between is a shared desk with a window that looks out to the pale birch forest. A tall mirror hangs on the front door, reflecting the beds and desk across from it. And on either side of the door are two sturdy wooden dressers. Two skylights above each bed offer a glimpse of the stars outside.

Nothing dangerous. No weapons for that voice to—

Mirror shards. Sharp and slicing, it whispers, interrupting the false safety from only a moment ago.

Stop, I beg. I hold my breath, letting my lungs scream louder than that voice.

Yes, it says. *Do it. Smash and stab and—*

I climb off my bed and move toward the mirror, hands clasped behind my back. I won't listen to that voice, but I need to reassure myself that I can't hurt Emma.

"Are you okay?" she asks, watching me slowly walk across our cabin. One drawer of her dresser sits open, her hand paused and holding some clothes, but I can't answer her as I creep closer to the door. My own warped reflection stares back from the wobbly-looking mirror.

"Penny? Is everything okay?" Emma asks again, dropping her clothes back in the dresser and turning around to face me.

Shaky relief floods through me when I notice it's not actually glass but one of those plasticky mirrors that can't break, like in my school's bathrooms.

"Yeah…yeah, I'm fine." I can't tell if she's actually concerned or being polite. Maybe both with how I'm acting. Should I have asked for a cabin alone?

Emma glances between the front door and the window at the

back of the cabin. She grips the pendant of her necklace, a long cylinder of some kind, black and smooth, and her breaths come a little too fast. I don't know if it's me or the room or something else making her nervous.

"Are you okay?" I ask her. *With me here* is what I want to say, but she doesn't know anything about me or my intrusive thoughts.

Emma nods but still holds her pendant tightly enough that her knuckles turn white.

"Um, do you mind if I open the window?" I ask, moving toward it. The short strands of my hair stick to the back of my neck from sweat.

"No!" she says quickly before hesitating. "I just… I don't do well with—" She takes a deep breath. "Do you mind if we leave it closed? For tonight?"

"Of course." I swipe my hair back from where it sticks to my temple. "It can stay closed."

She sighs, a sound so full of relief it makes me wonder why she's here.

I start to step away from the window when something dark flashes past, a blur of shadows in the glass that makes me jump. It's gone before I can even be sure anything was there.

"Thanks," Emma says, dropping her hand from her necklace.

"Did you see…?" I let the whispering question trail off, glancing out the window, but there's only a quiet forest. No need to stress Emma out over nothing.

"I like your hair," Emma says when the silence lingers long enough to turn awkward. She pulls a plastic grocery bag out of her backpack. "I wish I was brave enough to dye mine, but my parents would probably kill me. Yours don't care?"

"No." I tip my head down until my silver hair falls into view. "It doesn't rank high on my mom's list of worries." Besides, she knew letting me have that—this simple, stupid thing my father refused to allow—was one small way for both of us to start taking back our lives.

"That's so cool," Emma says. "I saw one of the other girls had pink hair. I would *love* to have some pink streaks. Or purple!" She sighs, and I wish I brought some dye with me for her.

"Want one?" Emma holds out a package of red licorice from her grocery bag.

"I didn't think we were allowed food in our cabins." Ms. Peterson mentioned it in the meeting, something about ants and mice. Still, I take the offered candy, too tempted to say no.

Emma shrugs. "I already had them. I'm not gonna throw snacks away." She sets the bag of candy on her bed and opens the drawer on her nightstand to show more: a bag of pretzels, a box of sour candies, some breakfast bars, and even a couple bottles of water. "Once we finish these, we'll follow the rules."

I take a bite of the licorice and smile as she shuts the drawer again, hiding away her contraband.

"So where are you from?" she starts to ask. "What brought you h—"

I'm glad when a knock on the door interrupts her. I'm not ready to talk about my home or family with her.

Emma shoves her bag of licorice under her pillow and jams the rest of what she's holding into her mouth. I follow her example and swallow my last bite.

The door cracks open after another knock, and Delaney peeks in. "Lights out in twenty," she says. "Better wash up before then."

I nod as Emma says, "Thanks."

The door starts to close, and Emma lets out a relieved sigh, digging her candy back out when the hinges creak and Delaney's face pops back in.

"I don't care about that." She points to the candy Emma tries and fails to hide again. "Just make sure Ms. Peterson doesn't see it, and neither of us will get in trouble."

"Okay," Emma says, her cheeks turning bright pink. "Thanks."

"You know that's an air conditioner, though, right?" Delaney points to a white box a little less than half my height sitting near my dresser. "Here." She comes over and clicks some buttons. A hum fills the room as cold air seeps through the heat.

"Oh, thank goodness," I say, letting the artificial breeze brush against my face. The room cools a little more as I step closer to the air conditioner and hold my hair off the back of my neck.

"You can adjust it however you want, but I'd recommend sleeping with it on." She starts walking out before veering over to Emma and snatching a piece of red licorice. "Thanks." She winks and heads to the door, closing it behind her.

Emma flops onto her back with a laugh. "Oh my gosh," she says before sitting right back up, licorice bag in hand. "I thought I was going to get in trouble on our first night." She giggles again, so bubbly that I find myself joining in as I sit on my bed across from her.

Emma lifts the bag of licorice, offering another to me. When I nod, she tosses one through the air. It hits my hand and bounces up before slapping me in the face and dropping into my lap. There's a breath of silence before both of us bust out laughing at what just happened and the last of any awkwardness from before disappears between us.

There's something so easy and comfortable about being near Emma. Maybe it's her welcoming personality or warm smile or how she reminds me so much of Beth. Of how easy it used to be with the friend I grew so close to through high school—until everything changed, and I spent more time in therapy than with my old friends.

"I thought she was going to yell at me," Emma confesses when our giggles die down.

"Nah," I say around a mouthful of licorice. "Delaney seems nice."

"Yeah, Ms. Evans and Ms. Peterson too. They all seem really great," she says as I finish the candy and start changing out of my clothes.

I pull on a worn T-shirt and cotton shorts while Emma throws on a pink-and-white-spotted pajama set. When I'm done, I grab my bag of toiletries off my nightstand.

"I'm gonna wash up like Delaney said." I hook a thumb toward the door, and Emma hops over to me like an excited rabbit.

"I'll come with." She grabs her toiletries bag before slipping her arm through mine as if we're already best friends. Together we head outside, walking through chirping crickets on a warm summer night.

Back home, I lost so much in the months since my father died. I lost control over my own thoughts and impulses. My art suffered when I couldn't hold a sharpened pencil. I spent my free time in therapy. Beth and our friend group distanced themselves from me when I couldn't act "normal" like them anymore. And maybe I'll never be that "normal" person again—whatever that is—but as I walk alongside Emma, I feel like maybe I can piece myself back together into someone new. Maybe even someone stronger than before.

FOUR

I startle awake as a chill crawls over my neck. The room is drenched in shadows, making it hard to see, but there's nothing to justify the unease filling my chest. There's only the cabin and Emma snoring lightly in her bed.

I'm snuggling back into my blanket when I figure out what's wrong. It takes longer than it should for me to recognize the smell, but when I do it's like a slap in the face. Sharp and astringent, it chokes the air and makes my hands shake.

Whiskey.

Memories rush in with the scent, filling my mind until it leaves me dizzy. Curled fists and blood on my father's knuckles. Mom's face, always coated in a thick layer of makeup. His leather belt in hand and his severe gaze on me.

I squeeze my eyes shut, willing the darkness to steal those memories away, and hold my breath until my lungs ache.

The tremors spread from my hands to the rest of my body, until I'm gripping my sheets too hard. Too tightly, like how my father's fingers would dig into my arm or grab Mom's neck.

You and him…you're the same, that voice whispers, a dark laugh sharpening the words. I clasp my hands over my ears even if it doesn't help. It's in my head—*my* voice, twisted with my father's gravelly tone and anger.

"No," I whisper, finally taking a breath.

But you are, it says back.

"I'm not!" I throw my hands down, uncovering my ears, and my left arm knocks into something on the nightstand.

Moonlight glints off clear glass as a bottle falls, smashing to the wooden floorboards. An explosion of shards and amber liquid coats the floor. The scent of alcohol grows stronger.

My heart thrashes when I look down, at the remains of a whiskey bottle—the same kind my father always had.

"No." I rub the wet splatters off my arm as my breaths come faster and faster.

How? I glance at Emma. She tosses and turns in bed. Did she put it there to mess with me? Did Ms. Evans or Ms. Peterson leave it out as some sort of twisted exposure therapy?

I throw my blanket back, needing to clean up the broken glass and spilled whiskey—to get rid of it. The smell turns my stomach.

"Penny?" Emma says, voice thick with sleep. "Are you okay?"

"I—I'm fine." I scramble to pick up the glass before she can see it, but a shard slices my finger, blood welling up on the tip, and I let out a hiss of pain.

"What are you doing down there?"

"It's nothing. I just dropped—"

The sound of a bird screeching outside makes me jump. I turn, and the window above the desk is pulled up, humid air seeping in through the crack.

"D-did you open that?" Emma slides to the end of her bed, blankets falling half onto the floor, and clutches her necklace.

"No." I shake my head, eyes darting from the open window to the air conditioner struggling against the warm night. If I didn't open it and Emma didn't either, then maybe whoever left the whiskey bottle came in through the window.

Take the glass, sharp and slicing, the voice says, and with it, images of Emma—cut and bleeding—flash across my vision. I swallow hard, trying to block out the commands.

"I'm closing it," Emma says, pulling my attention away from those terrible thoughts.

Emma drops her necklace and jumps off the bed. She passes so close to where I'm crouched on the ground that her rushed movements stir the air and the smell of alcohol.

"Wait, stop!" My hands skate over the floorboards, blindly searching for broken glass so she doesn't step on any, but when I look down, nothing is there.

No shattered glass. No spilled whiskey. Only bare wooden planks.

The impossibility is like a punch to the chest. The shock of it makes me tip back until I collapse from my crouch and my tailbone hits the wooden floor hard.

My hand trembles as I search for the cut on my finger, but even my skin is unmarred—no blood.

"I'm sorry, Penny. I can't sleep with it open," Emma says, and there's some desperate tinge to her voice that I might have wondered about any other time. But I can't rip my gaze away from the empty floor to look at her.

It was there. My arm hit the bottle. Broken glass clattered against the floorboards. The scent of whiskey filled our small cabin. And yet, there's nothing now.

I slowly stand, looking around for any proof I'm not losing my grip on reality.

Emma slides the window shut and locks the latch. She settles back into bed, and I mirror her, but neither of us fall back asleep. Or talk. Emma lies there, her eyes wide and darting around the dark room as she holds the pendant of her necklace. I can't stop staring at the empty spot on my nightstand, the ghostly scent of alcohol still stuck in my nose.

Minutes pass, only the silence of the room and our unsteady breaths filling them until I can't stay here anymore. I get up, my head spinning for a second when I stand too quickly, and rush toward the door.

"Where are you going?" Emma asks, voice shivering.

"I—I need to use the bathroom," I lie before shutting the door behind me and wondering if I'm losing my mind or not.

I pause on the small porch of my cabin and lean on the rail. I close my eyes and let the fresh air fill my lungs. It tastes like summer, the scent of silt-brewed water and night-blooming flowers. Of flourishing green grasses and sparkling stars.

Each breath helps calm me a little more.

It must have been a dream. A nightmare is more believable than an object vanishing into nothing. My intrusive thoughts are bad enough. I don't need to add hallucinations to the mix.

My fingers twitch even as my heart calms. I want to grab my art pencils and sketch my worries across a page until they spill out of me. But my supplies are tucked away in the drawer of my nightstand, and I can't bring myself to go back into the cabin.

As the pounding of my heart slows, another sound catches my attention. Quiet music drifts across the air toward me, and I turn to see a girl sitting on the porch steps of the cabin next to mine. She's situated at the bottom of them, just out of reach of the lantern's golden glow. Only silver moonlight shines over her, illuminating the cascade of her long dark hair and the guitar in her hands.

Her eyes are closed, pale face tilted up to the star-flecked sky, as her fingers dance across the strings. She sings softly, her voice too quiet to catch the words. But the melody reaches over to me, floating up and down in pitch.

The girl's expression is raw, open emotion drawn by tilted

brows, as she sings with a voice as sweet as honey. She falls into her music the same way I fall into my art, deep and all-consuming. It burns from within her until she's glowing under the silver starlight. She pours herself into every note and breath, and it's as heartbreaking as it is beautiful.

I can't stop myself from leaving my own porch and moving closer. My bare feet kick up dust as I walk down the dirt path before stopping a few feet away.

The song fades, the last note from her guitar hovering between us, as she opens her eyes—and squeaks. A discordant strum breaks the song apart as she clutches her guitar like a shield.

"Oh my god, you scared me," the girl says, relaxing her grip and taking a shaky breath. "Sorry. Did I wake you? I was trying to be quiet."

"No, you didn't," I say reassuringly. "I was…getting some air and heard you playing. I didn't want to just hover over there, but I didn't mean to scare you either. Sorry."

"Don't worry about it." She waves one hand, and a silver ring on her index finger glints under the moonlight. "I probably shouldn't have been out here this late."

"I'm glad you were," I tell her, and I am. Her music helped distract and calm me, better than finger tapping and counting or repeated mantras would have done. "That was beautiful. You're really talented."

Pink flushes her cheeks, barely showing through the darkness.

"Thanks." She sets her guitar on the ground by her feet. "Oh, I'm Harper."

Harper with the silky black hair, warm dark eyes, and captivating voice. Harper with the full curves that hug her pajama pants and tank top, and that keep drawing my gaze back to her.

"Penny," I tell her, shuffling awkwardly on the dirt path and feeling like I'm looming.

"Wanna sit?" Harper scoots over and nods to the empty space next to her.

I glance back at my dark cabin, wanting nothing more than to stay here with this beautiful girl and ignore whatever happened in there tonight. But it's late, and tomorrow will be a full—and probably exhausting—day.

"I should get some sleep," I tell Harper, even if I'm not sure sleep will come.

"Yeah." Harper turns to look at the vibrant blue door of her cabin, the number four painted across it. "I should too, I guess." She frowns before grabbing her guitar and standing up. The downward tilt of her lips makes me feel bad for not accepting her invitation to sit.

"But…maybe I'll see you at breakfast?" I ask, wanting to linger a moment longer.

"Yeah, that'd be nice." A small smile stretches across Harper's mouth. "I'll see you there, Penny."

She gives a little wave goodbye, and then Harper slips into

her cabin, leaving me alone with nothing but my thoughts and the memory of what happened tonight.

A shiver trembles my shoulders as I rub the tip of my index finger with my thumb, right where I felt the glass cut into me. Where I saw the bright red of blood.

And now there's nothing but smooth skin and my unraveling mind.

PENNY

A shout startled the little girl awake. The same voice that always woke her, nearly every night now. The door to her bedroom slammed open, making her jump and tuck herself deeper into the thin blanket on her bed.

Her father lumbered forward a step, a bottle in one hand, as her mother's protests from the hallway faded away.

"What did you do?" he asked, words slurred from too much drink.

The girl squeezed her eyes shut, her hands clenching tightly to her stuffed bunny as she pretended to sleep.

"Wake up!" her father shouted. "I asked you a question!"

Her father took another sip of his amber drink, the scent strong and bitter as it hung off of him and filled her small bedroom.

Slowly, the girl sat up, her back curved to make her smaller. She gripped her bunny to her chest like a shield. She knew exactly what he was talking about, what he wanted her to admit, but she couldn't bring herself to say the words.

"Pennnnnelopeeee," he said, drawing and stretching her name out. His voice turned deeper with each syllable, shifting into something that cut into the girl as hard and sharp as chipped porcelain. "You better answer me now."

"I...I broke a plate." The admission stuttered out of her. "It was an accident."

Her father's hand lashed out, faster than the girl's eyes could follow, faster than his drunken state should have allowed. She flinched, remembering the hues of mottled purple and bruising black that painted her mother's skin more often than not. But he didn't hit the girl. Instead, he slammed the door closed, pounding a fist against it for good measure, and watched the girl cringe.

"I'm sorry, sir," she mumbled, knowing he didn't care about her apology.

He whispered her name as he stepped closer. But *Penelope* wasn't a name anymore. It was her father's life sheared off, forked down a path of distaste and disappointment. The sounds of her name were curled with irritation from her father's mouth, annoyance at what could have—what should have—been, according to him. The letters of her name twisted like her father's lips when he spoke of her, and she hated it as much as he did.

Her father took a swig from his bottle and sucked his teeth as he glanced once more at his shiny gold watch. But his eyes didn't check the time, didn't catch the hour. They only stared at that relic of his old life as he mumbled all his regrets to the girl once more—as he reminded her, again, that she was his greatest regret.

His words, garbled by whiskey, wrapped around the little girl, until she had no choice but to believe him.

She had ruined his life.

It was her fault when her mother talked back to protect her and when her father left the bruises.

The little girl dropped her bunny to her lap as her father's words infected the room. As he hovered over her, wearing the shadows like a second skin until he was nothing but darkness and decaying words.

She clasped her hands over her ears and shrank into a ball. She wanted him to leave. But she knew, even when he would finally stumble his way out her room, that his poison would stay.

It was her fault, her fault, her fault.

It was all Penelope's fault.

FIVE

The first full day at Whitewood starts out with a soft chiming coming from outside, slow and repeating. Even with the window still shut after last night, it fills the cabin.

The light streaming in from the window is weak, a pale gray blue that tells me it's way too early to be waking up when I'm technically on summer break.

I stand, dropping my blanket onto the bed and stretching as the chimes ring again, clearly our alarm clock here.

"Ugh, what time is it?" Emma sits up, rubbing her face and groaning. She stiffens for a second, brown eyes darting to the window. Her whole body relaxes when she sees it's still closed, but I can't stop myself from staring at the nightstand and floor. Would it be better or worse to find shards of glass and a sticky dried puddle of whiskey there? To find proof that someone's seen my file and is messing with—or testing—me. Or to find nothing, only the damning evidence of my own mind fracturing even more.

The chiming sounds again, and I startle, lost in the memories of last night. Emma climbs out of bed and grabs new clothes as I start getting dressed, determined to forget about a broken bottle that never existed, a nightmare and nothing more.

Emma and I step out of our cabin and into an already humid morning. Down the slight hill, the sun glares onto the lake as heat wavers above. Even in shorts and a T-shirt, sweat gathers at my lower back. Ten steps outside, and I already miss our air conditioner.

We walk across the grassy lawn that separates the five cabins from the main building. In the center is a silver flagpole surrounded by bright yellow pansies. I glance up, finding a pale green flag. A four-sided outline, shaped like a curved shield, is stitched into the fabric, filled in and embroidered with white birch trees. Above it sits the name, CAMP WHITEWOOD, in ivory thread and bordered in black. I reach my hand out as we pass the flagpole, and pluck the rope strung through the pulley. It twangs softly against the metal and sings with all the birds hidden in the surrounding trees.

When we get to the main building, a set of double doors greets us. They're the same dark aged wood as the exterior of the building. A matching image of the flag's emblem is etched into the window of each door. I grab one of the doorknobs, the brassy metal rubbed away from being touched until the center of each pull handle is a bright golden color while the edges have become a bronzed brown.

Cool air smacks us in the face as we step inside, and I sigh. There's a small foyer painted in a pale green, with a table taking up a third of the space. Pens, sign-up sheets, and information packets are scattered across it. A serenity fountain burbles softly as if saying hello to anyone coming in. Next to it sits a diffuser, puffing steam that smells of lavender and something close to lime.

Behind the table, a bulletin board hangs on the wall, with more flyers about the different activities we can do tacked onto it. There's even a blue wooden box painted with colorful flowers attached to the wall—a way to let us talk to the counselors, anonymously or not, in a *nonconfrontational way* if we need it.

I slip past the comment box, doubting I'll ever use it, and turn down the hall to the right. My tennis shoes scuff the linoleum floor as Emma's flip-flops slap against it.

This whole building is all half-wooden paneled walls and pale paint, creams and mint and robin's-egg blue to give an inviting and calming atmosphere. Decorative signs line the hallway with various phrases. IT'S OKAY TO TAKE BREAKS. COME AS YOU ARE. BE KIND TO YOUR MIND. Layered around the text are floral designs, hearts, or rainbows, all in matching pastels. This building is definitely less camp vibes like our cabins and more therapist's office.

The hallway only leads two ways. Down to the left are Ms. Evans's and Ms. Peterson's offices and bedrooms—no cabins for them like the rest of us and Delaney. Emma and I take the right, passing the shared bathrooms and showers, and turn into the cafeteria, where the chatter of people mixes with the smell of breakfast. Farther down the hall are more rooms for art and music therapy, a rec room, and a group meeting space.

Some of the girls are already having breakfast when we step into the cafeteria. Harper sits at the long picnic bench–style table. Next to her is a girl with pink hair cropped short, and across from Harper is a blond with glasses. They're all chatting and eating, and when Harper glances my way, she waves and smiles in a way that makes my stomach swoop.

I wave back before heading to the buffet on the left side of the room. Emma and I grab plates and forks from a stack and scoot down the line. Silver trays full of food crowd the tabletop, and standing behind them is Delaney, ready to scoop eggs and fruit and pancakes onto our plates.

"Good morning," Delaney says. Her eyes are a dark blue that squint as she smiles at us. "What can I get you guys?"

"Some scrambled eggs and strawberries, please?" Emma asks, holding her plate out. "Ooh, and bacon."

"Um, some eggs and…" I look down the row of silver trays brimming with food, but something gold catches my attention. A thick metal watch wraps around my wrist, flickering under the fluorescent lights. I drop my plastic plate, ignoring how it bangs against the floor as my breaths saw in and out.

His watch is clasped onto my wrist. A piece of scratched and worn metal.

The second hand *tick tick tick*s as I stare at a chunk of gold that should be buried six feet underground, hundreds of miles from here.

It's not possible. Not real. Just like the whiskey bottle last night.

"Are you okay?" Delaney asks, still holding out a serving spoon filled with scrambled eggs.

"No—yeah." The flush rushing over my body is too hot for even the air conditioner to help. "I'm fi—" I start but choke on the words. My wrist is bare again, no sign of my father's watch.

Of course not. It can't be here. Not when it's wrapped around his rotting corpse.

"Here," Emma says, handing me a new plate before picking up the one I dropped and giving it to Delaney.

"Thanks," I mumble, trying to ignore the way the rest of the room has gone silent. If I turned around, I'd probably find everyone staring. Instead, I hold my new plate out as Delaney scoops eggs onto it.

"What else would you like, Penny?" she asks, her tone gentle and honeyed. "Emma?"

I release a sigh when the room fills with light conversation again, and Emma and I let Delaney load our plates with bacon and cut fruit and pancakes.

I try to shake off the whole watch thing, shove it to the back of my mind like my intrusive thoughts. *Compartmentalizing*, my therapist at home would say. *Avoiding* is what I call it.

Emma and I take a seat at the long table, across from Harper.

"Hey," I say and introduce Emma to Harper.

"This is my roommate, Samantha. But she goes by Sam," Harper tells me, nodding toward the girl with pink hair. "And this is—" Harper starts to introduce the blond girl with glasses, but another girl interrupts.

"I'm Reagan," the new girl says. She has a wide smile plastered across her face, making her chubby cheeks pinch tightly in the corners. She sits down, squeezing between Harper and Sam.

"Excuse me, we were—" Sam starts, but Reagan interrupts again.

"Hi," Reagan says, staring across the table at me. She sets her plate down and swipes back curly brown hair from her face, her gaze is zeroed in on me, and I have to fight not to squirm under her scrutiny. "I'm so glad to be here," she says. "Today is already so nice. This summer is gonna be so fun. Won't we have so much fun together, Page?" Reagan smiles and grabs the blond girl's hand, pulling it across the table toward her.

The bright cafeteria lights shine down on Page's pale skin. An angry red scar marks her forearm, looking like an old burn. Page yanks her hand out of Reagan's when she notices everyone's eyes on her and tucks her arms beneath the table, but the movement lets me see that the scar extends to her palm also.

Page pushes her glasses up with her other hand and fidgets in her seat as the rest of us glance around, trying to defuse the awkward moment.

"Don't you think this summer will be fun?" Reagan continues smiling at Page, waiting for an answer and oblivious to how she's turned things weird.

"What is wrong with you? Can't you tell how you just made her feel?" Sam says, anger filling her words as she glances at Page.

Page ducks her blond head and stares at her plate, but Sam keeps going. Sam stands up, pulling the long sleeves of her shirt down at each wrist, and shakes her head. "Not everyone is comfortable being grabbed like that. Weren't you sent here for therapy like the rest of us? God, be a little more aware, why don't you?"

Sam doesn't wait for an answer. She snatches up her plate of half-eaten food and storms away before slamming it down in the return bin and glancing back at Reagan. She hovers there, her lip curled, as if waiting for Reagan to respond.

Reagan's smile drops a fraction, her brow wrinkling. "I…I just…" Her fingers twitch again and again where she holds her fork, and I notice she's missing the tip of her pinky finger. A faded cerise-pink scar, edged in white, is all that's left above the single knuckle there. She shakes her head, curls bouncing with the movement. "I'm just happy to be here." Her smile stretches almost painfully wide.

"Well," Sam says, her voice flat as she calls across the cafeteria, "don't shove your excitement down our throats. Save that for Ms. Evans in our meeting." She turns around, speaking more to herself as she walks away and says, "Someone will need to be chatty for group therapy, because it sure won't be me."

Or me. I'm not ready to let these girls know every deep, dark thing about me. But I don't say that out loud. Instead, I shift uncomfortably in my seat as Reagan turns to me with that giant grin, seeming unbothered any longer by Sam's outburst. She goes around the small group, getting everyone's names and smiling far too much for so early in the morning.

SIX

After breakfast, Ms. Evans guides us to a room down the hall. A large round table and nine plastic school chairs take up one side. The other is filled with wooden easels set up with blank canvases and a rolling art cart.

Like the hallway, the walls are painted in pastel, soft periwinkle to cover the half wood panels, a speckled cream above. Instead of the decorative signs, there are posters tacked around the room. One is seafoam green and titled DAILY AFFIRMATIONS. I read a few off the list: IT's OKAY TO START OVER. ASK FOR HELP WHEN YOU NEED IT. TAKE CARE OF YOUR BODY AND MIND. LISTEN TO YOUR HEART AND HEAR YOUR VOICE.

I stop reading the posters as my stomach tightens.

TAKE CARE OF YOUR BODY AND MIND. How am I supposed to do that when it's my mind betraying me? Making me see things that don't exist.

Hear your voice. Isn't that my problem?

"Please, have a seat," Ms. Evans says, pulling my attention away from the poster, and I'm glad for it. She walks over to a small coffee table set against the wall and turns on an aromatherapy diffuser. A steady stream of air puffs out, spreading that same lavender and almost lime scent that was in the foyer.

"I thought we could all get to know each other a little first." Ms. Evans sits down in one of the empty chairs. A pile of notebooks and pencils wait on the table in front of her. She sets a stack of file folders next to them, each one with a photo of us stapled to it.

Ms. Evans looks around the group, nodding for us to sit as she straightens her pocketed vest, layered over a plain white T-shirt. It matches another pair of khaki cargo shorts and her tan hiking boots, and I'm struck again by how she looks more ready for the Australian wilderness than a therapy session.

I follow the group and take a seat at the table with Emma. A blush warms my cheeks when Harper sits down on my left, and I remember how beautiful her singing was last night, how openly she poured her emotions into her music. Her perfume wafts over me, lilac and sweet almond. And when she turns and smiles, tucking her dark hair behind her ears, my palms start sweating.

"Hey," she says, lightly bumping her elbow into me. "This should be…interesting."

I let out an awkward laugh but can't join in with her joking. Not when I realize how many girls are so close to me. Not when the pencils in front of Ms. Evans are in reaching distance, all of them sharp and pointed.

Stab them, the voice says. *One after another. Let them bleed. Watch them scream.*

I swallow hard and shove my trembling hands under my thighs, sitting on them to keep myself from giving in. I silently repeat some of my mantras, but when they don't help, I count in my head. I don't tap my fingers along with it and show everyone at this table how much those ordinary pencils affect me, though.

Instead, I turn my attention back to Harper, wanting to say something to show her I'm not completely weird, when the door to the room slams open and hits the wall. Flashbacks of my father crashing into my bedroom in anger fill my mind, and I nearly fall out of my seat. My hands fly up to my chest, tucking against my collarbone with clenched fists and shoulders curling as if to protect myself.

But it's only a redheaded girl—the one I almost pushed off the bus steps. Her face is flushed so deep that the amber of her freckles nearly blends into the splotchy pinks.

I take a trembling breath, trying to calm the racing of my heart. I'm at Whitewood, and my father is dead. His anger can't find me anymore…even if my body remembers it.

I'm not the only one affected, though. Sam jumps in her seat too, sending a scowl to the girl, and Emma actually does fall out of her chair. Her dark eyes dart around, and her brown skin turns a bright scarlet as she climbs back into her seat. I don't know what brought the other girls here, but part of me wonders if their own histories are similar to mine.

I hope not.

My heart squeezes too tightly at the idea of my warm and welcoming roommate—or any of the other girls—having dealt with some of the things I have.

"I'm sorry," the girl who rushed in says. "I overslept and missed breakfast, and Delaney said I could take this with me." She holds up a protein bar and bottle of water.

"Of course," Ms. Evans says. "Have a seat, Quinn. We were about to start."

The girl—Quinn—takes the last open spot next to Ms. Evans, almost directly across from me. Dark circles shadow her light green eyes, and she yawns, covering her mouth with the protein bar.

"Let's get started. Take one of each and pass them around." Ms. Evans hands the notebooks and pencils to Reagan, who takes them with a smile still painted across her face. I can't tell if it's genuine or for Ms. Evans's benefit.

The supplies pass from one girl to the next, and the closer they get to me, the more my skin flushes. Harper offers me what's left of the stack, and I take a notebook before letting my hand hover over the pencils.

You'll stab her, the voice says, and I don't know if it's a command or a premonition.

I snatch the pencils from Harper too quickly and let one slip from the bundle. It drops onto my notebook before I shove the rest at Emma.

Pierce her skin. Watch it bleed and bruise.

No. My own voice, untainted, hisses through my head, refusing to give in.

I tap the fingers on one hand, hidden under the table, until my attention snags on Ms. Evans. She watches me like an insect under a microscope. I look down to avoid her gaze and slowly pick up my pencil. Now that it's in my hand, I can see it's not as sharp as I thought. The tip isn't as dull as I keep mine, but it's blunted, more rounded than pointed.

Just in case, I smash the tip into the closed notebook even more, not caring at the mark it makes, just glad for the silence in my head.

"Good," Ms. Evans says after we all get our supplies. "These are for you to journal in, to write down any thoughts or feelings you have. Take notes on anything you might want to talk about, that sort of thing." I don't miss the way she opens her own notepad and scribbles something in it while glancing at me.

"Do we have to?" Sam asks, flicking through her empty notebook. She flips one page after another, each movement slow and precise. She stares at Ms. Evans, and with each flip she snaps her palm flat on the paper again and again. *Smack...smack...smack...*

Sam clearly doesn't want to be here, and it makes me wonder

why she *is*. Whitewood is voluntary only, so what made Sam come if she seems to hate it so much?

"Yes, we encourage each of you to journal your thoughts and feelings," Ms. Evans finally says after Sam's fourth slap. A slight admonishing tone fills her voice and makes Sam stop. "And," Ms. Evans continues, adding a smile to her words, "I think the more you write in them, the more you'll enjoy it. I know I do."

I open my notebook, my fingers itching to draw. I brought my art supplies, but for now, these will do. I sketch Emma first, shading in how her brown skin shines under the fluorescent lights and adding in the swish of her high ponytail, as Ms. Evans goes over group therapy expectations. I use the eraser to add highlights to Emma's sketched eyes, showing the warmth in them now that the fear from earlier has faded away. I take my time on the linked chains of her necklace and how the weight of her cylinder pendant pulls each one down heavily.

When I'm done with Emma's portrait, I switch to a blank sheet and draw Page next, her pale blond hair nothing more than negative space and a few light lines. I add her glasses and a shine on their lenses before shading in the scar on her arm and palm. Page tucks her hands under the table before I'm finished. I want to tell her it's okay. That she's not alone. Everyone has scars, even if they're not always visible. But Ms. Evans is still talking, and I don't know if Page would even want to hear my words.

I switch to another blank sheet and start on the next girl as she raises her hand slightly and asks, "Will you read what we put in the notebooks?"

"No, thank you for asking, Kylie. We respect your privacy here, and I won't be reading your entries unless you want to show them to me," Ms. Evans says before explaining more about our group meetings and the individual ones.

As my hand drifts across the page, letting my worries and fears and problems wash away—even if only for a moment—I fall into my art, the hum of scratching graphite blanketing my thoughts instead.

I draw Kylie with her dark skin and darker eyes, but this borrowed pencil doesn't do her justice with the shading compared to what my art pencils could do. Still, I let the sketch flow across the paper, filling in little spirals and curls for her hair.

"How many sessions will we have every day? The schedule has some spots that just say *extra session available.*" Sam crosses her arms over her chest, waiting with an unhappy scowl that says *any* answer won't please her.

"We'll tailor that to each of you, depending on how you're feeling and progressing," Ms. Evans says, tone calm and soft. "We're here for *you.* And you're all here for something *more*—more individualized, more immersive—than what you had back home.

"At Whitewood, we hope to create an environment that helps you meet your goals. We like to think of ourselves as more of a wellness center, a retreat to take care of your whole self, mind and body, mixing various types of therapy with fun camp activities also."

"And what if we don't come to your meetings?" Sam asks. Her thin lips nearly disappear as they flatten into an angry slash.

"It's our hope that you'll want to join in on everything, but we aren't here to force you if you're uncomfortable."

Sam rolls her eyes as I finish my sketch of Kylie and move on to Reagan.

"Now," Ms. Evans says, "I'd like to open up the conversation with what each of you hope to get out of our program, if you'd like to share."

A few groans and sighs echo around the table. Reagan's hair frizzes around her shoulders and head in wild curls, letting me sketch flyaway lines. I add the curves of her full cheeks, but when I get to her mouth, unease pinches at my stomach. She's still smiling, tight and dimpled—like it would hurt after this long. I draw the lines of it…erase and try again. And again. Until there's nothing but a messy smudge where her mouth should be, making me want to rip the whole page out.

"Um, can I…?" Page starts when only silence fills the table for too long. She shakes her head until Ms. Evans encourages Page to continue. "Can I skip the bonfire tonight? I'm…I'm not…"

"It's okay," Ms. Evans tells her. She shuffles through her file folders and scans the notes in Page's before looking up at her. "You can skip it. Or you could come and keep your distance. Ms. Peterson or I could stay with you if that makes you feel safer. Some of our activities might push you girls out of your comfort zones, but we never want to push you too far."

Page bites her lip and nods as I focus on my sketches again. Instead of tearing out Reagan's picture, I flip the page so hard it almost tears, and start a new portrait.

Sam sits next to Reagan, leaning away from the smiling girl, and I start on her next. I almost groan at not being able to capture the pink of her hair, so bubblegum bright.

"How about this?" Ms. Evans says when no one else seems eager to talk. "Let's move on to our art therapy session. You can all pick out an easel while I get Ms. Peterson."

She waves her hands, motioning for us to stand, before heading out the door. I close my notebook and go over to the easels with the others, slipping my pencil behind my ear. Emma and I take spots next to each other, and Harper grabs one near mine.

I set my notebook on the easel, laying it on the canvas already there, as Ms. Peterson bustles into the room. Her long skirt swirls behind her, and she has a warm smile on her face.

"Good morning, ladies," she says, flitting around the room and gathering supplies. "I'm so happy to have you all here. I thought it'd be great if we started today with a painting… Anything you want. Whatever comes to mind. Maybe try something that makes you feel happy or good."

My gaze darts to Harper, and a blush rushes over my cheeks when our eyes catch. She'd make a gorgeous painting, a contrast of obsidian hair and eyes set against the paleness of her skin—but there's no way I'm going to be the creep making an eleven-by-fourteen-inch acrylic portrait of a girl I just met, even if she's ridiculously cute.

Instead, images of a different painting fill my head until that *need* to put my feelings down on paper or canvas becomes too much. The empty white fabric begs to be transformed into something abstract. Something with shadows of dark gray and mournful blues overtaking the canvas—an almost overwhelming amount, like my own worries and fears. And shaky scribbles of bright red would be tucked and twining around the darkness, garishly loud like the voice in my head. And then…peeking out of the darkness, soft, subtle splashes of a pale pink, like flushed cheeks, the pearly white of stars on a summer night, the soft mint of Whitewood's emblem, and the faded periwinkle of a stuffed bunny, all the small spots of brightness or hope in my life.

"All right," Ms. Peterson says. She waves a hand toward a rolling cart full of supplies. "Everyone take a bucket, and you can get started."

Ms. Peterson steps over to a small side table with a stereo on it. It matches the one with the diffuser still chugging away in the other corner. She turns on some music, gentle and instrumental, the kind you'd listen to while mediating or doing hypnotherapy—relaxing tones that fade into the background. The combination of the aromatherapy and music spreads a calming effect through my body.

Emma rushes off and is back before I can even take more than three steps. "Here ya go," she says and hands a bucket to me.

"Thanks," I tell her as we each step in front of our own easels again. I reach into my bucket and fumble around for a paintbrush when Ms. Peterson calls my name.

"Oh, Penny, wait! I have a different one for you," she says, a hand held out as if to stop me, but it's too late.

My fingers wrap around a wooden handle. It's not a brush I picked up—it's a paint spatula with a pointed metal tip. My stomach drops, hard and heavy, and nausea spreads through me.

It's too sharp. Too dangerous in my hands.

Acid crawls up my throat and sweat coats my skin.

Stab her, the voice says. *Dig it into her skin.*

I don't know who *her* is, Emma next to me or Harper nearby or one of the other six women in this room, but it doesn't matter.

Paint with her blood. Smear it across your canvas.

My hand shakes, grip tightening around the wood. A flash of gold blinks into existence, and my father's watch is on my wrist again.

I drop the spatula, and it clatters against the linoleum. My heart slams into my ribs painfully while the scent of lavender and lime becomes overwhelming, making me dizzy.

"No," I say, not even realizing it's out loud. I back away, breath sharp and shallow, and stumble into someone. The watch disappears from my wrist.

"It's okay," Ms. Peterson says, her voice is soft, as if she's trying to coax a wild animal into calming down. "I've got you. You're safe here," she whispers. But doesn't she know? Hasn't she read my file? I'm not worried about myself. It's everyone else that's not safe.

She should be scared of *me*.

"I—I can't…have that." I shake my head, staring down at the spatula. Such a simple tool, one I've used countless times before.

"I know. I'm sorry. You were supposed to get the green bucket," Ms. Peterson says, letting go of my shoulders and crouching down.

I glance around the room at the other girls. Each of them has a cornflower-blue paint bucket. Except for Reagan, who holds a grass green one with that same stretched smile on her face as she watches the scene I've caused.

I tear my eyes away from Reagan as Ms. Peterson picks the spatula up and carries it across the room. Everyone is staring, but I can't find it in myself to care. Not until Ms. Peterson sets the spatula in a cupboard and closes the door, and I can breathe again.

"I'm sorry," I say, not knowing what else *to* say, but I don't want any of them upset with me.

"No, Penny. You don't need to apologize. This was my mistake. *I'm* sorry," Ms. Peterson says before turning her attention to the rest of the group. "Reagan, you mind switching supplies with Penny?" She takes the green bucket and trades it for my blue one. "This one will be yours during our sessions," she whispers to me. "There's nothing sharp in here."

I nod and take the bucket with hands that still shake slightly, but my stomach settles when I see only regular paintbrushes. The last jitters start to fade as Ms. Peterson moves to the front of the room.

"Now, what's everyone painting today?" Ms. Peterson asks, shifting the lingering looks away from me. Emma says something about painting the ocean as the rest of the girls slowly turn to their own canvases.

As the others start painting and Ms. Peterson goes around the room to stop by each girl, I only stare at my bucket, unable to reach for a brush.

"Penny," Ms. Peterson whispers next me. "I saw you sketching when I passed by earlier. Would you be more comfortable with that today instead?"

"Is that okay?" I ask, relieved at the offer but not wanting to disappoint her or ruin her session.

"Of course." She takes the green bucket from my hands, hooking it onto the easel.

"Thank you," I say before picking my notebook back up and sitting at the table again. I focus on my drawings as the scratching of my pencil mingles with the quiet music filtering through the room.

I start on a portrait of Harper, happy to distract myself. I add pressure to the pencil, darkening the lines of her hair as much as I can with the graphite but still unable to capture how dark it is. A flick of my pencil adds the tilt to her midnight eyes, a swipe of the eraser to bring light into them. The smallest dot to add the mole high on her right cheekbone. I fill in all the details I can, the Cupid's bow of her top lip and the long column of her neck. I add more and more, sketching her torso and the curves of her chest, even her hand holding a paintbrush and the silver ring on her index finger, a black stone in the center.

Once I'm done with Harper's picture, I realize how much detail I put into her portrait compared to the others. I flip through the previous pages, adding more to the others so it doesn't look like I'm obsessing over Harper if anyone sees them. As we all work, Ms. Peterson talks, her voice drifting into the background and telling the girls to paint what they feel or let their minds wander.

I follow her advice and relax as my pencil dances over the drawings, making them come alive with each new detail. The tip makes a soft rasping sound as my movements turn faster and more fevered, as if my mind is stuck in a haze and only my hand is in control. Lines and swirls race across a page, deep pressure until the tip nearly breaks through the paper. Faster and faster, my pencil vibrates over the image I work on. Graphite smudges the side of my hand, turning it gray as I drag it across the page. My breathing turns harsh, and it isn't until I'm done that I realize what I've drawn.

My father.

A shadowy version of him that used to haunt my nightmares as a kid.

I can't breathe. Horror makes my heart crash within my chest.

The drawing is nothing but dark scratches and smears in the faceless shape of my father—except for the watch drawn onto his wrist, eraser marks highlighting the details and shine of metal. His eyes are only blackened scribbles, hollow dips where the sockets are. I drew them so heavy-handedly that they nearly puncture through the thin paper.

A shiver writhes down my spine. I didn't mean to draw that—that nightmare version of my father.

I drop my pencil as that graphite-scratched image glares up at me. And then the horror that makes my stomach sink churns into something else.

Anger.

Rage heats my veins as I remember all the ways my father tried to destroy me. And now, even in death, he won't leave me alone. I'm sick of it. I pick the pencil back up and grip it too tightly, ready to stab the paper and rid myself of that sketch.

My jaw clenches until my teeth ache. I lift my hand.

Yes, destroy it. Destroy everything, that voice says. *Like he did.*

And as quickly as it came, that rage extinguishes. I won't be like him. I *can't*.

I'm angry at my father and everything he did—and I'm not sure if that will ever go away—but I won't let violence infect those feelings like he did.

The shadowed sketch of my father stares up at me with hollow eyes, making my skin crawl. I want to slam the book shut with all my strength, but I calmly—gently—fold it closed instead. And that takes a different kind of strength I wasn't sure I had.

REAGAN

The girl loved animals, and she loved living by the fields and woods where so many were. She spent her days barefoot in the mud and dirt, splashing through the stream and wandering far from her house—or it felt that way to the girl, at least. At eight years old, the world was enormous, unexplored, and full of secrets to discover.

She spent her mornings at home, doing school with her mother and wiggling in her seat, ready for adventures instead. At dusk, she'd trudge back home with all sorts of treasures, fallen feathers and shiny rocks and pretty flowers. Some days, she'd come home with a roly-poly or a worm in her pocket, a tiny snake or lizard in her hand, a fledgling bird or baby squirrel in her arms.

The girl wanted to have a million animals. She wanted to take care of them, let them see how much she could love them. She wanted the baby foxes that barked at night and the birds that flew above her head. She wanted the lizards with blue tails that ran too quickly for her to catch and the raccoons with their dark masks. She wanted a baby deer that would lose its spots in favor of fuzzy antlers. And she wanted the kittens and puppies that she sometimes found on the side of a dirt road by the woods. The girl couldn't understand why anyone would leave them there alone.

But they were lucky, those little kittens in gray and black and brown, the puppies that whimpered even as their tails wagged. Because the girl would bring them home; she'd give them love.

Only after the first litter of kittens, which the girl had gathered in her arms like baby chicks under the wings of a mother hen, and the second puppy she'd plucked from the brambles, did her mother say *no more*. They couldn't keep so many mouths to feed, so many medicines to buy for the little wild things that had never been given proper care.

Over time, the girl found more lost and abandoned kittens, more dogs that were all rib bones and large eyes, but instead of keeping them, her mother and father would gather them in boxes, tie them to leashes, and drive them too far away for the girl to follow. Even the tiny squirrels and baby birds she sometimes stumbled upon were taken. Her mother promised they went to a place that would care for the wildlings, but how could the girl believe that when she never saw them again?

So the girl became clever. Cleverer than her mother and father, or so she thought. She spent her days running through the woods and fields and streams, chubby cheeks smiling and frizzy brown curls flying behind her as she found new treasures. She carried them in her arms as they meowed or whimpered, barked, and even hissed. She'd take them to the old barn on the edge of their land, half-decayed but shelter enough. She stole blankets and folded them into beds and nests, snuck pet food from her house every day.

One day, the girl found a little raccoon, starved and scared. A tiny thing in gray and black and brown, dark eyes wild. It had eaten something bad, or so the girl thought. White foam coated its mouth. But the girl could help it. Like the others.

She bribed the tiny raccoon with a pocketful of kibble, but the wild thing wasn't tempted. So she pulled her jacket off and tried to catch it. To wrap it up in a hug made from fabric sleeves and the warmth of her own body. She'd done it before and had watched kittens and squirrels snuggle in with sleepy eyes.

And the raccoon, it came to her—except this animal was anything but tame. It was razor claws and pointed teeth and violent rage that the girl had never seen before. And when she got too close, it turned those weapons on her. It scratched her arms and pierced soft skin with knife-sharp teeth. Trapped in her jacket and arms, it hissed and growled as it bit and bit and bit.

Blood, too bright and painful, painted the girl's sun-kissed skin. Left smears and drips on her clothes, on the dirt-and-leaf-covered ground. On the animal's foam-filled mouth.

She tried to let go, but her arms were twisted into the jacket as the raccoon thrashed.

Until it bit down on bone, fracturing her finger. The girl screamed as blood gushed from her pinkie, as it filled the raccoon's mouth and poured out, staining the jacket and the little beast's own fur.

The girl dropped the growling bundle, freeing her hands. But the tip of her pinky was mangled and missing, only agony and crimson blood spilling from where it had been, only torn skin and a tiny broken exposed bone.

She ran, fast and far from the creature, leaving a trail of scarlet through the woods as she cried.

And when her mother found her, the girl was nearly faint. She tripped up the wooden steps of their porch as her mother's face went pale.

She was rushed to the hospital, her story stuttering from her lips as doctors swarmed. Her mother cried and her father paced while the girl was given stitches and shots. They wrapped her finger gently, neat as a birthday present, white gauze as spotless as freshly fallen snow.

Once home, the girl told her parents about all the little wildlings in the broken barn. And while she healed, her parents gathered the animals and drove them away.

But the girl didn't mind that they were missing. Because the fear that infected her with that raccoon's bite never left. She didn't want to collect the little animals anymore. Even the ones her mother had let her keep in the house, now grown, worried the girl.

Her finger ached and her hands shook when she thought of that raccoon. If such a tiny thing could turn on her, could break a piece of her forever, then she worried any of them might.

The girl went back to the hospital, again and again, getting shots from needles as piercing as that raccoon's own teeth. They kept her from becoming sick, but they couldn't make her finger whole again.

They couldn't heal the fear that spread through her body like a disease. They couldn't keep her from being both scarred and scared now.

SEVEN

A rt therapy ended with a blank canvas and a notebook I wanted to hide, especially from Ms. Peterson or Ms. Evans, who would only try to analyze why I drew my father in frantic lines and blurred features instead of a realistic style like the other portraits. And I'm not ready to talk about those nightmares yet, so I stash the book under my mattress before my session with Ms. Evans.

Even without it, my nerves swarm in my chest as I walk to her office. Each step feels heavier than the last, slower as I drag out the time. Sure, Ms. Evans has my file, sent over from Mrs. Ashley back home, but it's still hard, rehashing everything with someone new—and now there's something else going on with me that no one knows about too. I don't know why I'm suddenly getting worse and hallucinating things.

I pause in front of Ms. Evans's office, unsure if I should tell her about it.

"Come in, Penny," Ms. Evans says when I hesitate too long. "You can close the door behind you."

I step inside, and the scent of lavender and lime immediately wraps around me. A little glass diffuser swirls with steam on a table under a window. The view from Ms. Evans's office is gorgeous. A serene mountainside and lake that would be beautiful on canvas, with thick oil paint lines that bleed into each other. Softened but still detailed like a Monet. I can see why she chose this room for her sessions—something calming to look at when eye contact can feel too overwhelming.

"How are you doing, Penny?" Ms. Evans sits behind a heavy wooden desk to the right of the room. Papers are stacked across it in neat piles with a laptop resting open in the center. A tear-away calendar and framed picture sit there too, but with the desk looking out to the room, I can't see the photos.

Her office is like the rest of the main lodge, painted in cool pastel tones, soothing but bringing a brightness to the space. The walls are all a pale blue, with framed degrees and inspirational décor that screams *therapist's office*: BE PATIENT WITH YOURSELF. ALL FEELINGS ARE VALID. ONE STEP AT A TIME.

On the other side of the room is a narrow console table set against the wall. Another framed picture—this one of a girl around my age that looks a lot like Ms. Evans—and other little knickknacks decorate the top, while more essential oil bottles, a blood pressure cuff, and a couple machines that I can't identify sit on the lower shelf.

I walk over to the console table as Ms. Evans looks through folders on her desk.

"Who's that? Your daughter?" I point to the framed photo but keep my hands out of reaching distance, not wanting to provoke that voice in my head. The girl has the same light brown eyes and curly hair as Ms. Evans.

"Who?" Ms. Evans pauses her search through the manila folders. "My—oh. Yes," she says, but instead of smiling proudly, her face drops and her throat bobs as she swallows.

"What's her name?" I ask, trying to ease the tension suddenly filling the room.

"Clar—" Ms. Evans clears her throat. She looks down, flipping through the folders once more. "Clara." She takes a deep breath before glancing up at me. "One minute and I'll be ready, Penny. Just pulling up some of your information."

Silence fills the room as I wait, broken only by the shuffling of papers and Ms. Evans typing on her keyboard. My nerves rattle through me. Even knowing these sessions are meant to help me, I don't look forward to picking open my wounds again. So I fill the wait with questions.

"Is Clara here also?" I ask, staring at the photo. "Or coming?" Sunlight streams in through the window, leaving a glare across the frame's glass. I step slightly closer until the shine disappears. Clara looks around my age, sixteen or seventeen in the photo.

"Hmm?" Ms. Evans looks up. "Oh, no. Clara's not here. She…won't be coming. She never really enjoyed it out here." Her voice dips, softening as if she's speaking more to herself than me. "Sometimes…sometimes it still feels like she's here, though."

"It feels like it?" I shuffle from foot to foot awkwardly. Should I sit down?

"Oh…" Ms. Evans shakes her head and stands up, gathering up one of the folders from her desk. "I just meant with so many girls here, you all remind me of her." She waves a hand toward the two cushioned chairs. "Now, why don't we sit and get started?"

"Is it hard being away from your daughter all summer?" I take the closest chair before crossing my legs and uncrossing them. Fold my hands in my lap before tucking them under my armpits instead. Sitting here, across from a woman I don't really know, brings me back to that first session with my home therapist, too many emotions and stilted conversations, intrusive questions and awkward pauses. I delay the inevitable by rambling instead. "This is the first time my mom won't have me constantly around. She said she didn't know what she was going to do without me, being alone for once. And I didn't know if all moms felt like that with their daughters and—"

"Stop," Ms. Evans says, her tone turning sharp enough to startle me.

I shrink back into the cushions, worried that I've talked too much, like my father used to say. I don't want to anger her. Too many memories of my father slip through my mind.

"I'm sorry," I start, a knee-jerk reaction to calm and defuse the situation. "I didn't mean to—"

"No. No, I'm sorry, Penny." Ms. Evans takes one long deep breath in and slowly exhales, reminding me of a breathing exercise Mrs. Ashley once showed me.

"I shouldn't have pried," I say, muscles still tensed against a plush chair. "I ask too many questions sometimes."

"No, Penny," she says, voice feather soft once more. "I really shouldn't have spoken to you like that. I want you to feel comfortable asking me anything. I just…" She rubs her forehead like she's massaging a headache away. "I'd rather we talk about what brought you to Whitewood."

I nod, hoping not to upset her any more. She glances past me, at the framed photo of her daughter, and takes another deep breath, but I don't miss the way her hands tighten around the folder she still holds, leaving wrinkles behind.

"I really do apologize for my tone, Penny," Ms. Evans says, coming around from her desk. "Even adults—and therapists—can have a hard time with feeling overwhelmed with big emotions, and sometimes talking about my daughter…isn't always easy for me." She shakes her head. "But you're not here to worry about me and my complicated… Anyway, how about we get started with your session instead?"

She sits down across from me, smiling gently, but it's a strained thing that doesn't offer comfort. My eyes dart to the photo of Clara as Ms. Evans opens the manila folder with my picture stapled to the front. Why did it bother her so much to talk about her daughter?

I glance around the unfamiliar room and realize I'm sitting in a lodge in the middle of nowhere on an isolated mountain with a woman I've already overstepped with once. And somehow, I'm meant to share my most painful truths with her. But I don't have the same trust and connection with Ms. Evans that I built with my home therapist. And I don't know how I can do that now despite how much I *need* this place to help me. I can't go home without something getting better.

I swallow hard and watch the four feet of space between our chairs stretch into something that feels impossible to cross.

At home, Mrs. Ashley never snapped like that, and it makes me wonder how much help Whitewood can really be for me if I'm walking on glass like I did every day when my father was alive.

EIGHT

et's start over, please," Ms. Evans says. "I want this to feel like a safe place for you, and I'm sorry I haven't done that. It's my own issues and has nothing to do with you. Is that all right, Penny?"

"Yeah, okay," I say, even if I'm still left off-balance around her. But I'd rather smooth things over than cause another disruption.

"Thank you." She gets up again and steps over to the window, fiddling with the diffuser until the steam pours out in a thicker haze and perfumes the air. She sits back down as I push away the jitteriness her earlier tone caused.

"Despite my misstep before," Ms. Evans starts, smiling and opening the folder in her hands, "I want to make sure you know how glad we are to have you here and that, together, I believe we can work to meet your goals. So would you like to start by telling me what you hope to get out of your time here?"

"Um, well, I'm sure it's in my file, but—" I fidget in my seat and push my hair back, the silver flyaways leaving an itch on my cheek. Ms. Evans nods, encouraging me with another smile. "I feel like, maybe, I'm a danger to others. That I'll hurt someone."

"Okay," she says, and her gaze is too intense. I turn to the window, staring out instead. "When did this start for you?"

"Around the time my father died. Or a little after." I bite my lip. A wall slams down on my thoughts—my memories—and I let it, inviting a calm darkness to wash over my mind. I don't want to talk about my father at all, and I try not to even think about that night.

Of course, I have to talk about *him*, though.

"Can you tell me more about that?" The corners of Ms. Evans's lips turn down, showing either concern or pity. I don't want either. "Tell me more about your dad?"

"My father was…" My gaze goes back to the window. To the birch trees swaying in the distance. To the lake, little ripples breaking the surface as the breeze drifts over it. "He was awful. Abusive."

After a while, the more we talk, the less that weirdness from before lingers. It's almost like talking with my therapist back home, with the quiet room and the pleasant scent—though Mrs. Ashley's office always had the smell of oranges coming from her diffuser.

Ms. Evans scribbles notes in her folder, a blank page filling as she asks more questions. "And if you're comfortable with it, can you tell me what you remember about the night he died?"

I know what happened—even if I don't like to remember it. That wall starts to come down, but I stop it. Not that I want to. But if things are going to get better, then I have to tell Ms. Evans everything. I have to tell her how my father came after Mom again, reeking of whiskey and fueled by anger. Only this time, she wasn't the one left bruised and broken.

He was.

Still, I hesitate. My mouth opens, but the words won't come. They lodge in my throat and choke me until I look like a fish gasping for oxygen. The seconds tick by, but Ms. Evans only waits patiently. But it's harder with her—after her sharp tone.

But Ms. Evans is waiting, and I can't ignore the questions forever.

"He..." I swallow hard, as if I could devour the words until they don't exist. Until I don't have to admit how bad things were that night. "My father was yelling at my mom again, outside my bedroom." Each word is pried from my mouth like teeth being ripped out without Novocain. "I couldn't listen to it again. I went into the hall..."

The diffuser puffs lavender and lime into the room, cloying and thick, almost overwhelming.

"It's okay, Penny," Ms. Evans says, voice soft. "Remember, there won't be any judgment or blame. I'm only here to help you."

"It's…hard to talk about… I remember…" What do I remember? The night is seared into my brain like a list more than a memory. X, Y, Z happened. I've repeated the events before to others. Why is it so hard now? I squeeze my eyes shut and hold my breath until my lungs ache. I let the darkness wrap around me like a comforting blanket.

"Penny?" Ms. Evans nudges gently.

"I…remember seeing him shove my mom into the wall. And then…it's hazy." I open my eyes again. "Everything happened so fast. He was at the bottom of the stairs, and he wasn't moving."

"And you don't remember anything else?"

My brow scrunches. "Like when the police and paramedics came?"

"No. Like any other details from that moment."

"I—" I bite my lip again. "I don't know. He fell, right? What else am I supposed to say? Do you want me to describe it?" But even as I think about that night more, my head feels dizzy and nausea twists my stomach, and I know I don't want to dig into any of those gruesome details.

"Of course not. That's fine," Ms. Evans says. "I don't want you to feel like you're pushing yourself too hard."

I look away, unsure if any of this session has been helpful so far. I turn sideways in my chair and stare at the knickknacks on the console table instead. A glass sphere swirled with varying shades of blues and purples catches the light.

Pick it up, the voice in my head says. *Smash it into her head. Heavy and hard.*

I flinch at the words.

Such pretty colors. Watch her blood stain them.

"Penny?" Ms. Evans says, and I turn back to her, away from the glass sphere and those words. "What just happened with you?" Her brows are curved in concern, light brown eyes assessing.

"It's…the intrusive thoughts," I say, rather than telling her it feels more like a voice in my head. "My Harm OCD. I get these images in my head."

"Where you feel like you'll hurt someone?"

I nod.

"All right," she says, setting her folder on the floor by her chair and standing up. "I'd like to try something. Have you ever heard of EMDR?"

I shake my head as she steps past me and grabs one of the machines from the console table.

"It's a type of therapy treatment. Some of the other girls have done or heard about it before, so I thought I'd ask." She carries a long bar and grabs a tall tripod that was tucked into the corner behind the door. "It's called Eye Movement Desensitization and Reprocessing—or EMDR."

"What does it do?" I ask, eyeing the way she sets up the tripod near her chair and clicks the long bar into the top until it's sitting horizontally.

"It's for bilateral stimulation." She moves to her desk, tapping keys on her laptop until quiet music filters around the room—similar to the meditation-sounding playlist from art therapy. "The stimulation can be felt or heard or"—she points to the bar she set up before sitting down across from me again—"it can be visual. We'll start with visual."

"Okay, and how does that…help?"

I never did anything like this with my other therapist. Back home, we mostly talked or worked through breathing and finger-tapping techniques that never quite helped. But that's why I'm here, isn't it? To try something else that might be better—even if it seems…strange.

"I'll start by asking you some questions, and I'd like to you to follow the lights on this bar with your eyes while you answer them. We'll use this to help retrain how your brain processes those memories and events." She presses a button on the bar, and little bulbs brighten until it looks like a white light darting from side to side.

"Are you ready?" she asks, and I nod, even if the idea of staring at a light while talking to someone feels weird. She picks her folder up, flipping it open, and tells me, "Follow the light with your eyes." She offers another smile meant to be warm and encouraging, but my stomach is too twisted up, anxious about what she'll ask.

"When you get these images of hurting someone," she starts, "how do they make you feel?"

I follow the light back and forth. The knots in my stomach

turn heavy, pushing bile up my throat. They make me feel awful. Terrible. Like I'm becoming my father.

"Scared," I say. My head swims as I breathe, tasting nothing but lavender and lime. It's too much—the question and the smell.

"How do they scare you?"

"Can you turn the diffuser off?" I ask instead, glancing at her.

"Is it too much? I can turn it down."

"Can you just turn it off?" I press a hand over my mouth and nose, trying to get some fresh air as I inhale.

"Of course." She gets up, pressing buttons quickly before slipping back into her seat, and I drop my hand. The stream of air thins, but it takes a while for it to stop, and it doesn't clear the air of what's already there.

"Follow the light again," Ms. Evans says. "So how do they scare you, exactly? These images."

I blink away the dizziness and chase the light again. Back and forth. "I don't want to be like my father."

"Okay, you can look at me," she says, and I drag my attention away from the bar. "On a scale of one to ten, how worried are you that you'll hurt someone?"

"Ten," I say, too fast. I want to shove the word back into my mouth, let it burn my throat as I swallow the truth down. His anger is a smoldering flame in me, growing hotter. I hate him. I hate him for all the things he did. But most of all, for how he's poisoned me. Made me like him.

"Look at the light again. How did your father make you feel?" she asks when my gaze turns to the bar. Her tone is gentle—at odds with the emotions she's pulling out of me.

Back and forth, the light blips, and my thoughts spiral. "Like one misstep and his anger would take over."

"Did you feel like your actions or choices directly affected your father? That they'd make him angry?"

"Sometimes."

"You can pause with watching the light," she says, and I let my eyes drop to my lap. "On a scale of one to ten, how much did you feel like that was your responsibility? To try to keep your father from getting angry?"

"I...um... Ten?" I know, logically, his emotions weren't my responsibility. But he was always so...reactive, it *felt* that way. Like the bruises on Mom's body or the slap of his belt on mine were my fault. Especially when I was younger.

"Okay, follow the light again," she says, and my gaze shifts side to side once more. "Your father's anger was his own, Penny. It wasn't on you to keep him calm. To make him someone safe to be around. That burden was his, *not* yours. He made his own decisions that hurt and affected the people around him."

Ms. Evans keeps going, reassuring and affirming the guiltlessness of my role with my father. She asks more questions, which I answer while following the light. I don't know how long we stay like that, minutes or hours.

"Look back at the light one more time," Ms. Evans directs. "*You are in control of your actions, Penny. Not your father. His anger doesn't control you. That violence was his own. The guilt is on him, not you.*" She nods at me, as if the small gesture will cement her words in my mind. "You can make your *own* choices. And if you don't want to hurt someone, then you won't. You can tell those intrusive thoughts to be quiet. To go away. And the more we work on this, the more I hope you can see that."

The words are similar enough to what my home therapist has said, but there's something about focusing on that darting light and letting the rest of my mind take the back seat that helps me actually *listen*. And maybe believe them too.

I swallow hard, letting her words sink deeper and deeper into me—instead of automatically doubting and denying them like before. The smallest sliver of hope cracks in my chest, a flicker trying to replace the flame of my father's anger.

"Okay," she says, pressing the button on the bar to turn it off. "Since these images or thoughts started, have you hurt anyone, Penny?"

"I—no," I say, and that slice of hope tries to burn a fraction brighter. I've been too obsessed over the possibility of hurting people that I never believed it could end any other way. I never trusted that there was a chance I wouldn't turn into my father. But I want to believe that I won't. Desperately.

"On a scale of one to ten, how worried are you that you'll hurt someone?" Ms. Evans asks, the same question as before.

This time, though, I take a moment to think—to figure out how I *feel*. I want to be in control. To believe her words. I want that hope to survive, so I cling to it.

Or try to.

But it's hard. A lifetime of tiptoeing around my father. Years of him telling me it's my fault.

I take a deep breath, the scent of lavender and lime filling my lungs.

"Nine," I finally say, wanting things to change more than I've ever wanted anything.

Ms. Evans smiles, wide and warm. "Good. From ten to nine is good, Penny. It's progress. And I'm sure we'll continue to see more with our sessions."

She gets up, motioning for me to follow. I trail after, wisps of the aromatherapy clinging to me, and I'm grateful when she opens the door and fresh air greets me. But as I say goodbye and make my way down the hall, the acrid scent of whiskey curls my nose instead. The smell is suffocating, as if I've been dosed in the alcohol. I cover half my face with the collar of my shirt, but it doesn't help.

Kylie heads down the hall in my direction but pauses where I've stopped. "Are you okay?" she asks.

"Do you smell that?"

She sniffs the air and shakes her head. "Smell…what?" She leans toward me. "That oil blend they're always diffusing?"

"Never mind," I say and slide past her.

I thought my session with Ms. Evans had helped, but maybe not if I'm smelling my father's whiskey where it doesn't exist. Maybe Whitewood is only making things worse.

NINE

The night starts off better than my day. No hallucinations or phantom smells. No missteps with one of the adults. Instead, it's melted sugar from s'mores and sparking flames around a bonfire set close to the lake. The scent of silt and burning logs mingles with the air in a pleasant way.

Girls chat and laugh, and Ms. Peterson tries to get everyone to sing while she plays guitar and sits on one of the half dozen logs turned into seats. Harper joins and sings with Ms. Peterson, harmonizing with her for a few songs. A pinch of awe and jealously twines together within me as I watch the music consume Harper in a way that I wish my art could with me again.

And I hope it can someday. Despite the fear gnawing at me that Whitewood is only making things worse. Why did I smell whiskey after my session with Ms. Evans earlier? I wish I had my phone and could look up what EMDR really is. Does it mess with your mind more than Ms. Evans let on?

I shake the thoughts away as ridiculous and focus on the night instead. There's something calming here, under a dark sky stretched wide with a hundred stars. And with the heat of the fire warming me, I can almost forget all of those worries.

But this close to the fire, that voice whispers in my head. *Watch them burn. Push her in.*

It's a struggle to ignore the thoughts, but the more I try, the quieter it gets, until I can sit by the bonfire without every muscle pulled taut. If Ms. Evans asks, it still feels like a nine, difficult but... maybe not impossible.

And even if it's only a tiny change, the smallest improvement, I take a breath filled with hope.

"Want one?" Harper asks. She walks over with a s'more, chocolate melted and dripping onto her fingers and holds it out to me.

"Oh, thanks, but I don't want to take yours." I reach for one of the birch sticks, papery bark peeled and cleaned off, that leans against my seat. "I can make one."

"I...made it for you," Harper says, and a blushing warmth unfurls within me. "If you want. You don't have to."

Emma gives me a soft jab in my ribs until I take the s'more. Harper licks the drips of chocolate off her finger, and it's not the fire heating my cheeks anymore.

"Yeahhh, I'm gonna go say hi to..." Emma looks around the group, searching for someone.

Sam, Kylie, and Quinn all stand in a group, talking on the opposite side from where Ms. Peterson plays her guitar. Delaney packs up the s'more supplies, and Reagan sits on a log by herself, smiling too wide still and swaying along to the music.

"Reagan," Emma says finally. "I wanted to talk to Reagan." She gets up, shooting a wink at me, before motioning to her now-empty seat. "Here, Harper, you can have my spot."

Harper sits down and her lilac and almond perfume mixes with the woodsmoke, the sweetness a complimentary contrast to the deeper ashy notes. We stay like that, only Ms. Peterson's singing filtering between us, as I finish the s'more and try to keep my nerves from making me say anything stupid. She's too pretty for my brain to think straight.

But when the silence between us lingers a touch too long, I search for *anything* to say, and my gaze catches on Page. She's halfway up the hill, as far from the bonfire as she can get without technically not being here. Ms. Evans is with her, the two of them talking.

"Think she's okay?" I ask, nodding toward the hill. Ms. Evans drapes a long necklace over Page's head, silver metal flickering under the moonlight.

"I heard she was in a bad fire a few years ago," Harper says, "so she has a hard time around it."

"Oh." I watch as Ms. Evans guides Page away from our area and back to the main lodge.

"We're all here for something, aren't we?" Harper's dark eyes turn to me, firelight and curiosity dancing in them.

Relief rushes over me like a cool breeze when Ms. Peterson finishes a song and gets up, distracting Harper from asking why I'm here—though I can't help wondering the same of her.

"Well, it's getting late for someone my age, so I'm heading in now." Ms. Peterson picks her guitar up. "You girls are free to go back to your cabins or stay out a little longer. Delaney will be in charge for the night."

Ms. Peterson makes her way up toward the main lodge, and the group goes quiet until Sam calls out, "Well, what now?"

"We can hang around while the fire dies down," Delaney says. She moves to an empty log and sits.

"And do what?" Sam crosses her arms but follows Delaney's lead and takes a seat.

"We could tell scary stories?" Kylie offers as she and Quinn scoot onto a log. "You know, like campfire stories?"

"I don't know." Delaney hesitates, glancing around the group—from Harper and me sharing a log to Kylie, Quinn, and Sam all squished onto one to Emma sitting next to Reagan. "Ms. Evans doesn't want anyone getting triggered by anything."

"Come on," Kylie says, "you're telling me you guys never told ghosts stories around a bonfire any of the other years here? Wait, did you work here before?"

"Yeah," Delaney answers. "I've been here the last few summers."

"So?" Sam prompts.

"So yeah, we might have told creepy stories before." She turns her attention to the bonfire and laughs. "Last year there was this one time with my friend, Clara—I swear we almost peed our pants when a camper sneezed right at the scariest part of a story. And then we laughed so hard we almost peed again." Delaney chuckles to herself, but as quickly as it came, her smile fades.

"See. We'll be fine." Sam rolls her eyes. "We know ghost stories aren't real."

"You guys are sure?" Delaney asks, leaning in. She drops her voice to a whisper until we're all mirroring her, tipping forward to hear. "But this isn't a ghost story, and it isn't made up." She glances at the forest behind her and back to us. "It's all true."

Sam scoffs, but a smile curls one side of her mouth, betraying her disinterest.

"So yeah, I've been coming here for a few years, but I didn't tell you guys that I moved here year-round also. Not in the town we picked you up from, but close." The fire casts shadows on the hollows of Delaney's face while flames highlight the sharpness of her cheekbones, morphing her features into a living skull as she talks. "And there's one thing you learn living in these mountains: *Never* trust the woods."

Her dark blue eyes shift from one girl to the next slowly, building tension.

"Wh-why?" Quinn asks. She fidgets with her red hair, running a lock between her fingers and staring at the silver trees.

"I'm sorry," Delaney says. "Maybe we should stop?"

"It's just a story." Sam rests a hand on Quinn's shoulder, and the mask of annoyance always painted on her face disappears. "It's okay."

"I'm fine." Quinn drops her hands from her hair. "Go ahead."

"Never trust the woods?" Emma prompts when Delaney still hesitates. "They look normal to me."

"Looks are deceiving." Delaney finally continues. "There are several rules for *this* forest. One"—she holds up a finger—"never go in at night. That's when the creatures roam. When they'll find you."

"Like…a mountain lion?" Kylie jokes.

"Worse. Much worse." Delaney leans forward even farther. "Two, if you hear voices, stay away from them. They might sound like your friend, family—or even yourself. But *don't* call out to them."

I don't need any more voices haunting me. A shiver scrapes down my spine, and Harper inches closer, until the shaky unease turns to fluttering in my chest.

"Three," Delaney says, stealing my attention back, "don't whistle in the woods."

And there's something about her third rule that itches at my memory. That reminds me of a time Mom packed me up and drove us to her mother's house in Virginia. A week spent away from my father before Mom went back to him. A week of living with my grandmother and all her superstitions.

Don't whistle so close to the woods, Pen. Her raspy words echo in my head. *It ain't safe.*

"Why?" Reagan asks, and the memory of my grandmother drifts away like smoke from the fire, spiraling into the night. "Why can't you whistle?" Reagan's smile stretches, and there's something off about it—about her—that makes a knot twist in my stomach.

"Because the monsters that live in the woods—that hide in them…they'll hear you and listen," Delaney's voice is whispering, a melodic rhythm filling it. "And they'll come for you." She reaches forward with hands curled into claws as an owl screeches in the woods, sharp and sudden, making us all jump.

Harper grabs my hand, and the shaky nerves running through me are for a wholly different reason than fear now. I don't know if Harper is actually startled or not, but she doesn't let go as laughter breaks the silence and giggling spreads through the girls. And even though my palms are sweating, I don't pull away either.

"Made-up monsters in the woods?" Sam asks, skepticism drenching her words. "You were worried *that* would be too scary?" But her tone drops, her eyes darting from the woods to her cabin and back to us.

"They're not made up," Delaney says, and her face looks so serious I can almost believe her. "Last year—" She shakes her head, dark blond hair swishing around her shoulders and turning gold in the firelight. "No, never mind. I shouldn't."

Sam *tsk*s at the same time Reagan asks, eyes as wide as her smile, "What? What happened last year?"

"She's trying to bait us," Sam says.

"No, really. It's not my story to tell." Delaney looks toward the lodge.

"Come on, you already started," Kylie chimes in, and several others nod along.

"Fine," Delaney says. "But...don't tell Ms. Evans. Or Ms. Peterson, okay? They wouldn't like it." She waits for all of us to agree before continuing. "Last year...a camper went into the woods one night. She was upset, told some of the other girls that her therapy sessions made everything worse. I think she was trying to leave. Her m—Ms. Evans didn't know she left. *We* didn't know until the next day."

Delaney's gaze turns distant, staring into the fire.

"The woods are dangerous at night, hard to navigate," she continues. "Even without the monster lore, there's a ton of reasons not to go hiking after dark. It's too easy to get turned around or hurt."

"What happened?" Harper asks, a tremble tilting her words. I give her hand a soft squeeze, since the story seems to scare her. But dark forests and made-up monsters don't frighten me, not when I've lived with a real monster most of my life. But if it scares

Harper, then I want to offer her even a little bit of comfort. "What happened?" Harper asks again when Delaney takes too long.

"She showed up the next day," Delaney says, "more upset than before. Clara swore something was coming for her. For everyone."

"Did it?" Reagan asks, the smile on her face twitching.

"Of course not," Sam says, the crackle of the bonfire punctuating her words.

"Let her finish." Emma waves at everyone to quiet down.

Delaney opens her mouth to answer, but I cut her off, remembering the photo in Ms. Evans's office—the way Ms. Evans bit her words short when I asked about her daughter.

"Wait. Clara? You said her name earlier too." I almost didn't catch it, too distracted from Harper sitting so close. "Isn't she Ms. Evans's daughter? You knew her?" Maybe Delaney also knew why Ms. Evans snapped at me for asking about her.

"I—" Delaney raises one hand to her mouth, as if she can put the name back, swallow it into silence. Instead, she sighs and drops her hand. "Yeah...we were friends. Best friends."

"Wait, Ms. Evans's daughter was a camper here?" Sam asks, and Delaney nods.

"So, what happened?" Harper prods when the older girl doesn't elaborate.

"I really shouldn't have—"

"You don't have to tell us." Sam shrugs, but her lips curl sharply, a cat catching a mouse. "I'll just ask her in my session tomorrow."

"No!" Delaney shouts before pausing. She looks around the group and takes a deep breath. "Sorry, it's just… Please don't bring Clara up."

"You *were* friends?" I ask. "What happened?"

"She…Clara died," Delaney says and even the fire dims, the chill breeze sweeping around us. "Not long after that night."

A gasp slips out of Quinn. "The monster in the forest." Her eyes dart to the woods as she starts twisting her red hair around her fingers again.

"No. Not that monster. Her own. She was having a hard time after…" Delaney sighs again, and the sound is so defeated. "Nothing seemed to help Clara. The more sessions she did with Ms. Peterson, the more she lashed out. She was…erratic. Eventually, she…"

"What?" I ask, breaking the heavy silence pressing in on us. "Delaney. She what?" I ask again, slipping my hand out of Harper's. I lean forward, flexing my fingers to keep from prying the answer out of Delaney. What happened to Clara that made Ms. Evans so upset when I asked about her?

Delaney swallows hard and the seconds drill into me. "Ms. Evans didn't want you to know. She didn't want you doubting the work you're doing here. They helped all the other girls; they just couldn't—"

"What happened to Clara?" Quinn asks before I can jump up and shake the answer from Delaney. Quinn shivers as her eyes scan the woods again.

Delaney's gaze leaves the fire in front of us, tripping across the grass until she's staring at the forest also. The silver trees glow like ghosts against the dark night as she tells us, "Clara killed herself."

TEN

Ms. Evans's daughter is dead.

Her reaction when I asked about the photo makes sense now—a touchy subject like my father is to me—but there's something about Delaney's story that makes unease seep into my bones.

The more sessions she did, the worse Clara got. The more *erratic* she became.

Will that be me? The next failure of Camp Whitewood?

I pace back and forth at the end of my bed, unable to sleep after the bonfire, as Emma's light snores fill the cabin.

I told Ms. Evans I was at a nine, one small step better. But maybe I was only kidding myself. Those intrusive thoughts still scream at me, *and* I'm seeing things that don't exist now too.

Because you aren't getting better, the voice says, an ever-present shadow in my head.

But it's only been a day. I can't expect Whitewood or Ms. Evans to work miracles overnight.

You're like him. You'll only get worse.

No.

I tap my fingers as I pace, counting in my head to drown out the voice, but it doesn't work. I try some of the mantras next but give up when the words jumble in my head.

You'll hurt her, it says, and my eyes snap to Emma, splayed out and deep in sleep. *Wrap your hand around her neck. Like he would.*

I tuck my hands under my armpits, fingers pressing into my ribs.

Be quiet, I tell the voice. "Quiet, quiet, quiet," I whisper, speaking over anything else it might utter. I grab a mini bag of chips off Emma's dresser, knowing she won't mind, and open it, trying to let the crinkling plastic and crunch of each bite drown out my thoughts.

Am I like Clara? Unable to sleep and pacing around, speaking to voices that no one else hears? Is that what Delaney meant by *erratic?*

The cabin presses in, stiflingly warm. Even the air conditioner humming in the corner doesn't help. My skin flushes, and I need to get out of here, to breathe and let my mind calm down.

I open the door and take the three steps down the creaky wooden stairs outside until the shape of a person stops me. They sit hunched on the grassy lawn, staring out at the cabins—at me. They're only shadows and smudges like that nightmare version of my father. I hold my breath at seeing the creature that's haunted my dreams since I was a child. Another hallucination.

I *am* getting worse. Like Clara.

"What are you doing?" the creature—no, the person—asks, her voice soft but sharp. "Are you just going to stand there and stare?" She looks up as the moon slips out from behind the clouds until it bathes her face and highlights the pink of her hair.

"Sam?" I let out a heavy sigh. "What are you doing out here?"

I shuffle across the dirt path and grass to where she sits, not caring when dust and dew cling to my socks. I sink down onto the lawn across from Sam, folding my legs under me despite the way the grass itches against my thighs. A bare spot of dirt circles the flagpole where Sam sits, a ring of yellow pansies around her.

"Can't sleep." Sam looks behind me, gaze trailing over her cabin and the cobalt door. A shiver works down her spine. She stretches it out and cracks her neck. "What about you?" Sam turns her pale blue gaze to me. Her voice isn't harsh, but her crossed arms and frown clearly say I've intruded.

I can't bring myself to go back to my cabin though.

So instead, I lift a shoulder before letting it drop back down too heavily. "Can't sleep either." I hold up the half-eaten bag of potato chips. "Want some?"

Sam nods and scoots over a couple inches, pointing to the spot next to her. I step over the bright flowers and squeeze myself in before holding the bag of chips out to Sam.

"Thanks," she says, taking one. The soft crunch of our bites is the only sound as the minutes tick by, the chips dwindling and disappearing as we sit together.

The silence settles around the two of us, more comforting than awkward. Here, outside, with only the crickets and soft owl cries, it's peaceful. If only for a moment, I can ignore how my intrusive thoughts are ruining my life. And how I'm only losing it more each day, seeing things that don't—can't—exist.

"So," Sam says, breaking the hushed blanket that descended on us, "what brought you to Whitewood?"

I recoil against the question—literally—not sure I'll ever be ready to share my reasons with these girls. I bump the back of my head against the flagpole, sending an ache through my skull as the rope *thwacks* against the metal as if it were laughing at me. But I'd rather take the headache and imaginary mocking than answer Sam.

"You okay?" She glances at me sideways, and I nod. "So?" she prompts, drawing the word out too long.

"I…um…" I shrug and finally settle on, "My therapist at home told me about this place."

"You have something against paint scraper thingies?"

"What?" I ask.

"During art therapy," she says, voice almost bored. "You didn't paint."

The spatula and its pointed metal tip, which I didn't trust myself to hold. I don't explain though; instead, I ask, "What brought you?"

She turns her head to look at me, expression flat. "The bus." She rolls her eyes.

"Sorry," I mumble. She asked me, but is annoyed when I do the same?

"Hey, if you don't want to share, that's fine. But don't expect someone else to then."

Silence engulfs us. It rings in my ears, no longer a comfort— until a sliver of the truth bursts out of me.

"My dad's dead." The confession echoes in the soundless moments that follow.

I don't talk about him. Not if I can help it. But seeing his watch on my wrist and his whiskey in my room have felt like a whole new kind of assault, drowning me in those memories until I'm left gasping and whispering my secrets to a girl I barely know.

When I glance back at Sam, she doesn't show any remorse or pity. She doesn't offer condolences, which I wouldn't even want. She lets the seconds build and crumble around us until finally her voice comes out quieter than before.

"My dad's in jail," she says, the admission an olive branch, not a competition. The thumb on her right hand rubs a scar on her forearm, round and pink and only one of a few. When she catches me looking, she folds her arms and hides the scars. "I got sent here. Or...I was out of options." She glances around at the darkened night. "I'd rather be...anywhere else."

Sam pulls a necklace out of her shirt, fiddling with it instead of her scar. The silver chain is long, and the pendant looks as if it opens, hinges fixed on one side. A piece of felt or fabric peeks out from a front made of filigree, and the faint scent of lavender wafts from it.

Sam doesn't share more about her dad, and I don't ask. She rubs the pendant like a worry stone as her eyes drift across the lawn. She stares at the blue door to her cabin again and swallows hard, her throat bobbing as the moonlight turns her pale skin silver.

"My dad should have been in jail too," I finally whisper, my words dissipating into the night. I don't know why I tell her. I don't know Sam, and she doesn't know me, but…there's something that sits between us, a string tying two strangers together.

I see myself mirrored in her face. There are shadows in her eyes that reach too deep and a shine that gathers in the corners even as she refuses to let any tears fall. My own eyes prick and sting.

And when Sam turns her attention to me, I think she sees the same. Her gaze trails over my face, discerning details in the emotions I know are laid bare. I want to hide the hurt and anger and fear that burns within me at the thought of my father. But in this moment, alone in the middle of the night with a girl I don't know, I can't.

And neither can she. There's something almost liberating about finding a piece of myself in her. Of connecting with Sam without even needing to speak more of our awful truths to each other.

Sam clenches her jaw and breathes in deeply through her nose.

Slowly, she lets the air out, her chest deflating in a way that seems to calm her, before letting the necklace drop from her hands.

"Then it's good he's dead, isn't it?" Sam words it like a question, but I can tell she's not asking.

Still, I nod. If my father lived, he would've continued to hurt my mom. He would have eventually replaced the belt he used on me with his fists. I've never doubted that.

"Most people have no idea what it can really be like out there, do they?" I scan the cabins across from us. Five in all. Each with a girl or two sleeping behind those colorful doors. And each with her own story, maybe like mine and Sam's. Maybe different.

And maybe they understand too.

"No," Sam says, the single word barely audible. "Most people don't."

Another pause cracks the air between us before I finally speak again. "I envy them," I admit, hoping she understands. "The kind of people that go through life without..." I swallow so hard it hurts. "Without the shadows following them."

"Yeah...me too." Sam's pale eyes are bright, capturing the moonlight as she turns her face away.

We sit in silence and stare at the ink-drenched night and the silver stars, both of us trying to shove the memories of our pasts away.

I don't know who moves first, but without words, I find my hand in hers, gripping it for strength and comfort, and matching the way she clings to me. It's not the same as when I held Harper's hand at the bonfire, all fluttery nerves and flushed cheeks. This… this is like clinging to a life raft suddenly found in the middle of a storm.

We stay there, neither of us able to go back to our cabins. Every once in a while, Sam's gaze drifts to that blue door and a soft tremble shakes her arm.

I don't know what brought Sam outside, but she doesn't seem to want to go back to her room, and I can't force myself to get up either.

So I sit next to her, with the quiet wrapped around us as the minutes whisper by. My thoughts rage with memories of my father that I try not to dwell on. And I can almost feel the way Sam's memories plague her tonight too.

It isn't until a door creaks open and closed that we pull our hands apart. A flashlight bobs as Delaney heads down her little porch and up the dirt path.

"Think we'll get in trouble for being out?" Sam asks.

"Uh, just say we were going to the bathroom and you lost your shoe. Pretend to look around for it before she gets here." I start to get up when the look Sam gives makes me stop.

"Won't work." She points to her bare feet before glancing at my dirtied socks.

"Everything okay?" Delaney asks, stepping over to us.

I shrug, unable to come up with another excuse and hoping she won't tell on us.

"Couldn't sleep," Sam says. "We decided to get some air."

Delaney shines her light at the ground, off to the side so she isn't blinding us. The glow is bright enough to see the way a frown curves her lips down.

"All right, well, it's too late for that," she says. "Time to get back to your cabins and get some sleep. You have a full day tom—" Delaney flicks her flashlight over to my side. "What is that?"

I look down and nearly shove myself into Sam, pushing away from a whiskey bottle that sits next to my thigh. Delaney's flashlight catches the amber liquid, making it glow like fire.

"I—I don't know. It's not mine." I turn to Sam. "Do you see that?"

"Uh, yeah, it's sitting right next to you. It's not mine, and I'm not getting in trouble for it," Sam says, an accusation in her tone. She crosses her arms, staring like she's waiting for me to admit fault—until her forehead scrunches with confusion. "But...you had chips. You weren't carrying anything else."

"Okay," Delaney interrupts. "I don't know whose it is, but you're underage and Whitewood's rules specifically said no recreational drugs or alcohol. You knew that signing up."

"It's not ours," I say, not really caring if we get in trouble. Not when I *know* that's my father's whiskey. That squared bottle with curved corners and a black logo.

The *same* one I found on my nightstand, its shattered glass disappearing.

Only this time I don't know how Sam and Delaney see it too if it's another hallucination.

"I'm confiscating this." Delaney reaches down, and I almost expect her hand to pass through the glass. Instead, her fingers wrap around the neck of the bottle, it's cap still screwed on. "I'm…not going to tell Ms. Evans or Ms. Peterson, but don't make me regret it." She gives a stern look to both of us. "Did you bring anything else I should know about?"

"No—" I start as Sam says, "It's not even mine!"

"You two should get to your own cabins now." Delaney shakes her head. "Please don't make me regret not telling them. We'll all be in trouble."

"Okay." I don't bother to argue again.

Still shaking her head, Delaney makes her way toward the lodge, glancing back to check that we're leaving. I get up, wiping the dirt off my butt, as Sam climbs to her feet.

"Did you bring it?" Sam asks, confusion pulling at her face. "Did I not see—what the fuck." She steps back so quickly I'm scared to turn and find a giant spider or snake.

But when I do, it's so much worse. My stomach drops and I can't breathe. Sitting right where Delaney picked it up is an identical bottle of whiskey.

Sam glances toward the lodge, and I follow her gaze, but Delaney is already inside.

"No," Sam says. "I don't know what's going on, but I'm not

doing this tonight. Sorry, Penny. I—I'm out of here. I can't handle any more. I've got my own shit to deal with." She rushes away, bare feet kicking up dust as she goes to her cabin.

With a shaking hand, I reach down, needing to feel the realness of it like Delaney. But my fingers don't touch the smooth surface of glass or the paper label.

My hand passes through as if it were a mirage. And as my fingers scrape through air and emptiness, the image wavers until there's nothing left of my father's whiskey bottle—only grass and dirt and too many questions.

If I'm hallucinating, then how did Sam and Delaney see the bottle? How did Delaney pick it up, only for a phantom copy to appear? I haven't been able to trust my own mind for a while now. Not with the intrusive thoughts that keep filling my head. Not since I started seeing things no one else noticed. But this is different.

What if *I'm* not getting worse? What if this place is the problem?

EMMA

The girl woke to a sound, a noise that didn't belong. Not the normal creaking of the house or the heater turning on. It wasn't the snores of her parents, who usually slept down the hall, or the flushing of the toilet from a midnight bathroom trip.

It was a soft thump. A little clatter. So distant the girl could almost imagine it was her dream following her into the waking world, sleep and all its stories still clinging to her.

The girl dropped back down, letting her mattress and blankets hug her. She'd almost drifted off again when another sound came, jolting her awake. A muffled bang from downstairs.

She sat up, purple blanket dropping to her waist as a chill swept around her exposed arms. The girl listened, ears straining to hear until a buzzing white noise filled them.

And then it came—a soft thumping like footsteps.

The girl threw her blankets back and rubbed her eyes. She stood, shivering when her bare feet touched the cold wooden floor.

"Dad?" Her voice was scratchy and too quiet from sleep. She cleared her throat and tried again. "Dad."

Her father wasn't supposed to be walking around. He was still recovering from ankle surgery. But he never listened. And of course, the night her mother was gone, staying with her older sister who'd begged for help with a colicky baby, he would do this—test the limits of his healing.

The girl's door creaked open, and her steps drummed down the hall, turning into a rhythmic tapping on the stairs. She stood at the base, staring at the rumpled blankets on their living room couch—her father's makeshift bed. She glanced to the right, toward the kitchen, but no warm, glowing light spilled out. She looked to the left, to the bathroom door, but it stood ajar, dark and empty.

Another noise stuttered into the night, coming from down the hall, past the empty bathroom where her father's office sat.

A twist pulled at the girl's chest, an unknown anxiety yanking at her ribs. She looked back to the couch. To her father's empty spot.

She didn't know why he'd be up, but it had to be him. She breathed out slowly and tried to calm the silly racing of her heart.

"Dad?" She moved toward the hall, unable to shake away the anxious thrum.

Something lashed out at the girl, gripped her wrist, and yanked down. Her mouth opened to scream when she recognized her father. He crouched behind a console table that sat against the wall, right outside of the hallway.

"What—" she started, but her father lifted one finger to his lips as another clunking sound came from his office. And suddenly the girl understood. Someone else was in their house.

Her gaze dipped to her father's other hand, and she noticed the silver baseball bat he gripped.

"Do you have your phone?" her father whispered. His weathered face had even more wrinkles framing his eyes with concern. "We need to call the police."

The girl patted her sleep pants as if her phone would magically appear. She shook her head, breaths turning to gulps.

"Calm down, sweetheart. Go get it and call the police." He nodded toward the stairs. "Wait in your room."

"What about you?" The girl looked down the hall as another thumping came, like desk drawers closing or books falling. "Come upstairs."

"I can't." He glanced down at his ankle and shifted his foot, flinching against the pain it caused. "I'll be too loud."

"You can't stay here. What if—"

"Go," he told her, his voice low and commanding. "Now."

The girl hesitated but listened. She stood up, twisting too quickly and knocking into the console table. A little papier-mâché cat, which she'd made as child and always thought was too ugly for her mother to keep, trembled with the lamp it sat under. They tumbled to the ground together. Shattered ceramic broke and spilled too loudly.

"Go!" her father said, a shout-whisper slicing into her.

"Who's there?" a voice called from her father's office. Footsteps pounded against the hardwood floor, louder the closer they came. "Who's there?" they demanded.

The girl reached for her father, ready to pull him along, but he pushed her back. She stumbled toward the stairs, crashing onto the lowest step as a man's silhouette filled the hallway. He wore dark jeans, a black T-shirt, and a ski mask.

Her father stood, grunting as he put weight on his ankle, and lifted the silver bat in his hands. "Get out of here!" he shouted, but whether he was talking to her or the man, the girl didn't know.

She couldn't even stand up before the man rushed her father, shoving him hard against the wall. The baseball bat fell from her father's hands, bouncing off the wood before rolling toward the girl. She snatched it up as her father wrestled the stranger, grunting and shoving. But her father couldn't fight him off, not with his ankle so weak.

The stranger punched her father in the face. Scarlet blood

smeared against his brown skin as it gushed from his nose. The girl cried out for the man to stop, but he ignored her. She took a step closer and raised the bat high. With shaking arms, she swung as hard as she could.

The air whistled in her ears before the thud of metal hitting flesh sent an ache through her hands and reverberated up her arms.

The man let go of her father as she pulled her arms back again, as she swung and swung and swung—until the stranger fell to the floor with moans that slithered into the girl's ears. Until he crawled across the floor as the girl's father laid his hands over her forearms and stopped her from drawing the weapon back again. The stranger snuck away, stumbling out the front door instead of the unlatched window he'd climbed in from. The girl's father slipped his arms around her. He held her tight as the baseball bat fell from her grasp and her hiccupping cries filled the quiet night.

ELEVEN

The sun shines too brightly for so early in the morning as I stare at the notebook in my lap. My nail drags down the drawing of my father, scratching into that nightmare version of him. I pause when my fingers graze that graphite-drawn watch. I don't know what's happening to me, or what's going on at Whitewood, but I need to know why I keep seeing these reminders of my father.

And why Sam and Delaney could see what I thought was another hallucination.

The door to my cabin swings open, and I slam the notebook closed before shoving it into the drawer of the nightstand.

"You ready?" Emma asks, setting her toiletries bag on her dresser. She glances in the mirror. Matching sets of yoga clothes, formfitting shirt and leggings in powder blue, were dropped off for us this morning. "It's cute, right?"

"Yeah." I grab my sneakers and slip them on, but I don't care about yoga therapy, whatever that is. I have one goal today: figure out what's happening to me—what's happening here. And that starts with talking to Sam about last night.

We head outside, the morning already warm and bright. To my right, Harper and Sam step out of their cabin too.

Sam nods at me, and despite the unexplainable way the night ended, she doesn't avoid me like I worried she would.

"Hey, Penny," she says, coming over to us with Harper following. The two of them wear the same blue yoga clothes, making us look like little dolls dressed alike, except for the necklaces Sam and Harper wear. It's the same one Sam had on last night, only now Harper has its twin. Are they…friendship necklaces? A gift from one of them to the other? And why does that make my fingers crawl across my own collarbone, which feels emptier than ever before?

"Ooh, what are those?" Emma asks, stepping closer to Harper and admiring the silver locket with filigree openings.

"Oh, they're aromatherapy pendants. Ms. Evans gave them to us." Harper lifts hers up, and suddenly my neck doesn't feel so empty. "They've got that lavender blend in them."

I want to ask Harper why Ms. Evans gave those to them, but Sam shifts closer to me, leaning in and whispering, "Look, I don't know why you brought alcohol here, and it's not my concern, but next time don't have it out when I'm around. As much as I don't wanna be here, I can't get kicked out, okay?"

"I didn't—"

"You had to have brought it," she interrupts, and it sounds like she's convincing herself.

There's so much I want to say, but Harper and Emma are too close. "Okay." I let it go for now. "But...can we talk later?"

Sam hesitates. She glances back at her cabin as we walk down the dirt path to the main lodge.

"Wanna get spots near each other at this yoga class?" Harper interrupts, and any chance I had of Sam answering evaporates. But I can't be upset when Harper looks at me, a soft, hesitant smile decorating her round face, so I only nod.

"Yoga *therapy*," Sam corrects her, sighing loudly. "How's that supposed to help us?"

"I don't know, but no one's allowed to laugh when I fall on my butt," Emma says. "I've never done yoga before."

Harper leans in, slipping closer until that familiar scent of lilac and sweet almond perfume fills the space around us, now tinged with the smell of her aromatherapy necklace.

"I was wondering if you were busy later," she whispers, her steps slowing until Emma and Sam slide in front of us. "Or if you might want to hang out? With me?"

"Yeah," I say, stomach swooping at the idea. But I look around as we walk. There's the lake and trees. And more trees. "Uh, what would you want to do? Maybe a walk?"

"Oh, um...I..." She follows my gaze as I point to the birch forest.

"Don't worry. Delaney's forest rules only said not to go in at night," I joke, even if I don't really believe in them or the monsters.

"Uh, y-yeah, that's fine," Harper finally says. She takes a deep breath, her hand reaching up to fiddle with her necklace. "A walk. I can—we can do that."

"Great," I say, probably too quickly, in case she changes her mind. "Did you…want to ask Sam or Emma also?" I tip my head toward them.

"Oh…I was thinking it could be just us?" Harper bites her lip, and I can't stop staring at the way her teeth dig into the soft skin. "But if you want to, we can—"

"No," I cut her off, a grin pulling at my face. "No, that sounds good. I've got one of those small group sessions before free time, but I can meet you after."

"I'll come by your cabin," Harper says, and I can't stop the rapid beat of my heart when she smiles.

In front of me, Emma turns and stares, widening her eyes.

Is that a date? She mouths the words as she wiggles her eyebrows, and I pray Harper isn't watching.

I shrug one shoulder, wanting to read Harper's invitation as more than friends, but there's no way I'm going to outright ask.

"I've got that small group too." Sam twists around to look at Harper and me. Her pink hair is even brighter in the sunshine than it was under the moonlight. "Guess Ms. Evans put us in the same one."

Even if things ended weirdly last night, I tell Sam, "Well, it'll be nice having a friend with me." Someone that understands, I want to say but don't. Not in front of Harper and Emma.

I didn't think I'd actually find friends here, but the more I get to know the other girls, the more I find a connection with them.

But even with all of that, I can't stop the gnawing questions plaguing me about what's happening here at Whitewood.

———————

The door to Ms. Peterson's yoga room is open, and voices drift out as we make our way in. Meditation music is already playing at a low volume, while a diffuser sits in the corner, gently puffing that lavender and lime scent around.

Eight neoprene mats are spread out in two matching rows, all of them a muddy but soft mauve against the white floor tiles. Ms. Peterson's yoga mat, lilac with floral designs, sits at the front. The walls are a cheery, buttery yellow—brighter than the other rooms in the lodge, which are all creams and various cool-toned pastels. There's even a mural painting in here, a pink sun and fluffy white clouds, with the words BREATHE IN. BREATHE OUT, written in a deep plum and looping script.

"I'm sure she's fine," Ms. Peterson says to Quinn, standing close to the girl and speaking in a lowered voice that I barely hear but still catches my attention.

I make my way over to the front row with Emma, Harper, and

Sam. Kylie and Page sit and wait on two mats in the second row, while a third has Quinn's discarded shoes next to it.

"Shoes and socks off, girls," Ms. Peterson says, leaning around Quinn to talk to us. "And take a water bottle." She points to a table where reusable bottles sit, vinyl stickers with each of our names stuck on.

Penny—not *Penelope*—mine says. A warmth fills my chest at the small reminder that our counselors listened.

I grab my bottle, and even being made of only plastic, it's heavy, already filled with water.

Hit them, the voice in my head breaks the quiet. *Crack it against their skulls.*

Each word is louder than the last until my hand is shaking hard enough that I almost drop the bottle.

Instead, I repeat what Ms. Evans told me again: *If you don't want to hurt someone, then you won't. You can tell those intrusive thoughts to be quiet.*

When the shaking in my hand turns to a light tremble, I almost believe Ms. Evans's words.

"But I haven't seen her since last night," Quinn says to Ms. Peterson, pulling my attention back to the room.

"You probably just missed her this morning. I'm sure she's with Ms. Evans, needing some one-on-one time instead," she tells Quinn. "There's nothing to worry about. Any of you girls are allowed to skip group activities if it's because you're looking for more individual sessions. I'll check in with her after yoga."

"What's going on?" I whisper to Kylie and Page as I set my water bottle down and push it slightly away.

"Reagan is MIA." Page pushes her glasses up from where they've slipped down her nose. The movement flexes the muscles of her forearm, and the fluorescent lights glare down on the burn scar etched into her skin. "Did you guys see her?"

"No." Harper drops down onto the mat next to mine. "I thought she skipped breakfast and slept in. After how late we stayed up with Delaney during the bonfire, I sort of thought they'd let us all sleep longer."

I glance at Sam, who stayed up even later with me. Dark circles hang underneath her eyes, matching the bruising under my own. A shiver of unease crawls over my skin. I want to pull Sam aside and ask if she actually saw that whiskey disappear. I need her to tell me I'm not losing my grip on reality—that I'm not the only one feeling like something strange is happening at Whitewood.

"Quinn said she woke up at four in the morning to pee, and Reagan wasn't in bed," Kylie adds. She sits with her legs crossed on the yoga mat, gaze dancing around the group. Tired smudges rest under her dark eyes too.

Even her roommate, Page, has bags hidden behind her glasses. Emma and Harper are the only ones that look like they got decent sleep.

"But Quinn didn't find her in the bathroom," Page adds, leaning forward and whispering like it's a secret.

"So why would Ms. Peterson think she's with Ms. Evans?" I ask. First these hallucinations, then Ms. Evans's outburst in our session, and now Quinn can't find her roommate, and Ms. Peterson is acting like it's nothing? Too many things about Whitewood feel *not quite right* in a way that leaves my chest tight.

Kylie shrugs as Ms. Peterson tells Quinn to take a spot.

"All right." Ms. Peterson moves to stand on her mat. "Let's get started."

She directs us in stretches and breathing exercises to start. Each deep lungful tastes almost soapy from the lavender-scented air. But as the hour goes on and Ms. Peterson shows us poses, as she tells us to clear our minds and connect with our bodies, the scent changes, turning sharp and bitter.

"Breathe out. Release the tension," Ms. Peterson says as we lie on our stomachs, hands on the mats and backs arched with our heads tilted up. With each new pose, she talks to us, explaining all the different ways trauma can be stored in the body, how to let go of thoughts and feelings and tension. Telling us to breathe deep.

But each inhale is too sour. It fills my head with dizziness and turns my stomach, the lavender and lime of the diffuser overtaken by the stench of my father's whiskey. I can almost feel the sticky heat of my father's breath mingling with the smell and it makes me gag.

"Do you smell that?" I ask, whispering to Sam on my left. I face away from the diffuser quietly chugging away in the corner of the room, but it doesn't help.

"Smell what?" she asks, glancing around. "The oil?"

"Never mind," I say, dropping the pose.

"Are you okay? You look like you're gonna puke."

I raise my hand even as I stand. "Ms. Peterson." I don't want to cause another scene or upset our counselor by disrupting another session, but I can't stay here. The need to leave overrides my need to keep the peace. "I don't feel good. I have to go to the bathroom."

I don't wait for a response. I rush down the hall, but it doesn't matter how far I get from that room. The scent of whiskey follows me. It fills my head along with all the memories of my father. Of all the times he shoved and hit Mom. Of all the times his belt met my skin.

And of all the times I wished I could push him away but didn't.

A wall of blackness washes over my vision for a second, and images flash in the darkness. Hands shoving and pushing. A scream and a body falling.

I shake my head, willing the images—intrusive thoughts or whatever they are—to go away. Begging the scent of whiskey and my father's disgusting breath to leave me alone. But they don't. They chase me all the way to the bathroom, where I lean against the sink and gulp down quick breaths until the taste of clean air finally fills my lungs.

TWELVE

Dread clings like a shadow for the rest of the day. The phantom scent of whiskey and memories best left forgotten follow me for hours. But when I see Harper sitting on the steps of my porch, the worry fades, as if Harper's smile is the sun chasing the darkness out.

"Hey," I say, stopping before her.

"Hi." She's changed out of this morning's yoga clothes into cutoff shorts and a pale pink tank top. "You ready?"

"Just a minute. I need a new shirt." I pluck at the front of my black T-shirt, wanting to wear a tank top like her if we're going to hike through the woods.

"Okay." She slides over on the steps, and I slip past her as the scent of her perfume mixed with the aromatherapy necklace reaches out to me, soft and inviting.

When I open the door to my cabin, buttery afternoon light shines in through the skylights and gives the room a warm glow. The air conditioner hums in the corner, chilling the space and the sweat on my skin, but the window above the desk is cracked open, letting the cool air out. I cross the room to close it, wondering if Emma left it open. But…the way it upset her the other night makes me doubt that. Maybe the heat outside and the colder room are somehow warping the wooden frame and making it slide up.

I pull the pane closed, but as my fingers leave the window sash, a dark shape outside runs past, too close and too fast. A blur against the pale trees.

A gasp crowds my throat, a shock of adrenaline pushing through my veins before I take a deep breath to calm down, to stop *imagining* that nightmare version of my father. It's not real.

I turn away from the window and move to my dresser, not wanting to keep Harper waiting. I reach out for the drawer when a shine catches my eye. The brassy yellow of a fake golden belt buckle and the brown of worn faux leather, cracked with age, stare at me from the top of my dresser. I stumble back, nearly falling over, as my father's belt sits coiled like a snake ready to strike.

I flinch at the sight, remembering the pain of its bite.

Take it, those intrusive thoughts say. *Use it like he did.*

"No!" I shout, too loud in the small room. I swipe an arm out and try to shove the belt away, but my hand glides through. Another hallucination.

One, two, three, four, I count in my head, tapping my thumb to each finger with both hands. *One, two, three, four.*

It doesn't help. My breathing turns into short gasps that hurt my chest. I count faster, unable to stop the fear from taking over.

Onetwothreefour. Why do I keep seeing things that can't be real? *Taptaptaptap.* What's happening to me?

"Penny, are you almost ready?" Harper calls through the closed door.

I almost let Harper in and ask if she sees my father's belt. But what good would that do? Sam and Delaney saw the whiskey bottle. Delaney touched and took one. Sam saw the other disappear...didn't she?

Or am I making that up too?

If that whiskey bottle wasn't real, if my father's watch and belt aren't either—and I *know* they can't be—then have any of those conversations actually happened? Did I even see Sam and Delaney last night? Or talk to Sam today?

Maybe I've been imagining more than I realized. The thought makes my breath rush out, and I almost collapse to the floor. Only Harper's voice stops me.

"Penny?" she says, and the belt I haven't been able to take my eyes off of blinks out of existence, as if it was never there.

And it wasn't. It couldn't have been. After my father died, I burned it and threw the melted plastic and charred metal away.

"Coming," I yell out, pulling my T-shirt off. I grab the first tank top from my dresser and throw it on.

With a deep breath, I open the door and step out, shutting away all those worries and questions and focusing only on Harper.

On the girl that *is* real and standing on my porch.

"Did you say something to me in there?" she asks.

Push her, that voice whispers in my head. *Down the steps. Watch her fall and break.*

"No," I mumble, fighting against the images that fill my head. Hands reaching out. Shoving hard. I can almost feel the solidness of a body under my touch before it falls away, only empty air in my grasp. The echo of a shout fills my head.

"You okay?" Harper's face scrunches in concern.

"Yeah, sorry." I shake my head and push those violent thoughts away. I point toward a small trail that starts at the last cabin and leads into the forest. "This way?"

"Uh, yeah." Harper bites her lip nervously but nods, and we head into the birch forest.

The temperature dips slightly and makes the afternoon heat more comfortable. All around us, the birch trees stand like silent sentinels, their green crowns diffusing the sunlight. The gray knots on their trunks look like eyes, staring from a hundred different directions and watching our every move. The farther we go, the deeper the chill and the darker the woods become.

"So what brought you to Whitewood?" Harper asks, breaking

the silence. There's an edge to her voice I don't understand. As we walk along a thin trail, overgrown with moss and brush, Harper's gaze darts up and down the path, and she spins the ring on her finger. I can't tell if she's nervous because we're alone—or if, somehow, she realizes how dangerous I might be. Does she know *that's* what brought me to Whitewood and wants to hear me say it?

"My mom and therapist thought it would help," I say, falling back on that same flimsy line. "You?"

She shrugs and fidgets with her ring again, twisting the silver band and black stone around and around. "My parents thought it would help too. With, um, my…" She takes a deep breath that trembles through her shoulders. "I'm sorry, it's just—"

"It's okay." I pause on the trail, and she copies me. "You don't have tell me. We all have things that are hard to talk about, and I'm practically a stranger to you. Really, it's okay."

"No, it's not that—not you. I'm here 'cause…I tried to help someone and couldn't. And they…" Her breath shudders in again as if she can pull the words back into herself. It's like she does and doesn't want to talk about it at the same time. "They died. Because of me. Because I couldn't—"

Images I don't want to remember play across my vision like a movie. I squeeze my eyes shut for a second, letting starbursts cover the memories of splayed and crooked limbs. Not whoever Harper is talking about but my father, dead in front of me. A wall of darkness covers my mind, and then the memories flash like lightning strikes: blood from a broken body, a scream, and the fading anger of a dying man.

"I'm sorry, that was too much to share," Harper says, and I open my eyes again. She stares at me, face soft and pained.

"No," I say, wanting nothing more than to erase the discomfort in her gaze. "Never apologize for opening up to someone. Or for trusting me enough to tell me that." Harper looks like she still wants to crumple straight to the forest floor, so I offer her a truth of my own. "I…I know what it's like to see someone die too. And whatever the circumstances, I'm sorry you had to go through that."

Harper pauses and looks at me the way Sam did, like she sees something of herself in me. And I see it too. We are mirrors, different details to our frames—our stories—but still a reflection shared within them.

Her dark eyes start to shine as she looks at me. "It was…" She taps the fingers of one hand against her thigh. Not in the uniform way I tap mine. Her fingers press into her skin, one or two or more at a time, in different configurations.

It's more like playing chords. Like how, after yoga, she played her guitar in music therapy while I hit a silver triangle with a rod and tried not to listen to the voice in my head that told me to push the slender metal into someone's eye.

"It's okay." I rest my hand on her shoulder lightly. Gently. Her fingers go still. "You don't have to talk about it."

"Thank you." She turns back around, and I drop my hand.

Harper gives me a crooked smile. Another deep breath, and she shakes the sadness away. "My dad's the one that encouraged me to come. I wanted to try, to see if it helped, but—I don't know." She shrugs. "What about your dad?"

"Not worth mentioning" is all I say as we walk deeper through the birch forest.

"Oh, I'm sorry. I shouldn't have assumed—"

I wave her off. "It's fine. I just don't like talking about him."

Pink tinges her full cheeks, blooming across her skin in a way that only makes her prettier, that makes the darkness of her eyes stand out even more.

"So…um, got any pets?" I ask, hoping to shift the conversation to easier topics as we start walking down the trail again. I don't know how to do this, how talk to someone I like. The one and only date I went on back home went horribly. I was finally able *to* date without my father…around. And Silas was sweet enough, but my intrusive thoughts took over the night until I—quite literally—ran away from him.

"I've got a dog." She smiles, but it's tinged in sadness again. "My parents always said no, but Finn, he found me when I was… hiking, and he's been with me ever since. You?"

I let my hands swing by my sides as we walk. Harper is only a breath away, and if I moved a little closer, our hands would graze.

"My mom got a cat a little while ago." My father never let her before, but now she's free of him and his rules. "He's an old grumpy monster that she rescued from the shelter, but we love him." I glance around at the forest. "Do you go hiking a lot?"

"I—I used to." Her gaze goes distant as she twists the ring on her finger again before letting go and holding the pendant of her aromatherapy necklace instead. She takes a deep inhale of that scent. "You?" she finally asks.

"No, not really," I tell her. "My father…he didn't like doing stuff like that, so we never did. And besides, my grandma—my mom's mom, I mean—she had all sorts of superstitions like Delaney."

"Superstitions?" Harper asks.

I shake my head, trying to recall any of those old memories from before Grandma died, from before I was even old enough for school, when things were slightly better and Mom had somewhere to go when my father's temper started getting bad. "I just know she lived near the woods but didn't like it. Said the trees were always screaming. I remember *that*, at least. And she used to say, *Never listen to them.*"

"*Them?*" Harper's eyes dart around with a nervous energy. Maybe she believes in Delaney's story more than me. I should have suggested we go canoeing on the lake or something instead. But I don't know how to canoe, and I didn't want Delaney to chaperone us.

I shouldn't have brought up the stories from my grandma, but I can't ignore her question now.

"The trees," I answer, glancing at the pale woods surrounding us, glad they don't scream like my grandma thought her dark forest did. "Anyway," I add, laughing to ease the awkwardness. "You used to go hiking? What made you stop?"

There's a long pause as she fidgets with her ring again. So long, I start to wonder if she'll answer. Finally, she waves a hand at herself. "Yeah, believe it or not, chubby girls can love outdoor activities too." Her tone is light, but it's at odds with tension in her steps.

"I'm sorry. That's not what—"

"No, I don't know why I said that." She closes her eyes and takes another deep breath, smelling the oils in her necklace. "It's this place… It brings up a lot of stuff." She shakes her head. "I don't know. I'm just nervous." She tries to smile, but it wavers as her gaze darts around.

This place… Does she mean Whitewood? Does she feel how there's something off here too?

I scan the forest like Harper, as if I can see through the trees and back to the camp and our counselors. "Do you think Reagan is still with Ms. Evans? Doing one-on-one and…whatever else with her all day?"

"I guess?" Harper's brow wrinkles. "Why? Did you hear something?"

"No. I…" Harper doesn't seem concerned or suspicious, and it makes me wonder if I'm making things up. "I just haven't seen her yet," I finally say.

"I'm sure she'll show up for our next group thing or dinner."

"Yeah," I agree, pushing my unfounded worries away and wanting to enjoy the afternoon with Harper instead.

We head down the dirt path again, and I slide closer to Harper as the trail narrows and our hands brush. Harper doesn't pull away as our hands sweep past each other again, and this time I hook a finger out, catching her hand to intertwine ours, even as a swarm of bees seems to fill my belly.

We walk down the path quietly, fingers woven together, as the dirt trail dwindles. A small smile pulls at my lips, and my heart is thundering so loud in my ears, I wonder if Harper can hear it.

But the farther we make our way through the woods, the more a frown pulls at her lips.

I glance down at our hands, wondering if I shouldn't have taken hold of hers. I'm about to ask when I see it again—my father's belt. Wrapped impossibly around my waist, slid through the loops of my jeans.

My heart thrashes against my ribs, no longer a soft excitement about holding Harper's hand. I let go and grab at the belt, ready to rip it off, even if it can't really be there.

You'll use it, those thoughts hiss at me again, *like he did to you. You'll watch her flinch and cry.*

No, I tell the voice. I can't. I won't.

But even if Ms. Evans says I'm in control, it doesn't feel that way.

"Penny? M-maybe we should go back?" Harper stumbles over

her words, breaths coming fast as she stares from me to the forest and back.

I drop my hands from my waist. I don't know if she can see my father's belt, but it doesn't matter. The fear written across her face is clear.

Is it there because of me?

How many times did my father reach for his belt—just like I did—while I curled in on myself from fear?

Do it, those intrusive thoughts tell me. *You will eventually.*

I shake my head, but it doesn't make the voice go away.

You're like him. You'll hurt her.

No, I say, but the objection is small, quiet. And as I turn around and head back down the trail with Harper, I realize it doesn't matter why she's afraid. Because she *should* be afraid of me. I can't control my own thoughts, and I keep seeing things that shouldn't exist.

I can't tell what's real or not.

Before, I only had that voice to fight against, but this—it's too much.

I can't trust myself at all anymore.

THIRTEEN

Emma's snores cut through the night, covering the sound of the wind pushing against glass panes and the creaking of wood settling. A little diffuser, which she got from Ms. Evans, chugs away on her nightstand.

I stare at the beams in the ceiling above my bed and the small patch of sky framed by my skylight while trying to fall asleep, but it's useless. Even with the aromatherapy seeping into each breath, I can't calm my thoughts. I fidget under the blanket, unable to get comfortable. Reagan, the girl always smiling, with the curly brown hair and a missing pinkie fingertip, hasn't been seen all day.

Ms. Peterson went from saying she was sure Reagan was having a one-on-one session with Ms. Evans this morning to telling us that the other girl needed *more* than individual care.

Ms. Evans said Reagan is doing a special therapy program. But that doesn't explain *where* she is. She hasn't joined us for any meals or group sessions all day, and I didn't see her go to her cabin with Quinn tonight.

Reagan is having a hard time, they said, but confidentiality meant they couldn't explain more.

Maybe she's like me, seeing things that can't exist. Getting worse instead of better. Like Clara. Will I be next? Asking them for help like Reagan and getting shut away too?

There's nothing to worry about, Ms. Evans promised. *She's taking care of herself.*

But do Ms. Evans and Ms. Peterson not feel how something is *off* about this place? Do they know what's happening?

Turning on my side, I try to let my thoughts fade and to sleep instead. I take a deep breath, the air tasting of lavender, but it doesn't help. Too many worries keep me awake.

I couldn't get Sam alone earlier, but maybe I can find Reagan and ask her what's going on—if she's seeing things too. I sit up, throwing my blankets back. And if I can't find her, then I'll go to Delaney and make her tell me what happened to Clara.

My feet touch the chilled floor, but I don't stand. Not when a sound echoes through the room and makes me freeze. It's not the soft puffs of the diffuser or Emma's light snores but a rustling noise scraping across wood. A scratching *inside* the cabin.

I hold my breath, ears straining, and scan the darkness. Shadows cling to the walls and drape over the furniture.

I have to clench my jaw against the scream trying to claw its way up my throat when a shape near my dresser peels apart from the gloom, growing taller and taller. It turns into a person—into my father, the version from my nightmares. He is made of nothing but shadows, smears and smudges, and no defining features.

His head cocks to the side as he stands fully upright, shoulders tilted where the slanted ceiling is too low.

I squeeze my eyes shut, not wanting to see that waking nightmare. My heart pounds hard against my ribs, counting the seconds with me. My thumb and fingers tap in time, but it doesn't help, and I abandon the exercise.

I take deep breaths, trying to steady the air that shivers through my lungs. The lavender and lime are sharp on my tongue.

This isn't real.

I must have fallen asleep. I must be dreaming.

I tell myself to wake up. To count to three and open my eyes, and then he'll be gone.

One. Two. Three.

I force myself to look, squinting in fear like I'm a little kid again, and grab my blanket, holding it to my chest as if the thin fabric could be a shield against my nightmares.

He's still there, and it's so much worse seeing that *thing* than hallucinating about my father's watch or whiskey bottle. Worse than his belt.

The shadow man steps closer, and I scramble back, the

blanket and sheets twisting around my torso and legs until I fall off the opposite side of the bed. I struggle to stand, trapped by the slanted wall. Only the narrow bed frame separates me from the shadow man.

I spare a glance at Emma, still tucked in the comfort of her fluffy blankets, one foot sticking out as she snores loudly.

"Not real. Not real," I whisper to myself. It's another hallucination. That's all. It *has* to be.

Even with only pitch-black hollows for eyes, the shadow man stares at me, scrutinizing every detail the way I do to him. He holds my father's whiskey bottle, amber liquid sloshing within the glass as he takes another step closer. He lifts his other hand, and I almost sigh at seeing it empty, no belt curled within his grip, but my father's gaudy watch catches the moonlight on his wrist.

The creature lifts his index finger, and the shape of it grows longer and sharper, like a shadow-made talon. He rakes it across his featureless face and rips open a gaping mouth as I gag down bile.

A growl cracks and splinters up his throat, long and low, seeping out of the slice across his face. The nightmare creature points his clawed hand toward me, and my heart slams in my chest.

"Go away," I whisper, wishing he would listen. That he would disappear in a cloud of smoke like the whiskey bottle did. Like the belt and watch. "You're not here. Not real."

He opens the void of his mouth again, letting those same gurgled sounds and growls drop like stones to the floor, anger filling them more and more. He throws the whiskey bottle across the room. I flinch as the glass breaks and shatters, the sharp scent filling the room, so much like the night my father died.

I glance at Emma, but she doesn't even stir at the sounds, still snoring deeply.

My breaths heave as I back away.

You're just like your father, that voice whispers. *Violent and dangerous.*

The thought brands itself into me until it's a physical ache in my chest. All I want is to be myself. To make my own choices without those thoughts filling my head.

But I'll never be free of them—of him.

The shadow man lunges forward, and I stumble back into the wall. Another whiskey bottle is in his hand, as if he never threw it. He slams his empty hand down onto my nightstand. And every memory of my father hitting and punching…they all drown me until I'm a child made of nothing but fear and failure again.

I stagger to the side and run for the door. He follows, moving in a flash, as I fling the cabin open. Hallucination or not, everything in me is screaming to *get away, get away, get away*.

I stumble down the steps and trip along the dirt path. My breath scrapes, burning my lungs. Cabins blink by, one after another, a wall of white birch trees behind them and a crescent moon hanging above.

I spare a glance back, terrified that the shadow man will catch me, but my feet stutter to a stop. He's on the small porch of my cabin, not chasing me—only standing and staring like when he'd loom over the end of my bed in my nightmares.

There must be a reason I'm seeing him. But before I can try to figure it out or take a step in either direction, the campgrounds melt before my eyes. Fear like nothing I've ever known before paralyzes me. My muscles shake, taut and tense, and I forget to breathe until my lungs burn.

The cabins crumble and disintegrate into dust. Dark trees grow up from the ground, stretching taller and wider. The lake and the dirt paths waver like hot air before disappearing from existence. Birch trees bulge and darken, exploding in size until giant oaks have replaced them.

When I look up, there are a thousand stars scattered in a blackened sky, obscured by a canopy of branches above my head instead of the bare open expanse that was there only seconds ago. A full moon is pinned among the stars, no longer a thin crescent slice.

"What's happening?" I shout.

Turning in a circle, I search for the shadow man but can't see him through this dark impossible forest.

"How?" I ask, and my voice echoes. "How is this possible?" Am I dreaming, or is this another hallucination, worse than the others? Beneath my bare feet, brush and sticks poke into my skin, no worn path anymore. The temperature drops, nearly freezing, and I shiver in my long shirt and underwear. It *feels* real.

I spin around and search between thick tree trunks and darkened cracks for that creature. Terror that I'll be left here—alone forever—overwhelms me. Until a noise reaches my ears, the strangeness of it stealing my attention. The soft hiccupping cries of a child ricochets around the woods. With it come the sounds of the forest—insects buzz, bushes rustle with unseen animals, and in the distance wolves howl.

"Hello?" I call out, still hearing a child's cry. "Is someone there?"

This place, it can't be real—yet I feel the rough bark of the trees with my hand as I slip between them. The uneven dirt, grass, and sticks that litter the ground prick the bottom of my soles.

The crying grows louder, coming from all around. I clasp my hands over my ears, but it doesn't help. My steps move faster, searching for the child—for a way out.

The crying turns deafening. It smothers and consumes me from the inside out. I run as fast as my bare feet allow.

I don't see the rock until I'm tripping over it. Pain shoots through my toes, up my ankle. My hands and knees are scraped raw, dirt and blood staining them. My body aches as I sit up, palms stinging.

"What's happening to me?" I whisper.

I peer through the darkness, scanning every tree and bush, but I'm alone. The crying has stopped. Even the insects, the rustling wind, and the wolves' howls are gone.

Alone, except for a shabby-looking teddy bear, which sits on the ground a foot away, so out of place. On its chest is an embroidered red *Q*, which matches the blood on my hands and knees.

Slowly, I reach out to touch it, wondering why my mind has conjured up a lonely teddy bear. At least I understood the belt, the whiskey, and my father's watch. But this? I've never seen this forest or that teddy bear.

Before I can pick the toy up, a black shape rushes out of the darkness toward me. A scream tears up my throat as the thing jerks to a stop only inches away.

My hands shake as I slowly, achingly tilt my head up to find the shadow man hovering above.

He holds the whiskey bottle once more—the sight of it repulsive but at least familiar. His other hand lifts, skimming past my face as my father's golden watch flashes in the moonlight. I flinch, but he grabs my wrist, fingers digging into my skin.

"Let go!" I scream. He's nothing more than a figment of my own mind; I should be in control here. Not him—*it*.

But his grip is unforgiving, bruising. He drops the bottle in his other hand, the glass shattering and filling the air with the stringent scent of whiskey. He snatches the teddy bear off the ground instead, fingers clasping around its neck. With a growl, he shakes it in my face and yanks on my wrist, squeezing impossibly tighter. The creature's torn mouth twists open, a gaping chasm stretched into a silent scream.

"Wake up," I tell myself. "Wake up." I *have* to be asleep. My hand doesn't pass through the shadow man, and the forest doesn't blink out of existence like my other hallucinations did.

He growls again and finally lets go, but before I can move away, the same hand lashes out and grips my neck like he does with the teddy bear. I choke, gasping even as images fill my head, memories that aren't mine: shattered glass scattered across asphalt, a rotating glow of red and yellow and green lights, deer antlers that stretch up to the sky.

"Please," I beg the shadow man, real or not. "Leave me alone." The words are ripped from the depths of my heart. I whispered them a thousand times as a child, but never when my father could hear. I jerk away, breaking the connection as his fingers scrape the skin on my neck.

"Leave me alone," I say, voice firmer.

The creature growls, serrated mouth flapping with the grating sound as it wafts the scent of my father's whiskey-laced breath in my face. Another bottle is in his hand instead of the teddy bear. He throws it deep into the trees. Anger pulses off the creature as he rips the golden watch away next. He hurls it into the darkness, but in the blink of an eye it appears on his wrist once more. He takes a step toward me, then another, the whiskey bottle in his other hand once again.

He shifts closer as I slide away. Those hollow eyes, concave shadows and nothing more, stare at me. His tainted breath lashes against my face with each exhale, hot and sticky.

I don't wait to see what he'll do next. Instead, I turn and run, not daring to look back. The shadow man's enraged roar follows at my heels. I keep going, crashing through giant trees and trying to escape that creature and this place.

FOURTEEN

The forest blurs past me as I run. My bare feet are in agony, but I don't stop.

It isn't until a door appears that I jerk to a halt. A wooden one, painted bright red, stands between two large trees. There's nothing holding it up, no wall or frame, as if a door grew out of the ground. I reach one hand out to touch the painted wood, to prove it's real... Well, maybe even touching it can't do that anymore. But just as I'm about to grab the handle, something flickers in my peripheral.

I twist to the right, expecting to find my father's ghost, but it's another door, standing on its own like the first, yellow this time. Another and another appear out of thin air, vivid blue and a glossy green, all lined up. They're situated dozens of feet apart, nestled between the giant tree trunks.

I move back, passing the doors and enormous trees and wishing to wake up or come back to reality. The low growl of the shadow man rumbles through the forest, sending goose bumps crawling all over my skin. The blue door is closest, and I sprint to it. Anything to get away from that creature.

I grab the handle and rip it open. Darkness envelopes me as I spring through the doorway and slam it closed.

"No," a voice hisses, anger and fear suffusing the single word. "Not again."

"Hello?" I step farther into...a room? Moonlight shines in through two skylights and one regular window, but the space is still darker than outside. When my eyes adjust, I find myself standing in a cabin at Whitewood again, a mirror image of my own except both beds have the shape of a person in them.

"Get out," the voice says, tone severe. The person sits up, gripping a notebook like a shield—no, like a weapon, ready to throw it—and her pink hair catches in the silver light.

"Sam?" I glance around her cabin, more confused than ever.

I open the door again, peering out and unsure of what I'll find, a dark forest or the campgrounds.

"What the f—" I start but can't even finish the sentence. Outside the door, floodlights from the main building light up the grassy lawn and flagpole. To my left and right, more cabins sit in a line. I can't stop my gaze from darting back and forth, inside Sam's cabin and out onto the campgrounds.

I close the door only to open it again, staring at it like it's a portal to my hallucinations. Open and close. But each time, I'm relieved to see only the same view of the campgrounds.

"Penny? What are you doing?" Sam sets her book on the night-stand. She clicks on the bedside lamp, and I squint against the brightness. My eyes slide to Harper, worried we'll wake her, but she sleeps with a satiny purple eye mask on and doesn't stir.

"Yeah, sorry. I…" Slowly, I close the door behind me, even though I should leave. But the thought of going back outside and walking to my own cabin, where the world around me could change again, keeps my feet rooted to the floor.

"What's going on?" Sam's brows scrunch together, creating creases on her forehead, and I don't blame her. I have no reasonable excuse for barging into their room in the middle of the night.

"Is this a hookup?" She looks at Harper, still tucked beneath the blankets of her bed. "Because one of you really should have warned me or something."

"No," I say a little too quickly, embarrassment flushing my cheeks.

Sam glances past where I stand, her gaze lingering on one dark corner of the room before turning back to me. "If you're not here for Harper, then…what are you doing?"

How do I answer that?

"I…had to go to the bathroom and mixed up the cabins coming back." I take a step closer to the door, reaching for the knob, even though I absolutely don't want to go out there. "Sorry for waking you."

"Yeah, I'm not buying that."

"What?" I drop my hand from the doorknob.

"I wasn't asleep," Sam says, crossing her arms over her chest and staring at me.

"Okay? What does that—"

"Which means," she says, cutting me off, "that I saw you come in. *And* now that I'm not freaking out from you running in here, I saw how scared you looked. You didn't accidentally walk past your cabin. You ran in here. I thought maybe you were afraid of getting caught, but that's not it. So you want to try that again?"

"Why were you awake?" I ask instead.

Sam gives me a blank stare, the soft yellow light of her lamp highlighting every plane and angle of her face. She doesn't answer, and I don't blame her. She knows I'm deflecting.

"I was just—" I shake my head. What can I say? "I thought I saw…a rat?"

"Nope," Sam says, standing up and letting her blankets fall in a messy pile on her bed. "Even in the middle of a literal forest, this is the cleanest place I've lived. I know what conditions rats live in, and this isn't it." She steps around the bed, coming over. "And if you want someone to believe a lie, then you have to say it with authority."

"I just—"

"Wait. What happened to you?" she asks, and any of the reproach in her voice falls away. "Why are you bleeding?"

As soon as she says it, pain stings my skin. Sam stares at my knees as little rivulets of crimson trail down my legs. I hold my hands out and find scratches on my palms. There's even a bruise circling my wrist where the shadow man grabbed me.

I shake my head and try to swallow my panic. No. It was a dream—or a hallucination. All in my head, like those intrusive thoughts.

It *couldn't* have been real.

But even if I fell outside, hurt my hands and knees in a delusional haze, I didn't bruise my own wrist.

"How...how is that possible? What's happening?" I don't mean to say the words out loud, but they whisper around the room anyway. Sam stares so intently that I have to look away. "I mean, I...fell outside."

"With authority," she says. "If you're gonna lie, say it with authority."

"I don't know what's happening to me," I admit.

"That," Sam says, "I believe."

I turn to the door, ready to run, because how am I supposed to explain anything else if she asks more questions? I grab the doorknob, but Sam puts a hand on my arm. At least five inches taller, she looks down at me and stares as the seconds tick by.

Until finally, Sam takes a deep breath and asks, "It comes for you too, doesn't it?" She rolls her sleeve up to where a fresh mark sits on her forearm, an angry pink circle like a burn. "At night," she says, "do you see it too?"

SAM

The girl had never liked her dad. She'd always been afraid of him and had been thankful when his visits became fewer and fewer.

But now, tossed into the back seat of his car, with less care than if she were luggage, the girl was more scared of her dad than ever before.

His hand held her arm so roughly, she was sure it would leave a bruise, but what was one more mark on her skin? He'd already given her plenty over the years.

The door slammed behind her, and she flinched. Her palms dug into the rough carpeted floor as tears stung her eyes. Too old, she thought, she was too old to be crying over this—over him. She was thirteen, not three.

Her dad slid behind the wheel and slammed his door. He

muttered to himself as the car roared to life and sped away from her house. Her mother shouted and chased after. The girl crawled onto the back seat and pressed one hand to the rear window.

Her mom ran, pink bathrobe flapping in the air and one slipper gone. Her image grew smaller the farther her dad drove.

"Get down," her dad commanded, voice as hard as a fist to the face. The girl didn't listen; she didn't want to lose sight of her mom. "I said, 'Get down,' or you'll regret it." Her dad clicked the cigarette lighter in, a warning that made the girl shrink in the seat.

Outside, the road rushed by too quickly, and the artificial pine scent that filled the car made her sick. She wanted to rip that cardboard tree off the mirror and throw it out the window.

Instead, she pulled down her sleeves, hiding her arms and scars from her dad in case he went through with his threat.

"If your mom's not going to listen, then she doesn't get to have you." His eyes, so shockingly pale blue like the girl's, stared at her in the rearview mirror—only his eyes were full of anger and hate, and hers held nothing but fear.

The girl's heart thumped painfully, her breaths too thin. Her dad had never done this before. Never threatened to take her away.

Her stomach twisted, the fake pine scent only adding to the nausea. She had to find a way back to her mom.

The road stretched out behind them, and with every mile that fled past, the girl's heart clenched tighter. "I—I have to pee," she finally said, the only thing she could think of.

"I don't care," her dad said, not even sparing a glance at her as he jerked the wheel too hard and turned down a back road. "Hold it."

The girl sank down into her seat, fingers scratching nervously at her sleeve where one ugly raised scar hid.

"Are you…?" the girl cleared her throat, trying to stop the shake in her voice. "Are you going to take me back to Mom?"

"Maybe." He glanced at her in the mirror, and the girl ducked her head.

Her dad mumbled to himself as he drove, cursing and complaining, while taking the girl farther and farther from her mom and leaving her wondering what he might do next.

FIFTEEN

Sam stands in front of me, waiting for an answer. She rolls her sleeve back down, hiding the mark there. Her fingers inch up, twisting the pendant of her aromatherapy necklace.

"Penny." Her pale blue eyes are wide, begging me to reassure her. "Does it come to you too?"

"Um…" I glance toward the door as if I can see through the thick wood to where the creature was. "Yes?" I say, even though it's more question than answer.

Her shoulders curl in, and I can't tell if it's from fear or relief. "Come on." She glances at Harper, still asleep, and grabs my hand before opening the cabin door.

"I can't go out there," I say, digging my sore feet into the floor.

"It doesn't matter where we are." There's pity in her light eyes. "In here. Out there. That *thing* will find us if it wants to. The cabin won't keep you safe." A shiver trembles down her spine, and when she tugs my hand again, I don't fight her.

We step out onto the porch, and I hold my breath, scouring the lawn for that monstrous shadow. When I don't see it anywhere, I let out a stuttering sigh.

Sam lets go of my hand and sits on the first step, keeping within the glow of the porch light. I settle down next to her.

"Why does he come?" Sam asks, staring out at the grassy lawn. "*How* is he here?"

"Who?" I ask, because she can't know my father or the version that haunted my childhood nightmares. "Who do you see?"

"My…" She takes a deep breath. "My dad." Her voice is the softest whisper, and even with the quiet night, I have to strain to hear her, as if she believes that speaking any louder might summon him.

"No," I tell her. "It's *my* father." I don't even know what her dad looks like or who he is.

"You said he's dead." Her brow furrows, but how much more unbelievable is it than it being her dad, who she said is in prison right now?

"It can't really be him, but…it is. His ghost or…" I don't know. I never believed in the paranormal before, but now? I don't know what to think. But if Sam has seen things too, then it can't just be in my mind.

Sam shakes her head, pink hair rosier under the golden light.

"No, that's not possible. It's my dad—something pretending to be him. It…it doesn't look quite right."

"Is he shadows?" I ask, the words shuddering through me.

"No? It looks like my dad, but as if he's been drawn from memory. Like some things aren't quite right, but I can't figure out what." She shivers. "It's worse than if it were a perfect likeness."

"The thing I see, it's a man made out of shadows. But I've seen things that belonged to my father too. His watch. His whiskey." I stare at her, trying to see if she connects those bottles from the night of the bonfire to my comment.

She inhales sharply. "That was…"

"I thought I was hallucinating," I tell her.

"Me too." She swallows hard and grips her necklace like a life raft. "But real or not, it acts like my dad. It's left marks on me."

"I thought I was getting worse," I say. "Then…I don't know. I thought there was something weird about this place. Now…" I turn to fully look at her. Her pale eyes meet mine, urging me to say what we both know. "Something is *wrong* here. Something's going on."

"Yeah." Sam nods, and my stomach sinks when she agrees. "But what?"

"I don't actually know." I look toward the main lodge, wondering if Ms. Evans or Ms. Peterson are still awake, but the building is dark. Ms. Peterson backtracked about Reagan doing extra one-on-one sessions with Ms. Evans. And then they both glossed over Reagan missing from our group meetings and meals. Are they hiding something? "I'm not sure we should trust the therapists here."

Sam drops her necklace, blue eyes going wide. "You think they're doing something to us? Drugging us into hallucinating or whatever?"

"I—" A gasp scrapes my throat. Would they drug us? "What about that light bar? What was it called? ERMD?"

"EMDR," Sam corrects.

"Do think it could be doing something to us?" Nausea turns my stomach at the possibility. "Or would they really drug us?"

"I don't know." Sam fidgets with her sleeve, a scar peeking out of the edge. "Would that explain how I've been hurt?" She waves a hand at my bloody knees and the bruise on my wrist. "And you."

"I—" I'm about to try to explain it away, that I must have injured myself falling, but that doesn't explain her fresh wounds. "What about—" My mouth snaps shut when a soft, scratching hiss echoes across the yard.

Sam's eyes widen, screaming in silence as we stare at each other. Neither of us breathe. Slowly, so slowly, we turn our heads. Each second that passes, my heart thunders louder in my ears.

A shadowy creature slithers low on the ground, slinking through the grass and moving *closer closer closer*. It gets to the flagpole in the middle of the yard, pausing for a second before shooting forward so quickly it's only a few feet from the porch steps before I can blink.

I jerk back as Sam yelps and skitters across the splintery wooden porch. I can't take my eyes off the creature as it unfurls, rising higher and higher until the shadow man stands before us.

Only he's different. Wrong.

Where the shaded hollows of empty eye sockets have always been are now two disturbingly bright blue eyes. He—*it*—still wears my father's watch and holds that bottle of whiskey, but his hands are pale, no longer made of shadows like the rest of him. The darkness creeps down his arms before blending into peachy skin.

"What the—" Sam starts until the shadow man lurches forward.

The scent of alcohol envelops us, only this time it mixes and mingles with a pine scent, artificial and disgusting. My stomach twists at the combination.

"Stop," I say, surprised when the shadow man staggers to a halt before reaching the first step.

"What is *that*?" Sam nails dig into my arm as she pulls me to her. "Those are my dad's eyes, but…he's never looked like that before."

"That's the shadow man," I whisper. "From my nightmares. But he's never *had* eyes before."

"Make it go away. Please," she begs, and the fear trembling in her voice is nothing I've ever heard from her before.

"What…?" I clear my throat and stand up, facing the thing before us. "What are you?" Behind me, Sam climbs to her feet and hovers. She lets out a whimper as the shadow man lifts his hand, my father's watch glaring brightly in the porch light. He points one disturbingly pale finger at us.

A groan spills from his gaping mouth.

"Pennnnn…" he says, voice grating up his throat like concrete, "ellll…opeee." Penelope, not Penny.

"What are you?" I ask again. The shadow man takes a step forward, moving onto the dirt path. "*Who* are you?"

"Does it matter?" Sam whispers. "Go away!" She kicks one foot out in warning, but with the little staircase separating us from the creature, she only hits empty air.

The shadow man darts to the side before jumping up, clinging to the other side of the porch rails like a giant insect. The aged wood is the only thing separating us, and this close, those pale eyes shine too brightly under the moonlight.

"Saaaaaaaaaaam," the creature says, fixing its icy gaze on her.

"No, absolutely not." She grips my hand in hers. "Let's *go*, Penny."

The shadow man hooks one arm over the rail, a leg following. My heart clatters up my throat, choking me. These hallucinations have already hurt us, and there's no reason they wouldn't now too. We should run, but there are too many things I don't understand, and need to.

"Tell me what you are," I say, my voice somehow bolder than I feel. Is it real or not? "What's happening to us?"

The shadow man turns his head, creaking and slow, as he stares at the row of cabins and the forest behind them before bringing that piercing gaze back to us.

Sam's grip on my hand tightens, and she lets out another whimper as the world starts to change again, to mutate into something else.

"What's going on?" she asks, the words shivering through the air.

The cabins and lodge disappear, their lights winking out of existence, as towering trees replace the buildings and close in on us. Below our bare feet, dirt and grass grow out of the wooden planks.

The temperature drops, no longer a warm summer night. Goose bumps prick my skin, and Sam shivers as she steps closer.

"Penny?" Her eyes, so similar to the creature's standing before us, dart to me. She looks back to the shadow man. "Am I dead?"

"No, not dead," I tell her. Unless we're both in hell together. "I don't think."

"Then please tell me you see this too?"

I nod, swallowing hard. The shadow man claws his way over the railing, dropping down heavily next to us, and the rest of the porch vanishes into nothingness.

"Let's go." Sam yanks my arm and runs forward. I stumble behind her as we weave through giant tree trunks and away from the creature. We crash through the forest until we're both out of breath. Sam finally lets go of my hand and slows, but neither of us stop walking. I look behind us but can't see the shadow man. There are too many towering trees that cast their own darkness on the ground.

"Is it following?" Sam asks between gasps.

"I don't think so?" I stare out into the night, searching for that nightmare come alive.

Sam picks her way around sticks and small rocks. "Where are we?"

"I don't know, but this is why I came into your room. I was here, trapped in this forest."

Something shines in the dirt, silver in the moonlight. Sam leans down and grabs it. But she drops it just as quickly, gasping as if it burned her.

"No, no." Sam stumbles back, bumping into me. "What is this place?"

I move past her, toward whatever she dropped, and find a small silver car lighter in the dirt.

"Penny!" she shouts, and there's so much fear infused into my name. "Drop it."

The lighter falls through my fingertips and to the ground with a dull thud. I turn to ask her why, but stop when Sam rubs her arm, right where that round pink mark on her skin sits under her sleeve.

"How do we get back?" she asks.

"I don't know. Before, the door to your cabin just... appeared." I look around, but there are only trees and bushes and a thin dirt path.

"That way?" she asks, pointing to the trail.

I don't have a better idea, so I nod, and together we walk deeper into a forest that shouldn't exist.

SIXTEEN

I have no sense of time here. The moon doesn't shift in the sky to bring dawn, and even the silver clouds are still. They're like a painting, stagnant and flat. Not real.

I don't know how long Sam and I have been walking, minutes or hours or forever.

It seems like forever.

I can't help feeling like the shadows are watching us, like that creature is following our footsteps unseen. The hair on my arms and the back of my neck rise, and an itch scratches down my spine.

The farther we go, the more the scent of pine fills my nose, but when I glance at the trees, they look like cedar or oak.

"Is that…?" Sam hurries her steps, her bare feet scuffing up dust, before grabbing something off the ground. "Whiskey."

"Put it back," I tell her, my voice whispering and severe.

Her eyes catch mine, understanding filling them. It's left for me, the cigarette lighter for her. They litter the path as we walk, silver and glass catching the moonlight and screaming for our attention. More and more of them cover the ground, until Sam and I are picking our way around the discarded nightmares, not daring to touch any again.

Everything about this place shouts *wrong wrong wrong*.

Sam stops, pausing at a tree with low-hanging branches. She reaches one hand toward a leaf, plucking it. Only, as I step closer, it's not a leaf, and that artificial pine burns my nose. She turns, hands shaking, and holds a cardboard air freshener in the shape of a tree.

"My…" She swallows hard. "My dad always had these in his old beater car." Her gaze falls to the ground, where more of those horrible trinkets are scattered.

More air fresheners fill the branches—canopies of cardboard that smother the sky above. The smell crawls down my throat, so strong it burns.

But it's not the air fresheners that hold my attention and make me shake. It's the gold watches that blink into existence, draping the branches like some twisted version of a Christmas tree. Even the trunks of these trees aren't normal. Gold flickers on the bark, embedded in that dark wood. I lean closer, until the sight of my father's belt appears, hundreds of copies weaving and layering over each other to create the trunks and branches. They shift as I stare, opening a hole half my size. I panic, worried that this false tree is about to eat me—until something pushes its way out.

A bulky tan box falls at my feet with a crash. Tubes and wires snake out behind it, and the hole in the tree mends itself with copies of my father's belt. A screen on the box flickers to life, and moving lines pulse across, bringing a high-pitched beeping that echoes around the forest.

"Is that a heart monitor?" Sam backs up, stepping slowly toward the path again. "You know what? Screw this. I'm not doing it anymore." She shakes her head and makes her way down the trail again. "Let's get out of here, Penny."

I follow after her, not wanting to be near those trees or the heart monitor they vomited out. Just like the teddy bear from before, I don't know what that's about, and I don't know if I want to. Maybe they're connected to Sam, because I've never seen them before. But…she didn't have the same flicker of recognition when they showed up, not like the lighters or the cardboard pine trees.

Sam picks up her pace, nearly running, and I have to rush to catch up—careful to avoid all of the objects on the ground. Each inhale brings the scent of pine and alcohol. Each flicker of gold in the trees has my heart racing faster—until my steps match the wild beat of Sam's. And no matter how far we go, the beeping from that machine screams louder and louder. Until the high pitch of it starts saying a single word.

Soon. Soon. Soon.

I don't want to learn what *soon* means.

The trees press in. The beeping yells louder. And all around us are the reminders of our trauma.

Soon. Soon. Soon.

It's only when I trip on something and slam to the ground that Sam stops running and the sound of the monitor silences. My palms, already scraped raw, sting all over again as I sit up.

"Are you okay?" Sam reaches down to help, but I pick up the thing that tripped me instead. Fuzzy fabric and button eyes. Round ears and a short tail. And stitched onto the chest is the letter *Q* in red thread.

Sam gasps and pulls my attention away from the bear until I'm staring at the monster again. Half shadows and half human. He fills the small space of the dirt path, only a few yards away. I scramble to stand up and drop the toy to the ground.

Those glacial eyes—so different from the dark hollows I saw before—pin me in place.

"What do you want?" I ask, and my voice trembles through the trees.

Next to me, Sam takes a step back as the creature cocks its head at such an unsettling angle it makes my skin shiver.

The shadow man's gaze dips down to the teddy bear I dropped and then to one he holds in his hand.

"What is this?" I scream, and I'm not surprised when no birds or animals startle at my outburst. This forest might be filled with their squawking and chittering, but there's nothing normal about this place.

"Don't." Sam grabs my hand, gripping tightly enough to crush my fingers. "Don't talk to it." Her eyes dart down to the creature's feet, where a pile of cigarette lighters and whiskey bottles surround it in a perfect circle.

The shadow man steps over them, abandons the teddy bear to the pile, and flies at us faster than possible. He slams into me, and I crash to the ground, into the pointed corner of something hard— another heart monitor, which screams in high-pitched tones as it comes to life.

The monster's fingers grab my shoulder, digging in like shards of ice. His other hand clutches my head. A hollow gasping sound scrapes out of his throat, his serrated mouth stretching *open open open*.

This isn't real. It *can't* be real, but searing pain explodes in my head as his face draws closer. Sam yells my name as my hands scramble over the dirt, desperate to claw myself away.

An earsplitting shriek from the shadow man wails through the forest, and he jerks back. Behind him, Sam's chest heaves, and she shakes her right hand before balling it into a fist and dropping her weight into a fighting stance, ready to punch the creature—again, I'd guess, by the red on her knuckles.

I twist onto my hands and knees and crawl away before staggering to my feet as a scream caroms around the trees, high and piercing. I look up in time to see the shadow man grab Sam by the throat, choking her with pale fingers. He takes his other hand and grips her head, tufts of short pink hair slipping between fingers that clench too tightly. Sam tries to scream, a gurgled sound that only squeaks through the harsh grip on her throat. The creature opens his mouth, dark and empty, and that same hollow sucking sound scrapes my ears, burrows in. I don't know what it's doing to Sam—what it tried to do with me—but I have to stop him.

"Let her go!" I shout and crash into both of them, limbs tangling as we fall. The shadow man skitters back, more bug-like than human. I grab Sam's arm and pull her away.

"Pennnn…" the creature starts, its mouth gaping, "elllll… oooope." It lurches toward us, crawling on all fours. It lifts a hand, that ugly gold watch flickering under the moonlight, and points one pale dirt-stained finger at me.

But I don't know what this creature wants.

And I don't know what any of this means. My father's whiskey and watch. The cigarette lighters and pine air fresheners that make Sam flinch. Or the teddy bear with bloodred stitching and the heart monitor that still shrieks through the trees.

I don't know.

I don't know.

I don't know.

SEVENTEEN

P enny!" My name is shouted through the forest, but it's not the creature in front of me slowly saying *Penelope*. It's my nickname, higher in pitch and frantic.

The shadow man's gaze slices past where I stand, but when I turn, there's nothing behind me. Only those same trees with their garish horrors, the same dirt path.

"Sam!" the voice shouts.

Something touches my arm, invisible, and I scream. It grips my shoulders and shakes me until I think I've lost the last bit of my sanity.

"Penny!" it says again, and I swear it sounds like Harper.

For a blessed second, the shaking stops. But Sam's pale eyes go wide, and she cries out when that invisible thing starts shoving at her.

Her chest heaves with each breath, matching my own. I glance at the shadow man, but he's exactly where he was, crouched in the brush.

"Penny. Penny, wake up," the voice says, coming from right in front of me. I blink as Harper's face wavers into existence.

She grips my shoulders, shaking my body, as the forest melts away and Whitewood slowly comes back. Trees shrink and shift back into the campgrounds. The dirt below me morphs into Sam and Harper's porch. Air fresheners and cigarette lighters, whiskey bottles and watches fade away. The heart monitor's beeping is replaced by the soft chirping of crickets. Nothing of that nightmare forest is left.

Except the shadow man.

He stands at the bottom of the wooden steps. His icy gaze darts to Harper, and a hiss falls from that empty, torn mouth. His form darkens and folds in on itself like twisted origami before the shadows flee across the grassy lawn and disappear behind the main lodge.

Hot air replaces the cold of that false forest, and clouds skim by above our heads. I could collapse in relief at seeing that sky, real and not frozen like a painting.

In front of me, Harper barely breathes, while Sam stands still at my side, and my heart thunders so loud in my ears.

For nearly a minute, that's how we stay. Silent and staring at where the shadow man fled, hoping nothing else happens.

Harper breaks the quiet. "What was that?" She slowly loosens her hold on my shoulders. "You guys saw that too, right?"

I nod, not sure how to explain anything to her as Sam leans heavily on the rail.

"Penny," Harper says, panic seeping into every letter of my name. "What. Was. That?"

I shake my head. I have no idea what she saw. Just the shadow man or everything?

"Why did it…why did it look like that?" Sam's face scrunches in confusion, but the fear from earlier is gone. "Before, it always looked like…" Her gaze goes distant for a moment. "Like…like my dad. He…" She shakes her head, voice trailing off.

"I need answers." Harper's dark eyes are wider than I've ever seen them. "What was that, and why were you guys just standing there?" She glances around as if the answers to her questions will appear. "I woke up, and Sam was gone, and then I heard noises out here, and you guys were…" A shiver of unease shakes her body.

"We were what?" I ask. What did she see while we were fighting for our lives?

"You were both just standing out here, staring at nothing like you were possessed or something. You guys scared the shit out of me."

"We were standing still?" I ask. Sam and I might not be in the exact spot we started in on the porch, but we were still here despite running through a forest.

"Umm, you were shuffling a little? Like a zombie." Harper scuffs her feet in place, moving about one slow inch. "I thought it was a real *28 Weeks Later* situation."

"A what?" I ask.

"Doesn't matter." She waves the question away. "I tried shaking you and calling your names, but you didn't answer." Her gaze drifts across the lawn. "I didn't even see that…thing at first."

"Did you see it? The, um…?" Sam's face scrunches up, in confusion or pain, or both. "The forest and the…the…?"

"Are you okay?" I ask her when she trails off again.

"I… Yeah." Her expression relaxes, the confusion melting away. "I'm fine."

"Hello? Somebody tell me what's going on." Harper looks behind the cabin, to where the white birch trees stand like ghostly beings. "What was that *thing*?" She flings an arm out, motioning to where that melded figure of mine and Sam's fathers stood.

"I'm kinda tired." Sam yawns and stretches. "I'm gonna use the bathroom and then get some sleep."

"What?" Harper asks, the single word ricocheting around us with disbelief. "You're just going to go to sleep after that? I—I have questions!"

"Okay." Sam shrugs, unfazed. "Ask Penny."

"Seriously, are you okay?" I step closer to Sam.

"Yeah, of course." She nods, and a smile—so out of place—slips across her face. "I'm just tired. Why?"

"*Why?* What do you mean?" I flail my arms around us, trying to encompass…everything. "Because"—I lean closer, whispering—"the shadow man and the cigarette lighters? The air fresheners?"

"What?"

"Everything in that forest!" I nearly shout. What is *wrong* with her? "The cigarette lighters?" I say again, touching her arm gently above the fresh pink mark there.

Her pale eyes widen as she stares down at her arm "I… That's…" Her brow scrunches but she shakes her head, smoothing the lines of confusion away. "Tonight was…weird. I don't really understand what happened, but we're okay." She smiles down at me. "Everything's fine, Penny."

"How can you—"

She slides past me, patting my shoulder and walking away.

"Sam," Harper calls after her. "What are you doing?"

Sam glances over her shoulder, still smiling. "Going to the bathroom." She walks across the lawn, almost following the creature's path, before veering toward the front doors and heading inside.

"That was…" Harper shakes her head. "What's going on?"

I look toward the lodge, where Sam went. Is she pretending? Disassociating? Why is she's acting like nothing happened? Like tonight wasn't completely terrifying?

I give another shrug. "I have no idea."

A rising chime jolts me awake, growing louder as it continues, but it's the girl in my bed that startles me even more. As the morning's soft alarm sounds and Harper groans under my blanket, it takes me a minute to remember everything.

Harper had a million questions last night. And I had no answers. Not really. But after she saw the shadow man, we left a note for Sam, telling her we'd be in my cabin, so Harper and I could talk. If Sam wanted to sleep, I didn't want to keep her up if that's what she needed. I guess Harper and I eventually passed out too.

We spent last night whispering so as not to wake Emma—though her snoring was deep enough that I was sure she would have stayed asleep anyway—as I told Harper everything I could. About my hallucinations, and how they started out small before becoming…whatever last night was. How the shadow man came to my room and looked different when Sam was with me. I even showed Harper my sketch of him.

Harper's guess is that something is triggering us to hallucinate. Or *someone*. Maybe drugs like Sam suggested, maybe something else. But if it's the camp's therapists, then I don't know how they're making us see the same things. If there's something in the food, wouldn't everyone be experiencing it? Until last night, Harper hadn't seen anything strange—anything *impossible*.

The soft chiming sounds again, and this time, Harper yawns and sits up, squinting against the sunlight.

"Penny?" She rubs her eyes before looking around the cabin. "Am I in your room?"

Even with messy hair and the shadows starting under her eyes, Harper is pretty. I want to freeze this moment, immortalize it on paper. My hands twitch, wanting to draw her in charcoals and colored pencils, in strong lines for her profile and soft smudging for her hair. A blushing rose for the flush on her cheeks and a porcelain white to add light to the depths of her midnight eyes.

But when I realize how close we are in my narrow bed, my hands start to sweat and a heat fills my cheeks.

Smother her with the pillow, that terrible voice hisses in my head. *Watch her turn red and purple and dead.*

Shut up! I yell back. I don't want those thoughts ruining this moment with their vile words.

Thankfully, the voice in my head stays silent as Harper looks from me to Emma still lightly snoring. She winces when the chime goes off one last time.

"Oh no, I didn't mean to sleep here. I don't want to get you in trouble." Harper jumps up and rushes to the door, pausing to ask, "Meet me at breakfast? I'll bring Sam and we can"—she shrugs—"talk with her too?"

"Okay," I tell her and start getting ready as she heads out of the cabin. I wake Emma up, a job that takes ten minutes itself, and then throw on some shorts and a T-shirt. But before I can even grab my toiletries, the door to our cabin slams open. Emma shrieks and I gasp, but it's only Harper.

"I can't find Sam anywhere," she says, out of breath with panic painted across her face. "She wasn't in our cabin."

"Maybe she's—"

"No, I checked all over the main building and even the other cabins. She's not *here*, Penny."

"She has to be," I say, but dread fills my mouth as I speak. It pours down my throat and sinks to my stomach. Because it can't be a coincidence that she's gone after last night. After she walked away so unbothered and unconcerned. "She has to be," I repeat anyway.

"No." Harper shakes her head. "I think she's gone."

EIGHTEEN

The morning was a rush of barely eaten breakfast, hushed conversations, and pretending to follow our schedule. But no one's really focusing on therapy sessions or outdoor meditation, let alone the more camp-y activities like archery. And it doesn't exactly seem like a good idea to arm a bunch of distracted girls with pointed weapons.

But Ms. Evans is acting as if nothing's wrong—as if another girl isn't gone. *Doing special individualized therapy*, she said about Sam. Like Reagan, supposedly, but I don't believe her.

So here we are, six rather than eight, following along despite the missing girls as we stand across from round targets of painted hay. Delaney calls out directions and encouragement as the others notch arrows and tug on bowstrings.

I stand to the back, away from the weapons, no matter how

dull-tipped they are. Just being nearby made the voice in my head too loud. I asked Ms. Evans to be excused, but she went on about exposure therapy and getting as close as comfort allowed.

I didn't tell her my comfort would be at least a hundred miles from here.

Arrows fly through the air, some whistling with speed and punching into their targets while others wobble and crash to the ground. Emma is surprisingly good, firing off arrow after arrow and nearly hitting the bull's-eye a few times. She looks like a woman on a mission...or like if she stops moving for even a minute, her thoughts will drown her. I know the feeling. When my mind won't stop obsessing, all I want is my sketchbook and pencils. To turn my mind off and let the scratching of graphite distract me.

The *thwack* of bowstrings is a discordant song mingling with the whispers in my head.

Shoot them, the voice says. *Watch their blood bloom. Let it stain their clothes and paint their lips.*

I want to cover my ears, but it won't help. I tried my finger tapping and counting earlier, the mantras too—but they aren't enough. They never were.

Pick one up, those intrusive thoughts say as my gaze darts to the unused bows laid out on the grass. *Shoot them.* There's a tube-shaped bin filled with arrows sitting next to Harper.

I shake my head, trying to dislodge that voice, and step back again. Ms. Evans stands behind us, her stare so strong it's a heavy weight on my skin.

Screw archery and exposure therapy and being examined like a germ under a microscope. I take one step away, ready to leave, when Harper sets her bow down and comes over to me.

"We need to figure out where Sam is. Reagan too." Her attention shifts from me to Ms. Evans before skimming over the other girls.

Kylie and Page follow along with Delaney's archery lesson but pause every few attempts to whisper to each other.

But Quinn...she doesn't even try. She hugs her bow to her chest with both arms, standing between where Kylie and Page are clustered together and where Emma is firing arrows one after the other. Quinn's gaze darts around, jumping from the empty field where the targets are set up to the forest of birch trees at our backs. She must be barely sleeping. Her red hair has snags and tangles, and the shadows under her eyes are a deep bruised color darker than her freckles.

Quinn stiffens suddenly, the blood draining from her already pale face. She stares at the forest, and I follow her gaze, stumbling back when something moves within the soft shadows. It's there and gone so fast, I can't be sure of *what* it was.

That shadow creature? One of the missing girls?

But no, whatever it was looked taller than Kylie, who, at around six feet, towers over the rest of us.

How big do deer get?

Quinn rushes away from Delaney's lesson, across the lawn and toward our cabins as Ms. Evans follows—chases—after. When I check the birch trees again, they're empty and quiet. No sign of deer or anything else.

"Did you hear me?" Harper asks, and I yank my attention back to her.

Shoot her! that voice shouts, and I flinch. *Grab her bow. Take an arrow. Plunge it into her pretty chest.*

Stop! I shout within my own head. I take a deep breath, inhaling the warm air, the smell of the grass, and the summer sun. *You don't control me*, I say, willing the statement to be true. And when those thoughts drift to the back of my mind for a moment, I almost believe it.

"Sorry," I tell Harper. "What did you say?"

"We should go look for them on our own. Tonight. We need to figure out what's going on, and that starts with finding Sam and Reagan. Are you in?"

"Of course," I say, watching as Ms. Evans guides Quinn up the hill to the main building and away from the cabins. "I don't think they're telling the truth."

Harper follows my gaze as Ms. Evans and Quinn disappear into the lodge. "Me neither."

"You still think there's something in the food?" I ask. We had breakfast this morning, and nothing seemed out of the ordinary. No new hallucinations, at least.

"What else could it be?"

"Maybe something from those EMDR sessions?" I ask. "I've never done them before. Could it be hypnosis instead?" I ask, still not wanting to believe that our therapists would drug us.

"I don't think hypnosis can make us see things. Or...can it make us believe we did?"

"I don't know." I think back to my sessions with Ms. Evans, trying to figure out if the light bar could cause hypnosis, but... the visions started before my first session. The realization brings a phantom scent with it—and for once, it's not my father's whiskey.

"The aromatherapy," I say. "What if that's how they're drugging us?" That overpowering lavender and lime has been around every time I've had a hallucination, diffused into the air or worn in a pendant. Even Sam had her necklace on last night.

Harper gasps at my suggestion and looks down at the silver necklace she wears. The faintest hint of those oils reaches me, and I step back.

"That would make more sense than the food. I didn't see that... thing, until after I got my necklace." She pulls the chain over her head, cringing when it gets tangled in her long black hair, before shoving it into the pocket of her shorts.

"We have to figure out what's in that," I say, pointing to the length of chain sticking out.

Even if I don't understand how or why the camp therapists would drug us, there's one thing I'm sure of: I don't trust Ms.

Peterson or Ms. Evans. They're doing something to us. I just need proof. And that starts with finding Sam and Reagan, figuring out what they know and why they disappeared.

QUINN

The girl was lost, with only the company of the trees and the insects that screamed from hidden places.

And she had her teddy bear. A scruffy brown thing, button eyes scuffed up and fabric worn thin over a plastic nose. She clutched it tight to her chest and shivered in her T-shirt and shorts. She only had one shoe left and no idea where the other had gone. Her socked foot was dust-covered and dirt-stained. Blood dripped from hands and knees that stung.

The little girl didn't know how long she'd been alone. The night had gone from dusk to dark and darker still. She'd been with her parents, hiking on vacation to a forest that she couldn't even pronounce the name of.

She'd been trailing behind them when she'd seen a butterfly, a sapphire blue and midnight black, so beautiful she was sure she'd found a fairy in disguise. She'd followed it instead of her parents, stepping off the trail and hoping to find out if she'd really found a magical creature. Even after she couldn't see the trail behind her, she tottered along. Another step, and she had been sure she could catch the butterfly.

And then she had fallen, down a steep, rock-covered hill. Her head banged against the unforgiving earth, her knees and hands scraping as she fell and fell and fell.

When she finally stopped, she was bleeding, and every part of her small body ached.

Somehow, the girl had held on to her teddy bear as she fell, but now it sat a few feet away, coated in dirt like the girl.

She snatched it up, hugging it tight, and stared at the forest around her. The girl had fallen too far for her screams to reach her parents. She tried climbing back up the rocky hill but slid down again and again, scraping away more skin until she finally gave up.

The girl stared up at trees that reached high into the sky, green leaves blotting out the fading sun. She held her teddy bear and took one step after another into the forest. She walked until her feet ached and the sun abandoned her and only a full moon lit the dark night.

Tears trailed down her cheeks as her breath stuttered. The girl sat on the ground and curled against a tree. The night grew cold, and the girl cried harder. She was alone in a forest alive with strange sounds that scared her. Insects shrieked and bushes rustled. Shining eyes spied out from behind leaves. She didn't know if her fear conjured the sound of howls and scraping claws or if the animals were coming for her.

The girl looked down at her teddy bear, scruffy and dirty like her. She stared at the red *Q* embroidered on the bear's chest. A vibrant scarlet that matched her hair. She hoped this bear could protect her from any others that might lumber through the forest looking for a small child the perfect size to eat.

The girl trembled, the cold seeping under her skin until it became a part of her. She grasped her teddy tighter and stared out into the dark until her eyes hurt.

The girl startled at every sound as she waited for her parents—all night, and the next day, and the night after that. She sat there alone.

Holding tight to her teddy bear, the little girl waited and waited and waited.

NINETEEN

I get to Ms. Evans's office for my EMDR session, but she's not here. The door is open to an empty room. I look up and down the laminate-tiled hall, but I'm alone. Stepping closer to the doorway, my heart starts to race as I make a quick decision.

One more check of the hall, and I'm darting inside. I might not get a chance like this again. Instead of taking a seat in one of the cushy chairs, I hurry over to Ms. Evans's desk to search for any answers about what she's doing to us.

That same laptop from before sits closed on her desk. I lift it open, and the screen blinks awake, a password bar staring at me. Of course, she wouldn't leave her computer unprotected, and I don't dare try to guess at it.

I glance at the open doorway. Still no one.

I scan her desk. A framed photo of Ms. Evans and her

daughter—with what must be her husband and son—sits near the laptop. They look younger, happier. Clara can't even be thirteen in this photo, compared to the one across the room, where she's closer to my age.

Ms. Evans's screensaver comes to life, startling me. More photos of her family fade in and out of existence, but it's obvious something happened between her and her husband. All the photos where Clara is older than about thirteen, where Ms. Evans has more gray in her hair, are missing him. The more I watch, I realize her son is missing from them too.

But family photos won't give me answers, so I search the desk instead. A plastic holder sits to one side, filled with files that have a photo of each girl here stapled to them. I flip through, finding Sam's and Reagan's. I start to open Sam's when footsteps squeak against the hallway's tiles.

Quickly, I shuffle the folders back together and set them in the holder before slamming the laptop closed. I rush around the desk and across the room. I barely drop into the chair, trying to steady my breaths, when Ms. Evans steps into her office.

"I'm so sorry I'm late, Penny. It's been…a busy day." She swipes some flyaway hairs back and moves to her desk, looking through the folders I just set down.

I hold my breath, wondering if she'll be able to tell. But she only picks mine out and comes over.

"Are you ready?" Ms. Evans drops my folder onto her chair

before setting up the light bar for another EMDR session. Only this time I don't plan to watch the light—not until I figure out if she's doing something to me. No, this time, *I* want answers from *her*.

"Actually, I wanted to ask how Reagan is doing. And Sam. What are they actually doing? When will they join us again?"

Ms. Evans's hand hovers over the light bar for a second before pressing a button on the side to power it on. She clears her throat. "They're doing fine. They'll rejoin the rest of you when they're ready. I'd rather focus on you, Penny."

She steps over to the side table with the diffuser, and I don't miss the way she didn't answer my question and changed the subject. When, exactly, will they be *ready*?

"Can we keep that off today?" I ask as she taps a button on the diffuser, making it glow with a soft purple light as air puffs from the top. "I…have a headache, and the smell is too much," I lie, but I can't take the chance that it's the aromatherapy making me see things.

"Of course." Ms. Evans turns the diffuser off before taking a seat. "Do you mind?" she asks, pulling a tube out of one of her vest pockets.

Before I can figure out what she's asking, she uncaps the tube and rolls it under each ear. The scent of that lavender and lime blend drifts across the space, almost too faint to notice.

"I find the aromatherapy helpful for my own focus, and the rollers aren't as strong as the diffuser."

"I—okay." There's no point arguing now.

"If you'd like, I can give you one. You can roll the oil on your wrists or neck. It's not as overwhelming as the vapor diffusers. Or I have necklaces also. You can take a bottle of oil and add drops to the felt. I'm sure you've seen a few girls wearing them already."

"No," I say too quickly. "That scent isn't…my favorite." But what I really want to ask is why she's pushing it and what's actually *in* the blend.

"The lavender and bergamot?" she asks, a wrinkle pulling between her brows. "You might be the first person I've had say they didn't like it. It's good for both focus and calming. But that's okay"—she smiles—"I have others you might like, ones to help calm or relax also."

"I—"

"Here…" She gets up and rummages through a drawer at her desk before coming back with two roller bottles, handwritten labels on each: *Sweet Orange* and *YlangYlang with Chamomile*. "Take those and see if you like either of them better."

"Thanks." I shove them into the pocket of my shorts despite knowing I won't use them.

"Now, are you ready?" Ms. Evans settles back into her seat and picks up the remote for the light bar.

I look away from Ms. Evans, and my attention catches on that photo of Clara on the side table. "What made you start this camp?" I ask, delaying the EMDR session while wanting to know more about why Ms. Evans would create a therapy retreat in the middle of nowhere.

"We can talk about that later if you'd like." She shifts my folder to her lap. "But I don't want us wasting your one-on-one sessions, Penny."

"It's just," I say, staring between her and the light bar, "you know so much about me already, and maybe I'd feel more comfortable if I knew a little about you and this place?"

"I can understand that." Ms. Evans's smile is soft and warm enough that it really seems like she cares, but then the corners of her mouth drop, and sadness is painted there instead. She hesitates a moment before speaking. "I had a son. He was two years older than Clara. But…there was an accident. He didn't make it." She swallows.

"I'm sorry."

"The point is, I know what pain and loss are, Penny," she says, and I don't mention how Delaney told us about Clara. I can't help but wonder what happened to her son or why she didn't mention losing her daughter too.

"I know how hard it can be," she continues, "and how sometimes the people we lose can feel like they…linger—in both good and bad ways. So believe me when I say I understand some of the things you're going through and I want to help you. I want Whitewood to make a difference." Tears shine in her eyes but don't fall. She clears her throat. "Now, enough about that. Let's get started. If it's not too difficult, I'd like us to talk about your intrusive thoughts and also the night your father passed."

She might have lost family too, but it's not really the same. And while I *do* want to get better, how can I do that with Ms. Evans when I don't trust her?

"All right, Penny," she says, "follow the light and focus on those intrusive thoughts. Think about how your Harm OCD has made you feel lately. Do you feel like they're less powerful than before? Easier or harder to silence?"

I try to *pretend* to follow the light but can't stop my gaze from actually drifting to it and chasing that bright dot back and forth—until I'm thinking about the questions she's asking and not possible hypnosis.

"Okay, now look back at me," Ms. Evans says, pausing the light with her remote. "On a scale of one to ten, how worried are you that these thoughts will take control? That you'll hurt someone?"

A heavy silence fills the small office as I think. That voice still commands me to do horrible things, but…I haven't acted on those thoughts. That voice has gone quiet once or twice when I've told it to.

"Maybe…maybe a nine still?"

"All right," she says, smiling before going through the same sort of questions as last time. Again and again, follow the light and focus. Stop and reply. The pattern repeats until I tell Ms. Evans I'm still at a nine…but maybe getting closer to eight.

She turns the light bar off and looks back at me. Her light brown eyes are almost too intense.

"I'd like to ask you about the night your father died." She folds her hands in her lap. "These intrusive thoughts started shortly after his death, so if it's not too much, I'd like you to tell me, again, what you remember about that night."

"It was..." I hesitate, not really wanting to think, let alone talk, about it.

"It's okay, Penny," Ms. Evans says. "You can tell me as much or as little as you'd like."

"I just..." I shake my head, silver hair itching against my jawbone. That night is a fragment of memories better left in the dark. "He was drunk again. Yelling at my mom. Hitting her. It went on longer than it ever had before, so I came out of my room. I couldn't stand it. I wanted to get my mom and leave. Just leave that house—and my father—forever. But..." I squeeze my eyes shut, trying to remember. Hazy images flit through my mind. "It's kind of a blur. My mom was bleeding by the time I came out. I remember the corner of the wall jamming into my spine when my father shoved me. He tried to grab my mom and...and then...I don't know, my father was at the bottom of the stairs, and he didn't get back up."

"Mmm-hmm." Ms. Evans hums as she flicks through the papers in my folder. She lifts one up slightly and reads it. I can't see what it is, but it looks like there's the emblem of a police shield printed on the corner. Is it the report from that night?

"What is that?" I ask.

"Is there anything else you can remember?" she asks instead and tucks the paper away. "Sometimes, when a person has faced something traumatic, the brain tries to protect them. Is there anything different that you can recall? Any other details or—"

"What are you saying? You think I'm lying?" I lean back in my chair, trying to get even a few more inches of distance from her.

"That's not it, Penny." She shakes her head. "It's just important to try to remember everything possible so we can work through that night. That's all."

I know the facts. My father was drunk. Grabbing us. Hitting Mom. And he fell. My memory might be hazy, but I *know* that's what happened. Is she trying to make me doubt myself? To make me feel like I can't trust my own mind so she can continue to drug us—or whatever she's doing?

"I already told you what happened," I say. "I don't want to talk about it anymore."

"I understand. We don't have to push it more today. But you *can* tell me anything. If you ever want to. If you remember something else." A small smile tips the corners of her mouth. "I want you to know I'm here to help you. In any way I can. We'll face the shadows together."

TWENTY

I make it back to my cabin without anything strange happening after my session with Ms. Evans. No hallucinations triggered by aromatherapy or hypnosis pretending to be EMDR. Maybe Ms. Evans's light bar is nothing more than that. And maybe her oil roller wasn't strong enough.

Still, I can't stop thinking about our session. *The brain tries to protect*, she said. What did that mean? Does she think I'm hiding something from her—or that my own memories of that night are messed up?

I pull my notebook out of my nightstand and drop onto the bed, flipping through sketches until I stop on the drawing of that shadow man, all harsh lines and deep pressure.

Are these hallucinations related to my memories from when my father died?

"Are you trying to tell me about that night?" I ask, speaking to that sketch.

A knock on my cabin door startles me, but before I can get up, Harper hurries in.

"Sorry," she says, standing in front of me and twisting the silver ring on her index finger. "I saw you leave the lodge, and I don't know, I was hoping we could talk more? About Sam and..." She stares down at the notebook still open in my lap. "That."

Harper shivers before sitting down next to me, and I shouldn't be distracted, but when the scent of her lilac and almond perfume enfolds me in its sweetness, I can't help noticing the thickness of her lashes as she looks down at my sketch or the fullness of her lips as they tilt down.

I lean closer without meaning to...and pretend to show her the notebook to save myself the embarrassment.

But the door to my room flies open, and I jump so bad the book falls from my hands and slides under the bed. Emma comes in, smiling as her eyes dart from me to Harper and the too-small space between us.

"What's going on?" she asks, letting the words singsong across the room. "Am I...interrupting?" She winks at me, and I could die—because there is no way that Harper didn't see that. "I came to tell you we're supposed to be going to Ms. Peterson's mediation thing, but I could cover if you need me to."

I glance at Harper out of the corner of my eye, and the nervous flutters in my chest calm slightly when I see pink staining her cheeks too.

"No. You're not interrupting," I say.

Harper clears her throat and sits up straighter, but she doesn't scoot away.

"We were…talking," I say, the last word fluttering through the air like a lie. Not that we weren't, but I still haven't told Emma about the hallucinations. I have no idea what she'd think.

Emma's smile drops. "Wait, what's going on?" Her gaze searches over us, taking in the tension she missed before. "Is something wrong?"

"No," I say at the same time Harper says, "Yes."

Emma glances between us. "Okay, what's happening?"

"Nothing." The word rushes out of me too fast.

Emma crosses the room and folds her arms, waiting for the truth.

"You can't keep her in the dark," Harper whispers, even though Emma is only a foot away and can definitely hear. "It's not fair to her."

"Ummmm, what?" Emma drops her arms. "What does that mean?"

Harper stares at me, a silent command, but the words are stuck in my throat. I haven't known Emma long, but I don't want to lose the friendship we've found by scaring her away. I've already been through that with Beth. I don't want to do that again.

"Don't make her find out like I did," Harper says, her voice turning so quiet I'm not sure if Emma can catch her words anymore. She takes my hand in hers, warm and comforting. "I was so worried about Sam. About you—" Her eyes rake over my face, fear and concern filling their dark depths.

Harper is right. Whether I freak Emma out and she wants nothing to do with me doesn't matter as much as telling her truth. She deserves to know what's happening.

I turn back to Emma, and the truth spills from my mouth like a Catholic confession, hushed and hidden within this small space.

And when I'm done, Emma's face fills with both dread and disbelief until I worry that all I've done is scare her while also pulling her into my problems.

Outside, the sun is bright and cheery, the wind brushes gently against my skin and brings the sweet scent of grass and growing things, and the lake glitters as if diamonds are delicately laid across the surface. It's calm and peaceful and completely at odds with the fear churning within my chest like a winter storm.

As Ms. Peterson instructs us, I sit on the sun-warmed hill, surrounded by the other girls, and try to calm my swirling thoughts. But whatever sort of meditating or grounding exercises Ms. Peterson wants us to immerse ourselves in don't distract my mind enough. Those hallucinations—I don't know what else to call them—started out small—the flickering image of a whiskey bottle or my father's watch at first. But now they're consuming, pulling others in as well. How is it possible?

"All right, girls," Ms. Peterson says, sitting cross-legged on the ground and facing us. Her wavy hair catches the wind until it frizzes even more. "Now that we've listened and tuned in to our environment, and really brought that into ourselves, I'd like to go around the group and talk about how you're all feeling."

She shifts positions, sliding her legs to the side and fanning her tiered skirt across the grass. It's a patchwork of ruffles and various patterns, all in earth tones that contrast too sharply against her pumpkin-orange T-shirt.

But before we can talk about our feelings, Ms. Evans rushes out of the main lodge and across the grassy yard to where we're gathered.

"Sorry to intrude, but can I speak with you for a moment?" Ms. Evans asks the other therapist. She moves a few steps away and motions for Ms. Peterson to follow.

"Just a moment, girls." Ms. Peterson frowns before climbing to her feet and following, her skirt flowing in the breeze and sandals slapping against the ground.

They both start speaking in low voices, too quiet to hear their words. Next to me, Harper twists her silver ring around her finger and watches them as Emma plucks grass out of the dirt and Kylie and Page whisper to each other. I'm about to ask Harper what she thinks we should do to look for Sam and Reagan when Ms. Evans's voice hisses across the space toward us.

"It's working," she says before glancing at where we sit and lowering her voice. Their conversation is broken by the distance. "Did you…?" Ms. Evans starts, the rest of her words snatched away by the wind.

"I don't think we should—" Ms. Peterson's reply is cut off when Ms. Evans gives her a stringent look, gaze dancing to us and back, a clear warning to the other woman.

"We'll figure it out," Ms. Evans says, her voice barely reaching us. "Meet me in my office after *this*."

Ms. Evans doesn't wait for a reply. She turns on her heel, hiking boots digging heavily into the grass with each step, and makes her way back to the lodge.

"You were the one that interrupted," Ms. Peterson mumbles to herself, coming back over. A frown still tugs at her lips and forms lines on her brow, but when she sits down, she shakes it off and smiles.

"Sorry about that. Let's get back to what we were doing." Ms. Peterson turns to Quinn at the end of our row. "Let's start with you. How have you been doing so far, Quinn? I know your parents were a little concerned with you spending your summer in the woods. Are you finding it difficult at all?"

"Nope," Quinn says, the single word too chipper. "I'm fine." She shrugs, the movement so carefree it leaves me jealous.

"That's great to hear." Ms. Peterson picks up a notebook from the ground next to her, a pen clipped to it. As she scribbles comments, it's like gears clicking into place.

Quinn, with her crimson hair that matches the embroidered *Q* on that raggedy teddy bear. Shock surges through me like lightning. Has she seen those visions also?

The teddy bear. The heart monitor. I wondered if they were connected to Sam, but now…that teddy bear has to be related to Quinn. Is the monitor also? Or that forest I'd never seen before?

"Have you felt any negative emotions since our last conversation?" Ms. Peterson asks Quinn, drawing my attention back to the redheaded girl and the smile decorating her face.

"No, it's been a lot of fun so far," she tells Ms. Peterson. "Why would I?"

"Well—" Ms. Peterson tips her head to the side. The fine lines that decorate her forehead carve deep into her skin. "Okay, well, what about this morning during archery?" she asks. "You wanted to get away from the woods. How are you now?"

"I'm okay," Quinn says, the statement more like a question. Like she doesn't know why Ms. Peterson would ask that, but I do. Or I think so. Because these hallucinations seem to be a mix of memories, mine and Sam's—probably Quinn's with that forest, if Ms. Peterson is asking these questions.

But Quinn doesn't seem like someone being plagued by twisted visions. Dark smudges shadow her eyes, but a wide smile stretches her cheeks tight.

I gasp, and everyone turns to me.

"I…saw a spider," I say, grimacing at the dumb lie. Ms. Peterson turns back to Quinn, but out of my peripheral I can see Page staring at me.

An uneasy feeling crawls over my skin, but it isn't from the way Page watches. It's from the grin on Quinn's face, which shows too many teeth. From the way she seems unbothered by anything, even whatever issues that brought her here or the fact that two girls are gone and all we have is a flimsy excuse about special therapy sessions.

That look on Quinn, empty yet calm, is the same one Sam had before she left and didn't come back. Sam was terrified before the shadow man even showed up that night. She was scared and screaming when he threw us into that forest full of nightmares. But after he grabbed her, after Harper shook us back into what was real, *that's* when Sam wasn't scared anymore.

There's something else happening besides these hallucinations.

They aren't just tormenting us. They're *changing* us somehow.

PAGE

The girl felt too old for costumes and candy, stuck between childhood and womanhood. She wanted candles and creepiness, scary stories and Ouija boards. She was done with trick-or-treating and trading candy with her little brother.

But she spent the night walking from door to door, holding her brother's hand after refusing to dress up. She put on black clothes and tucked glittery red devil horns into her blond hair, but that was it. Her friend came along, cat ears perched on her head and dark clothes too but nothing more.

Together with her friend and brother, the girl walked through their neighborhood for hours, and if she sometimes added candy to her purse, it didn't mean she was trick-or-treating. It was only the fee for taking her brother out.

When the night grew late, the trio went home. While her brother settled down to sleep and her parents headed to their own room, the girl and her friend were free to stay up, to pull out the Ouija board and show they weren't scared. One by one, she lit candles around her room, saving her favorite for last: a black skull candle she bought with her allowance money. She set it on the floor next to the Ouija board. The black wax melted into a bloodred color as it dripped down the skull's temple and jawbone before piling onto the paper plate she'd placed under it.

The girl turned the lights off in her room, letting the flickering candles glow brightly. She sat opposite her friend, the Ouija board between them, and pushed her wire-framed glasses back up. Gently, both girls placed their hands on the planchette. They whispered questions to the other side. They giggled and gasped as the spirits spelled out their responses, while each girl swore it was the other moving it.

They spent the night wrapped in blankets on the floor of her bedroom, telling scary stories until their eyes grew too heavy to keep open.

Then the girl woke to heat and smoke as her friend's screams tore through the night. No alarms rang; her father had always forgotten to replace the batteries.

All around, fire blazed. It ate away at the wallpaper and the furniture and the toys the girl couldn't bring herself to get rid of. It devoured her pictures and posters taped to the walls until they curled and crumbled into nothing.

The candle on her dresser lay tipped over, eating the wood and clothes within, creating a wall of flames that made the window crack. The girl scrambled to stand up, tears hot on her cheeks as smoke clogged her glasses.

The fire was ravenous. Hungry for her blanket, for her room—for her. It seared her arm and gorged itself on pale skin. She cried out but grabbed her friend, who stood frozen and staring at the raging flames.

She reached the door, gripped the brass knob. The metal scorched the tender flesh of her palm as she ripped the door open. Smoke spilled out, and the fire chased the girl. As she dragged her friend and rushed to her brother's room.

Her arm felt useless, burning and bleeding and screaming with pain. But she woke her brother, pulled him out of bed with her good arm. Urged her friend to *go go go* as she half carried her brother.

Her lungs ached, coated by the smoke that filled their house. Her throat felt raw as she screamed for her parents to wake up—to get out.

She heard their confusion, their cries and thundering footsteps, as she got to the front door and fresh cold air greeted her.

The girl's friend stumbled down the porch steps as she followed behind with her brother and his tear-soaked face. Her parents came crashing out, relief replacing their fear when they saw their children.

The girl's arm and hand were consumed with an agony that made it hard to think, to breathe. To feel any relief at seeing her family and friend outside, unharmed. Her parents rushed to her as the girl held her brother and trembled.

Her father called the fire department, and her mother pulled the children farther from the house. And then they waited, as the fire ate away at their home—but not their lives.

As the lights of fire trucks streaked the sky in red and white, the girl couldn't help but feel guilty. She'd forgotten to snuff out the candles.

TWENTY-ONE

You and Harper are going? Now?" Emma asks as I search for my flashlight. I left it on my nightstand, but it's not there.

"Yeah," I say, stretching my arm under the bed. It must have rolled away. I pull my empty backpack out and shove it behind me. My fingers crawl over the wooden floorboards, but only dust clings to my hand. I shake it off and glance toward the window. The sun has already dipped below the horizon, painting the sky in shades of bruised indigo and smoky coal.

"I'm coming with you guys," Emma says. She picks up a bottle of the essential oil blend that Ms. Evans gave her and holds it up. "I want to find out what's in this too."

"No, I don't want you getting in trouble if we get caught." I reach even farther, until even my shoulder squeezes under the bed.

The muscles in my arm stretch, fingers skimming over dirt settled on the wooden planks.

"I don't care about that." Emma walks over to my side of the cabin but trips on my discarded backpack. The bottle she's holding smashes to the floor, glass shattering until the scent of lavender and lime—*bergamot*, Ms. Evans called it—fills the room, suffocatingly thick.

"No. Oh no—" I start to say, until something grabs my wrist and I scream instead. Cold fingers burn into my skin, gripping harder and harder as I try to yank my arm away, unable to free myself.

"Penny!" Emma shouts. "What's happening? Are you cut?" Her gaze races over me, searching for a wound.

I can't answer. Not as I stare under the bed and the darkness separates. It peels apart until the face of the shadow man is staring out from that small space, hollow spots for eyes and blackened fingers.

He moves closer, slithering under the bed frame. His hold on my wrist is unforgiving, but as he slides closer, I move too, trying to rip my arm away as the two of us shift backward together until we're no longer under the bed. His fingers dig into my skin, never letting go. His hunched form slowly stretches and straightens, uncurling, until the shadow man is looming over me.

Emma gasps, stumbling backward. Her hands fly to her mouth, covering it as she stares at the serrated skin of his torn face.

Now she knows. Now she sees all of him.

Only…something is different. Those glacial blue eyes—so similar to Sam's—that he had last time are gone, along with his pale-skin-covered hands. They've been replaced with shadows and darkness once more. But there's something else too. It niggles and itches in the back of my brain, but I can't figure out what's…wrong. Different.

The shadow man's ink-drenched hand still grasps onto me, the other holding that same bottle of amber whiskey that he always has. He doesn't have my father's belt, but he's been without it before. And yet, it still feels as if he's changed in some way, missing… something I can't quite place. But as his grip tightens on me, I don't care about anything besides getting free.

I yank my arm back, but he holds firm. Again, I pull, as hard as I can. Fear spreads through my veins, until finally, he lets go. I stumble back as Emma grabs my shoulder, drawing me back and putting distance between us and the shadow man.

"You see it too, right?" Emma asks, her voice shaking and whispering.

"Yeah." I bump into her as I move away again.

"H-how?" She grips the long pendant on her necklace, not an aromatherapy one but the same black cylinder from before. "How are we both seeing it? Is this…real?"

"I don't know," I tell her as the creature standing before us cocks its head to the side at that same harsh angle. My wrist aches from where he grabbed me. He—*it*—doesn't feel like a hallucination.

The shadow man's attention shifts to Emma, and my heart thrashes, an inconsistent beat that spreads pain through my chest. He lifts his hand, and the yellow lights in our room glint and flicker off the glass bottle. His other hand holds the black flashlight I was looking for, but he pushes the whiskey bottle closer.

"Get that away from me!" I step back, shoving Emma along as a moan rumbles through the creature's chest. I have no idea what it wants, but there's no way I'm touching that bottle.

"Penny," Emma whispers in my ear. "L-let's just go." Her hand trembles against my shoulder, where she still holds on.

I nod. Hallucination or not, the pain the shadow man inflicts feels real enough, and I don't want anything happening to Emma.

"Pennnn—" he starts.

"No!" I yell. I can't hear that name coming from his ragged, lipless mouth. I step back again, until I knock into the desk, Emma stumbling with me. "*Never* say that name again."

The shadow man opens his empty mouth, a roar pushing past that dark maw. But his anger only fuels my own. I'm sick of this. Of seeing him—a nightmare version of my father. Of being scared. Of not understanding anything.

"You're not him! You're not my father!" The words ricochet off the walls, and it's as if they break the room apart, melt the window and wood panels. Everything shifts and changes until the cabin is replaced with a small bedroom.

But even crowded with shadows, I know that thin mattress and even thinner blanket. The single window layered in a film of dirt and the wooden dresser missing two knobs. The mirror on the wall, fractures spreading across it like cracked ice.

I've been dropped into my bedroom. From before Mom and I fixed it up—from before my father died. Emma is here too, standing next to my narrow bed.

The shadow man is too large compared to the tiny space. That skeletal face, shrouded in darkness, stares at me. His head cocks right, then left, taking in every detail, every emotion that I display.

I hold the air in my lungs, afraid of letting it even whisper across the too few inches left between the shadow man and me. It's too much. Him and this room and the terror keeping me frozen.

"Pennnn"—he starts again, and this time I don't dare yell at him—"elllll…opeeeee."

His fingers slam into my sternum, and the world erupts in colors, blinking green, yellow, and red, a shower of sparkling glass.

As quickly as it started, my dingy bedroom comes back into harsh focus as the shadow man grabs my shirt. He yanks me toward him, and it feels as if he's wrenching my pounding heart out of my chest.

Emma gasps, heaving and panting. "Not real, not real, not real," she whispers.

Eyes appear within his dark sockets, their colors flashing from dark brown to light green; back and forth, they shift between the two colors—no pale blue like Sam's this time—as this monster stares at me.

Something grabs his attention, and his head turns as he focuses on the blank wall behind him. He lets out a loud growl before dropping his hand from my shirt and shoving me away. I fall back, caught by Emma, as the shadow man's shape folds and bends in on itself. He flies toward the empty wall before disappearing *into* it.

"Where are we?" Emma asks, but I can't bring myself to tell her as I look around the small room I grew up in—only it's not an exact replica.

Hidden in one corner by the bed is a heart monitor, on a stand this time. A quiet beeping starts as the screen begins to glow. And on every surface in my room, vases full of decaying flowers flicker into existence. Nestled between the bouquets are dozens of cards standing like little headstones.

"It's blank," Emma says, picking one up. She grabs another and another. On the front of each card are words full of condolences, sympathy, and prayers, but inside is nothing except white space. "Why are they blank?"

I shake my head, fingers trailing on a dying daffodil. Her guess is as good as mine. I drop the flower and wipe the feel of those velvety-soft petals off on my jean shorts.

"What. Is. That?" Emma lets the cards in her hand fall like ash to the ground and points at the twin bed.

My pulse throbs faster as the thin blanket on the bed starts to *inflate*, filling the shape of a body underneath.

Soon, soon, soon, the heart monitor says, making Emma scream as it suddenly grows louder in the stiflingly small room.

I move toward my bed as the machine's beeps shriek in time with each step. *Soon, soon, soon.* I reach a trembling hand out, and my fingers grip the blanket.

"Don't," Emma pleads. But I have to. I have to know who—or what—is under the covers.

Soon, soon, soon.

I rip the blanket back and gasp. Lying in the bed is a woman, frail and thin, and covered in tubes. Needles dig into her dark skin, and an ashen pallor has drained her face of any signs of life. I drop the blanket to the floor.

There's a dead woman in my bed.

The monitor goes silent, and my head fills with dizziness until I realize I'm not breathing.

Even in death, the woman clutches a silver picture frame to her chest. In it, she smiles, eyes twinkling and cheeks dimpled, vibrant and full of life—everything missing from her now. Next to her is a man, handsome and happy, and standing before them both is a girl, a young teenager with dark skin and bright eyes that match her mother's. Her black hair is braided in perfect rows, and her own smile highlights the prettiness of her face. There's something familiar about the girl, but I can't figure out what.

"Wh-who is she?" Emma asks, glancing between the woman and me.

"No one I know." I peel my eyes away from the bed. "You?"

She shakes her head.

Screaming and yelling spreads through the room, replacing the beeping of the monitor. My heart drops to my stomach as my father's anger seeps through the walls. I glance back at the dead woman, but the bed is empty again. Emma's eyes go wide as she follows my gaze.

"What's—"

A dull thud sounds, cutting off whatever Emma was about to say. It's followed by a cry from Mom, and then it's my voice in that hall, shouting at my father.

There was only one time I yelled at my father like that. I know this night. And I don't want to relive it.

But even as my legs shake in terror, I can't stop myself from rushing to the door as my voice and my father's shouts crescendo together. Emma calls my name as I yank the door open.

My father stands in the doorway.

"Penelope!" he shouts. He yells my name over and over, his face turning an ugly shade of red...until shadows fissure over his skin, turning it darker, replacing his features until only that nightmare version of him towers over me. The shadow man's hand lashes out, grabbing my neck, cutting off my air as his grip tightens.

He yanks me out of the bedroom and toward the stairs. My fingers scrape against the wooden railing, unable to grab it as hands shove me and the sensation of falling makes my stomach heave.

"Penny!" Emma cries out, but when I look up, it's not my roommate or even the shadow man standing at the top of the stairs. It's me—a copy of myself, watching as I crash *down, down, down*.

Only it isn't the hard stairs or foyer I land on but the softness of a bed in a different world and time. My cabin at Whitewood solidifies. Emma stands next to me, breathing too quick and shallow.

Dark wood panels and matching skylights materialize in our room. No dead woman or broken bedroom. There's only a night gone dark, too many questions, and the spreading scent of lavender and bergamot. The phantom words of that heart monitor echo in my ears like a promise. *Soon, soon, soon*. But what do they mean? What else could possibly be coming *soon*?

TWENTY-TWO

A soft knock on the door makes me jump, and Emma flinches. Neither of us move, still disoriented from the hallucination. The only sound is my still-heavy breaths and the reverberations of those piercing beeps splintering against my eardrums.

The knock comes again, and with it, Harper's whispered voice. "Penny? Are you there?"

"Yeah," I say, shaking myself and glancing at Emma, making sure she's okay. "Come in. But leave the door open." I climb off the bed and shove the window up, hoping to air out the room. Emma glances at the open window, biting her lip and holding her pendant, but doesn't ask me to shut it.

Harper comes in, her gaze darting between the shattered glass on the floor and Emma standing next to my dresser with all the blood drained from her face.

"Did something happen?" Harper asks as I step away from the window, and Emma nods silently.

I'm about to answer her when I notice my nightstand. My flashlight is propped on the little table, standing tall like a lighthouse.

The shadow man had it in his hand, but now…it sits there as if waiting for me to take it.

Harper waves her hand in the air, pulling my attention back. "What happened?"

Emma starts cleaning up the floor with one of her towels as I fill Harper in.

"Come on," Harper says, nodding toward the door. "Let's figure this out and find Sam."

"I'm coming too," Emma says, following as Harper moves toward the door. "I don't want to stay here alone." She holds a plastic bag that used to have her snacks in it but is now filled with the broken bottle and oil-soaked towel. Her grip on it tightens, knuckles turning pale.

"Then let's go," Harper says.

I grab the flashlight off my nightstand, hand shaking slightly. Following Harper and Emma, I click the cabin lights off but leave the door wide-open. Emma glances back at the doorway and grips her necklace.

"We should air it out," I tell her.

She nods, but her hold doesn't loosen, and I can only hope the scent of lavender and bergamot is gone before we get back and we won't need to leave the window or door open overnight—and that no more hallucinations are brought on by that broken bottle.

Together, the three of us hurry down the steps of the cabin and across the lawn, skirting around the flagpole and its ring of yellow flowers, which nearly glow under the moon. It's well past midnight, and the camp is covered in a blanket of quiet that makes my breathing feel loud.

"What's the plan?" Emma asks as we stop in front of the lodge's main doors.

Harper looks at me, biting her lip and giving a small shrug.

"We search their offices and any other rooms?" I ask. "Sam and Reagan have to be here somewhere. There aren't any other buildings."

"Should we stay together or split up?" Emma stares through the etched glass windows to the darkened foyer.

"Split up," I say at the same time Harper says, "Stay together."

I shake my head. "If we get caught together, no one will believe any excuses. Plus, we can search faster."

"Okay, but…" Harper glances from me to Emma and back. "Be careful."

"You too," I say, grabbing the door and holding it open for them. I'm about to follow when something near our cabin catches my attention, a quick blur of movement. "I'll meet you guys in there.

I'm gonna peek in the cabins, make sure Delaney and everyone else is asleep."

"Good idea," Harper says as I let the door close between us.

The night wraps around me, still warm, as I make my way back to the cabins. But I don't check them. Not when I catch another glimpse of movement within the woods. A dark shape darts between the trees, and I hold my breath as if that will help me see better.

Is it the shadow man again? Even without the aromatherapy blend?

I pick at the front of my shirt, sniffing the cloth and worrying the scent is on me and I'm too used to it to notice.

Before me stands a wall of white birch trees reaching for the sky with emerald fingers. Another shadow-clad shape slips between the trees, but whether it's a deer with spindly antlers or only swaying tree branches, I don't know.

"Penny!" a voice calls out, and it takes me a moment to recognize Sam's voice. Relief floods me. She's here. "Help me! I'm stuck!"

"Sam? Where are you?" I step closer to the edge of the forest.

"In here!" she yells. "Please, help me!"

I glance back at the camp once, but when Sam yells my name again, I rush into the forest, following a narrow dirt path. The temperature drops, the moonlight dimming with it. I finally remember the flashlight in my hand and turn it on. Its bright glow covers the ground at my feet.

"Sam!" I call out, sweeping the light around. The relief I felt moments ago twists into worry. What if it's not really her? I sniff my shirt again, catching the faintest scent of bergamot. What if this is only another hallucination?

"Help!" she shouts one more time, and I can't take the risk that this isn't real. Not if she needs me.

"Tell me where you are!"

But Sam doesn't shout out again. The forest goes quiet, only the creaking of the trees and the chittering of insects calling back.

The trunks of the birch trees are glaringly bright with their pale skin, shining like specters in the night. The breeze rattles their leaves, whispering secrets between them, too soft and foreign for me to know. But as I pass the trees, I can't help feeling as if their quiet murmurs are meant as a warning. A plea to turn away.

With every step I take deeper into the forest, the more those trees close in, as if angry that I don't listen to their warning. And when the small dirt path I'm on dwindles away, the air in my lungs also tightens.

Maybe I should listen. Maybe I don't want to discover the secrets this forest hides.

But I can't turn away if Sam's out there. So I keep going, walking blindly through a forest of peeling bark that curls away as if even it doesn't want to be here.

Only the incessant whine of insects breaks apart the ringing in my ears—until the sound of a stick, cracking like a rib bone, shatters the quiet. My flashlight beam flies in that direction, and a dark shape lurches behind a cropping of trees. It's half-hidden, but I catch a glimpse of something toweringly tall, even hunched over, as antlers reach toward the star-flecked sky. The shape rushes away too quickly, but there's no denying it was too large to be a deer.

I stand there in silence, listening. Waiting. Too afraid to breathe and wondering if moose live in these woods.

A chill rushes down my spine. This place feels too close to that fake forest I saw with Sam. The trees are different, silver with spindly trunks, but it doesn't stop the way my heart begins to stutter in displeasure against my sternum. My vision blurs, shadows filling my view. I try to leave, to turn away and get Harper and Emma, make them help me find Sam so I'm not alone in these woods, but all I do is stumble through the darkness.

A blink, and my vision clears enough to see the forest—only even in this foreign place, I know I'm not in the same spot I was a moment ago. A sharp drop-off sits before me, only a few yards ahead, where before it was flat ground.

How did I get here?

I lean against a tree, try to catch my breath.

I want to call out for Sam again, to find her so neither of us are alone, but the words stick in my throat like phlegm, growing and clinging to my insides until I'm afraid if I cough it out, it will turn into a panicked scream. Tacky blood smears onto my hand where I hold onto the tree. Crimson stains its curling bark.

My flashlight bounces from tree to tree, each swipe of that

yellow glow showing another trunk marked by brushstrokes of blood.

I can't stop staring. Scarlet handprints stain the pristine white trees, leaving a gruesome trail for me to follow.

Come, it seems to say. *If you dare.*

And I do.

I follow the crimson path, moving closer to that drop-off as my flashlight finds more blood seeping into the dirt, dripping onto the brush. Sam called for me, for help—before going silent. My head screams that it's her blood, that she's hurt or worse. Panicked gasps saw in and out of me as I move *faster, faster, faster.*

Each splash of blood I see stabs into me. Each swipe of a handprint is proof that someone is—or was—hurt. My vision goes dark again.

So much blood, that voice in my head says. The words are a praise.

The world around me is nothing but the pitch-black of my own mind. I can't see. I take slow steps, knowing the drop-off is nearby.

What have you done? the voice asks, a purr of approval. **So much blood.**

Nothing! It wasn't me. I didn't—

The ground falls away until I'm crashing down the hill. My body slams and tumbles against the earth and rocks and trees. Pain explodes through every part of me. Dirt kicks up into the air, filling my lungs.

I collide with something, sharp pain bursting across my ribs as my fall is suddenly stopped. I reach one shaky hand to my side, feeling the tender spot as papery bark scrapes against the back of my hand. A tree.

Is this how he felt? Those intrusive thoughts whisper at me. *Falling down the stairs. Dying. He hurt you. While you...*

True darkness takes me, silencing both my mind and that voice.

———————

Waking up, I groan against the aches and pains spreading through my body. My head is dizzy, but at least I can see again. The world comes back in sharp focus. Silver trees lit by the moon surround me, their knobby eyes staring with accusation. I shake the feeling away as I sit up and lean against the trunk at my side.

I need to get back to Whitewood. How long have I been here? Have Harper and Emma realized I'm gone? I look around the forest, trying to figure out which way to go, when the sight of Sam's face next to me makes a scream crawl up my throat.

I stare down at the forest floor—at the body lying in a broken pile. Blood, too much of it, soaks the ground, painting it in death and decay.

The ringing in my ears becomes so loud that it turns into an all-consuming silence. Tears sting my eyes as I stare at...her.

Sam's body rests on the hard ground in a horrible image of twisted limbs and devastating loss. Wrists bent back, one leg wrenched into a V shape, an arm lying under her torso.

A pool of dried blood spread under her makes it look like she's lying on a blanket. Her head is tilted in a way that reminds me too much of the shadow man and how he always cocks his. Twigs and leaves are tangled in her short pink hair, and her pale blue eyes, now coated in a film of white, stare unseeing at the canopy of emerald leaves.

You killed her, that voice whispers, pleased at the idea. *You did this. You were always going to be like him. Hurting others.*

No. I scramble to my feet. No amount of finger tapping and counting can help me now. *This wasn't me.*

But it was, those thoughts tell me. *Look at your hands.*

I stumble back with a gasp. My flashlight is gone, probably somewhere on the hillside I fell down, but in its place is my father's belt, cracked fake leather and garish gold buckle. Blood coats my palms, soaks into the belt, and stains the front of my shirt.

You are more like him than you want to admit, the voice hisses. *No...you're worse. You killed her.*

I drop my father's belt as if it's a brand burning into me. It falls next to Sam's body.

It isn't possible. It has to be another hallucination—only there's no essential oils to trigger it this time.

Slowly, I take a step closer to Sam, needing to prove to myself that it's not really her. She's not dead. None of this is real.

But it is, those intrusive thoughts say. *And it's your fault.*

The moonlight slips through the branches, highlighting the

way Sam's skin has turned a gruesome shade of gray. Bruises ring her neck, and I'm terrified to see if they match the width of my father's belt. Traces of dried foam coat her mouth and nose, and there's a bloat starting to take over her body that makes my stomach sick.

Only there's a fluttering—a soft movement—on her chest. A breath, both impossible and terrifying. My heart catches in my throat. Is Sam…alive?

I lean forward over her body, and her chest shatters apart. Dozens and dozens of little gray things swarm into the air as I scream.

And it's only when one flies into my mouth that I realize they're moths. I gag and lean over, coughing hard enough to spit it out.

More moths surge around me, their powdery wings brushing against my skin and tangling in my hair. I flail my hands until they finally disperse into the night, but they leave an even harsher truth behind—a gaping hole in Sam's chest where they were teeming.

The emptiness sits there now, exposed and mirroring the hollowness filling my own chest. Jagged ribs, broken like frail twigs, stick into the air and reach up for me, while others stab even deeper into her.

Yet they don't hide the way her heart is missing. Gone.

You did this. All that blood, the voice says. *On your hands.*

I look down at my crimson-stained palms, unable to stop the panic rising in me when I find a ruined heart cradled there. I jerk back, dropping Sam's heart. It thuds and bounces on the ground in a way that makes bile burn my throat.

You are dangerous, the voice purrs again. *Deadly.*

Images of Sam standing at the top of the drop-off fill my head. Of me, pushing her down, watching as she falls to her death. I blink, and then it's my father's face staring up, my hands still outstretched. Another blink, and Sam's sightless eyes are watching me again.

"No." I shake my head. It's impossible. "I...I didn't do this."

But you did. Her blood is on you.

"No," I say again, even if I don't believe my own denial.

The crack of a twig pulls me back to the moment, stops my panic from spiraling for a second. I glance around at the shadow-filled forest and stumble backward when a shape even darker than the night slips behind a tree several yards away. Did Harper and Emma come looking for me? I can't have them see this.

I need to leave. Not just this forest, but Camp Whitewood and everyone here. They aren't safe around me.

TWENTY-THREE

The trip back to camp is a blur that has nothing to do with my vision messing up and everything to do with the horror consuming me. I stumble through the forest and rush to my cabin before Harper or Emma can find me.

I grab my duffel bag and my empty backpack and start shoving everything in, taking a minute to yank off my bloody shirt and put a clean one on. I want to wash my hands, but I don't dare go to the bathrooms in the main lodge.

I don't have a plan—don't know where I'll go—but I'll walk through the woods to town if I have to. I pause, wondering if I'm following in Clara's footsteps, but does it matter anymore?

Slipping my toiletries bag into the side pocket of the duffel, my hand slides against something hard. I pull it out only to find the plastic razors Mom tried to give me before leaving. She must have stashed them there.

I drop the package, unable to hold those dangerous blades. But it's *me* who's dangerous, not them. They're special—safe. And yet, I'm sure I could still find a way to cause harm with them.

Sharp enough to slice skin, those intrusive thoughts whisper as I stare at the razors. *Pick them up*, it commands.

My hands shake at my sides. I need to pack, not struggle with some stupid razors. I grab more clothes, jamming them into my duffel, when a voice startles me.

"What are you doing?" Harper steps into the cabin and moves close enough to rest a hand on top of mine, to stop my frenzied packing. Her breaths are fast, her hair windblown as if she ran here.

"I have to go," I tell her, unable to admit the darker truth.

"What? Why?" She looks around the cabin.

"What are you doing here? I thought you were looking for…" I can't bring myself to say Sam's name.

"I saw the light on. Did something happen?"

"I can't be here." I slip my hand out from under hers. "It's not safe."

"I know," she says. "We'll figure this out together. But you can't leave in the middle of the night. That's not safe either."

"No, you don't get it." Those damned plastic razors stare up at me from the floor.

Pick them up. Slice her skin. Watch her bleed, that voice urges.

I ball my hands into fist to keep from giving in—to keep Harper from seeing Sam's blood on them.

"It's not safe for you to be around *me*." I turn away from her. "I was sent here because…because I get these intrusive thoughts. And they tell me to hurt people," I admit, hoping and not hoping it will make her leave.

"Have you had thoughts like that about me?" she asks, but there's no judgment in her tone. I nod, and she rests a hand on my shoulder, gently pulling until I face her. "And look, here I am. Unharmed. You might have those thoughts, but have you acted on them?"

There's so much trust in her dark eyes that I have no choice but to warn her away with the truth.

"I can't even look at those stupid razors without hearing in my head that I should cut someone with them. I'm *not* safe to be around."

Harper leans down, picking up the package before holding it out to me. "I trust you. You haven't hurt me yet, and you won't now."

You're just like your father, the voice says. *Take them. Cut her. Do it now.*

"I can't even *touch* that." I step back. "I found Sam," I say, knowing it's the only way to make Harper understand. "She's dead. Because of me." I hold my hands out, palms up, for her to see the evidence. "This is her blood."

Harper looks down, her face scrunching. "There's nothing there, Penny. Well, some dirt—but no blood."

"That's…that's not possible. I saw her body." I grab my discarded shirt, but the front is no longer soaked in blood. It couldn't have been a hallucination. It felt so real. "Did you find Sam? Or Reagan?"

Harper shakes her head. "No, they weren't anywhere in the lodge."

Was that really Sam, her body, abandoned in the woods? I don't know what's real and what's not anymore. Did I hurt—kill—Sam? Every part of me screams that I would never do that, never *want* to, except for the voice in my head. If I stay, will I only hurt more of my friends?

That voice laughs, a harsh chuckle curling around my thoughts. **Yes**, it says. **You will.**

There's a part of me, small and frail but there, that desperately wants to prove those intrusive thoughts wrong.

To show it that I *didn't* hurt Sam. To find out what's real or not.

"Come with me," I tell Harper. "I need your help." I need her to see if Sam's body is out there or not.

Before Harper and I can step out of the cabin, Emma comes rushing in.

"I found something," she says, nearly breathless. "I think." She glances at the still open door and inhales deeply before closing it. "Good, the smell is gone."

"What is it?" Harper asks.

"This," Emma says, holding up a notebook, similar to the therapy journals we were given.

"Look." Emma flips through pages filled with neat, looping

script before stopping on one that has a photo tucked into it. Ms. Evans smiles up from the picture, along with a teenaged Clara.

"Read the back." Emma flips the photo over, and in the same looping script is written:

I miss you, Clara. I'd do anything to have you back. I can't change the past, but I can promise that I will do <u>anything</u> to keep from ever failing again.

"And look," Emma says, flicking through the pages until she gets to some of the newer entries.

Emily doesn't agree with how I'm doing things, but we have no choice. It's the only way to make this work. To not fail again.

"Who's Emily?" I ask.

"Ms. Peterson," Harper answers. She points to the open page with one finger, the package of razors still in her grip.

"It was dated a day ago." I take the package of razors from her and drop them onto my abandoned duffel bag. "So it's true? They're really doing something to us?" I look at Harper and Emma. Worry wrinkles their brows, pulls their lips downward.

Emma swallows hard. "I think so."

Then maybe…maybe Sam is fine, even if we can't find her. Maybe it was only another hallucination. There wasn't any blood on me.

But I have to know for sure.

And I can't leave Whitewood until I figure all of this out.

———

The next morning, I stand in front of an easel, surrounded by the other girls in Ms. Peterson's art therapy, as if everything is normal when it absolutely isn't. I promised to pretend everything is fine even though it's so very *wrong*. My hands are clammy and won't stop shaking. My stomach is so nauseous I can't eat. And there's a weight pressing on my chest that makes it almost impossible to breathe. I can't stop thinking about last night.

It took Emma and me a half hour of trekking through the woods before finding the drop-off I fell down—before finding Sam's body. She's dead, that much is real.

Sam is dead. Heart torn out. The feeling is mirrored in me. There's a hollow spot in my chest every time I look at our therapist, every time I see the image of Sam's broken body seared across my closed eyelids.

And the women leading this camp might be responsible for that. Not me. Emma pointed out that Sam's death couldn't have happened last night; her body was already starting to decompose. The thought makes me sick.

And Reagan is still missing. Maybe dead like Sam, for all we know.

I almost wish that we didn't find it—Sam's body. I could still hope everything was a hallucination. But there was no aroma-therapy or anything to mess with our heads when Emma and I found Sam again.

My heart aches. I didn't know Sam very long, not even a full week at Whitewood. But we shared something, an understanding. Two discarded girls with dads that still haunted us—our histories, different but somehow similar, tying us together. My breathing tightens, a sadness seeping into each inhale. Sorrow for what our friendship could have become—and for all the possibilities of Sam's life that were killed along with her. I wished I'd had more time with her, gotten to known her better. We stood over her body, eyes averted, and said our goodbyes. And as I racked my brain for the right thing to say, all I could recall was how Sam was blunt and defiant, but underneath, she was kind. She cared about me—practically a stranger—and the others. There was empathy in her eyes if you could get past the wall she'd built to protect herself.

I saw glimpses of it, and I wish that I could have known more of her.

And while Emma and I were in the woods with Sam, Harper put Ms. Evans's journal back. But even if the book is in her office, I can't get the words written there out of my head. My palms sweat, heart racing at the possibility that Ms. Evans is willing to do *anything* to not fail again—whatever that means. Maybe even kill or hide an accidental death?

We're trapped here with the very women that might have killed

Sam, and there's no one for us to go to for help. Unless we can sneak into their offices again and try to call the police—but will they listen to a bunch of teenagers with no real proof? If we bring the police to Sam's body, will they deem her a runaway who got attacked by a bear or something? And what will Ms. Evans and Ms. Peterson do to the rest of us if they realize we're suspicious of them?

A loud screech fills the art room, and I flinch as Kylie jerks away like she's ready to run. But it's only Quinn, her easel sliding against the linoleum floor as she sets a canvas on it.

Everyone looks exhausted, dark circles and slow blinks. Page's eyes are red and puffy behind her glasses, like she spent the morning crying. Kylie has the same far-off stare as Emma, and Harper chews her lip, spinning the silver ring on her finger. The others don't know about Sam. At least, Emma, Harper, and I agreed not to say anything yet. Not until we can figure out what's going on. So why do the other girls all look as worn down as us? Are these hallucinations plaguing them too like I think they must be?

Quinn is the only one not frowning. There's a frozen smile on her face. If it's meant to be comforting, she's failing. All it does is send an itch crawling down my spine.

Ms. Peterson comes around the group, passing out little buckets full of paintbrushes and supplies and pulling my attention to her. I want to step back when she comes close, the overwhelming distrust urging my feet away, but I stay rooted in place. She hooks my special green bucket onto the easel and moves to the next.

But my stomach tightens when I see the metal paint spatula sitting in my bucket. Did she put it there on purpose?

Next to me, Harper sees me shaking, and her gaze follows mine to the paint supplies. "It's okay," she whispers, stepping closer. "You won't hurt anyone."

"I will."

Do it, the voice hisses. *You are your father's daughter. Dangerous and violent.*

"No, you won't." Harper takes my hand before I can even try my useless finger tapping. "You didn't last night. Do you even remember that? You took the razors and set them down. You didn't even think of hurting me or Emma, did you?"

"I…" I didn't realize it, but she's right. I took the package from her, those blades new and sharp, and I didn't hear those intrusive thoughts.

"You're in control. It's okay. I won't push you, but if you want to try…" Harper guides my hand slowly toward the bucket, waiting and watching. "Trust yourself." She lets go.

Hand shaking, I pick up the metal spatula, the tip sharp and pointed.

Stab her, the voice says.

Be quiet, I tell it—not a plea this time but a command. And I'm surprised when it listens, when that voice fades away. I can still feel it there, waiting to strike, but for the moment, it's blessedly silent. And for the first time, I wonder if I might be stronger than those intrusive thoughts.

I look up at Harper, smiling slightly, but a frown yanks it away when Ms. Peterson turns on the aromatherapy diffuser.

"Can we keep that off?" I ask, tucking the paint spatula into the bucket again, not wanting to tempt fate any longer. "I have a headache, and the oils have been making it worse," I lie.

"Oh." Ms. Peterson glances from me to the diffuser before clicking it off. "Of course. Now, for today—"

"Where are the others?" Kylie asks suddenly. "Why aren't they with us?"

There's a sharpness to her tone that makes me wonder *why* she's asking. But there's something else too, a thought—a memory—that tries to climb to the surface.

Kylie bites her lip, chewing on it, and when she catches me staring, the memory slams into me.

The dead woman in my childhood bedroom—the vision the shadow man threw Emma and me into. The woman was clutching a picture, framed in silver: a mom, a dad, and a girl only a couple years younger-looking.

Her hair might be different, a halo of tight curls instead of the braids in the photo, and her smile is gone, but it was Kylie.

Was that woman—that hallucination—real in some way? Connected to Kylie somehow?

I need to know.

There must be an intensity to my face, because Kylie flinches and looks away, but I can't stop seeing her image frozen in time with a smile, can't stop hearing the echoing beeps of that heart monitor. And I swear the scent of decaying flowers fills my nose and twists my stomach.

I have to talk to her.

KYLIE

The girl sat in the hospital chair, the sterile antiseptic crowding her lungs with every breath, as an incessant beeping droned on around her.

The high-pitched beeps dug into the girl's ears like ice picks, but at least they meant that her mother was still there. Still alive.

For now.

But she knew—everyone knew—it wouldn't be that way much longer.

The girl, barely a woman herself, was losing her mother when she needed her most. She wanted to scream, to rage, to shout that it wasn't fair. That this shouldn't be happening. Her mother had always looked so healthy, so alive.

Until now.

The girl stared at her mother, tucked into the bed with tubes and needles hooked into her arms and blanketed over her face. Her mother had never been so frail before, as delicate as spun sugar. It would only take a breath to break her.

The girl held her own breath, let it scream in her lungs as she tried to hold time still. As she listened to each gasp that rattled through her mother's body.

But time wasn't something her mother had. It wasn't something the girl could hold frozen if only she wished hard enough.

Time ate away at her, at her mother—at both of them. As her father paced the hall, unable to sit still, the girl couldn't do anything.

So, she sat and waited and cried over the inevitable. Her reflection stared at her from the window. Tears trailed down her cheeks, leaving a shine over her dark skin.

The girl loved her mother.

She didn't want her to leave.

But as she waited, she heard words in those constant beeps, the machinery speaking to her. *Soon. Soon. Soon.*

The harsh hospital lights glared down at an even harsher truth. At a space filled with too much stark white and pale blue and pastel green. At the flowers that surrounded her. They wilted in their vases, alongside her mother, from days and weeks of sitting there, their water turning murky and dark. The scent twisted the girl's stomach, aged perfume that mixed with sting-ing disinfectants.

In only a month, the girl's entire world had crumbled along with her mother's health. Each second and minute consumed her mother. From paper-frail skin, her mother's bones protruded, stark and severe, a broken cage trapping what was left of the once vibrant woman

The girl begged to hear her mother's voice one more time, to hear sweet words spoken warmly. But she knew her mother had no strength to even whisper an *I love you* anymore.

The girl wanted to destroy the room that held them both prisoner. She wanted to throw those flowers out the window, vases and cards along with them.

She knew she'd never get the sickly scent of decaying flowers out of her nose or the droning tones of those machine out of her ears. They burrowed into her like ticks, sucking and stealing the memories of her mother from before. Before she got sick. Before they found the cancer. Before they knew she wouldn't survive.

Her mother's breath rattled, long and slow...until it stopped.

The girl trapped the air in her lungs once more. Let it burn and blaze and consume her. She waited for another labored breath to come from her mother. She waited seconds that lasted an eternity. And as the machines screamed the truth and her father raced into the room, as nurses and doctors barreled past, the girl still let her lungs scream when her voice couldn't.

She stood in the corner of the room, watching the rush of people around her mother's body as the machines spoke to the girl once more, one long flat cry that fractured the girl's heart.

Gooooone.

Her mother was gone. Dead.

The inevitable had always felt, if only a little, deniable to her until that moment.

The girl collapsed to the ground, the hard tiles slamming into her knees, as she wished for the earsplitting sounds of the machines to say anything else. As she wished for time to spin backward until the memories of this day didn't exist.

But even as the machines stopped and silence filled the room, the girl knew nothing could bring her mother back.

TWENTY-FOUR

As soon as art therapy ends, I try to catch Kylie, but she rushes out with Page before I get the chance, and Harper steps in my way without realizing it.

"Can I go with you?" Harper asks, twisting her silver ring around. "I don't want to be alone in my cabin."

"Of course." I reach out and take her hand, smiling when she entwines her fingers with mine.

Emma joins us, and Harper rubs her thumb over the back of my hand as we walk. I'm not sure she's even aware of the motion, but it's suddenly all I can focus on, the soft touch of her skin against mine. Harper steps closer, and I don't want this moment to end. I want to stay with her and forget about everything else.

But I can't hide from our problems.

"Do you guys know where Kylie might have gone?" I ask.

"To her cabin?" Emma says, pointing to the front double doors as we make our way to the foyer. "Why?"

"Because," I glance at them, "that vision in my bedroom back home, with the woman…" I glance at Emma, not reminding her that it was a *dead* woman. A chill races down my back, and I shiver. "I think it was Kylie in that photo."

––––––––––––––

A bright yellow door stands in front of us, the number two painted in dark black like the center of a sunflower. I hold my hand up, ready to knock, but pause, fist hanging in the air.

"What if I'm wrong?" I ask, looking back at Harper and Emma. What if it wasn't Kylie in that photo, and she doesn't know anything about these hallucinations or the shadow man? She could end up telling Ms. Evans or Ms. Peterson, thinking I need more help.

If it wasn't for Harper, Emma, and Sam all seeing things too, maybe I'd think it *was* all imagined, but not after everything we've been through.

"You're not wrong," Emma says. She fidgets with her ponytail, but her eyes have a faraway look, like she's reliving that scene all over again. "It was her."

"Well, we won't know for sure without asking." Harper slips past me and knocks on the door as I drop my hand.

Whispered voices seep out from the cabin before someone shouts, "Coming."

The door swings open, and Page stands there, pushing her glasses up from where they fell down her nose. Her pale hair shines like gold as she tips her head to the side, curiosity and caution filling the movement.

"Hey," she says, but the word sounds more like a question.

"Can we talk to Kylie?" I don't wait for an answer; I step into their room as Page shifts out of the way.

"Okay...about what?" Page walks across the room and drops onto her mattress, facing Kylie and waving a hand between the two beds. "Do you...want to sit?"

Emma takes a spot next to Page, but Harper and I stand near the end of Kylie's bed, hovering and unsure if I should say anything in front of Page. I don't even know if Kylie will believe us, let alone the other girl.

Their cabin is an exact mirror of mine. Two beds with skylights shining down on them. Matching dressers that are scattered with makeup and toiletries, books, and several half-empty water bottles. Their shared desk has a couple more books and the journals Ms. Evans gave to all of us.

Grab one, the voice says as my gaze travels over a couple more books on Kylie's nightstand. *Throw it at her. Hit her.*

I squeeze my eyes closed for a second and take a deep breath. *No.* I try to silence the voice. *I won't*, I say, half a command and half hope. And as I open my eyes, I'm thankful when the voice doesn't shout anymore.

My attention turns back to Kylie and her drawn face. "I wanted to ask Kylie some questions...alone?"

Kylie folds one foot under her, and the other bounces on the wooden floor. Her shoulders curve in, and dark circles smudge the space under her eyes.

Something in the room beeps, and Kylie startles. She glances around the room frantically, eyes wide as they search every crack and corner.

"I'm sorry!" Page slaps her wrist, pressing buttons on her watch until the beeping stops. She turns back to Kylie, an apology written across her face. "I thought it was turned off."

Kylie nods, but her chest heaves with each breath. "It's...it's okay. We're fine. We're safe." She mumbles the words to herself.

"Are you okay?" Harper asks, stepping closer to Kylie.

"Yeah, fine," she says, even as her foot bounces faster. "What did you want?" She crosses her arms and scratches her bicep, leaving faint lines etched there.

She reminds me of Sam, the night I found her outside, nerves frayed and wrung out. The shadow man visited me that night. Sam too.

How many of us are being haunted by Whitewood's manipulations?

My eyes slip from Kylie to Page's watch, now silent. And even if the tones are different, it reminds me of the beeping of that heart monitor.

"Have you…?" I shake my head. How do I ask Kylie if she's been hallucinating—if she's seen my shadow man creature or anything else?

Emma nods, encouraging me to continue. A week ago, I was worried I wouldn't make any friends at Whitewood, and now I have Emma, ready to stand against monsters and memories come alive.

Harper too. Another friend—or more? She rests a hand on Kylie's, gently stopping the other girl from scratching herself.

"Go on," Harper says. The quiet words fill the room and help steady my nerves.

"Have you seen anything strange? At Whitewood?" I finally ask.

Instead of answering, Kylie looks at Page, and there's an unspoken conversation between them. I shift from foot to foot, waiting.

As the seconds tick by in silence, I wonder if Kylie will even answer. More questions crowd my mouth and press against my teeth until I can't stop myself from shattering the quiet.

"Did you ever know someone that…was sick? And maybe needed to be in the hospital?" I ask, not sure how to explain seeing a woman and a heart monitor in my childhood bedroom or what it even means. "Your mom or aunt or someone like that? Maybe a few years ago?"

Kylie is quiet, assessing, before she finally says, "My mom. She died three years ago." Those few words suck all the air out of the room, leave a shroud of grief draped over Kylie. But a second later, that sadness turns to wariness, and her dark gaze slices into me. "How did you know that?"

"Because I saw it." I point toward Emma on Page's bed. "*We* saw it. I don't know how, but there's this thing—"

"The monster," Page whispers and pushes her glasses up again. Page balls her right hand into a fist before flexing the fingers straight out again and again. The scar on her arm and palm shift with the movement.

My blood goes cold, keeping me rooted in my spot with both shock and regret. Part of me hoped I was wrong and that they've been spared.

"You've seen it too?" Kylie stands, pacing the room.

Page hops up from her bed and darts over to their shared desk, fiddling with an aromatherapy diffuser set there. She clicks it on, and it glows a pale green as air puffs out.

"No!" I shout, rushing over and almost colliding with Page as I try to shut the machine off. But it's too late. The scent of lavender and bergamot seeps through the room, and my chest tightens.

TWENTY-FIVE

W hat was that for?" Kylie asks after I turn the diffuser off, the last puffs of air sputtering and dying out.

"It's the oils," I say. "They're doing it."

"What?" Kylie glances between all of us. "What do they have to do with the monster?"

"I call it the shadow man," I say. "It looks like a nightmare of mine."

Kylie shakes her head, her halo of curls swaying with the movement. "It looks like my mom sometimes. Or Page's little brother. But wrong. Sometimes the figure is pitch-black or the eyes don't match." She shivers, and I don't blame her.

"It comes here at night," Page says, hesitating until Kylie nods for her to keep going. "It makes us see stuff. Our memories, but also other things that neither of us know what they are."

"We saw your mom," I say, "when she…"

"When she died," Kylie finishes. She stares down at the floor as she talks. "It keeps showing that day to me. You'd think three years is long enough to…grieve. But it's not. I was supposed to come here, do the therapy, and"—she swallows hard—"heal or whatever. But how can I do that when I have to keep reliving that day?"

"We don't think it's a real monster," Harper says. "Maybe more like…experimental therapy or something? And the aromatherapy is triggering hallucinations."

"What?" Kylie stares at the diffuser like it's a bomb about to explode. "You think it's our therapists?"

I nod as Page shakes her head. "No, it's real," she says, her attention fixed on her palm—on the scar there. "The fire…my memories. It's…" She takes a deep breath before looking up. Her face pales, and a quick inhaled gasp slices past her teeth. "No!" she shouts, scrambling back on the bed until she's climbing off the other side.

Her gaze is stuck on a spot behind me in the room, and I'm almost too afraid to turn around. Emma clasps her pendant with one hand, knuckles turning white, as she stares in the same direction.

My neck is stiff as I twist around. All the air in my lungs flees, a silent scream leaving me, when I see the shadow man standing behind us.

But again, he's wrong. Not wholly *my* shadow man. Plastic tubes grow out of his ink-stained arms. But they aren't hooked to any machines or fluid bags; they only twist around his arms and dig into his skin. Little red horns grow from his head, and I wonder if maybe he is real like Page thinks—a demon come to torment us.

Only, the horns flash and shimmer in the light like glitter—and I don't know much about demons, but I don't *think* they accessorize with sparkles.

He takes a step closer, and any curiosity I had about those horns vanishes. Hallucination or not, dread sinks heavy in my stomach as he lifts his hand, always holding that bottle of whiskey, and points at us.

"Go away!" I yell, begging whatever this is to listen.

The other girls all rush to their feet, to the other side of the room behind Page's bed, and I move with them, unable to keep my eyes off the shadow man.

"Pennnnelllllopeeee." The words coming from him are guttural and grating, those serrated lips fluttering with each syllable. His head turns, and with it, dark brown eyes appear in the hollows of his face.

"Kyyyyylieeeee," he says, making her whimper and shift closer to Page. He tilts his head at that horrible angle, and the eyes disappear, replaced with nothing but silver wire-framed glasses.

"This isn't real. *You* aren't real!" Harper shouts at the creature.

He pauses, shifting his attention to her. His head turns up, noseless face seeming to sniff the air until we all take another step away, our backs pressing against the slanted wall of the cabin. The shadow man inches forward, smelling the air with heavy breaths.

And then his head drops to one side completely, until his neck looks broken and those brown eyes that stand out too much stare at Harper. She grabs my hand, grip fierce and unforgiving.

His gaze rakes over our group, moving slowly down the line of us before slamming back to Page like a rubber band stretched too far and snapping.

"Paaaaaage." Her name stretches out of his gaping mouth as glasses appear on his face. They reflect an orange light that flickers like flames.

Page's breaths race, one after the other, as fire starts to grow from nothing behind the shadow man. It races up the walls and licks across the floor. The wood paneling darkens as it burns.

Push her, that voice whispers. *Watch her burn.*

No, is all I say back to it. There isn't time to argue with my intrusive thoughts. Not when the shadow man's growls get louder and the flames grow hotter. The voice doesn't speak again, but even if it did, I'm not sure I'd hear it over the pounding of my heart or the crackling of a growing fire.

"Not again," Kylie says. She shakes her head as Page crouches on the floor, rocking on her heels.

Pain sears my forearm, and I let go of Harper's hand. Someone screams, and a scar matching Page's appears on my arm. My palm bubbles with angry red blistering before it fades into pale pink. When I glance up, each girl has the same mark, mirroring Page's.

The shadow man takes my father's whiskey bottle and smashes

it into the fire, letting the heat flare as a growl explodes out of the creature.

"We need to get out of here," Harper shouts as the room grows hotter. She grabs my hand, no hesitation or disagreement from the rest of us. Kylie crouches down and pulls Page up as Emma grips her necklace even tighter.

I don't want to get closer to the shadow man, but we don't have a choice. He stands in the middle of the small cabin, blocking the exit.

We huddle together, hugging close to Kylie's bed and trying to skirt around the shadow man while avoiding the flames. We only make it two steps before he growls. His voice echoes the roar of the fire.

He's only a few feet away from us, unharmed by the fire surrounding him. Half of the tubes in his arms pull out of his skin, sharp needles appearing at the ends. The tubes lengthen and drape to the floor as the needles scratch across the wooden planks. The horns on his head, glittery and looking like they're stuffed with cotton, shift also. They twist and grow. Grooves and lines replace the glitter until bloodred horns—almost goatlike—are perched there instead. His arms and legs lengthen until he grows taller and taller. Inhumanely large. His back presses against the ceiling, curved and hunched, even with his legs bent.

My heart slams against my ribs, and fear pumps through my veins. His hands graze the floor, and his head is tilted to the side as he examines us, those glasses still the only thing decorating his formless face. I bite my lip to keep a whimper from escaping. He really could be a demon, with devil horns and surrounded by fire.

"We have to run," I say, nodding toward the space between his legs. The thought of this enormous monster reaching out and snatching us up, little dolls to toss around and discard into broken heaps, makes my legs shake.

The fire crawls closer and closer, and if we don't get out of here soon, it will consume us. The smoke swells until the room is a haze of cloudy gray.

Kylie nods, but Page shakes her head. Emma lets go of my hand, grabbing her necklace again and holding it out like a talisman meant to protect her.

"*Now,*" Harper says. She darts forward, yanking me with her.

Terror chokes my throat as I pray the others listen and try to escape. Smoke swallows me, stinging my eyes and clouding my vision.

The shadow man roars as the cabin fills with the sounds of rushing footsteps, coughing, and the crackle of fire. He swipes his arm out, and I pull Harper down with me. We crash to the floor. Hot air whips over our heads, the shadow man barely missing us.

A scream echoes all around. Through the haze, I see Kylie on the floor and Emma pressing herself against one bed, only inches from the fire. But it's Page who screams. The shadow man grabs hold of her. His fingers stretch almost entirely across her chest, squeezing her tight. He brings his head closer to hers, and his mouth widens, opening obscenely large.

"Let her go!" Kylie yells, climbing to her feet and standing against the monstrous creature. His gaze snaps to her, and his eyes change again, glasses dissipating until that dark brown stare replaces them.

He growls at Kylie, about to lunge forward, when something stops him. He jerks to a stop and glances behind him, toward the door, head cocking to the side as if hearing something.

The shadow man's attention turns back to us, and the air in my lungs is as searing as the flames. He looks from us to the door, back and forth.

With each turn of his head, his gaze changes. It shifts from the hollow sockets of my shadow man to dark brown eyes like Kylie's. From a pale green stare to wire-framed glasses. They shift too quickly, until the shadow man screeches out a sound that's more scream than growl.

And with it, his shape shrinks, shadows collapsing in. He lets go of Page, and she stumbles back as Kylie catches her. He races *away* from us, the flames extinguishing themselves as he flies across the cabin. The door swings open, and the dark shape of the shadow man races into the night.

I don't move, not a single step. I hold my breath and wait to see if the shadow man will come back. The others must feel the same. They stand still. Harper grasps my hand. Emma keeps herself pressed against the bed. And Kylie pauses, crouched next to where Page fell after the shadow man threw her down.

The seconds tick by, but when the shadow man doesn't come back, I take a deep breath—one that seems to break the spell on our group.

"Now what?" Harper asks, looking around. The fire is gone. No singed walls or burnt wooden floor. No evidence it existed even when it felt so real.

I take a step toward the open door, when it slams shut all on its own. Screams are ripped from our group at the sudden movement, but we fall silent when another sound starts crawling through the cabin.

The echoing beeps of a heart monitor wraps around us. And within them, words are whispered, a hissing voice that melds with the mechanical beeping.

Soon, soon, soon, the monitor calls.

"Nope." Emma shakes her head. "No. I'm not staying here for this again."

Kylie takes a deep breath in. Holds it tightly within her chest. And slowly, so slowly, she lets it out again before taking a step. Page grabs her hand, scrambling to stay by her side.

"Let's get out of here," Harper says. Her dark eyes are solemn and serious. Scared. I want to take an eraser and smudge the fear out of them, but it's impossible. And my own must reflect that same fear back.

"And follow that *thing*?" Page asks as Emma takes my free hand, the burn scar still marking her brown skin. Still marking all of us.

"Do you want to stay here?" I ask, and she shakes her head before we all head toward the door.

We only make it a few steps before little nightmare trinkets wink into existence. A glass bottle glints under the skylight. A teddy bear, bloodred *Q* stitched over its heart, appears next to my father's drink. A flash of gold blurs into a black skull candle near my foot. Another candle appears by Page, with a flickering flame and crimson wax dripping down its sightless face. More matching candles fill the room.

Decaying flowers and sympathy cards sprout out of the wooden floorboards. Kylie reaches one hand out, fingers shaking as she touches the petals of a brown-tinged lily. She yanks her hand back, and it passes through one of the cards as if the paper were made of air, but I don't have time to wonder about it when a dozen or more heart monitors tumble out from under the beds. Their beeping words crash even louder as the flames of too many candles make the room grow swelteringly hot.

Soon, soon, soon.

"Well…shit," Emma says, her gaze skipping over the scream-ing machines. "That can't be good."

Page stays in the very center of our little group, refusing to get close to any of the candles and their flames, and after this place was filled with a searing inferno, I feel the same. The five of us cluster together, holding hands and inching toward the door as more of those horrific trinkets materialize. The cabin feels pulled and stretched too long, and I don't know if the dizziness in my head is making it look like that or if it's another part of this nightmare.

Whiskey bottles clink together as they grow in numbers, spilling out from the walls and clattering to the middle of the floor. Teddy bears with worn noses and dusted with dirt multiply at our feet, making it hard to move through the small cabin. But there are no shiny cigarette lighters or pine-scented air fresheners. No hint of Sam's past—of her at all.

A pair of glitter-coated devil horns on a headband shine like freshly spilt blood in the candlelight, and Page pauses in front of them, a frown pulling her lips and a crease gathering on her brow. But as she tilts her head, staring at the object while firelight dances across her glasses, the headband disappears. I look around, but there are no clones or copies of them hidden between the multitude of whiskey bottles, teddy bears, and dark skull candles.

Page shakes her head, pale eyes blinking away cobwebs only she can see. The glittery headband blips back into existence again, but Page doesn't seem to notice. She keeps walking with Kylie at her side, stepping onto—through—the headband in her path. Her foot passes into it as if the red horns are made from mist. She doesn't even spare it a second glance as more appear, tucked next to candles, glass bottles, and teddy bears. I pick up one of the headbands near my feet. It's solid under my touch, every individual sequin scraping under my fingers.

"Penny?" Page asks, glancing over at me. "What are you doing?"

"What is this?" I ask her instead, holding the headband up for her to see.

"What is…what?" Page glances around at our group, brows knit together with confusion.

"Come on," Harper says, taking my hand again. "We need to get out of here."

Soon, soon, soon, those sharp tones scream—a promise and a threat tucked within the curves of those repeated words.

I nod at Harper, but as I drop the headband to the floor, a candle burns too close to a broken whiskey bottle, and fire erupts in one corner of the room, quickly spreading around and behind us.

"Not again," Page cries, tears already streaming down her face as the heat licks against our skin.

Soon, soon, soon! the warning continues, shrill and sharp, the sound growing louder.

"Let's go!" Emma finally shouts over the machines' cries. We're only a few feet from the door when a loud bang erupts around us, deafening, and followed by a furious growl that rattles the floor.

"Was that—"

"A gunshot," Harper interrupts Page.

The fire and all those items from our nightmares flicker in and out of existence for a second before solidifying again. Something slams against the cabin door, and I jump. Kylie screams. Another thud and another, like a fist pounding on the wood.

"Help!" someone, a girl, shouts through the door.

Soon, soon, soon! the heart monitors continue. The high-pitched beeps—somehow turned into words—stab my eardrums like knives, and I want to yell at it to *shut up!*

I get to the cabin's door and grab the knob, twisting and yanking, but nothing happens.

"Open it!" Page shouts, but the latch won't pull free.

"Come on!" Kylie yells, and when I glance over my shoulder, the cabin is a raging firestorm of rust red and spiced orange and a blazing aureolin yellow. It consumes everything in its path, moving closer and closer to us.

"Help me!" the girl on the other side of the door yells again. "Let us in! Let us in!"

"Let us out!" Kylie screams, her words crashing against the walls as the fire burns hotter at our backs.

A screeching roar shatters the air, a very human scream chasing behind it.

I pull on the door with all my weight, all my strength—until another scream, not from any of us, splits the air. And all at once, every single teddy bear, with their crimson stitching, vanishes, little empty spots that make my stomach sink at what their absence could mean.

"Hurry," Harper pleads as she crowds closer. As they all press in. Until the smell of sweat and ash and their desperate fear wraps around me.

"I'm trying!" I want to beg and scream for the door to open. End this nightmare and let us be free. Each panicked gasp brings searing heat down my throat.

Sweat coats my skin as the fire becomes a wall around us. Page's scar on my palm fits perfectly over the doorknob as I twist it back and forth again. But it only hits against the lock.

The *click, click, click* of the doorknob rattles in time with the screaming machinery. *Soon, soon, soon!*

But I won't let it be true. *Soon*, it called for Kylie's mom—but not for us.

I jam my shoulder into the door, throw my weight against it, and turn the knob. The latch slips free, and we tumble through the doorway, out into the cool night air. Dark shades of indigo and charcoal paint the sky, and diamonds gleam across the expanse. Crickets chirp, toads croak, and the air has never smelled sweeter, free of any smoke souring it.

I glance back through the doorway. Only Kylie and Page's cabin is there. No fire or objects from our memories. Even the heart monitors' screams have gone silent. A sigh slips out of me, and I slump against the closest person—Harper.

But a strangled cry makes me jolt upright. Kylie's wordless shout dies out, turning to sobs. Her gaze is fixed on the lawn, and when I follow it, my heart freezes and my stomach revolts.

Lying on that green expanse, in a halo of golden light from the camp's floodlights, is Ms. Peterson. Deep, ugly gashes are clawed across her chest, carmine-red blood drenching her peasant shirt. More slashes have ripped a face with unseeing eyes. An abandoned shotgun sits in the grass next to limbs splayed out all wrong.

And beside Ms. Peterson is Quinn's body too, all impossible angles and that same blank gaze. A hole is torn through her chest, and even from here, it's impossible not to notice how her heart is missing like Sam's was.

TWENTY-SIX

Across from us, one of the front doors to the main lodge slams open, and we all jump. Our stares break away from Ms. Peterson's and Quinn's bodies lying in the grass as Ms. Evans stumbles to a stop when she sees them.

Yellow light spills out behind her, lengthening her shadow. It creeps over the cement porch, the dirt path, the lawn. It crawls longer and longer, reminding me of how the shadow man's form stretched and grew in the cabin. A shiver skims down my back, and I rub the goose bumps on my arms.

But a flicker of movement near the lodge makes me freeze. The shadow man watches us in the darkness, hunched and half-hidden around the corner of the building. He looks so much like the nightmare version of my father again, that barely sketched outline of a man, all heavy-handed shading and hazy features. He's the same size as my father now too, no longer too large like before. He grips both hands on the corner and peers around the edge. The glow of the floodlights barely touches him, but it's enough to show the shine of blood coating his hands.

"No," I whisper, and his sightless gaze snaps to me. A whiskey bottle blinks into existence in one hand as the blood slides from his skin down the crystal-clear glass. Crimson drips from his mouth into the open neck, a bloom of scarlet mixing with the amber whiskey.

Another door bangs open, shattering the horror-filled quiet that's trapped us all. The purple door of Delaney's cabin swings on its hinges.

"What's going on?" Delaney steps out, pulling off headphones and letting them hang around her neck. She looks at the five of us on Kylie and Page's little porch, squinting in confusion—until her gaze sweeps over the lawn.

Delaney rushes down the porch steps, tripping over her feet. The question, or her presence, seems to pull Ms. Evans out of her spell. She races over, and the rest of us follow, steps faltering and stopping only a few feet away from the bodies of Ms. Peterson and Quinn.

"Everyone back up," Ms. Evans says. Her eyes are wide and wild, searching all around for the threat. I swear her gaze lands on the shadow man, still hunched in the dark. She pauses, body tense for a split second, but she doesn't cry out or say anything about the monster lurking in the dark before she moves on, scanning the rest of the area. And when I glance back at the creature, he's gone. Only a stain of ruby red handprints from where he grabbed onto the wooden siding is left.

"Did anyone see what happened?" Ms. Evans's attention is trapped on the claw marks that mar Ms. Peterson's chest and face.

Everyone shakes their heads, fear in their eyes. I don't know what to think anymore—what to believe. I thought the therapists were behind this, but Ms. Peterson... Is that monster real like Kylie and Page thought? Did *he* kill Sam? I almost speak up, the secret of Sam's death burning my throat. I hate that she's still out there, moldering away in the woods alone. It isn't right, but I don't know what to do about it yet.

I glance at Ms. Evans, distrust twisting my stomach. Is the horror on her face a façade? She admitted in her journal that Ms. Peterson didn't agree with whatever they were doing. If she killed Sam, then what would stop her from hurting anyone else—even Ms. Peterson, who didn't seem to agree with her?

"We didn't see anything," Kylie finally answers. "We were in our cabin and heard..." She shakes her head, pressing one hand to her mouth.

The shadow man left us in the cabin, and then we heard their screams. We heard the gun. And then the teddy bears disappeared, and now Quinn lies dead at our feet, and that can't be a coincidence. They had to be from her memories.

And now they're gone with her.

My gaze skips from Harper and her dark eyes shining with unshed tears to Emma and the way she grips her necklace. To Kylie, hugging her arms around herself as if to hold everything in, and Page, who can't stop rubbing the burn scar on her forearm. Will one of them be next?

I swallow hard. No. We need to stop Ms. Evans or that monster or whatever is happening. I don't know how, but we have to.

"What could have…?" Delaney's question trails off. Her hands tremble at her sides as she looks to Ms. Evans. "An animal? A bear?" She turns toward the tree line, to the sea of white birches and everything they could be hiding.

Ms. Evan nods, eyes lighting up at the possibility—or the easy cover. She takes a deep breath and lets it out. "Everyone back to your cabins for now," she says. "No one leaves until we have this sorted. There must be a predator around."

"What about…?" Delaney shakes her head, blond hair tangling in her headphones. "Do we leave them…there?"

Ms. Evans shakes her head. "It could attract predators back. You and I will have to take care of them—somehow." She swallows hard. "But first, I need to call the police. And the rangers." She glances down, flinching at the sight of Ms. Peterson and Quinn, and I wonder if she's really going to call anyone or only pretending. Her jaw clenches as she reaches down, picking up the shotgun so close to Ms. Peterson's fingers.

Take it. You can shoot her, the voice hisses. *Shoot them all.*

I recoil hard against the suggestion, too horrific to imagine. I swallow those violent words down, until they sink so heavy in my stomach they can't find their way back to my thoughts again.

"Now, girls. Go." Ms. Evans stands back up with the shotgun and twists around, not waiting to see if we listen. She calls to Delaney and rushes back to the lodge before disappearing inside.

None of us move.

My attention is trapped on Quinn and the gaping hole in her chest. Her red hair is splayed across the grass and splattered with blood only a few shades darker. Pale green eyes stare unblinking at the night sky, the stars a reflection of the freckles scattered across her blood-drained face. Her arms and legs lie at discomforting angles, one hand nearly touching the bright yellow pansies that grow in a circle around the flagpole by her head. A metallic tang hangs heavy in the air and makes bile crawl up my throat.

The image of her body, broken and abandoned, burns into my mind until even when I blink, she's there behind my eyelids.

"Come on," Harper says, gently touching my shoulder and making me jump. I nod but don't follow. I can't stop my gaze from being drawn back to the lodge and the bloody handprints still there, left behind because they're not a hallucination. They're real.

He is real—the monster that wears my father's nightmarish face.

And the bodies lying on the grass are more proof. It's their blood that coated the shadow man's hands.

The realization slams into me and squeezes my chest as if it's my heart being ripped out right along with Quinn's.

"Penny?" Harper says when she notices me still standing on the edge of the grassy lawn.

"I'm coming." I follow the others back toward the cabins. Kylie and Page hesitate at the entrance of theirs.

Emma stops walking down the dirt path and turns to them. "Come with us."

Kylie and Page don't say anything; they only follow behind silently. The five of us pile into my and Emma's cabin.

"What now?" Page asks. "You said you thought the aromatherapy was causing hallucinations, but that…was real. They're dead. They're…" She pulls her glasses off and shows them to us. "There are smoke stains from the fire on my lenses." She cleans her glasses and puts them back on.

"That monster is real," Kylie says, conviction filling her words.

"Monsters don't exist." Emma grips that cylindrical black pendant on her necklace, knuckles sharp from her harsh grip. "People are the *real* monsters. I still think this has something to do with Ms. Evans."

"Maybe it's not one or the other." Harper paces the room. "Maybe the monster is real and Ms. Evans is using it?" She turns to me. "Delaney said there were stories of creatures in the woods—"

"Folklore," Emma interjects, but Harper continues.

"What if Ms. Evans found that creature and realized she could use it?"

"For what?" Kylie drops onto Emma's bed.

"Experimental therapy," I tell her. It's only a guess, but it feels right. I face Emma. As much as she wants to believe that monster isn't real, I don't think it can be denied any longer. "You found her notebook. She said she'd do *anything* not to fail again. And you've seen what that monster is capable of." I hold my hands out to show the scrapes and cuts I've gotten over the last few days, the bruise on my wrist where he grabbed me. I tilt my neck and swipe my fingers down the skin. To keep our therapists from seeing them and asking questions, I've been using makeup to cover the marks there, so similar to what Mom used to do. But now I wipe the concealer away—if it even lasted through the night—and let Emma see the mottled purples and greens from where the monster has choked me too.

"Okay," Emma says, dropping her hand from her necklace. "Let's say the monster is real. And Ms. Evans is controlling it somehow. What then? What do we do?"

"I don't know." I plop down onto my bed, and the movement throws my notebook onto the floor. I took it out of my nightstand and stared at Sam's portrait while wrestling with whether we should tell anyone about finding her body or not.

Harper picks my notebook up, and I hold my hand out, but she doesn't pass it back. Instead, she flips through the pages, taking in all the sketches I did of everyone that first day. Normally, I'd be anxious to have her see my hastily done drawings, but right now there are too many other pressing issues.

Harper stares down at Sam's face on the page. "It looks just like her," she says, words tinged with sadness.

I nod, not sure what to say.

Harper turns the page slowly, until it's her face she's staring at, more detailed and drawn out than the rest. This time my stomach dips, filling with nervousness despite how this should be the least of my concerns. I reach for the book again, but the movement jostles her arms and makes her flip several pages, landing on my sketch of the shadow man.

Even with only hollow eye sockets, his impossible gaze seems to follow me as I stand up and move closer to Harper. He looks exactly like I remember. Except for the watch decorating one wrist. There's something about it that scratches at the back of my brain, but when I try to focus on that feeling, only an empty blank spot fills my thoughts.

I stare at the picture. *Gold*, my mind supplies, even though the drawing is done in black and white. So…why do I feel like the watch should be gold?

And whose is it? My father never had a watch. The shadow man never wore one.

"Why did I draw that?" I ask, even if I don't think Harper has an answer. I point to the watch, not caring how my finger smudges the graphite lines slightly.

"The monster?" Harper asks. A shudder runs down her back as she stares at the image of him. "Or his watch?" She glances at the other girls as they all press in closer to see what we're looking at.

"*His* watch?" I ask. "What do you mean?" That wall of blackness crashes down on my thoughts when I try to remember anything about it.

They all stare at me, faces scrunched in confusion at my question.

"The one that he always wears. He had it on tonight," Emma adds.

"There were a bunch of them on the floor of our cabin too," Kylie says.

"But…" I shake my head, looking down at my notebook in Harper's hands. Dread crowds my chest, turns my breathing tight. "I didn't see any watches. I don't know what you guys are talking about."

"You told me it was your father's," Harper says. She shifts the open notebook into one hand and rests her other on my upper arm, her thumb gently grazing the skin there.

"No," I tell her. Each inhale turns jagged. "My father didn't have a watch like that. I would remember if he did."

"You…" Harper looks from me to the notebook and back. "You *told* me he did. When Sam disappeared and you showed me this sketch, you said he always shows up wearing your father's watch and holding a whiskey bottle. You told me about seeing his belt too."

"What?" My questions rings through the cabin, too loud. That's not possible. "Why don't I remember it, then?"

Emma and Page shrug. Kylie shakes her head, no answer to give, and Harper bites her lip.

My mind races back to Kylie and Page's cabin and a flash of gold near my feet that disappeared in a blink. And then to the red headband that flickered in and out of existence.

"The headband," I say, turning to Page. "Do you remember a red headband with devil horns?"

"Umm…what?" She shakes her head slowly. "I don't know what you're talking about."

"The horns you wore on Halloween," Kylie tells her. "The night your house caught on fire."

"What?" She shoves her glasses up.

"You told me about it only a few nights ago," Kylie continues, "after that thing showed up in our cabin looking like your brother."

"I…I don't…" Page touches her head as if she is going find a headband sitting there. "I don't know."

"What did you see tonight?" I ask Kylie, thinking about the different objects that came from her memories. "The flowers and cards?" Kylie nods. "Did you see the heart monitors? Hear them?"

Kylie shivers, her whole body twitching against the memories. "Yeah, I heard the beeping. The words they turned into—wait, cards?"

"They were with the flowers," Harper says. She looks around my cabin as if waiting for them to appear.

"I didn't see those," Kylie says, voice solemn and scared.

"Why can't we remember them? Why can you guys see...my father's watch? But I can't? I can't even remember anything about it. How come I remember the headband but Page can't? Why can't Kylie remember the cards, but the rest of us can?"

Only silence fills our cabin as we all realize that Ms. Evans or the shadow man or both aren't just tormenting us with our memories. They're stealing bits and pieces of them too.

"We need to do something," Harper says, pacing around the cabin. "We need to stop this."

Kylie and Page sit together on one bed as Emma busies herself with checking the lock on the window. I watch Harper's path from where I stand and grip my notebook tightly.

"What are we supposed to do?" Emma asks. "We don't even know what's happening. How are we supposed to stop Ms. Evans or that creature?"

"We can't sit around and do nothing," I say, agreeing with Harper. "We need—"

A knock on the cabin door stops our conversation.

"Girls?" Delaney's voice seeps past the wood. "Are you all in here?" She doesn't wait for an answer as the door swings open. "Good," she says, relief thick in her voice. "The other cabins were empty, and I got worried." She bites her lip, glancing around. Her eyes are an itchy red and swollen with puffiness that comes from crying. "I came to tell you that Ms. Evans is leaving for the night. She—"

"Leaving?" I ask. "What do you mean?"

"She tried the satphone but couldn't get through to the police. She's going to drive into town and get them, but it'll be at least four hours before she's back. Ms. Evans left me in charge until then, and I'd feel better if we were all together. Grab some blankets and pillows and whatever else you need, and we'll set up in the cafeteria for the night."

"She's already gone? Without telling us herself?" I ask. Is she running? Like I tried to after finding Sam?

"Yeah, she left a few minutes ago." Delaney glances out at the grassy lawn still stained in blood and shudders. "Don't take long, and stay together, okay?" she says before leaving and closing the door behind her.

DELANEY

Two words changed the girl's entire life and shattered her heart.

Sadie's dead.

Two sisters broken apart by two small words.

Sadie's dead. Gone.

It felt impossible to the girl. Her sister couldn't be dead. They were supposed to always be there for each other. To fight and make up, tease and encourage. Be each other's maids of honor and have their future kids play together. They were supposed to grow old together.

The girl loved her sister, but now she was suddenly alone.

Her best friend just…gone. A phone call, with her father's grave voice and her mother's broken cries in the background, changed everything.

The water took her sister. Stole her breath and blood, and left her family with a white sheet draped over a truth that none of them wanted to see.

The girl, more a woman than child at eighteen, stepped into a cold room at her parents' side while a stranger led the way. Fluorescent lights glinted too harshly against silver tables. Her tennis shoes squeaked on the tile of a nauseatingly pale green floor. Each step was hesitant—full of denial. If she didn't see her sister, then Sadie couldn't be dead.

But there she was, nothing more than a shape under a white cloth.

The girl took another step on weak legs, feeling as if even a breath exhaled too hard would send her stumbling and crashing down.

A silver grate sat nestled in the tiled floor, breaking the perfect uniformity of those tiny squares. The girl skirted around it, not wanting to think about why a drain was necessary here even as images of blood—bright against the pale ground—flashed across her vision.

It was too easy for the girl to imagine her sister's death. A long fall that led to rocks only barely showing the teeth of low tide. Of crimson blood staining the dark blue water. Her sister's body caught on the unforgiving stone, blond hair draped and swaying like jellyfish tentacles in the bay, and eyes staring into a place unknown to the girl.

But the girl hadn't been there—hadn't actually seen it happen. Yet the scene played across her mind every time she closed her eyes. Her sister cliff diving, like so many times before. A mistake, miscalculation. Low tide letting jagged rocks reach out of the bay's depths. A water-drenched death.

The girl shook her head, blond hair that matched her sister's sliding over her shoulder, and moved closer to the table. She stopped only inches away.

"You don't have to be here," her father said. He placed one hand on her back, meant to comfort. But the warmth of his touch sent a shiver over her skin, too sharp in contrast to the cold temperature of the room.

"I have to—" The girl shook her head, unable to say what she needed as her mother's sobs filled the room. "I can't leave... I need to"—she clasped one hand to her chest, feeling her heart shattering apart—"say goodbye."

"You can—" Her father's voice cracked right along with the mask of strength he tried to wear. He took a deep breath and let it out slowly, controlled. "You can say goodbye at the funeral. You don't need to see this. Either of you." He glanced at his wife. "They only need one of us to confirm ID."

The girl's mother cried out again, and the noise was a knife through her chest. It was a sound that reached deep inside the girl, like claws carving her heart out—leaving her hollow.

Her mother's hand gripped the girl's forearm, as if afraid

she would disappear next. Shaking fingers dug into her skin, hurting her, but the girl didn't care as her mother's weight leaned on her. As she leaned back.

"Go on," her father said. "Take your mom with you."

The girl shook her head, refusing to leave. This was her sister. Her best friend. She couldn't…walk away.

"No," her mother said. "I'm staying." She straightened, her grip loosening and fingers sliding from the girl's forearm to entwine their hands instead.

They stood before the silver table, a landscape of lost love and possibilities shrouded in white before them. Sadie.

"Are you ready?" the man that led them here asked. But none of them answered, their gazes trapped on the white cloth and the truth they couldn't hide from once he lowered the sheet.

Finally, her father nodded, the smallest motion but enough. Eyes cast down, the man lifted the fabric and folded it to bare shoulders. Sadie's light hair had been combed, and a papery sheet had been left over one side of her head, sparing them from seeing the gaping wound that had killed her.

The girl could almost pretend her sister was only sleeping, eyes closed and face blank, if not for the gray tint to her skin. No flush of life filled her cheeks, no slow breaths moved her chest.

Her sister was a wax doll, a nightmare version of the person she once knew.

"That's our daughter," her father said. "Sadie."

"No," her mother cried, stumbling around the girl and to her father. She crashed into his chest, and her tears soaked his shirt. "My baby, my baby. My Sadie."

Her father wrapped one arm around her mother and the other over the girl's shoulders, pulling them close.

The girl couldn't stop staring at her sister. At what was left of her—an empty thing. She turned, hiding her face in the crook of her father's shoulder as tears stung her eyes. They burned down her cheeks in a room cold enough to leave a chill deep in her bones.

The girl looked back at all that remained of her sister and the white sheet now covering her body again. But even as she closed her eyes against the sight, the girl couldn't stop seeing those made-up images plaguing her—bloodstained water and mist-shrouded eyes, pale skin, and the ugly crack splitting her skull.

The girl's heart squeezed tight with grief, clenching at the loss until it seemed to falter to a stop. Until her chest felt silent and still, as unmoving as her own sister's.

TWENTY-SEVEN

We gather in the cafeteria like Delaney asked, backpacks stuffed with clothes and toiletries, arms filled with blankets and pillows, but Delaney isn't waiting for us, and an eeriness fills the empty lodge with only the five of us huddled together.

"Should we look for Delaney?" Page asks. "What if something happened to her?"

"Give it a few minutes," Harper says, dropping her bedding on the floor. "I'm more worried about Ms. Evans leaving."

"I think she's running. Maybe things got out of hand, and she can't cover up what happened. Not when we all saw it." I set my blanket and pillow down and drop my backpack on the floor. "She doesn't know we found Sam, but this—"

"You found Sam?" Kylie asks, and I realize they don't know

about her. We didn't get a chance to explain everything before the shadow man came for us in their cabin.

"She's dead," I say, a lump clogging my throat.

You killed her, that voice in my head says—not gone but biding its time. Only now it's not as strong—not as loud and overpowering. *You're dangerous. You'll hurt them.*

No, I tell it. I start to tap but stop before my index finger even touches my thumb. It's never really helped before, and I don't think it will now. Instead, I say, *I'm not dangerous,* determined to have it be true.

You are. You'll—

Quiet, I say, the single word a severe command of my own. I have more immediate things to deal with than my intrusive thoughts. And when the voice fades away again, I take a deep breath. Tentative relief spreads through my chest at the small bit of control I've started to claw back.

"I found Sam's body in the woods," I tell Kylie and Page and catch them up on everything with Harper and Emma's help.

"Sam, Quinn, and Ms. Peterson," Page says, her voice hollow. "They're all dead."

"And Reagan's still missing," Emma adds.

I don't add that she's probably dead also—but as I look around the group and the somber faces on all the girls, I don't think I need to.

"We're not safe until we figure out what's going on and how to stop it," I tell them. "Harper and Emma, can you guys search through Ms. Evans's office and room again? Look for anything about what she's been doing." I turn to Kylie and Page. "Can you two try to find any signs of Reagan?" I ask, hoping—maybe futilely—that my suspicions are wrong.

"What about you?" Harper asks, taking my hand in hers.

"I'm gonna find Delaney and see what she's knows."

"Alone?" Harper's grip tightens.

"I'll be okay. I'll find her, and we'll come back here."

Harper nods reluctantly and lets go of my hand. Our small group dissolves as we search for answers that might not exist.

I slip my flashlight out of my backpack and head for the front doors. Outside, the night is dark, and so are the cabins. I move to the corner of the lodge where the shadow man stood, and I click my light on. The yellow glow illuminates the blood left there.

Swallowing hard, I swipe one finger through it, already knowing the truth but needing to confirm. Crimson comes away at my touch and marks my skin—real.

I wipe my finger off on my shorts and make my way across the lawn with heavy steps. I pass the flagpole and the blood still there too, but the bodies were already moved before we left our cabin earlier. I turn away from the stained grass and see the shape of a person sitting down by the lake. Delaney.

My sneakers punctuate the quiet night with loud slaps when I get to the pier's rough wood.

"Hey, we were getting worried about you," I say to our only remaining counselor.

"Oh!" Delaney startles at my voice. She yanks her feet up from where they were dangling above the water and twists around to look at me. Her eyes are redder than before. "Penny, you scared me."

"I wanted to make sure you were okay." I glance around at the quiet night and the calm, dark lake. The only sounds are the gentle call of insects and a soft splash here and there from the water. No shadow man growling or moaning as he comes for us. Still… "We should probably get inside."

"I was about to grab my stuff, but I…needed a minute." She rests one hand on her chest as if to calm her heart and lets her feet drop above the lake's surface again.

The night air wraps around me, filled with the scent of algae and mineral-laden water. I take a seat next to Delaney, the weathered wood rough under my hands as I turn my flashlight off and set it down. The moon is fastened high in the sky, a slice of glowing white surrounded by swirling clouds and more stars than I can count. The silver light glitters on little ripples from the fish. All around us, hidden crickets sing from the grasses, and a bird calls quietly from somewhere in the line of birch trees that surround the far side of the lake. Out here, it's almost peaceful enough to forget about everything that's happened tonight.

Almost.

I blink, and the image of Quinn's body lying in the grass next to Ms. Peterson burns itself into my eyes.

"Are you okay?" I ask Delaney, knowing she must have helped move the bodies.

She nods slowly, blond hair glowing almost white in the moonlight, while her gaze is fixed on the lake. Her profile is all curves and sharp cheekbones, haunted eyes and more unshed tears. She is a painting of highlights and shadows cast by the moon, and my hands itch to draw her.

"I just..." Delaney takes a deep breath, still staring ahead. "I can't believe what happened." She swallows and turns to me. "What if something else happens, and it's my fault? I didn't think I'd be left alone and in charge of you all. I'm only twenty-one; I'm not trained for...any of this. I thought last summer was difficult for us—for Ms. Evans—but this..." Her rambling tapers away, as if saying what happened will make it worse.

"It'll be okay." The words spill from my mouth, but I'm not sure they're true. My gaze trails up the hill, toward the flagpole, where we found Ms. Peterson and Quinn.

A shiver shakes Delaney as she looks there too. "Ms. Peterson is—was—a really nice person." She turns back to the lake, and so do I, letting the ripples that skate across the water replace the memory of those death-clouded stares. "I hope Ms. Evans is doing okay. She and Ms. Peterson were friends for years."

"How'd you meet them?" I ask, trying to learn anything that might help us.

"Ms. Evans was my therapist after my sister died; we—my

parents—found her, and she helped me." Delaney shakes her head again.

"I'm so s—"

"And when Ms. Evans told me how she was starting this camp, a place for girls like me to feel safe to talk—to find peace—I wanted to help. It was great at first, and then there was everything with Clara, and now…" Her dark blue gaze is searching. "I know each of you have something you're dealing with, and I'm sorry all of this must only be making things worse."

"It's not your fault." More than she could even know, it wasn't her place to apologize.

"Do you know where Reagan and Sam are?" I watch her reaction, trying to catch any information from it.

She shakes her head, brow scrunching. "That wasn't part of last year's program."

"Before she left, did Ms. Evans tell you where they are, though?" Does Delaney know Sam is dead? Does she know what happened to Reagan?

"Ms. Evans said she partnered with the therapist in town. That's where they've been. They're safe, Penny." Relief saturates her words so strongly there's no doubt she believes them.

"Good," I say, even if what she's been told is a lie.

"It's getting late. We should probably—"

Water splashes under the pier as her words cut off. Delaney's scream slices through the dark night, and the sharp tang of fear coats my tongue. My gaze darts around frantically, looking for the threat but finding none.

Delaney jerks back, trying to lift her feet but unable to. "Something's got me!" She tries to yank her leg back again and again. "Help!" she yells, and my heart pumps fear through my entire body.

A pale waxy hand grasps onto Delaney's ankle, reaching out of the midnight-dark lake. Water drips from ghostly white fingers and soaks into her sock and sneaker.

Delaney's scream is an arrow burrowing into my chest. I grab her arm and pull hard, knowing this must be the shadow man. Her foot slips out of the creature's hold, and we fall back as a shriek slices through the air, inhuman and terrifying.

Push her in, that voice says, but I don't have the patience for it right now. My hands hesitate for a second before I do the opposite.

"Run!" I yell and get up, helping Delaney as she scrambles to stand, one shoe missing.

But we both hesitate as another screech ricochets around us. Two ghostly hands grip the end of the pier, as slowly, a head peeks over the edge. Drenched blond hair hangs over a girl's face in ropey tendrils that cling to her skin like seaweed. With her face tipped down, she stares up at us with clouded eyes and climbs out of the water, arms and legs hooking over the pier's edge as she crawls like a spider.

I trip back, and Delaney mirrors me.

"Please," she says, the single word trembling on a shaky breath. "Not again. Please, Sadie."

The girl stands at the end of the pier, staring with milky eyes as we move away. A large gash pours blood from her head, staining the wood at her bare feet. She wears a white sheetlike dress that somehow isn't wet from the lake like the rest of her. Only the blood spilling from her head wound seeps into the dress, horridly vivid against the stark white cloth.

Her skin has a deathly cast to it—until her image flickers like a TV flipping through channels. Her skin shifts from swirling dark shadows to chalky gray, back and forth. Until there's absolutely no doubt that it's the shadow man standing before me.

"Please, Sadie," Delaney begs. "Leave me alone."

"That's not Sadie," I tell her, even if I don't know who that is. I glance between Delaney and the false Sadie, so similar in the curves of their faces, in the lightness of their hair, the slim build of their bodies. The shadow man must be making himself look like Delaney's sister.

Sadie's neck clicks to a tilted angle, and I grab Delaney's hand, refusing to wait and let the monster torment us. Our feet slam on the wooden pier as we run, a staccato of hard bursts until we make it to the grass. My breaths rake in and out, but when I spare a look behind us, the pier is empty, no splash of lake water or blood painting the wood a darker shade. No sign of the fake Sadie at all.

"Come on. Before that thing comes back," I say, pulling Delaney along.

Tears stream down her face, but she nods.

We get five feet up the hill when my heart drops, my stomach twisting into knots. The shadow man—Sadie's version—blocks our path up to the lodge.

The creature opens her mouth, bloodless lips stretching. Water pours like a flood from it as her white-skimmed eyes stare unblinking and unbreaking. A choking sound scratches my ears as the creature twitches and jerks until something far too large falls from her mouth. It tumbles down the hill, flashing in the moonlight, until it crashes into my feet.

I swallow down a gasp and stare at the whiskey bottle now nestled against my sneaker.

"What...what is that?" Delaney asks, staring from the glass at my feet to the creature wearing her dead sister's face.

Without answering her, I kick the bottle away, but more and more fall from Sadie's gagging mouth. They cascade down the hill, pile up around us, until I can't take it anymore. I snatch Delaney's hand and drag her away—to the safety of the woods and away from where it can find the other girls waiting in the lodge.

We race into the forest, but with only one shoe left, Delaney limps and stumbles. Still, we run until breathing hurts, until a stitch pinches my side—until we are surrounded by the white forest and a thousand eyes made of gray knobs and papery bark that stare at us from every angle.

"Is she—it—gone?" Delaney lets go of my hand, turning in a circle.

"I think so?" There are only pale trees and dark bushes surrounding us.

"What was that?" Delaney turns to me. "Have you seen it before?"

"Yeah," I admit. "Not your sister, but…yeah."

"I saw Sadie for the first time"—she glances down, counting on her hands and mumbling—"two nights ago, I think." She shakes her head. "I'm not sure. These last few days have been…a lot. I thought it was stress. I haven't been sleeping great. But if that's not it, then what was that thing?"

"I'm not sure." I scan the forest, but all of the trees look the same. "I'll explain as much as possible later, but right now we can't stay here. How do we get back?"

Delaney glances behind us, at the direction I think we came from. "This way." She points, confident in where to go. "We need to make sure the others are okay."

I follow along next to her, but as we walk, objects blink into existence like in Kylie and Emma's cabin. First, a skull candle, throwing glowing orange light against the gray skin of a tree to my left. Another whiskey bottle by Delaney's foot. I flinch against a stark white glow that suddenly shines above our heads, only to find a single fluorescent light hanging from a branch, swaying precariously and buzzing. I blink away the spots it leaves in my vision as something falls from above and hits me in the face—a sympathy card. More drop from the boughs of the trees as the sickly perfume of rotted flowers fills the air. Red headbands with glittery horns hang from the branches also, and I wonder if there are gold watches there too.

"How...?" Delaney starts, but she doesn't even finish the question as more objects crowd the ground, decaying flowers and blank cards from Kylie's memories, my father's whiskey bottles and his belt, and too many of Page's skull candles to count.

A door appears, but when I touch the knob, it's searing hot, and I yank my hand back with a cry, knowing it won't bring us to safety like that one that led to Sam's cabin.

Behind me, Delaney screams, sharp and high-pitched. She points toward the closest tree. It takes everything in me not to scream too when one milky eye blinks. Tucked within the knobs of the birch trees are a hundred mist-stained eyes, staring at us from every direction. They look exactly like Sadie's death-shrouded gaze, and panic claws at my chest.

A screech pierces the night, turning into a low moan and bouncing off curling bark as those eyes continue to blink and blink and blink at us.

The trees scream. Another of my grandmother's old phrases whispers through my head, and now, more than ever, I think she was right. The woods shouldn't be trusted—or listened to.

I cover my ears against the noise and back up, ready to run *anywhere* but here until I bump into something. I jerk away and turn, only to find the shadow man—a mutated Sadie version of him. The creature's groaning shout dies off as water starts pouring from Sadie's mouth and blood cascades over pale hair. Only now shadows creep over the death pallor of her skin. Hands stained like ink smudged across a page. The darkness crawls past her wrists, up her forearms, and above the elbows. My gaze is trapped on her wrists, no watch like my sketch had.

I'm so busy thinking about a watch that doesn't exist, I don't see the creature's hand lash out until it's grasping my throat, cutting off my air. Nightmare Sadie lifts me, my feet dangling inches off the forest floor as Delaney cries out.

Sadie's grip is ruthless, stronger than any girl her size should be capable of—but she's not a girl; it's a monster stealing her form.

Images flash in my mind at her touch. Red, yellow, and green blinking lights. A shower of shattered glass. Antlers. I don't know what they mean; if they're someone's memories or not. And when her grip squeezes impossibly tighter, they disappear, replaced with the sight of Sadie's stolen face as darkness edges into my vision.

My heart strikes my sternum, hard enough that I swear it splinters and cracks. No air squeezes past the creature's brutal grip, and my head feels as if it will burst from the pressure, fracture apart like the wound in Sadie's skull.

Delaney shouts, but the words are snatched away, a blurred

sound in the darkening night, which buzzes with insects. The noise crowds my ears until I worry the buzzing is coming from my own head.

And it's not the night becoming darker, but my vision going black. Nightmare Sadie leans in, sniffing my temple. Her mouth opens, blue lips pulling tight and revealing a bloated purple tongue, and the sight of her—of this creature—makes fear freeze my veins.

Water pours from her mouth and carries the strong scent of seaweed and salt. Her jaw stretches until she looks ready to devour me whole. I flail uselessly as her grip on my neck turns deadly. As she makes an inhaled gasping sound through the salt water that continues to gush out of her open mouth. Dizziness fills my head and the world spins, but whether it's from whatever the creature is doing to me or the lack of oxygen, I don't know. Her fingers lengthen, turning into sharp claws made of shadows. They dig into my throat and bring a stinging ache.

A hundred dead eyes, nestled within the tree trunks, watch as the creature wearing Sadie's body like a costume tries to eat away at my mind. As the monster tries to siphon my memories away while it chokes my neck tighter and tighter.

And I know that my heart will be next. That this creature will rip it out if I don't get free. I thrash in its unforgiving grip, bruising my neck as my body screams for even the smallest gulp of air. My eyes burn, and unwanted tears spill over. I can't die. I can't leave the others to fight this thing alone. I have to help them—have to save myself. We have to get away from Whitewood. Make it home. I can't leave Mom to mourn me like this.

I fight against the creature's hold even harder. I have to get free, but I can't. The darkness closes in on my vision, and I know this monster will steal my memories and my life—just like it did to Sam and Quinn.

TWENTY-EIGHT

Another scream comes from Delaney. I think it's Delaney. My throat is still clenched in the creature's grasp, claws stabbing into my skin and blood dripping down to the collar of my shirt. I kick my legs, trying to make it harder for this beast to hold me as I curl my fingers around its talons and attempt to pry them off my neck. My nails dig into darkened flesh, but its grip is unrelenting, and my vision turns even darker as this monster cuts off my air.

The shadows on Nightmare Sadie's arms climb over her skin while her arms and legs lengthen—until it's no longer Delaney's sister but that horrid version of my father. Her milky eyes and pale skin disappear, eaten away and replaced by the dark hollows and the formless face of the shadow man, and I thrash even harder in his hold.

"Stop!" Delaney shouts from behind him. She swings an ashen branch at the monster. It cracks against his skull, and he lets out a growl so loud and deep it reverberates in my bones. She slams it into him again, and he finally drops me.

I crash to the ground hard, underbrush poking into my skin and bruising my body. The shadow man lashes out, one clawed hand slicing into my upper arm. I cry out at the searing pain as blood gushes down my arm.

Delaney swings her makeshift weapon again, a wordless cry roaring out of her. Again and again, until the shadow man is bleeding and cowering and backing away as his whine whistles sharply. Her branch slices through the air one more time, spinning her along with it when the shadow man darts away. He vanishes into the forest, another smudge of gray and black blending into the night.

Delaney drops her hands, her stick falling to the ground and painted in the shadow man's blood, a red too dark and thick. A red tainted with the shadows that coat his skin.

"Are you okay?" Her breaths are labored as she stares at the wound on my arm and the scarlet staining my shirt. My fingers dance lightly over my neck, finding four puncture marks on the left side and one on the right. Four jagged slices rake across my bicep.

I nod, even though I'm not okay. The wound on my arm makes it hard to move, a sharp agony enveloping it with even the smallest twitch. Delaney crouches down and carefully shifts my arm as she examines the gashes.

"I'm not trained for medical stuff," she says. "That was Ms. Evans, psychiatrist and doctor. But I don't think these cuts are too deep. It doesn't look like it went through muscle." She lets go of my arm gently. "Can you move it?"

I lift my hand, hissing against the pain, but she's right. I have control, even if it hurts.

"Good." She unwraps a blue bandana from her wrist and ties it around my arm, helping to stop the bleeding, but the crimson color stains through almost immediately. "That's not enough." She grimaces at her handiwork. "We need to get back and bandage that for real. Can you stand?"

"Yeah," I say as she helps me to my feet before searching the forest around us. Thankfully no trinkets litter the ground. They vanished when the shadow man fled.

I look down at the branch Delaney used to fight him and the stain of blackened blood. "At least we know he—it?—can be hurt," I say, even if that means the creature is undeniably real—something alive and not a hallucination. At least we aren't helpless.

"I've never seen it like…that. Only my sister." Delaney takes a deep breath and shakes out her trembling hands. "How is it possible? A shape-shifter?"

"You're the one that told the story about monsters in the woods." I shrug, but the motion brings a sharp pain to my bicep.

"I didn't think those stories were actually real! This can't—it's not…" She trails off as her gaze turns to where the shadow man left.

"It's shown up looking like something different to Kylie and Page too," I tell her. "For me, it's that last one, the dark form of a man." I don't take the time to explain *why*.

"The others have seen it too?" she asks, and I fill her in quickly, even telling her about finding Sam's body in the woods, heart missing like Quinn's. There's no doubt in my mind now that the shadow man killed them. But does Ms. Evans know? She must be connected to that creature—using it. Did she lose control of her monster?

"Sam's…dead? No, she's with Reagan. In town."

I shake my head, but Delaney doesn't want to believe it, so I don't push.

"What does it want?" she asks.

"I think it's doing something to our memories," I say, and explain as much as I can about our guesses and what we know about the creature.

"I can't believe it," Delaney says when I finish. Her blond hair cascades around her as she shakes her head. "I mean, I can. I saw… all of that, but—" She shakes her head again but doesn't finish the sentence.

"Also…" I bite my lip, unsure what she'll think of my theory. "It's Ms. Evans," I finally say. "I thought we were hallucinating. That Ms. Evans was drugging us with the aromatherapy for some sort of experimental—"

"She wouldn't do that." Delaney shakes her head, tone adamant.

"Besides, I've been using her aromatherapy for years and never saw…that before."

"I know that now," I tell her, glancing at a spot of too-dark blood on her shirt from the shadow man. "The aromatherapy part, at least. But…" I pause, knowing how much Delaney seems to trust Ms. Evans. "I think she's using that creature, making it force our trauma on us. Making us—"

"No," Delaney says. "She *wouldn't* do that. I don't believe it. She helped me, and I know she wants to help all of you too."

The note Emma found on Ms. Evans's photo slips through my mind—or the part I can't forget:

I will do anything *to keep from ever failing again.*

Followed by the journal entry:

Emily doesn't agree…but we have no choice. It's the only way…

I don't waste time arguing with Delaney about it, not when we have to get out of this forest before the shadow man finds us again.

"We need to make sure the others are okay." I doubt Delaney's attack will keep that creature away for long. I scan the trees around us, turning in a circle, but it's all the same.

"Maybe…this way?" Delaney starts leading us, hobbling with one shoe still missing. "We're bound to find one of the trails at some point, and then we can read the markers and find our way back to camp."

We walk in silence, both lost in thought, as the cry of insects keeps us company. A bird screeches sharply, and I jump, too afraid that any noise is the shadow man coming back. I place my hand over my heart but wince at the pain it causes in my arm. The puncture marks have stopped bleeding as freely, but they still ache.

"Are you all right?" Delaney asks. "We need to get that cleaned and bandaged as soon as we get back."

"I'll be fine." I pick my way over a fallen log and around a bush. "Thank you though—"

"Thank me? For what?" She stares at the ground, careful of where she places her shoeless foot.

"I think that creature would have killed me if you didn't stop it." I push a low-hanging branch out of the way for Delaney and let her pass. "It was going for my heart. Like it must have with Sam and Quinn."

"And Reagan," she says, stumbling to a stop. I'm about to ask her what she means—we don't *know* what happened to Reagan— when the smell hits me. A foul stench slaps me in the face and burns my nose. Bile inches up my throat.

Delaney steps to the side, one hand covering her mouth and nose, and reveals a body.

Reagan.

She's clearly been dead for days, if not the entire time she's been missing. I wouldn't even recognize her if not for her right hand and the missing tip of her pinky finger, the smoothed-over scar proving it happened long before her death. Unlike the other marks marring her body.

A dark hole sinks into her chest, ribs broken and exposed, and similar to how I found Sam. Only the rest of Reagan is far worse. The forest has claimed her.

Animals have scavenged and stolen bits and pieces of Reagan, gouging out eyes and chunks of flesh to devour. Maggots swarm and wiggle within the wounds as flies buzz around. Leaves have fallen over her, and dirt coats her skin, the forest trying to take its prize completely. Her curly brown hair is matted and tangled with dried blood and twigs. Her limbs are bent at terrible angles, one leg torn apart so much that her foot rests unattached inches away.

I gag and twist to the side, letting my stomach empty onto the ground. Vomit splashes at my feet. I need to get away from here— from the sight of Reagan's broken body.

It's too much. One dead girl after another and another, and I don't think I can take it anymore. That fragile slice of hope I had that Reagan was still alive snaps apart until it feels like my whole chest is fracturing. How can the rest of us survive this? It seems impossible, and I almost want to give up.

I stumble a step, and Delaney catches me, letting me lean on her shoulder. And the small act helps so much more than she'll ever know. Because I can't give up. Not when I look at Delaney and the support she offers me even through her own fear. Not when I think of Harper and her soft kindness. Or Emma with her warm and welcoming personality and how tragic it would truly be to lose either of them. How bitter it would be to witness Kylie's or Page's death next when they've been so strong, facing their traumas again and again.

The shadow man ripped out Reagan's heart and left her, abandoned and alone, for the forest to swallow away. And he almost did the same to me. But I won't let him do that again. Not to me or any of the other girls. Together, we can—we *have to*—survive.

"They said she was in town…" Delaney shakes her head, disbelief and tears filling her eyes.

I stand up straight, taking my weight off Delaney, and wipe my mouth with the end of my shirt before turning to her. "I'm sorry, but Ms. Evans can't be trusted. She's lying and hiding things from you—from us."

Delaney's shoulders curve in on herself. "We should go."

"What about…?" My eyes dart toward Reagan's decomposing body, watering as the smell stings them.

"There's nothing we can do," she says, moving past and waving for me to follow. "When the police come, they'll take care of…her."

"Sam too," I say, feeling a weight crush my chest. "We can't leave her there either."

Delaney nods and leads the way again. I follow, my stomach sinking with every step we take, leaving Reagan behind—alone once more. We walk through the forest, searching for a trail or marker to show the way back. But no matter how far we get from Reagan's body, the rancid smell that came with discovering her lingers in my nose.

"There!" The single word bursts out of Delaney like a gunshot, loud and sudden. A bird sitting in a nearby tree startles and flies away. "The road! Do you see it?"

I peer through the dark night, following the line of her finger as she points, and there it is. We hurry, nearly running to get to it. The closer the road comes, the more the trees spread out, giving a clearer view.

A twig snaps behind us, deeper in the forest, and I jerk around, sure that the shadow man is following. But there's only a glimpse of antlers, there and gone in a quick bound.

"What was that?" Delaney asks, gaze frantically searching the forest.

"Just a deer," I reassure her. "We're okay. That monster isn't here."

We keep going until we step onto the dirt road, and I let out a deep exhale—let the fear and worry dissolve for a moment.

"This way," Delaney says, nodding to the left, but I pause, catching sight of a color to the right that shouldn't be there.

"What's that?" I ask. But I already know. The shape is large, the color too bright to be natural. The moon shines down on a cherry-red car, and my feet carry me to it, faster and faster, matching the rushing of my heart.

Delaney's lopsided jog echoes off the hard-packed dirt, but she doesn't answer my question or tell me to stop. "That's Ms. Evans's car" is all she says between heavy breaths.

I pause near the trunk of Ms. Evans's sedan. The front is smashed into a tree, the back end swung out into the road. There's a trail of tire prints that swerve across the dirt.

"No," Delaney says, her voice barely a whisper. "Is she...?"

I don't know. I'm not sure I *want* to know.

But we have to.

With hesitant steps, we creep toward the front of the car. "Careful," I tell Delaney as shattered glass crunches under my sneakers. It sparkles like glitter under the moon, almost beautiful if not for the grim omen it might signal. "Wait. Stay there." I glance back at her, making sure she's listening. "The last thing we need is for you to not be able to walk."

Pick up a shard of glass, the voice whispers. *Slice her instead. Watch her—*

Shut up. I try to steady the shake of my hands, but I'm not sure if it's from what those intrusive thoughts are telling me to do or the way my feet creep closer to the wreckage.

Delaney nods, waiting for me as she chews at her fingernails and tries to peer into the car. "Is she...in there?"

I gulp down the panic trying to tear its way out of me and move closer. The soft crunch of glass under my shoes mingles with the gentle chirping of crickets.

I inch my way toward the driver's-side, praying and begging for Ms. Evans to have gotten out, to have walked back to camp. Maybe I don't trust her, but I don't want her dead either.

But my brain understands what I don't want to see. A door ripped open. Blood pooling in the dirt. No shoe prints in the dust.

I bite my lip to keep another scream from escaping when I peer inside the car. Ms. Evans's upper body hangs over the steering wheel, a bloody gash on her head. Claw marks rake down one side of her torso, exposing cerise-red muscle tissue and dove-white bone. Blood saturates her side, staining her hip and the beige seat. A pool gathers on the carpeted floor and has dripped onto the dirt road, thick and congealing at the edges.

I turn back to Delaney and shake my head, unable to say the words aloud, but it doesn't matter. She understands.

Ms. Evans never made it off the camp's property. She wasn't controlling that monster or using it on us—not if it killed her too, right? And now we're alone. No help is coming.

We're trapped on a mountain in the middle of nowhere with a monster hunting us.

TWENTY-NINE

elaney and I head down the wide dirt road back to Camp Whitewood as the sky lightens to pale blue and golden yellow. My arm aches with every step, and my breathing scrapes across my bruised throat.

Next to me, Delaney wears a dead woman's shoes that are a size too big. We took Ms. Evans's hiking boots off her—or *I* did, to keep Delaney from stepping on any of the shattered glass. Her white sock was caked in dirt and speckled with blood, but at least now she can walk without injuring it more.

I almost cry when the arching sign with the camp's wood-carved name comes into view. Delaney and I pick up our pace, ignoring our aches and pains. The white birch trees dwindle away and spread out to the sides, curving around the campsite as the main building with the little cabins and lake appear. I barely keep myself from collapsing in exhaustion and relief—I would have, if the sight didn't remind me that we aren't really safe. Maybe we made it through the night, but staying at Whitewood is dangerous, too many bodies piling up while a monster lurks in the shadows.

We rush past the school bus and Ms. Peterson's Jeep. The camp's flag still waves high in the sky, but sitting beneath it, next to the ring of yellow pansies that border the pole, are puddles of rust brown that stain the juniper-green grass. Dew sparkles under the cresting sun and highlights the blood-soaked ground.

I turn away from it, refusing to let that happen to any more of us, and follow Delaney. She swings the front door open and holds it for me. Cool air-conditioning rushes against my skin, and I take a moment to thank the universe for it. My shirt is sticky with sweat and blood, my skin covered in scratches and dirt. We pass the bathroom, and my feet almost carry me straight to the showers until voices drift out from the cafeteria.

"We can't just sit here and hope they're okay," Harper says. Her words curl around the open doorway and down the hall.

"But wandering around trying to find them isn't a good plan either," I hear Kylie say. "We should be smart about this."

"Maybe we should wait to see if Ms. Evans is actually getting the police," Emma says, and my stomach sinks at the news we'll have to give.

"Wouldn't they be here by now? Delaney said four hours. I can't just—" Harper stops when I step into the cafeteria. "Penny!" She rushes over and throws herself at me, arms wrapping around my neck, but let's go when I hiss at the pain in my arm.

"Thank god," Emma says, coming over with Kylie and Page. "We were freaking out when we couldn't find you guys."

"What happened?" Harper takes the hand of my uninjured arm, softly rubbing her thumb back and forth. "Are you okay?"

"We'll survive," I say, wanting to lean into her and let myself be enveloped by that lilac and sweet almond scent. But knowing I must smell horrible, I pull back instead, not letting go of her hand. "We *did* survive," I correct myself, glancing at Delaney. "The shadow man found us. We got away but ended up lost in the woods."

"What?" Kylie's dark eyes widen. "He came after you?" She glances at Page, who stands next to her, smiling softly and not seeming concerned at all. The image makes a flush of anxiety rush over my skin. It's so at odds with the frowns pulling at everyone else's mouths.

"He came here," Emma says. "A little before dawn."

Harper nods and shifts closer, whispering, even though all of us can still hear her. "He did something to Page. She's…" Everyone's attention turns to Page, but she only stands there with that same small grin. "She's been like that. She's just… I don't know. She's not…"

"Not scared or worried or anything," Kylie says. "We were all pulled into another vision thing, and he grabbed Page. He did something to her. She couldn't see that headband before, but now…"

"It's like he ate her memories," Emma says, opening her mouth and leaning close to Harper's head, mimicking the monster. "She doesn't remember the house fire at all now."

I gasp, and Harper's sharp gaze rakes over me. "What's wrong?"

"I just—the shadow man, he showed up looking like Delaney's sister—"

"My sister who's…dead," Delaney interrupts and shivers.

"It tried to do that same thing to me, but Delaney hurt it. She stopped it." I look around the small circle of girls before turning to Page, who has the same creepy smile that Sam had after the shadow man attacked her. The same look on Quinn before she turned up dead too. Even Reagan had a smile like them, that first full day here, before she disappeared. I thought she was just happy to be at Whitewood, but now… "You're right, Emma. I think it's eating some of our memories, stealing them away. Our more…traumatic ones?" But is that so bad? To forget what hurt us? I don't want to die, but to forget my father and the pain he caused…would I give those memories up?

"How?" Delaney asks.

"Ms. Evans *has* to be controlling that creature, then. Making it do this," Harper says.

"She's not in control of it," I tell them, voice grave. "Even *if* she was using the creature for her own purpose, she's not now."

"Isn't that what you—" Kylie starts, but Delaney interrupts.

"Ms. Evans is dead." Delaney swallows hard, tears gathering in her already bloodshot eyes. "And she wouldn't have done anything to hurt you guys. I know she wouldn't have."

"The creature is real. And we know it can hurt us." I lift my injured arm, even though the others have proof too, cuts, bruises, and burns. "But it can be hurt too," I add, filling them in on our night. On Delaney hitting the shadow man and making it bleed, making it run. I tell them about finding Reagan in the woods too, heart missing like Sam and Quinn.

"But Ms. Evans's journal," Emma says, gripping the pendant of her necklace again. "She said she'd do *anything* not to fail again. What else could that mean?"

"She wouldn't have kept us here if she knew about that creature. She didn't want to fail *you*. All of you," Delaney says, voice so certain.

"How do you know?" I ask.

"Ms. Evans talked about how she failed her daughter. That she couldn't help Clara, and because of that, Clara…took her own life. Ms. Evans didn't want to see that happen to anyone else. When she talked about failing, she meant failing to help other girls like Clara. She wouldn't do something that would endanger you. *Everything* she did was to keep anyone else from dying like her daughter."

"Then why did she lie about Sam and Reagan?" Harper asks, her words gentle.

"I don't know," Delaney says. "I heard Ms. Evans and Ms. Peterson arguing about them. About what to do. Ms. Peterson wanted to call the police. I thought the girls must have done something, broken one rule too many." She turns to me. "Like when you and Sam had the whiskey bottle. I thought maybe Sam got in trouble again, with Reagan." Delaney's blond hair sways as she shakes her head. "Maybe they knew the girls were missing, and Ms. Peterson wanted to call the police, but Ms. Evans didn't, hoping they'd show up again. Ms. Evans wouldn't have wanted to involve the cops if it meant camp could've been canceled. After last year and everything with Clara, she only got enough funding for one more year—kind of a trial before sponsors would give more."

"That's a lot of guessing," I say.

"Yeah," Delaney admits. "But if there's one thing I'm sure of, it's that Ms. Evans would never do something that could put you—us—in danger. Ever."

Her tone is so adamant, her belief in Ms. Evans so unfailing that I believe her too. I wanted someone to blame so I could make sense of all of this, but maybe Ms. Evans only wanted to help, and my fear made it easy to put the guilt on her.

"We have a bigger problem than worrying about that now anyway," I say, nodding toward Page. "Sam and Quinn looked like that too. Before the creature killed them. I think it's going to come for Page next."

We all turn, staring at the girl in question.

She shakes her head, that eerie smile pulling her cheeks. "Maybe it's not trying to hurt us," Page says. "I can't explain it, but

I feel…good. Lighter. You guys keep telling me I can't remember some sort of fire, but maybe that's not so bad?"

Yeah, maybe, except… "And the dying part?" I ask, but Page only offers that same soft smile.

"Okay, that's it," Delaney says. "We're leaving camp. All of us. Today."

Delaney calls out instructions, telling some girls to get our bags and others to grab some prepackaged food and water before she points a finger at me. "We need to get you cleaned up. Come on, there's a first aid kit in the foyer."

"I can help her," Harper offers as Kylie tugs Page toward the kitchen and Emma starts piling our backpacks together.

"Do you know what to do?" Delaney asks. She waves a hand toward my haphazardly wrapped arm. "That needs cleaning and new bandages and—"

"I took a first aid class," Harper cuts her off. "I can help."

"All right," Delaney says, her attention already scanning the room and the other girls. "Go ahead, but don't take too long. There's a first aid kit attached to the wall in the foyer." She darts off to help Emma before we can even respond.

"Come on," Harper says, guiding me out of the cafeteria and to the lodge's entrance. She finds the first aid kit and tugs it off its hook as I unwrap the dirty bandana from my bicep.

Harper gasps a little when she sees the gashes. "Does it hurt?" She pulls out bandages and antiseptic wipes.

"A little," I admit before hissing when she dabs the cuts with a sterile wipe.

"Why do you think that creature is doing this?" Harper asks, and I don't know if she actually wants an answer or if she's trying to distract me. But she's so close that the heat of her body mixed with the scent of her perfume is distracting enough. "Why is it torturing us with our worst memories?" she continues, pulling me back to our impossible situation.

"*Our?*" I ask, as she carefully unwinds a roll of gauzy bandages and starts wrapping it around my arm. "Has it…" I'm not sure how to ask her if the monster has started targeting her now too. I hope not. "Has it used your memories?" I ask as she secures my new bandage with little elastic clips.

"While you were gone"—she twists her silver ring around her finger, fidgeting with it—"it came, and I saw…I saw…"

"You don't have to talk about it." I reach out to rest my hand on hers to try to calm her fidgeting, but Harper's ring slips from her finger before I even touch her. It clatters to the tiled floor and bounces around our feet.

"No!" she says, the word more an inhaled gasp than anything else. She drops to her knees, hands skimming the floor and searching for her ring. Her breathing turns sharp, suffused with panic.

"Hey," I say, crouching down and helping look for it. "It's okay. We'll find it."

"You don't understand." She shakes her head, long black hair draping to the floor. "It's a reminder." She swallows hard. "It's *my* reminder. I need it."

"Okay." I let my voice turn soft, soothing. "It's here somewhere. It's not gone." My gaze searches over the speckled laminate. It couldn't have gone far.

I swipe my hair back behind my ears, the short length of it curling under my chin, as something glints under the brochure table, a silver shine that flashes like a beacon.

"There." I pick it up and hold it out for her to see.

Harper sighs. "Thank you." She stands up, reaching down to help me up as well.

"What is it a reminder of?" I ask but immediately want to take the words back. To swallow them to the bottom of my stomach and erase the grimace that pulls across Harper's full heart-shaped face.

"It's…" She shakes her head.

"Never mind." I take her right hand in mine, draw it to me, and gently slip her ring back onto her index finger.

"No, it's okay." She squeezes my hand but doesn't let go, and neither do I. "It's why I'm here. I told you before, I saw someone die. I tried to help them but…couldn't." The last word is almost too quiet to hear. A secret, a story, an admission—heavy and weighted as it hangs in the air. "But I— tried."

"I'm so sorry." I don't know what else to say.

"It's my reminder that I *did* try to help." She gulps air down, lets it out slowly. There's a shine that catches the light in her dark eyes. "Even if something is hard or terrifying, I can look at my ring and it reminds me. To hope. To try. To not give up."

We stand there, alone in the foyer, holding on to each other in the silence that follows. The quiet isn't uncomfortable, though; it wraps around us like an embrace and gives me the courage to admit my own secrets.

"When my father died," I start to whisper, and pity creeps into Harper's eyes. "No," I say instead of finishing my sentence, stopping the sadness spreading across her face. "It was…a relief."

Her brows tilt, but she doesn't let go of my hand. She doesn't shove me away with disgust or shout at me that I must be heartless, callous.

No, she only waits patiently to see if I want to say more.

"He hated me," I tell her, staring down at our hands. At her ring—her reminder to try even when things are hard or terrifying. And opening up like this is exactly that. But I like Harper, and I want her to know me. All of me.

Hard and terrifying.

To hope. To try. To not give up.

"I don't mean we didn't get along or anything small like that." My words tremble quietly between us. "I mean he blamed me for everything wrong in his life. His family was really rich, but they cut him off when he married my mom. And it took him a few years, but by the time she got pregnant with me, he realized he regretted it. All of it. Me, my mom, leaving his family. He tried to go back, but they treated him like he didn't exist. They hated my mom that much.

"And over the years, my father got…worse. Violent. And he died because of it."

Images of that night slam into me, but they're half-remembered, shrouded, and hazy. My father drunk and tripping—no, not tripping, but hands outstretched. His hands? Reaching for me? No…they weren't his large hands that reached out. I try to focus on that memory, but a wall of darkness slams down on my thoughts, and I don't know if it's something with me or something the shadow man has done.

It doesn't *feel* the same as my missing memories stolen by that monster. This feels just out of my grasp, still there but hidden. The gold watch and whatever else the shadow man might have stolen are just…blissfully gone. Maybe for the better, even.

I shake my head. That's a worry for another time. I look back at Harper as she patiently waits for me to continue.

"I thought I would turn into him, and it terrified me so much I couldn't function the same. I was scared of hurting anyone. It's why I came here."

"Being worried about others," she says, "is how I know you wouldn't hurt anyone."

"I want to believe that," I say, still staring down, unable to look at her because I'm not sure it's true.

"Penny," Harper says, tipping my chin up with her free hand

and pulling my gaze away from her ring. "You shouldn't have had to live like that."

"My mom…she didn't know how to leave him—"

"That's not what I meant." She steps even closer. Until the sweet scent of her perfume is all I can smell.

"I know," I tell her. "It's strange… He didn't want us, but we were also the only thing he had left. And even if he hated us, he didn't want to lose anything else that he felt he *owned*."

"Penny…"

"He was terrible, and maybe part of him will always be in me, like a splinter stuck under my skin," I say, thinking about those intrusive thoughts, easier to snuff out now but still not gone.

"No, Penny," Harper says, tears in her eyes. "I didn't know him, but I do know you're nothing like that. You've been trying to protect all of us this whole time. You tried to figure out what was happening here and how to stop it." Her gaze burns into me. "Penny, you're so brave and strong and…amazing."

I don't let the doubts and fears and worries crowd my mind. Instead, I lean forward, pull Harper close. She's only a few inches shorter than me, and I have to tilt my head down, tip hers up. But then our mouths meet, and she lets go of my hand to wrap hers behind my neck. Her fingers curl into my hair as my palms slide up her arms and shoulders and neck to cup her face as we kiss.

She is all curves and softness, sweet almond and lilac, and an intoxicating taste that fills my chest with champagne bubbles, with strawberry effervescence and sparkling fizz. Her kiss is a brand, searing into the delicate skin of my lips as her ChapStick paints itself across my mouth, becoming mine.

We're both breathless as we slowly pull apart, giddy smiles spreading across our faces.

"You're kind of amazing too," I tell her, unable to stop my smile from stretching wider.

But the feel of it only reminds me of the shadow monster. Of the eerie smiles that decorated the other girls' faces before they died.

Harper notices the shift in me. Her gaze drifts down the hall where the others get ready. "As much as I want…more of that, we should get back."

"Yeah," I agree. "And finally get the hell out of here. Together."

HARPER

The day started with so much promise for the girl. A warm spring morning with the sun shining. A new hiking trail that boasted a gorgeous waterfall view.

It was supposed to be a perfect day.

The girl loved spending her weekends going on hikes when she could, forgetting about the stress of school, bad breakups, or the pressure about which college to choose. She could let her mind clear and her body take over. She could let nature envelop her.

The girl glanced at the map posted on a large sign situated at the trailhead and checked which color-coded markers would take her to the waterfall.

The hike was easy enough that the girl didn't mind going alone. That she didn't feel the need to drag a friend along to have a safety buddy. For half an hour, the girl walked through a sun-dappled forest just starting to turn green again. New shoots sprung from the ground, early flowers dotting the grass with patches of purple, yellow, and white. Every once in a while, she'd see another hiker, wave hello, and pass them by like ships at sea.

Out here, the girl could breathe deep and enjoy the quiet. The cool air filled her lungs, refreshing, clean, and hinting at the taste of last night's frost already melted away.

She walked for another hour, following blue color-coded signs to the waterfall. The girl hadn't seen any other hikers in a while, but it was still early in the day, not so unusual.

But the loose dog bounding around a curve in the trail toward her was strange. The girl backed away, unsure if the dog was friendly or not. She glanced up and down the trail, into the dense woods, but didn't see an owner.

When the dog got to her, it didn't jump or bite. It dragged an orange leash along the ground and whimpered, circling the girl before looking from her to farther down the trail, back and forth. The girl had never had a dog, but she'd always liked them and imagined having one someday. This one looked like some sort of cattle dog or shepherd, brown, black, and white mixing together in patches and speckles.

The girl reached her hand out slowly before letting the dog come the last few inches. She petted its head, scratched its ears. A silver tag on the collar said *Finn*.

"Where's your person, Finn?" the girl asked, looking around again.

The dog whined, glancing down the trail. It moved away from the girl a few feet and stared at her. When she followed, the dog went farther. And again waited for her to follow.

"Is your person down there?" Her gaze wound along the path, a sinking feeling weighing her stomach down.

Another whimper from the dog, and a bark that startled the girl. She flinched but kept trailing after the dog. The faster she went, the faster the dog moved. Until they were both running.

"Wait," the girl called, but the dog didn't slow, so neither did she. "Finn!"

Trees blurred by, ribbons of brown and green, as the chilled air sawed at her lungs. Her attention was trapped between her fevered steps—keeping careful not to stumble and twist an ankle—and the orange leash flailing behind the dog like a snake with its head cut off. The crashing of the waterfall reached the girl's ears, growing louder but still unseen.

The dog rounded a bend in the trail, and the girl followed only seconds behind, nearly tripping over him. He'd stopped short, whines cresting and nose nudging at the ground.

No. Not the ground.

At a body lying there. A woman—unconscious.

She was older than the girl by at least a couple decades, with hair half-grayed and wrinkles decorating her face. Her eyes were shut, expression empty. Her body was twisted across the ground as if she'd collapsed. No blood or wounds to be seen.

The girl dropped down next to the woman, dirt stirring up around her, as Finn circled and whimpered and circled again. She reached out one trembling hand and touched the woman, searching for a pulse. The woman's skin was warm—normal— but the girl couldn't feel a heartbeat. Either it was too weak... or it wasn't there.

She tried to feel for any breathing, but the woman's chest wasn't moving.

"Help!" the girl called out, her words swallowed by the roar of the nearby waterfall, still hidden but somewhere close. "Is anyone there? We need help!"

No answer came. The only reply was Finn's whimpering while he nudged the woman's shoulder.

The girl had taken CPR classes—had been taught what to do when someone wasn't breathing or moving.

She pulled her phone out and dialed 911. Hit speakerphone. She set it on the ground as she tried to remember everything she'd been taught. She put her hands on the woman's chest, one on top of the other over the sternum. There was a song, something ironic and stupid and old that she'd been told to match the beat of.

Dun, dun, dun. And another one gone. Dun, dun, dun—was all that the girl could remember of it.

She breathed into the woman's mouth before pressing down on her chest again, hard. Over and over. Repeating the steps and the song's chorus while hoping it wouldn't come true.

Bones cracked and crunched as an operator answered the line. As the girl shouted replies to their questions and half sang a nearly forgotten song in her head, trying to balance the chaos. And all the while, the dog whined and whined and whined.

The girl focused on her ring, a silver band with a black stone. She kept her gaze on it as her hands pushed down as fear tried to take over. If she stared at the ring and not the woman's face, then she could do this. She could keep going.

Dun, dun, dun. She pressed down, over and over, as the operator promised help was on the way. But as the girl tried to breathe for the woman and pump blood through her heart, she worried how long it would take. She'd walked the trail for nearly an hour and a half. Even if they rode motorized bikes to get all the way out here, the girl feared it wouldn't matter.

Because the woman under her hands wasn't responding to the chest compressions or air forced into her lungs; the girl's stomach twisted with worry—with fear that maybe she'd found the woman too late.

But the girl continued.

Dun, dun, dun. Another one gone. Dun, dun, dun.

Push and press and breathe. Sing the song and repeat all of it again and again.

And as the minutes ticked by with only the dog's whines and the waterfall's roar for company, the girl grew tired, arms aching and sweat clinging to her brow.

Until the paramedics arrived and they carried the woman away on a stretcher while pumping air into her lungs with a plastic bulb.

"Miss," one of the remaining paramedics said. He guided the girl to follow, handing her Finn's leash, mistaking the dog as her own after his real owner was sped away on a small all-terrain vehicle. "Are you all right?" the paramedic asked, but the girl barely heard the man. Her head was filled with the crashing of the waterfall she never got to see and the drumming of a song she barely remembered as she stood there, holding the leash of a dog that wasn't hers.

"Will she live?"

He didn't answer her question. He only checked over the girl for any injuries of her own, but it didn't matter. She'd seen the truth in his eyes, and as Finn whimpered at her feet, the girl started to cry.

THIRTY

No sooner do Harper and I pull apart than Delaney comes speed walking down the hall with the other girls in tow. She hands Harper her backpack while Emma gives mine to me, and Kylie holds onto a smiley-dazed Page.

"Is everyone ready?" Delaney asks. She glances around at each of us as if expecting anyone to object. I almost wish I could ask to take a quick shower, to wash off our night in the woods, but it's the least of my concerns.

Delaney counts our group, her finger tapping through the air as if we're about to go on a camp-related hike and not fleeing for our lives. "Good. Everyone has their bags?" she asks, and we all hike our backpacks higher on our shoulders. "Then let's go."

We step out to the morning sun shining down on the camp. To birds chirping and a fresh breeze coming up from the lake.

To the grass and flowers swaying in the wind as if saying good morning.

It's almost idyllic—if not for the bloodstains by the flagpole.

Delaney leads us over to the bus, keys jingling in her hand as she walks, but when we round the side and get to the door, we all stop. Large claw marks scrape down the hood, twisting the thick metal. A chemical scent fills the air, and liquid leaks out from under the bus, trailing across the dirt. My heart drops at the sight, sure that it wasn't like that when Delaney and I got back this morning.

"It's...it's destroyed," Harper says.

"No." Delaney shoves the door to the bus open. "It can't be."

She rushes up the steps and drops into the driver's seat. But when she slips the key in and turns it, there's nothing but a clicking sound. She tries again and again, met with only a *click click click*. Finally, she hangs her head and takes a deep breath before trudging down the stairs.

"Wait. Ms. Peterson's Jeep!" Delaney darts around the front of the bus, and we all race after her, but any hope we had is snuffed out like a flame. Sitting next to the bus is a white Jeep, the same gouging lines torn through it—four claws marks that match the ones on my arm, only much larger, and I can't stop thinking of the way the shadow man grew impossibly huge in Kylie and Page's cabin.

"Now what?" Kylie asks, looking between the bus and Ms. Peterson's Jeep. Neither one looks salvageable. And with the way

Ms. Evans's red car was crushed, there's no way it would work, even if we could all fit.

"We try the satphone," Delaney says, heading back to the main building with all of us following her like lost ducklings. Delaney slides her backpack off, and the rest of us copy, piling them by the front door.

Everyone's faces are filled with worry lines—except Page with her eerie smile, which hasn't left. Harper bites her lip. Emma runs her hand down her long ponytail, unable to keep still. Delaney takes deep breaths, one after the other, as if calming herself. Kylie can't stop scratching the skin of her upper arm in a nervous tic.

And the voice in my head hisses its violent thoughts to me, telling me to lock them all in here, to let them die at the hands of the shadow man—or my own.

I follow Delaney, doing my best to ignore those whispers and reminding myself that there's nothing more that I want right now than for all of us to get out of here alive and safe.

I am in control of my own actions, I say, letting the mantra grow louder than my intrusive thoughts until they fade away for now.

Delaney holds the door open, and we all file into the foyer. "This way," she says, and leads us down the left hallway.

Ms. Evans's office is the same as before: a desk to the side, two chairs facing each other in the middle, a console table where the EMDR machine is stored once more. And under the large window is the small table with the diffuser, the faintest scent of lavender and bergamot still clinging to the room.

"Is this it?" Emma asks as she opens a desk drawer and lifts up something that looks more like a walkie-talkie than any phone I've ever used.

"Yeah," Delaney says, holding her hand out.

Before Emma can give the satphone to Delaney, or even turn it on, a deep voice crackles out of the speakers.

"*Who's there?*" it asks.

Emma gasps and drops the phone. It bounces onto the desk as the blood drains from her face. She backs up, bumping into the rest of us and grabbing her necklace tightly.

"*Who's there?*" it asks again.

Kylie reaches forward, but before she can pick the satphone up, the image flickers. And for a split second, there's a different phone sitting three inches to the right, the plastic smashed to pieces and the long antenna ripped off. It's there and gone in a blink.

The unbroken one sits on the desk, that same gravelly voice repeating its question.

"*Who's there?*"

"What's happening?" Delaney asks, moving closer to Emma. We all inch forward, trying to see the satphone.

But when Page speaks, we freeze. "It's here," she says, facing the door as the small smile on her face stretches and grows into a full grin that sets my teeth on edge. "It's back."

We follow her gaze, and all the air is trapped in my lungs when I see the shadow man, another mutated version of him, filling the doorway.

"*Who's there?*" that voice asks again, the words echoing from the satphone and burrowing into my ears.

"*Who's there?*"

"*Who's there?*"

"*Who's there?*"

THIRTY-ONE

The monster fills the doorway, his form larger than normal again. Medical tubes weave in and out of his shadow-stained skin as filmy gray eyes stare at us. Growing from his head are horns, so dark they're more oxblood red than crimson.

My muscles tense with fear. He's a terrifying collection of all our worst memories, a physical manifestation reminding us of Kylie's mother dying in the hospital. Of my father and his violence. Of Delaney's dead sister and the house fire Page survived.

Only now there's something new. He holds that same amber-filled bottle in one hand, but a bright orange leash is smashed between his grip and the glass as it trails down onto the ground. And in his other hand, he holds a silver baseball bat that drags across the floor as he steps closer. The scrape of the metal on linoleum mixes with the staticky voice still coming from the fake satphone.

Who's there?

The words are low and severe, and they make Emma shake in a way that tells me the monster has finally started preying on her own history.

"Get back," Delaney says, waving for us to move, but there's no place to go, no other exit than the doorway the monster blocks. Still, we shuffle away, bumping into the wall and window. Except for Page; she stands there and stares with a wide smile stretching her cheeks too tight. Until Kylie drags her back.

The shadow man's milky eyes dart to Kylie, and he growls, a low rumbling that clatters within his chest as the sound of a heart monitor starts beeping, coming from everywhere and nowhere at once. The noise twists into that high-pitched word, repeating over and over.

Soon. Soon. Soon.

It curls and coils around the voice from the phone until the two are screaming at us, stabbing our ears with the intensity of it all.

Who's there?

Harper grabs a glass paperweight and throws it at the shadow man. He barely notices as it bounces off his shoulder and drops to the floor. "Leave us alone," she shouts, picking up a pair of scissors sitting in a mug and holding them out like a knife.

Delaney picks up the desk lamp, yanking the cord out of the socket, and launches it at the shadow man. It slams into his head, and he drops both the bat and bottle to grip his head, a sharp yelp coming from him. I want to help, to fight back too, but the idea of using something as a weapon pleases that voice in my head too much.

Do it, it says, gleeful and too loud. *Grab the scissors from Harper. Stab the monster. Stab them all.*

No, I'm not listening to you, I say, balling my hands into fists to keep from doing anything. *I won't hurt my friends.*

The creature's form begins shifting, flipping rapidly: the shadow man I've always known, normal size once more; Kylie's mom, weak and withered; Delaney's sister, white dress and water pouring from her mouth; Page's little brother and a ring of fire circling him on the floor. And then a man—dressed in dark clothes and a black ski mask, pale skin and light brown eyes barely peeking through. A weird animal, almost catlike, weaves around his feet. But it looks wrong, made of crumpled paper and paint—not alive yet somehow moving. And another person I've never seen before: an older woman with graying hair. She wears hiking boots with a vest so much like what Ms. Evans always wore—only this fake woman holds an orange leash, unattached to anything as it trails to the floor.

I can't help glancing at Harper, remembering her story about the dog and the woman on her hike. Harper's eyes widen in fear as she stares at the appearance of the older lady.

Round and round the images rotate as the creature clutches its head, blood trickling down every version of its stolen faces from where Delaney threw the lamp at it.

Who's there? Who's there? WHO'S THERE! The question repeats with every change of the monster's form, a staticky cry that echoes louder each time.

"Go," Delaney shouts.

She shoves Emma past the monster. It shifts to Page's little brother, and I grab Harper's hand, drag her behind me as we slip by his smaller form. I glance back, and Kylie is pulling Page, Delaney helping to push her along. But Page doesn't cooperate. She shuffles her feet, staring at the shadow man with a smile—as if that monster is her savior.

He turns into the masked man and throws his arms out, ramming the other girls. Kylie crashes into Harper and me. Harper gets shoved hard enough that the scissors are knocked from her hands, clattering down the hallway, as we catch Kylie before she can fall to the unforgiving floor. Delaney is thrown to the ground, though, hard enough that her body slides across the smooth tile and smashes into the hallway wall. She groans before lifting one hand to her head.

The catlike *thing*, weaving around the shadow man's legs, jumps out into the hall after us, sharp claws swiping the air. Emma rushes to it and stomps one booted foot down over and over again, until there's only a strangled hiss dying off and a crumpled pile of unmoving paper under her shoe.

"God, I wanted to throw that thing away years ago," she mumbles as Harper lets go of Kylie and takes Delaney's arm.

Harper lifts Delaney up, helping support her weight. A bright red mark spreads across the counselor's cheekbone, but at least she's free of the room—away from the creature.

Only Page is still trapped inside Ms. Evans's office.

And she doesn't try to leave. She stares up at the creature with a smile that doesn't belong.

Soon, soon, soon! the machinelike words continue to warn.

The monster turns to Page, one hand lashing out to grip her neck.

"No! Stop!" Kylie shouts as the monster shifts from the man in the ski mask back to the amalgamation of our nightmares. A gash splits open its shadow skin, dark blood trickling down. But it doesn't seem to care about its own wound anymore. His shadowy fingers stretch and lengthen into claws that dig into Page's chest.

Emma rushes forward, pushing past Harper and me, and grabs the silver bat from where it rolled into the doorway. She steps inside the room as the shadow man's nails rip through Page's skin and muscle and bone.

Holding the bat up, Emma pulls it past her shoulder and swings at the creature's back. But instead of hitting him, the baseball bat passes through the shadow man, dispersing like smoke before coming together again. Emma spins, thrown off-balance, but rights herself. She stands, jaw clenched as she stares at the monster. It lifts Page up, her feet dangling above the floor, like it did to me. She doesn't fight to get free or struggle against the monster's hold. She only smiles at it with a grin stretched far too wide, a rubber band pulled taut—tight enough to snap.

The shadow man shoves his hand into her chest, and Page doesn't even cry out. Her eyes glaze over as it rips her heart out. Kylie lets out a scream, so raw and full of anger and grief that it makes my skin prick, a chill full of terror that scrapes down my spine.

Kylie snatches the bat from Emma's trembling hands, slicing it through the air. But again, it doesn't harm the shadow man. It slides through him as if it doesn't exist—and it doesn't. He's making us see it. It's not real, and it can't hurt him. Not like the lamp Delaney threw, which left a gash on its head.

The shadow man drops Page's lifeless body, and the smile on her face finally falls away. Her blood pools onto the floor, a vivid scarlet that grows larger and stretches sticky fingers across the tiles to reach for us.

I step back as the creature turns around, cradling Page's heart in one clawed hand. That serrated mouth of his opens, gaping wide and dark, an endless pit. Blood drips between his clawed fingers, splattering onto the floor. He shoves her heart into his mouth and swallows it whole as we stare in horror, watching as this monster kills our friend and *eats* her heart.

The shadow man sighs, a soft whispering sound that wraps around us. Acid burns my throat, and I gag. The room is filled with the sharp scent of death, with the metallic taste of blood suffocating the air, and it turns my stomach even more.

A smile curls the edges of the monster's bloodstained mouth, and he stretches out his neck as the horns on his head shrink and disappear with Page's death. The burn marks on its shadowed arm also fade.

It's like Quinn and how the teddy bears vanished with her death.

Like Sam and how I never saw another cigarette lighter or pine-scented air freshener after she died.

What did it take from Reagan? She disappeared—died— before I even got to know her. What stories and suffering did this creature thieve away from her?

This monster is stealing our memories, torturing and killing us. Eating our hearts and our histories.

"Run!" Delaney shouts as the shadow man lurches forward. Emma screams as the papery cat-thing inflates again, hissing and spitting around her legs like a possessed kitten as she rushes down the hall.

Kylie drops the useless bat and runs out of the room, leaving Page's body behind, as Harper and I follow and the creature chases us.

Soon, soon, soon! the phantom beeping still cries, and it feels like a warning. A promise. Our deaths are coming. Soon.

Our feet pound against the hard floor, but the shadow man is faster. He slams into Kylie and me. We crash into a door—*through* a door that breaks open from the impact—and sprawl across the floor, legs and arms tangling. Pain shatters through my ribs and back. My head bounces against the floor. One of Kylie's hands smacks my face. She grunts as her body smashes into a wooden piece of furniture.

Harper shouts my name from the hall as shoes screech against the linoleum. "Penny!" she says again, rushing into the room. I want to yell at her to get away from the shadow man while she can. But my head is dizzy, and speaking feels too hard while the room spins and the monster towers above.

"No!" Harper screams as the creature reaches a claw-tipped hand out to Kylie and me each. "Stop!"

And miraculously, he does.

But dread chokes me when he twists around to face Harper. Her body shakes as she takes a step back, but the shadow man's arms are long. He reaches out, trailing fingers down Harper's cheek as she whimpers, and a shiver of delight creeps down his own spine.

More footsteps fill the hallway, coming closer as Emma and Delaney shout for us. The shadow man rips his arm away from Harper and growls. He waves one hand in the air as Emma and Delaney skid to a stop in the hall. The open doorway disappears, replaced with a blank white wall that traps Kylie, Harper, and me in the room with the shadow man.

Soon, soon, soon, the warning screams again, in time with the pounding of Emma and Delaney's fists against the false wall.

Soon, soon, soon, it cries, each word punctuated by the shadow man's footsteps coming *closer, closer, closer*.

The creature pivots, turning to Kylie, and Harper edges around him. She crouches next to me, her dark gaze darting to my face before shifting to keep an eye on the monster.

She pulls on my arm as I scramble to get my feet under me. The shadow man looms over Kylie as she tries to push herself away, but she's stuck between him and a bed.

I swallow down bile, the realization of where we are—trapped in Ms. Peterson's room—makes acid crawl up my throat. Ms. Peterson's and Quinn's bodies lying on the bed, covered with that stained blanket. Kylie jerks back as the creature reaches a hand down and something slips off the mattress, bumping into her shoulder.

A scream rips out of Kylie when she sees the gray-skinned arm touching her. Long red hair drapes down the side of the bed frame and tangles around the arm.

Quinn.

"Please," Kylie begs, tears streaming down her face as the creature leans down. "Please, let me go."

"We have to do something," Harper whispers, and I nod.

Next to the wall, where the door was, is a thick wooden walking stick.

Pick it up, those intrusive thoughts whisper. *Smash its head.*

And for the first time, I listen to that voice. But not to hurt someone—only to protect the people I care about.

I dart toward the walking stick as Harper snatches a book off the nightstand, the monster's gaze so intent on Kylie that he isn't paying attention to us.

Harper throws the book, and it bounces off his shoulder. He doesn't even seem to notice.

Do it, Harper mouths as I grab the heavy stick, hands trembling.

I tiptoe forward, shaking as I hold the walking stick up like the baseball bat Emma and Kylie tried to use. Only this has to work. It's not a figment created by the monster. It's real. Solid.

I hope.

The shadow man hunches over Kylie, his back curved and showing every single bone in his spine. His hands latch onto her head, arms still covered in a tangle of medical tubes.

Soon, soon, soon, the unseen monitor screams, a never-ending litany, repeating in time with my frenzied heartbeat.

My hands grip the walking stick too tight, and nausea twists my stomach. Pain bleeds into my bones, everything in me shouting to not hurt *anyone*, to ignore that voice in my head rejoicing at finally being listened to.

But the creature in front of me isn't a person. And if I don't do this, *it* will hurt Kylie—kill her like it did to the others.

Soon, I agree with that screaming machinery. Soon, this night-mare will end.

It has to.

The monster sniffs the air around Kylie's head as she squirms in its hold. It looks more like the nightmare version of my father again, no nose or features to its face—except the dead eyes of Delaney's sister.

With trembling arms, I bring the walking stick down on the monster's back, the impact sending shock waves up my arms. But the creature doesn't let Kylie go. Its mouth stretches as it makes that sucking sound once more, like wind through a tunnel.

Again, that voice hisses in my head. *Again!*

And I listen, even as my entire body tenses too tightly at giving in. I slam the stick into the monster. Over and over, but he doesn't stop.

Soon, soon, soon! Fear crowds my chest, panic that this time the warning is meant for Kylie alone. That her death is coming.

No. I won't let this monster take anyone else.

Anger burns in my veins. Kylie screams, Emma's and Delaney's fists pound against the wall, and Harper is yelling something, but there's only a ringing in my ears and that voice in my head as I strike the creature over and over, unable to stop.

Soon, soon—

The warning cuts off. Silence fills the room.

Darkness crowds my vision, and my jaw clenches. My hands ache, but I don't let go of the stick until the monster drops its hold on Kylie.

A smile has replaced the terror on her face, a placid thing that sends a new fear skittering through my body. The medical tubes twisting around the shadow man's arms sizzle and hiss, burning away to nothing—and I know Kylie's memories of her mother in that hospital are disappearing with them.

Her memories. They might have been painful for Kylie, but they were hers if she wanted them. Not his to take—to steal.

The sight of it all breaks me, and I swing the stick again, as hard as I can while aiming for the shadow man's head. I'm trapped in a room with the girl I have a crush on, two dead bodies, and now another girl that's more smiling zombie than person—and the monster that created this nightmare.

The shadow man turns to me, his death-clouded eyes and bloodied mouth a reminder of all he's done.

My muscles tremble and burn as my stick whistles through the air with speed.

THIRTY-TWO

The walking stick—my makeshift weapon—slams into the shadow man's head, and he collapses, half on the bed and lying over the bodies of his victims. Kylie jerks away, but that placid smile doesn't leave her face.

Hit her, those intrusive thoughts command.

No, I say. *I saved her.*

I drop the stick, breath shaking at having used something as a weapon, even if it was to stop the shadow man. The wood clatters as it bounces on the floor, half muffled by a rug under the bed, and all my muscles loosen once it's out of my hold.

"Come on," I say to Kylie, not wanting to stay long enough for the creature to wake up. I reach a hand toward her and almost sigh when she takes it and steps away from the shadow man instead of waiting for it to kill her like Page.

The busted doorway appears again, the wall the monster created disappearing as Emma and Delaney fall into the room.

"Are you guys okay?" Delaney asks. "What happened?"

Next to her, Emma holds the papier-mâché cat by the neck and a plastic lighter in the other hand. She flicks it with her thumb, but before the flint can catch, the fake cat disappears like the wall.

Emma stares at her empty hand. "What in the demented kid's craft," she mumbles before shoving the lighter in her back pocket and stepping closer, Delaney following. The two of them stare at the unmoving shadow man at my feet.

"Is it…dead?" Harper asks.

"No," I say as his form starts switching again, changing between the man in a ski mask and Delaney's water-drenched sister. My shadow nightmare and Kylie's frail mother. The older woman from Harper's hike, half her face smashed into the blankets and obscured.

Harper fidgets with her ring, twisting that silver band with the black stone around her index finger. The creature's shape changes again, back to the shadow man and then Delaney's sister, flipping through memories and masks.

"We're getting out of here now," Delaney says, and none of us disagree. She takes Kylie's hand, drawing the girl along.

"It's okay," Kylie says, a small smile tilting her lips. She pulls her hand out of Delaney's hold and takes a step closer to the bed.

She doesn't look quite the same as Page did, no tight grin stretched too far, but there's also no fear there.

"It won't hurt us," Kylie adds, glancing at the creature slumped over on the bed.

"Yes, it absolutely the fuck will," Emma says, voice stern as she points to the obvious proof—to where Ms. Peterson's and Quinn's bodies lie unmoving on the bed.

She follows the line of Emma's finger, and her smile tips slightly higher. "No, she won't," Kylie promises.

"Come on. Let's go," Harper says.

"Before it wakes up." Delaney grabs Kylie's arm and pulls her out of the room. Emma scurries behind while Harper and I hurry also.

"Wait," I say, scanning the room. The door is broken, the latch busted, but we can't just leave it wide-open for that thing to wake up and follow us. We have no car and no working phone, and if we have any hope of getting free of Whitewood without it finding us, then we need whatever advantage possible.

I start dragging Ms. Peterson's heavy wooden dresser across the floor, wincing when the cuts on my bicep burn with pain.

"Here." Harper grabs the other side and helps me push the dresser. We get it close to the doorway before slipping into the hall, pulling the heavy furniture into the opening and blocking the way out. It's not enough, but it's all we've got.

We race down the hall, and I can't stop myself from glancing back every few steps, checking that the shadow man isn't about to attack. Each time I look and the hall is empty, it becomes easier to breathe.

Delaney leads us through the foyer and out the front door. The summer heat is sticky and thick compared to the cold air-conditioning, and sweat gathers across my forehead almost immediately.

"What do we do now?" Harper asks. She looks through the windows. Even with the lights still on inside, the foyer is dark compared to the bright sunlight.

"We trap that thing inside and get out of here," Delaney says, pulling out a key ring from her pocket and moving next to Harper. She slips a silver key into the door, and a satisfying *click* sounds. "I'm going to lock the others," Delaney adds, jaw tight and eyes determined.

"That thing already threw them"—Emma points in the direction of Kylie and me—"into a door and broke it. Do you really think that's gonna work?"

"Probably not!" Delaney says, tossing her hands in the air and dropping them heavily. "But it's all I've got!" She takes a deep breath and lets it out. "I'm sorry. I'm just a little—" Another deep breath. "I don't know what else to do. It's better than nothing, right?"

"Of course," I say to calm her—reassure her. Even if I think locking the doors won't really stop that monster. Just like the dresser I shoved in the doorway. "If it helps even a little, we should do it."

Delaney nods, her movements a little less frantic now. "Okay," she says, "everyone grab your bag." She waves to the pile of backpacks we left by the front door.

I pick mine up, a black one stuffed with some clothes, plenty of food and water, and even Bunny. Emma and Harper grab theirs from the pile, swinging the heavy bags onto their backs as Delaney hands Kylie's hers, urging the girl to put it on.

"Guys," Kylie says. That straight smile is still tacked across her cheeks, pinned into place with her dimples. Her teeth show too many and too bright against her dark skin. "We're gonna be fine. It's—"

"Yeah, if we get out of here, *then* maybe we'll be fine," Emma says, running a hand down her long dark ponytail. She stares at the windows, shifting from foot to foot as if ready to run at the slightest movement from inside.

My gaze drops to the ground, to the single backpack left there. A bright teal one with Page's name written in marker. No matter what Kylie thinks, we aren't safe near that monster. Page is dead because of it.

Page, Quinn, and Sam. Ms. Evans and Ms. Peterson. Reagan too. The list is too long, already too heavy. Our small group is less than half of what it was. I can't lose any more of them.

No one reaches for Page's bag. No one picks it up.

"We're gonna have to walk," Delaney says, snapping my attention back to her. "I can't fix the car or bus, and the satphone is smashed. Our only option is to hike out of here and get to town."

"That'll take all day, won't it?" Harper asks.

"Probably longer," Delaney says. "I'll grab a tent and some of the sleeping bags, and then lock the side door." Her eyes skip from me to

Harper to Emma before stopping on Kylie, assessing. "I need you guys to stay with her—away from the doors and windows, but keep an eye on the lodge. And shout if you see that creature moving inside."

"We should get weapons," Harper says. "We know it can be hurt—but not with anything it…creates. We need real weapons in case it finds us again. What happened to the shotgun Ms. Peterson had?"

"I looked for it after Ms. Evans left." Delaney shakes her head, blond hair slipping over one shoulder. "I couldn't find it, but there's a shed behind my cabin. It has a couple axes and hatchets for chopping wood." She slips a key off her ring and hands it to me. "Two of you go get them while one of you stays with Kylie and keeps an eye out."

"I'll stay," Emma says. Her hand slides up to the cylinder pendant on her neck. "I've got pepper spray," she adds, and for the first time, I notice a discreet cap on the black cylinder that looks like it could flip up.

"And you haven't used it already?" Harper asks, mouth hanging open.

"That creature's always had its back to me or wasn't close enough when something was happening. Or someone else was too close! We also thought it wasn't real until, like, this morning!" Emma lifts the black cylinder. "It's kind of a one-time use. One chance." She swallows hard. "And…when I saw the baseball bat…I couldn't think straight. I—"

"It's okay," Delaney says, waving her hands at us to walk. "Let's just go before it wakes up."

"The archery supplies!" Emma says. "Get them too."

"Good idea." Delaney looks at each of us again as we all walk away from the main building. "Five minutes, and we're all leaving. Together."

I nod, veering off with Harper toward the cabins. Delaney darts in the opposite direction, her keys jingling as she runs around the building. Emma walks with Kylie, half guiding the other girl to the grassy lawn. She turns away from the flagpole and the dark stains soaked into the earth, and watches the main building, fidgeting as she scans one window and the next.

Page's backpack still sits there, alone and left behind. My stomach clenches at the reminder of another girl dead and gone. Stolen away like her memories.

I turn, following Harper toward the shed and hoping we can get out of here safely.

"Do you think we'll be okay?" Harper asks. She steps to the side when we get to the shed and lets me pass with the key. She twists the silver ring on her index finger, the black stone spinning like the moon in orbit with each turn.

I want to lie to her. To brush the worry off her face with gentle false words. She bites her lip, the fullness of one cheek pulling in with the movement, and the memory of our kiss makes my cheeks warm. That's one memory I *never* want to forget, even if there are others I could do without.

But the fear in Harper's eyes shifts my focus away from that kiss and the hope for more. Instead, I want to tell her that of course we'll be fine. That nothing will happen to her.

But I don't know that.

"I hope so," I finally say, climbing the three steps up the little porch of the shed. I turn around to face Harper, wanting to comfort her more. She stands one step lower than me when that voice in my head shouts.

Push her, it hisses. *Watch her break and shatter. Just like your father.*

I recoil against the words, against the images flashing through my mind—Harper falling down the stairs, a dozen more steps than this porch has.

A vision, of me pushing her until she crashes to the bottom of the stairs in my childhood home, slams into my thoughts so strong that I fear the shadow man is here, causing another hallucination.

Harper gasps as her bones crack and break, limbs bending at awful angles as she tumbles *down down down*. And then it's not Harper but my father. His face flashing in my memory. His body broken and dying as my own hands hang in the air after watching him fall to his death.

*Push her—just like what you did to **him***, that voice whispers through my thoughts before memories I buried so deep surge up and overwhelm me.

PENNY

The girl's father was angry again. And he let his anger infect their house with both his words and his hands.

A loud smack echoed from the hall, and the girl flinched from where she hid in her room as her mother's cries followed behind. The girl's own anger and fear burned within her chest as her father raged, longer and louder than ever before.

Another crash came from the other side of her door, and she couldn't take it anymore. Her mother had always tried to protect her, always taken the bruises and breaks for the both of them. But tonight, the girl couldn't listen to the sounds of her father's fist or her mother's cries.

On trembling legs, she walked across her room and reached out for the doorknob. She hesitated long enough to hear her father yell again, to hear her mom try to quiet him and face his wrath once more.

The girl ripped her door open and stepped into the hall. Her father gripped her mother's upper arm, his other hand drawn back.

"What do you want?" he asked, voice laced with poison. "Go back to bed." Her father tapped his belt buckle, a warning to the girl, but she shook her head, pulling her gaze away from the fake gold that glinted too yellow in the light.

"Let her go," the girl said, her words barely louder than a whisper as they stuttered like her heart.

"Go back to bed, Penny," her mom begged. "It's okay. I'm okay."

"No," the girl said. "You aren't." She faced her father again, her throat clogged with years of fear. "Let her go."

"Or what?" her father asked. He pulled her mother closer, his grip on her upper arm making her flinch.

"Please," the girl said, wishing for any care or concern from her father but knowing she'd get none.

His anger was all she knew of him. His violence was all she saw from him.

He shoved her mom back, releasing his hold as she crashed into the wall. Her head smacked the plaster as she cried out, and the girl stepped toward her mom, wanting to take her and run from this place.

But her father staggered forward, blocking the girl's path. The scent of whiskey seeped through the hall, nauseatingly thick.

"Go back to your room," her father said, his words starting to slur as he took another sip from his bottle. Behind him, her mom nodded. But the bruises and blood tarnishing her mother's skin filled the girl with anger.

"No," she said to her father, the word shaking but strong. "Leave her alone."

"You don't tell me what to do," he said, reaching back and grabbing her mom by the hair, dark strands fisted in his ugly grip.

The sight of her mom's pain was too much.

"Let her go!" the girl yelled, shoving both hands into her father's chest. His hands came free of her mother's hair as he stumbled back, bumping into the corner of the wall and the open stairway. He caught himself on the banister and turned to the girl, eyes flaming with fury.

"Penny, don't," her mother cried. "You'll only make him mad."

"He already is!" the girl yelled. "That's all he ever is!"

"Come here," her father said, lurching toward the girl.

She ducked away, grabbing the bottle of whiskey from his meaty fist. "All you are is anger and nothing else." She held the bottle up as if to throw it. "And I won't let you ruin our lives anymore."

"You better remember who's in charge here, Penelope," her father said, his tone darker than she'd ever heard.

"You think you're strong when really, you're weak," she told him, sounding braver than she felt. The girl's chest heaved with each breath. "All you care about is your drink and the money you don't have, and it *controls* you." She threw the bottle over the railing, watching it fall to the first floor, watching it shatter into a hundred pieces as amber liquid splashed everywhere.

"You'll regret that." Her father's hand lashed out, grasping punishingly onto her bicep. He pushed the girl toward the stairs, but she caught herself before the first step could claim her.

She moved away from the stairway as her father grabbed her shoulder and stumbled forward on drunken feet, the momentum making them twist until they switched spots. Her father let go of her and pulled an arm back, fingers curling into a fist. But the girl ducked and threw her hands out to protect herself. And she felt her father's chest under her palms. Felt fear take control of her. And she felt her fingers press against the resistance of his body, felt them push until only air touched them and her father was tipping backward.

His arms waved in the air, one hand slapping against the wall for purchase where there was none. Until that first step took him, slowly at first and then down the rest too fast. He rolled and crashed as bones cracked and moaning cries were pulled from his lips. A blink, and he was at the bottom of the stairs. He lay crumpled against the wall, his chest unmoving and eyes unseeing as the girl stared down in horror even as her mind darkened and hid the memory of that night from her.

THIRTY-THREE

P enny?" a voice calls, and at first, I think it's Mom—or the memory of her calling my name from that night, lingering in my head. But I blink and blink until Harper's face comes into view, the summer sun shining behind her. "Penny, what just happened?"

"I…" I remember the night my father died. I never like to dwell on it. Every time I do, the memories are hazy—fuzzy. It isn't like the blank absence of my past being stolen by shadow man but more…like it was pushed down. *The brain tries to protect*, Ms. Evans said before. And it did, trying to save me from an unwanted truth.

I told myself that my father fell down on his own, but…I pushed him. He grabbed me, and I killed him. Too many emotions clog my throat. Guilt sinks heavy in my stomach, but interlaced is also shame—shame at the relief and freedom I still feel with his death, even now, knowing it was my fault.

I didn't mean to shove him. It wasn't anger that made me do it. Not like my father, whose rage was always the reason he put his hands on us. I only wanted to get away from him. To protect Mom.

Push her, that voice says again, but this time I stop to listen to it. Not to follow its orders, but to hear it—the tone, the cadence. It's less my father's and more...mine. *You could do it*, it adds, and I could.

But I won't. Because that voice isn't really my father's twisted memory infecting me. It's mine, lighter and higher in pitch as it speaks to me. It's *my* thoughts and feelings. Not his.

That voice in my head whispers all the things I *could* do, if I were to follow my father's footsteps. But I should stop thinking of it as a demand for violence and more of a manifestation of my fears. Think of it as a *warning* telling me what I'm capable of—so I can do the opposite. So I can choose to *not* be like my father.

When I pushed him down the stairs, it wasn't on purpose or premeditated. It was to save Mom and myself. When I gave in to the voice and attacked the shadow man, it was to protect myself again but also Kylie and Harper.

It's as if gravity shifts under my feet, leaving me off-balance before righting itself again—a change in my perspective, so simple yet so hard to get here. But now that I see it, I can breathe easier than I have in too long. Because there is a difference between my father and me, a gulf so wide I could never cross it. My father was fueled by anger and resentment, and he took it out on my mom and me—the people closest to him. But my motives have always been to protect—*not* hurt—the people I care about.

"Penny? Are you okay?" Harper asks again, pulling me back from realizations that make my legs shake as much as they make me feel…better.

"I'm fine. Sorry. Everything's been…a lot."

"I know that was hard for you," Harper says, glancing back to the lodge. "Using that stick and protecting me. And Kylie," she says instead of describing how I attacked the shadow man. "I wanted to say thank you."

"You don't have—"

"No, I do." Harper takes my hand in hers. "Even if I don't know everything about your situation, I know that was huge for you. You're so strong. Brave," she adds, and I wonder if she can see the change I feel in myself.

I don't know how to respond, so I only nod, and she gives my hand a soft, reassuring squeeze before we turn back to the shed, knowing we can't waste any more time.

I unlock the shed, pushing the door open. A dark maw opens to us, and Harper follows me inside. It takes a moment for my eyes to adjust, to find the pull string for a light bulb that hangs from the center of this small space. The light flashes on, and I blink against the brightness until it settles into a soft golden glow around us.

The shed is tight, smaller than even a third of our cabin, and packed with shelves and all sorts of tools. One wall has a pegboard with two axes and a hatchet hanging on them, along with a Weedwacker, rakes, and a couple shovels. Fishing gear and extra archery targets lean against one corner. Broken arrows are piled haphazardly in a bin at the very back. The other wall has an assortment of bows and quivers hanging from another pegboard.

Take them. Those thoughts filter through my mind as I stare at the weapons. *Gut her. Stab her.* Again, I take a moment to stop and hear what they're really saying. To not just flinch in fear from them. The voice is softer, taking on more of my tone than my father's gravelly depths. *Watch her bleed.*

No, I tell those thoughts, but it isn't a plea this time. The word seeps calmly through my mind, full of my own command. I let those intrusive thoughts become a warning instead of a demand. They can show me what is possible—what any person is capable of if they let themselves become the kind of monster my father turned into. But they also show me exactly how different I am from him.

My father died because of his own choices and actions. Even if it was my hands that pushed him, it was only out of protection.

I spent too long believing his violence infected me, that it filled my blood and my thoughts. But I am not my father's daughter— and I never have been.

You could do it. The voice tries one more time, softer but not gone.

Enough, I tell it, coaxing that creature inside me to sleep. *Enough.* The voice fades, curling into the back of my mind. My father thought he was strong when really he was weak.

I'm tired of believing I'm weak when really I've been strong all this time.

"Come on," I tell Harper. My hands only shake a little when I grab one ax off the wall, knowing now that I'd never hurt Harper with it. "We should get what we need and go."

She nods and plucks a smaller hatchet off the wall and picks up some of the quivers full of arrows.

There's still a monster trying to hunt us. A creature stealing our memories. And we might need to stop it on our own.

Good or bad, my memories are *mine*. Not something to be taken away, even if I wished for that before—even if my own mind tried to protect me in that same way too.

And maybe I don't want to dwell on every terrible moment of my life or remember everything about my father—but that's my choice to make. Already, I can feel the edges of certain memories turn to smoke, blanks spots that I can't keep in my grasp. Memories stolen by the shadow man that I don't know if I'll ever get back.

But for better and for worse, my past has made me who I am. And that creature doesn't get to decide what memories I get to keep and what I forget. I am a collection of it all—a constellation of all my hopes and desires, of my memories and history, of my choices then and now, and for the future. Together, they shape who I've become and who I will be. And I won't let some monster take that away. I won't let him steal pieces and parts of my life anymore.

"Let's go," I grab two longbows off the wall and hook them on my shoulder as Harper hefts the larger ax off its hooks. We make out way out of the small shed. Those intrusive thoughts are blessedly soft in the back of my mind, even as I carry weapons we might need to use against a monster made from our literal fears.

"Is everyone ready?" Delaney asks. Her eyes rake over Harper and me as we get back to the group. They stand on the grassy lawn where we left Emma and Kylie, far enough from the flagpole so we don't have to stare at the blood staining the ground.

"Yeah, I think we got enough," Harper says, juggling three quivers full of arrows looped onto one shoulder. She carries an ax and a small hatchet in each hand, while I have another ax and the longbows—and no voice in my head yelling at me to hurt anyone right now.

Delaney reaches out to help grab some of the weapons. She takes the three bows, but I keep the ax.

"See anything in there?" My gaze darts to the main building, only a dozen yards away. It's quiet. No flashes of movement in those dark windows. No hint of the shadow man.

But it's only a matter of time before it wakes up and finds a way out. We need to leave.

Harper sets her ax and hatchet on the ground before slipping the quivers off her shoulder and holding them out for someone to take. "I don't really know how to use a bow. I think someone else should take them."

"I will." Emma grabs a quiver and slips it over her head, letting the strap fall diagonally across her chest, but with her backpack on, it sits closer to her side than her back. "I've done archery before. I'm not a bad shot."

"Me too," Delaney says, taking a quiver for herself and wearing it the same way.

"Do you think…?" Harper looks at the weapons before turning to the lodge. "Do you really think we'll have to fight that thing? Kill it?"

"If we don't get out of here already, then yes," Delaney says.

But Kylie finally speaks up. "No," she says, and her smile is still there, soft and serene, light mauve lips across dark skin. And even if it's not the same grin that stretched Page's mouth too wide as the shadow man killed her, it still sends a skittering of unease down my back. "I've been trying to tell you," Kylie continues, "we're not in danger."

I look from Harper to Emma to Delaney, an unspoken conversation happening between us. Maybe it's better not to put a weapon in her hands if she won't use it. Still, we can't leave her completely unarmed in case whatever the shadow man did to her wears off and she realizes the gravity of our situation.

"Okay, no more wasting time," Delaney says. "We're leaving *now*. Grab a sleeping bag and strap it to your backpack, and let's go." There's a folded tent and sleeping bag attached to hers already, which is more of an actual hiking pack than the regular backpacks the rest of us have. Emma and Kylie already have sleeping bags hooked to theirs.

Emma helps Harper and me attach ours as Delaney slides one of the extra bows and quivers over Kylie's head. Harper slips her hatchet into some bungee cords that crisscross on the back of her bag before hefting it on. I grab my backpack, and the added weight of it digs into my shoulders as I pick my ax up again.

Delaney glances around the camp, taking a deep breath and letting it out slowly before nodding her head once, as if saying goodbye. "Follow me and stay close," she says, gripping her bow tight and leading us.

Emma carries her own bow and walks with Kylie, whispering something softly to the other girl. I grip my ax tight, knowing I'll only use it to protect these girls, not hurt them. Harper picks hers back up also, and together we trail behind Delaney.

We make our way across the lawn. Fluffy clouds cascade across a vivid blue sky. Warmth fills the air, not quite the blistering heat of midday yet.

Above our heads, the flag with Camp Whitewood's crest snaps awake in the breeze, and Emma flinches. The air carries the hint of silt and algae from the lake, of earthy loam and fresh growth from the forest—but there's also something else. Something foul that turns my stomach. A rancid stench that grows. It isn't until we pass the flagpole that I realize where the smell is coming from. Morning light shines down in bright rays and highlights the death-stained grass, marring the picturesque scene. But hidden among the grass is more than just blood. There are bits and pieces of...flesh. Of ripped muscle and chipped bone and torn organs that have all rotted in the last day. My stomach heaves, and I swallow down acid.

Harper follows my gaze, covering her mouth and nose with one hand. "Don't," she says, nudging me with her shoulder to look away.

I turn my attention to the girls in front of us, to the way their eyes also dart to the grassy lawn as we make our way between the cabins. We get to the edge of the birch forest and pause. It feels as though we take a collective breath before gripping our weapons a little tighter and stepping under the canopy of trees, leaving Camp Whitewood and all its horrors behind.

We get five steps in when an angry growl echoes from the camp, muffled by walls and windows and distance. Fear spreads in my veins, but I take a deep breath and hold the handle of my ax until my hands hurt, refusing to let anything else terrible happen to our group.

Together, we rush deeper into the forest, stumbling over sticks and underbrush. Delaney leads the way, glancing back to make sure we're all here, all safe. Emma holds Kylie's hand, urging the other girl to move faster. Kylie doesn't fight against Emma, but her steps are slow and calm, unlike the rest of ours.

Harper glances over at me. Her fingers clench around the wooden handle of her ax, and with her other hand, she takes mine, holding tightly.

THIRTY-FOUR

We walk for what feels like hours, for miles and miles through pale trees and shadow-stained woods, until even the marked paths we started on have left us. The sun filters through the canopy of leaves, sneaking in through cracks and openings until the forest is dappled with sunlight and mottled with shadows that flicker and move all around us. They make me twitch, checking out of the corner of my eye for anything amiss.

Every crunch of a stick or crumbling leaf has me flinching, hearing the phantom growl of the monster coming for us. Despite the minutes that trail behind us, the hours that carve our path through the forest, everything about me is still on high alert, heart fluttering too fast like moth wings, grip punishing around the handle of my ax.

"What was that?" Delaney asks, pausing at the front. She scans the woods, the sea of spindly white trees becoming more infiltrated with tall oaks, spiky pines, and dark maples the farther we go. She slips an arrow out of the quiver over her shoulder, the movement awkward from where it sits against her backpack.

She lifts her long bow up and notches the arrow, searching through the trees.

"What did you see?" I ask.

"There!" Emma says, pointing to the left.

"Is it the monster?" Harper lifts her ax.

A flash of movement. A blur.

Dark horns and a large shape.

The shadow man—but no. His horns were either small and glittery crimson or ram-like and oxblood red. And they disappeared when Page died.

Another streak of movement in front of us now. A dark smear of brown. Antlers?

"Where'd it go?" Delaney asks, and we all look around, turning in little circles, but it's gone.

We wait for a minute in hushed silence before Harper speaks. "A deer? I saw antlers."

"Too big." Delaney's eyes still search, but nothing moves.

"A moose?" Emma asks, taking another turning step and crunching a twig under her sneakers.

"They're not usually this far south, but it's not imposs—"

"No." The answer comes from Kylie. "No," she says again, voice edged in panic. Her smile is still in place, a ribbon from dimple to dimple, but for the first time since the shadow man attacked her in Ms. Peterson's room, there's fear too.

"No?" I hand my ax to Harper and move toward Kylie, hands raised as if approaching a wild animal. "What do you mean? It wasn't a deer?"

"Or a moose?" Emma asks again, her tone pleading for Kylie to agree with her.

"No," Kylie says, her eyes so wide that the dark brown of them is fully surrounded by white. She stares out at the woods. "Something else. Something *more*."

"More?" I rest a hand on her arm.

Her gaze flicks to me, sharp and sudden. "Something terrible." Her words are an omen spilling from her mouth, one that crawls down my throat and makes my stomach sink. I drop my hand and stumble back.

"Maybe…we should keep going," Delaney says, and I agree. I don't know what Kylie means, but nothing good will come from staying here.

Delaney looks around, realizing that we've all turned and twisted while searching the forest, that we've lost our direction. She puts her arrow back in the quiver and slings her bow over her other shoulder. From her pocket, she pulls out her compass, the one she used when the last of the marked trails curved back the way we came and we had to step off them.

"Wait…" Delaney says, staring down at the compass. "Huh?"

"What's going on?" I step over to Harper and take my ax when she offers it back.

"Something's wrong." Delaney holds the compass up. The arrow spins round and round. "It's not working."

Dun, dun, dun, a sound slips between the trees, a deep bass-filled thumping.

"What…is that?" Emma asks, staring up at the canopy of leaves as if she can pluck an answer from their branches.

The sound comes again, a melody following along. A twig snaps behind us, and I whirl around. My heart stutters and stops, crashes twice as fast, when the shadow man steps out from behind a thick tree trunk.

He's more shadows than skin again as he creeps across the forest floor, movements slow, teasing. Cloudy eyes stare out from a ski mask over his face. An orange dog leash trails from each wrist, writhing along the ground behind him. He holds a whiskey bottle, the amber liquid sloshing with his steps, in one hand. In the other is a metal baseball bat that digs a path into the dirt and leaves. My father's belt is around his waist, and at his feet, that ill-formed cat weaves around his ankles again, a papery rasping echoing with each of its movements.

Dun, dun, dun.

"Umm…is anyone else hearing that?" Emma takes a step back, away from where the shadow man slowly moves closer and closer.

"Yeah, but…what is it?" Delaney notches her bow again, pointing it toward the monster.

Dun, dun, dun.

"Is that a song?" My gaze darts to Harper as the shadow man's hunched form straightens, standing taller.

Harper's head shakes, dark hair slipping over her backpack, as her hands tremble. The blade of her ax and the silver of her ring both catch a fleck of sunlight, glinting sharply.

And another one gone.

"Shit," Harper says. "It's mine. It's my memory."

And another one.

"You've gotta be kidding me," Delaney says, lifting her bow and taking aim.

And another one gone.

"Absolutely not. I'm not dying to *this* song," Delaney adds, letting her arrow fly, not seeing the way Harper flinches at her words.

Dun, dun, dun.

The arrow flies through the air, a sharp whistle in my ear. But the shadow man darts to the side, and it only slices his arm. Dark blood flows from it, matching the dried stain on his head. The creature roars, pain and anger saturating the sound.

The song grows louder, seeming to come from everywhere at once. It's joined by the staticky voice of Emma's nightmare.

Who's there? The words crackle around us. *Who's there?*

"Run!" Delaney shouts as the shadow man lunges, racing across the distance between us. The paper cat takes off after Emma, hissing and showing sharp claws.

Emma and Harper run behind me. But Kylie doesn't move. She only waits for the shadow man to come to her—to kill her.

"Penny!" Harper shouts, her footsteps getting louder, coming back. "Come on!"

But I can't. I can't lose anyone else. I rush in front of Kylie.

And another one gone.

I *won't* lose anyone else. I shove Kylie to the side. She stumbles and falls to the hard ground.

And another one.

I grip the ax until my fingers hurt, knuckles going white.

And another one gone.

The shadow man's growls are so loud they rumble through my body. Closer and closer, he rushes toward me. His dead stare pins me in place.

Who's there? that staticky voice asks again. The bat and bottle disappear from his hands as the shadow man lunges, replaced with claws that rake through the air toward my chest. *Who's there?*

"I am," I say and swing my ax, protecting both myself and Kylie. Protecting Harper and Emma and Delaney too. "And I'm not afraid of you!"

An earsplitting whine slices through the forest, and the shadow man drops to the ground. Sticky blood sprays across my torso and splatters to the forest floor. It pours out of the gash in the creature's forearm. He howls and curls in on himself, his form flipping through masks and bodies again.

"No!" Kylie shouts. She runs over, hovers above him as if she can help.

"Get back," Harper says, stopping at my side. She takes Kylie's arm and pulls the girl away.

"Stop!" Kylie screams as I lift my ax again, ready to end this for good. "She doesn't want to hurt us!"

Her words stop me, make me pause long enough for the monster to start crawling away on hands and knees. But an arrow whizzes past, close enough that I gasp. It slams into the creature's shoulder and another long whine splits the air.

"Wait," I yell, holding up one hand, my ax too heavy in the other. I turn to Kylie. "What do you mean *she*? Who do you see when you look at the creature?" Even though the monster doesn't look like Delaney's sister right now, I still ask, "Does she have blond hair? A white dress?"

"No, she has brown hair." Kylie glances from me to the monster. It leaves a trail of blood as it drags itself slowly away. "You don't see her?"

The creature is a shadow-stained mixture of all our nightmares. It has Sadie's pale eyes, clouded in death, but it's definitely *not* a girl.

I shake my head. "What is it you see?"

"It's a girl," Kylie says, voice barely more than a whisper. "And she's sad. She's so, so sad."

"What?" I say, but I'm not really asking. My gaze is stuck on the shadow man—on the different forms he flips through again. Each time the creature is hurt, it seems like it can't hold on to one image. First, Kylie's frail mom, and then Delaney's water-drenched sister. The man in a ski mask and the older woman in hiking gear. The shadow man of my nightmares.

Then—a girl. So quick I could blink and miss it. A girl with pale skin and brown eyes that match her long hair.

A girl I've seen before but only in pictures—from a photo sitting in Ms. Evans's office.

"C-Clara?" the name stutters out of Delaney. It bounces off the trees and vibrates all around. "Did you guys see her?"

"I told you," Kylie says, "it's not a monster. It's a girl. A sad girl."

The creature's form switches again, flickering like candlelight. Is it another trick of the monster? Another memory to torment us? Clara is dead. It can't be her.

"Help," the creature says, wearing Clara's face in the space of another blink. She lies on the ground, gripping under her shoulder where the arrow hit. The paper cat that was chasing Emma before now crawls over to Clara—to the monster—curling into a ball at her neck and meowing. "Help," she says again, and the single word fills my stomach with heaviness.

Then her image is gone, replaced with the man in the ski mask, lying in the dirt and leaves.

Who's there? that same deep voice that crackled through the satphone asks.

The old woman, empty orange leash and dirt-stained hiking clothes.

Dun, dun, dun, the bass-filled thumps of Harper's song drum as hard as my heart.

Kylie's frail mother, looking wholly out of place with medical tubes over her face.

Soon, soon, soon, those mechanical beeps scream again.

Delaney's sister—death-clouded eyes staring at us while water pours from her mouth.

Another one gone.

The shadow man, no face or features to him. Only darkness and that half-empty bottle clutched in his injured arm.

And another one gone.

The words overlap, the song, the voice, and the beeping all scream louder and louder until they are a cacophony of noise and pain, coming from everywhere and nowhere.

The monster's form switches again, and it's Clara, large brown eyes staring up at us, tears streaming down her cheeks. She lets go of her injured arm, hand painted in blood too dark, and points to the forest behind us.

"It's…coming," she says before collapsing and turning into a combination of all of our nightmares once more.

CLARA

One night changed everything for the girl. One night that ended in disaster and death.

The girl's father drove his family home after visiting aunts, uncles, and cousins. Having dinner and drinks and playing games. But the girl's father didn't drink, knowing the long drive home he'd have to take. He celebrated the New Year with his family and then packed them all up to go home.

But that didn't stop others from drinking at their own parties, from being reckless and uncaring as they got in their cars.

It didn't stop one stranger from drifting across the road.

The girl was dozing off in the back seat beside her older brother when the world crashed and crunched and broke apart. When the scream of tires mixed with her own and with her mother's. The car didn't tilt or flip. It collapsed inward with a bone-breaking impact. The girl flew forward in her seat, her belt yanking her back, bruising her chest, as a shower of glass flew through the air, catching the glint of yellow streetlights and red brake lights and the glaring green of the stoplight in front of them until unconsciousness took over.

"Mom?" the girl said, opening blurry eyes and blinking away the dizziness and darkness that had claimed her. "Dad?"

They didn't answer.

The girl touched her head, hissing at the pain. Blood trickled down her temple and slicked her hand. She turned to her brother.

"Logan?" she asked, almost too afraid to whisper his name. His body was slumped to the side, head hanging forward. Blood painted the window next to him while fissures and cracks spiderwebbed across the glass.

The girl's mother groaned and slowly lifted her head. She looked to her daughter with unfocused eyes.

"Clara?" she mumbled. "Are you okay?"

"I think so," the girl said, trying to ignore the sickening spinning of her head. "Dad? Logan?" she called again, but no answers came. No waking groans or panicked questions.

"Logan?" the girl asked one more time. She shook her brother's shoulder. His body slumped lower. An empty airbag sat deflated at his side, dusty white and drenched in too much blood.

"Dad!" she shouted, turning to him as the sounds of sirens screamed through the night. Her hand wavered over her father, unable to touch his unmoving form. A crack split his forehead, too deep and too wide. Blood poured down his face, over his brown eyes, which always smiled at the girl. It soaked his shirt, turning from pale blue to deep scarlet.

The girl's father didn't wake up. Her brother didn't open his eyes. Not when the paramedics came and helped the girl and her mother out of the car. Not when they carried the other driver away. Not when bystanders wouldn't stop staring and the stoplight flashed from green to yellow to red, round and round again.

By the end of the night, the girl's entire world had changed. Her father and brother gone. Only her mother left sitting beside her.

———————

And then another night changed everything for the girl again. A night spent speaking sorrows and secret hopes to a forest better left alone. To creatures better left unspoken to.

But the girl wasn't from the forest. She didn't know the whispers and the rules.

She didn't know to never wander the woods at night, especially on her own. To never speak your wishes out loud to the creatures that lived there. To never whistle in the forest or look to the trees.

Because you might call the creatures to you, dark and terrible things that will eat you, bind you, bury you. If you call to the shadows of the forest, they will gladly answer in such terrible ways.

The girl had been brought to the camp with her mother, was meant to heal here. She'd spent months in a dark place, in dark thoughts and memories that plagued her. And her mother's work was to help people like that.

But the girl knew this camp wasn't the answer her mother wished it would be. She didn't want to relive that night, to talk about it with anyone. So the girl had left, snuck away in the night with her backpack and bag. She would walk to town, no matter how far, and then…she didn't know. She only knew she needed some space away from her mother's camp.

"I don't want to talk about it," she whispered to the night. "I don't want to share that story ever again."

The girl shook her head, swallowing down the words she wanted to scream. She wanted to forget that night. But she couldn't—and she couldn't bring herself to beg for it either. Instead, she took a deep breath, and she trudged on. She whistled to herself, a tune her father used to sing to her as a child. A song that made her feel not so alone in these dark woods.

But the girl wasn't alone.

And she froze when she realized it.

A large shape slid out from behind a tree, its form hunkering and large. It stood like a man, on two feet—and yet it was anything but human. It loomed tall, twice the size of the girl, with thick antlers that reached for the branches above. A bone-bleached skull, long and narrow, sat where a face should be.

The girl stumbled, tripping backward in her haste to get away. She crawled on the ground, clawed at the dirt. But it didn't matter. The creature took large steps as it whistled her song back at her, a twisted mimicry that set the girl's teeth on edge.

The creature pointed to her, a spindly finger with one too many knuckles.

You will never have to talk about it again, little thing, the creature told her, but the words didn't come from its mouth. They thundered in the girl's head.

Before she could object—could take back the words she'd whispered to the forest—pain split her skull, and the world went dark. The stars snuffed out, and the pale trees disappeared. Her body stretched and constricted, felt all wrong. She was being twisted inside out, altered and remade.

And then the world exploded around her again, burning stars and blinding white trees. A cold ground and a sharp breeze. She glanced around, found herself still in the woods. She watched as the creature crowned in antlers turned away. It glided through the forest as its laugh echoed in her mind.

The girl knew she was something different—changed.

Something wrong.

A creature of the forest now.

She stood up, as ungainly as a newborn fawn, as her form stretched and tightened, trying to recall what it used to be. She thought of her mother, despair filling the girl's chest. And suddenly she was her mother. Her taller height and longer limbs.

As quickly as it came, the girl's body changed again. Unable to settle on her own face, flipping through memories and taking the forms of others. Panic filled the girl, and she fled, leaving her bags behind, searching for a place to hide what she'd become.

But agony twisted her stomach. She wasn't just a creature of the forest now. She was a monster that hungered.

A creature that craved fear, that drank memories soaked in sorrow.

And she was powerless against the need to find and devour them.

THIRTY-FIVE

I creep closer to the shadow man, to the creature that is a smattering of our memories come alive. Is it really Clara or another trick of the monster?

It lies on the ground, covered in dirt, leaves, and twigs, blood dripping down its shoulder. Milky eyes stare, blinking slowly and watching as I stand over the creature.

Who's there? The question bounces around.

"Penny," I answer, not sure if that's what it wants. If what I'm doing is stupid and reckless.

"Pennnn…" the monster starts, "ellll…opeeeee."

"No," I say. "Just Penny."

"Pennnn…" The single syllable is a growl rumbling up his throat. "Eeeeeee."

"Clara?" I lean down, trying to see a hint of the girl that might be under this monster's mask. Those death-shrouded eyes flicker to brown and back again, quicker than a breath. "Are you…Clara?"

"Don't!" Harper yells as I touch the monster that has been tormenting us. My hand rests on his forearm, and the world is a starburst, a supernova of exploding light. Images and memories flip like flash cards in my mind.

The glare of yellow, red, and green lights. The same colors and flashing brightness I saw before when the creature touched me. Of glowing yellow streetlamps and burning red brake lights and the vivid green of a traffic signal. All three colors caught and trapped within the glass of a shattered windshield.

More memories that don't belong to me pour into my mind.

Of Clara leaving camp and walking at night through the woods alone.

Of a creature that feels ancient and terrifying finding her. Changing her into something like itself. Something dark and dangerous and *hungry*.

More images flicker by. Clara, going back to camp but unable to hold on to her form. Feeling everyone's memories and fears around her, overwhelming and uncontrollable. Tempting. She fed on her mother's fear. Nearly killed her. So Clara pushed new memories into her mother's head, false ones, to fake her death and keep her mother from searching for her. And then she ran. Back to the woods and the isolation she'd hoped for.

Still hungry and starving and empty. But as she stayed away, she found a place to sleep, to keep herself from truly becoming the monster she'd changed into.

Until a group of girls, filled with delicious fear, woke her from hibernation—woke older creatures that had fallen into slumber also. Their fear was too enticing for her, for the famished beast inside.

More memories seep in with a pain that makes my skull throb.

Reagan in the woods, killed by the monster Clara had become. Sam and Quinn.

Clara, a creature out of control. Begging us to listen—to hear the words she couldn't say. Clara, satiating her hunger with our fear.

Telling us to run to safety. To stay and be eaten.

Clara killing the women that wanted to let her prey get away— Ms. Peterson and her own mother.

Clara screaming, a beast and a girl fighting within herself.

"Penny!" I hear my name shouted as I'm yanked back. I blink, and the world comes into focus. Harper holds my arm, pulling me from the monster—from Clara. "Are you okay?" Harper asks, gasping and out of breath.

"Yeah," I tell her. "I'm fine."

"You looked like you were having a seizure."

"You were right. It's not a monster. It's Clara," I say, turning to Kylie, who nods. I shift my gaze to Delaney. "She didn't die—she changed."

"How?" is all Delaney asks, but it's too much—too confusing—to explain.

"It doesn't matter right now." I look down at my empty hands, wondering where my ax went. "She's not in control. She's more monster than person."

"Then let's kill it," Emma says. She rushes forward, picking up my ax from where I must have dropped it next to the shadow man—next to Clara. She raises it, and the sunlight glints off the sharp blade.

"No!" Kylie shouts at the same time I do. The creature whines and tries to get away, but she's too injured to do more than crawl.

"We can't kill it—her," I say. "She's still…in there."

"Then what do we do?" Harper asks. "If we leave, won't it follow us?"

"Kill," a voice says, soft and strained, and when I turn around, the creature flickers with Clara's form. She flashes between bodies, becoming one person after another too quickly to tell the difference. "Kill it," she says, clinging to her own face. She raises her bloodstained hand, pointing with one finger. "It's here," she says and collapses, unconscious. I startle when the papier-mâché cat, still cuddled against her neck, disappears in a puff of shadows. Her form switches back to the mingling of our memories again but doesn't move.

"What?" Delaney asks, turning around to search the woods. "Kill what?"

"The real monster," I say. Some ancient and eldritch creature that found Clara in a forest no one should go into.

A forest *we* are in.

My eyes skip from one spot to the next. From oak trees to maple and pine to a few remaining birch trees, with their knotted eyes that stare back. Mottled light and shadows dance among the woods, making it look as if everything is moving.

"There!" Harper says, pointing to the right. "What is that?"

A dark shape slips out from behind a thick tree. The creature from Clara's memory. It's twice my height, even hunched over. Thick, heavy antlers crown a head—a skull. There's no skin on the thing's face. Only bleached bone, narrow and long, with empty eye sockets that somehow still see us. Brown fur covers an emaciated body, and while it walks on two legs, its feet end in hooves, and its hands are large, fingers too long.

A sharp whistle darts between the trees, curving and curling into a tune, coming from the creature.

The trees scream. Don't listen to them—my grandmother's warning echoes in my head, and I wonder if she knew they also whistled. If she knew what monsters hid within the woods. Her phantom words mix with Clara's memory, with how the girl's tune called to the forest, to the creature.

"Don't whistle back," I tell the others, not sure exactly what doing that would mean but not wanting to risk becoming like Clara either.

"Umm…I wasn't planning to!" Emma shouts, her voice edging into hysterical.

"Don't talk to it either," I say. Clara spoke, words only to herself, but the forest heard her—*it* heard her. And it twisted her wish into a nightmare.

"Maybe we stop saying what we *shouldn't* do," Emma says, slipping an arrow out of her quiver, "and figure out what we *should* do." She notches the arrow and aims.

"Kill it," Kylie says, and I agree, knowing deep within me that this creature will kill us or turn us into monsters like Clara.

Emma looses her arrow, and it flies through the air, straight toward the creature. But it darts to the side, too fast, and her arrow bounces off a tree.

I rush toward the shadow man—to Clara—and grab my ax. A burst of air hits my cheek as Harper screams my name. I twist, ready to slice my blade, but stop when I see Harper standing before me. I yank my ax away, let it drop from my hands, horrified at almost hurting her.

Kylie snatches my ax off the ground. She moves quickly, carving the blade through the air. It slams into Harper, cutting through flesh and bone as a spray of blood hits me.

"NO!" The scream rips out of my throat and tears me apart as I watch Harper collapse to the ground. Blood gurgles and bubbles out of her mouth. Her skin goes pale, her eyes glaze over, and everything in me is splitting apart and dying right along with her.

THIRTY-SIX

et away!" someone shouts, and I swear it sounds like
Harper, but she's at my feet. Dead.

I push Kylie away and collapse next to Harper's body.

Only, there's something wrong with Harper. There's no silver
ring on her hand, and her eyes are too light, not a brown so dark
they're almost black like my own. Even her curves and weight are
wrong, her face too thin and the plumpness of her stomach larger—
though I can't tell if that's from the ripped-open wound or not.

Something crashes into me, and I'm thrown sideways. All the
air is pushed out of me as someone falls on top of my chest. But
I don't care about the pain filling my ribs or the dirt in my lungs,
because Harper is there. Alive.

"Come on," she says, scrambling up and pulling me along. She
snatches her ax from where she dropped it. "It wasn't me."

I look back to where I thought she died. In her place is that ancient creature, one sharp-clawed hand swiping at the space where I was standing.

The monster climbs to its feet, and there's a slash across its stomach, but it's shallow, nothing like the image I saw on Harper. Blood trickles out of the wound, thick and sticky, dark and oozing like tar.

The creature laughs, a sound like scraping bark, and turns away from Harper and me. Its long deerlike legs carry it across the forest floor and to Emma faster than I could run. Emma already has another arrow ready. It flies into the creature's chest, knocking the monster back on stumbling feet, but it doesn't stop it from coming for her. The arrow doesn't pierce its heart.

No, these arrows are meant for novices learning archery at camp, not for hunting. They aren't sharp enough to stab through thick hide. And that's what the creature has, pelt like an animal, coarse brown fur and leathery skin. The creature rips the arrow out as if it were nothing more than an irritating splinter.

It lumbers forward and slices a clawed hand at Emma, and my throat is raw from my scream.

Emma holds the bow up like a shield, but the creature's nails saw through, wood and string falling to the ground. She drops what's left and steps back, staring up and up and up at the skeletal face of the monster.

"Emma, move!" Delaney says, holding her own bow up, arrow ready except for Emma, who stands in the path. She darts to the side, but the arrow misses, and Delaney curses. She tries yanking another out of her quiver, but her hiking pack is too large, and the remaining arrows spill to the ground.

"Help her!" I shout at Kylie, who still holds my ax. She stands behind Delaney, next to the unconscious Clara creature. I want to scream at Kylie to wake up, to move! There's no way we'll all survive if we don't work together.

"No, no, no," Delaney says, dropping to the ground, frantically pawing around to pick an arrow up.

The creature moves closer to Emma, and I rush over, ripping my ax out of Kylie's hands as I pass, but Emma is too far. Yards away. I trip on sticks and underbrush.

"Watch out," Harper shouts, running behind me. I feel her catch my backpack, but it doesn't stop me from falling. The bag slips down my shoulders, and Harper is knocked off-balance. We slam to the forest floor, sticks and rocks digging into my hands as I try to cushion my fall and hold on to the ax.

"Get back!" Emma screams. She holds her necklace up toward the creature. She flips the lid and presses down. A fine mist sprays toward the monster's face, and when the pepper spray sputters out, Emma backs away.

Another laugh, dry and scraping up the monster's throat.

Emma drops her necklace. "One chance, Emma!" she shouts at herself. "And I use it on an animal man with no eyes?!" She stumbles back, but another sound replaces the creature's laugh—a rattling cough.

"No eyes," Emma shouts, pointing at the monster in victory, "but try breathing with pepper spray in your throat!"

"Emma!" I yell. "Get away from it!"

"Oh, right. " She backs up, ready to run but pauses when the creature changes. Its form shrinks down until someone else is standing before her, gasping air that brings the hint of capsaicin my way.

And it's me—or it *looks* like me—choking on pepper spray in front of Emma. Tears trail down my—its—cheeks, face turning red.

Only the silver of my doppelgänger's hair is more of an ash gray, and the skin a shade too pale.

This creature isn't like Clara, who uses our memories to make us see things and turn into people. This creature mimics those it sees. But not quite right. As if sketching a drawing without the source material—despite me standing here.

"Why Emma?" Not-me says, the voice a perfect match from an imperfect copy, even with its breaths still wheezing. My duplicate reaches forward, fingers stretching out to Emma as her gaze darts between me and Not-me. "Help me," it begs her.

She hesitates long enough for the false copy to lash out, to grab her by the neck and choke her too.

"No!" I yell, running toward her, fingers aching from the grip on my ax. Harper drops her backpack and follows, holding her own weapon up as the creature throws Emma. She slams to the ground, her face a startling shade of red as she gulps down air.

Harper and I split apart, each taking a side of my duplicate. But as we swing our axes out toward the creature, it changes again, growing taller and wider until it's wearing its true form, long arms easily shoving us back before our blades can cut it.

I crash into a thick tree trunk, and my ax flies from my hands, landing four feet away with a heavy thud. Harper cries out as she falls, her ax nearly slicing into her calf as it drops and slides away, skittering across dead leaves and pine needles.

The monster turns to Harper, its body growing smaller until Delaney is standing there—another copy. Imperfect again. Her hair a light brown instead of blond, and her face longer and less rounded.

"Why are you doing this?" Harper asks. Her voice shakes like the leaves that quiver in the treetops. She searches the ground for her ax, one hand flailing over sticks, dirt, and forest litter. Her fingers touch the handle.

"Please. Please don't hurt me. Please," Doppelgänger Delaney begs, the words wheezing out of the creature. Its steps start to falter, its breathing turning into an almost grating whistle because of Emma's pepper spray.

"That's *my* face!" the real Delaney shouts. She holds her arms above her head, and something flashes in her hands, silver and sharp. She throws her arms forward and releases the hatchet that was tucked into Harper's backpack.

The weapon flies through the air, end over end in a brilliant arc, before striking the other Delaney, burying into her shoulder and collarbone. Muscles and ligaments split apart. Bones stick out, and dark blood pours from the wound as the creature rips the hatchet out of its shoulder and drops it to the ground.

A roar shakes the trees, cutting off into a rattling cough that makes the creature slam one hand into a tree trunk, the sound louder than anything I've ever heard—ever felt—as wood splinters apart. It echoes in my bones, the very marrow of my being, and I worry it can't be killed—that we've only angered it.

Bones crack and vertebrae grow more pronounced as the monster shifts back to its true self, taller and taller. Its roar turns to a rattling growl, breaths coming in shallow gasps through a skeletal face. It stares at Harper on the ground, slowly inching her ax closer, before shifting its gaze to Emma, still swallowing air from a bruised throat, and then to Delaney, standing yards away as her arms drop to her sides. Its attention slides to Clara, the creature she's become, and then to Kylie, still standing nearby as if ready to protect her.

And then its stare turns to where I'm pressed against the rough bark of a tree with my ax too far to reach, too close to Clara.

The antlered monster staggers toward Harper. Each rib sticks out sharply from a chest covered in hide, and with each stumbling step, its breaths grow more labored. Terror crowds my throat as the creature moves closer to Harper, but the sight of it weakening gives me hope. And even with the hatchet wound, I'm not sure this thing would be losing strength if it weren't for Emma's pepper spray.

I start to creep toward my ax—to end this horror for good—but another groan stops me. It doesn't come from the towering monster but the thing Clara has become. She shifts on the ground, waking up as her image flips through the masks from our nightmares again.

My legs tremble as I take one slow step after another, trying to reach my ax before Monster-Clara can, before the skeletal deer creature gets too close to Harper.

I reach for the handle, but Clara snatches it first. Not the shadowy creature she's become, but her—Clara the girl. Her face and body flicker, staticky and grainy, as if it takes all her energy to keep hold of her true self.

"Help me"—her breath is labored and blood trails down her shoulder, where an arrow still sits—"kill it."

I don't let doubt stop me. Not when the real monster lurches toward Harper.

Harper scrambles back and swipes her ax in a wide arc, raking it through the air in front of her. The blade catches on the creature's leg, digging deep even as the ax is yanked from Harper's grip. The creature staggers back—toward the flickering version of Clara and me—and rips the ax out of its skin before throwing it deep into the woods with a roar.

"Kill it," Clara shouts, her voice as grainy as her image.

I grab one of the monster's arms and jerk it back, its hoofed feet stumbling over rocks and twigs. Emma jumps up, snagging the monster's other wrist, pulling hard as Harper springs forward.

She lunges, driving her shoulder into the creature's sliced-open stomach. Delaney rushes over as the monster falls like a rotted tree, hard and heavy and taking us down with it. Harper grabs its legs, pinning them down, careful to avoid its sharp hooves, as Delaney grips the monster's antlers, holding its head in place while it growls and gasps for air.

"Now what?" Emma asks, eyes darting from one girl to the next. Harper climbs to her feet, about to raise her bloodied ax again, when something else slashes down. Delaney lets out a scream and covers her head, forgetting to hold down the monster with us—but it doesn't matter. A spray of blood flies up, and I flinch, closing my eyes against the warm liquid as a heavy *thunk* rattles my teeth.

When I look up, Clara—face flickering—is standing above us, chest heaving. She stares down at the monster, a look of relief washing across her face right before she collapses into an unconscious pile at the head of the skeletal monster.

At the *detached* head of the monster.

An ax is buried in the ground, separating the creature's antlered skull from its body as its thick blood soaks the earth.

THIRTY-SEVEN

A stillness fills the forest. A silence. Everything hushed and unmoving, as if afraid. As if the death of a god has just been witnessed, and now even the trees and wind, the insects and animals don't know how to breathe.

"Are we...alive?" Delaney asks, shattering the stillness. "Is everyone okay?"

"Well, not *everyone*," Emma says, sitting back and staring at the monster and its severed head. "Oh no, I think I'm gonna be sick." She swallows hard but doesn't throw up.

"Is it over? Can we finally get out of here?" Harper asks. She's covered in dirt and that tar-black blood.

A moan rumbles out of Clara, and she stirs, sitting up and rubbing her head. We all watch, waiting to see her face change—to flick between our nightmares once more.

But her image doesn't shift. She doesn't project our fears back at us.

She's solid, human and nothing more.

Her gaze trips over her bare feet, her legs, and a pair of tattered shorts. She stares at her arms and the scraps of a shirt too dirty to even tell what color it originally was. Her skin is coated in dirt too but no longer shadow stained. She lifts one hand, touching her cheeks and feeling her face, while the arm from her injured shoulder—an arrow still sticking out—hangs heavy at her side.

"Am I...me?" she asks, wide brown eyes begging us to say yes.

"Yeah," Delaney says, reaching out for Clara and gently helping her stand. But Clara collapses against Delaney, sobs racking her body as our surviving counselor wraps her arms around one side of the girl and holds her, careful to avoid the arrow Emma put in her.

"I'm sorry," Clara mumbles into Delaney's shoulder. "I'm so sorry. I did..." A cry of agony wrenches itself from her, and whether it's emotional or from her injuries, I'm not sure. Maybe both. "I did so many terrible things. My mom. I killed—"

"It wasn't you," Delaney says, voice soothing and low. She runs a hand over Clara's hair, a sea of knots and tangles, but it seems to calm the girl. "*You* weren't yourself. We don't...we don't blame you."

Clara lifts her head, hesitantly looking at the rest of us. "I—I'm sorry. I didn't mean to. But then..." She gulps and pulls away from Delaney. "Your memories, they were all too much. Overwhelming. They were all I could hear. All I could see. Until I killed—" Another sob breaks her words apart. "And then, with each girl…the world went a little quieter. My hunger—the creature I was, its hunger—dimmed. I couldn't stop myself. I'm sorry. I'm so sorry."

I glance at the other girls. At Kylie, Emma, and Harper. All of us a little broken by our pasts but stronger than we could have ever known. While I'll never forgive my father, I can accept my past and know it doesn't control me. I can find a way to live my life without those memories and fears wrapping around me like chains.

And I hope the other girls can too.

"I'm sorry," Clara says one more time before her apologies turn to cries and Delaney mumbles soft words to her. She guides Clara away and starts grabbing things from her backpack—clean clothes, the first aid kit, and even some granola bars and a water bottle.

The rest of us get up, gathering our bags and giving Clara space. Emma helps Kylie stand, and I'm so relieved to see the creepy smile gone from her face that I could collapse all over again.

Harper takes my hand in hers, squeezing tight, and I never want to let her go.

"I thought you died," I say, the words pushing past a lump in my throat.

"I thought you were going to die," she says.

We stand there, letting the quiet wrap around us as I realize how close we all really did come to death today.

The sun still shines, sprinkling through the treetops in dazzling rays. A soft breeze rustles the leaves and cools my skin. Birds chirp again, and a gentle buzz of insects calls out through the woods. It's a sharp contrast to the blood and death at our feet.

"I'm glad you're okay," Harper finally says.

"Me too." A bubble of ridiculous laughter fizzes in my chest. "I'm glad you're alive too."

A bark of laughter bursts out of Harper, short and sharp. "Yeah," she says, "me too."

"Hey, so…" Emma glances from Harper and me to Delaney and Clara. "We're more than ready to leave," she says, pointing between herself and Kylie, who nods vigorously.

"Yes, please," Kylie adds.

"Can we get out of here already?" Emma asks.

"Definitely." Delaney hikes her bag onto her shoulders. She comes over to us, and Clara follows—now in clean clothes, wearing a pair of socks and sneakers, and eating a granola bar. The arrow is gone from her shoulder, and gauze bandages are wrapped around all her cuts and wounds.

"What are we going to tell people?" I ask, wondering how we could possibly explain any of this to the police.

"Bear attack?" Delaney says, shaking her head. "I don't know. We'll figure it out. First, we get out of here."

"B-before dark," Clara adds, her voice soft and whispering.

"Before dark," Kylie agrees, and we all nod, not eager to find out what other horrors the heart of this forest might hold.

"Let's go." I drop Harper's hand for a second and pick up my ax, my hand no longer shaking at holding it; I would never hurt any of these girls.

Harper grabs her hatchet, the ax she had long gone, and wipes thick blood off the blade. I take her hand in mine again, holding tight, and heft my ax up, resting it against my shoulder.

Exhaustion fills my body, but I push it away, glad to be able to feel the strain of my muscles, the heaviness of my breaths, and the drumming of my heart. To hear the crunching of leaves as the girls around me walk. As we make our way through the woods, more a family of survivors than simply friends. And together, we leave the monsters, but not our memories, behind.

EPILOGUE

My paintbrush drags across the canvas in front of me, trailing a pale blue over the stretched fabric. The shade is an exact match to the color of Sam's eyes. I spent nearly ten minutes perfecting it, adding a dab of phthalo blue and a heavy hand of pearlescent ivory onto my palette. I mixed them together with my paint spatula before adding a touch of dove white and the smallest dot of ultramarine. Another bit of pearl to lighten the shade even more.

"Are you still working on that?" Mom asks, stepping up behind me. She rests one hand on my shoulder, squeezing gently before letting go and smiling at me.

After I made it out of the forest with the other girls—exhausted and aching—we found the closest town, and Delaney took over explaining everything to the police. They labeled the deaths an animal attack, a strange incident, but we knew the authorities wouldn't believe us about the monster, so we kept quiet about it.

And in the days that followed, we were looked over by doctors and bandaged up, families were called, and each of us who survived had to give our own accounts to the police. We repeated the bear attack story Delany had given. They even sent rangers armed with tranquilizer guns to search the area, but of course they didn't find any deadly animals. Because the monster was with us, only now she was an emaciated girl with no family left.

Explaining a dead girl coming back to life was also hard, but Clara stuck with a story close to the truth, saying that she ran away for the year but came back to Whitewood to see her mom again. With everything else to figure out and explain to our families, the police didn't question her too deeply.

And if the rangers found the remains of that eldritch creature, they didn't tell us. Though I wouldn't doubt it if the forest claimed its body, scavengers picking it apart before the plants and ground swallowed it whole.

"Shouldn't Harper be here soon?" Mom asks, pulling my attention back to the here and now. She picks up some of the paint tubes and places them in their case on the little table next to me. Her hands flutter around my supplies, needing something to do—needing to help.

Mom still hovers, but it doesn't make me feel anxious or like I'm walking on glass like it used to. She doesn't hover because she's afraid I can't handle myself or my intrusive thoughts anymore, but because I almost didn't make it back to her. And I get it. Even if Mom doesn't know the *whole* truth, death was a lot closer than I want to admit even to myself, and I'm grateful to be home again—in a house that finally feels safe and full of love with her caring presence buzzing around me.

While I was gone, Mom even started to make a little corner of the dining room into an "art studio" for me. She set up my easel, in the corner that had the best lighting coming in from the windows, and spread a drop cloth on the wooden floors. She found a second-hand side table to organize and set my supplies on, hoping that when I came back from Whitewood I'd want to paint again; I might have cried a little at seeing the gift she'd set up—at seeing how she wanted to help and give me the things she couldn't before, when my father wouldn't let her.

"I just want to get this done." I glance at the clock across the kitchen and realize how late in the day it is. I pick up the paint spatula—before Mom can tuck all of my supplies away—so I can finish the painting.

Stab her, those intrusive thoughts say. **You could do it. Watch her bleed.**

Quiet, I say back and slice the metal blade of my spatula across part of the canvas instead, creating a line through that pale blue paint.

That voice is still in my head, in my own tone and cadence—not my father's any longer but not gone. And maybe my Harm OCD will never go away, maybe it's something that will always cling to me like a shadow, but now I trust myself enough to know it doesn't control me. I still see Mrs. Ashley and talk to her almost weekly, but fear doesn't fill me at hearing those thoughts in quite the same way it used to.

I've chosen to change my perspective on them. To look at those dark whisperings like a warning of what I—or anyone—could be capable of, rather than as a command. It doesn't mean I enjoy hearing those violent thoughts pop up, but I'm learning to live with how my Harm OCD affects me instead of letting it take over my life.

And part of that is painting again. Summer is almost over, I'm going back to my old school, and I'm woefully behind on having any recent projects to add to my portfolio to show colleges during my senior year.

But this painting…it isn't for my portfolio. It's for me. For Harper, Emma, and Kylie, for Delaney and Clara too.

"Well, you should probably hurry up, Penny." Mom puts the last cap back on my opened paints and sets it in the case. "You don't want to look all paint splattered when your girlfriend gets here," she says, her voice pitching higher with excitement. She looks at me, and her eyes sparkle with a happiness that has been absent too long in her life.

"Mom!" I drag the spatula through the paint one more time

before deciding it's finished and turn to her. "Don't call her that. She hasn't—we haven't talked about..." I set the spatula on my palette, needing to wash both of them and a few brushes still. "We haven't talked about labels. Don't call her that when she's gets here."

"I promise you, Penny, she's not driving three hours to visit if she's not thinking of you like that," Mom says, a soft laugh filtering through the dining room. "Now go, get changed. I'll take care of this." She shoos me away with her hands and collects my dirty palette, brushes, and spatula to take them to the kitchen to clean. "Oooooh, I can't wait to meet your *girlfriend*," she adds, walking away as I take my apron off and set it on the hook Mom hung for my studio corner.

"Moooom," I say, but the admonishment in my voice is weakened by my own laugh. "Don't call her that."

"Mm-hmm" is all she says as the sound of water comes from the kitchen.

I check my phone for an updated ETA from Harper and see a missed text saying she'd be here in fifteen minutes—and that was ten minutes ago.

My nerves flutter as I rush upstairs to change out of my painting clothes, and I've only just gotten a clean shirt on over my head when the doorbell rings.

"I'll get it," Mom calls up the stairs, but I'm already racing down them.

"Nope," I tell her, getting to the foyer before she's even turned the kitchen sink off. "I've got it!"

My hands turn sweaty, nervous excitement flooding my veins as I twist the knob and open the door. And then Harper is standing there, backlit by the golden glow of a late afternoon sun. Her dark eyes crinkle with a smile when she sees me, and my own lips tilt up to match hers.

"Hey," I say, opening the door wider for her to come in.

"Penny!" she says before pulling me into a tight hug and letting the scent of her lilac and sweet almond perfume envelope me. "I missed you."

I wrap my arms around her also. "I missed you too," I tell her. The one-on-one texts and calls—and even the group chat, nicknamed *Badass Ladies* by Emma—haven't been enough. But at least in the group chat, we can all keep in touch, and it's nice to see how Clara is doing better while living with Delaney and recovering.

"Oh, is that one of yours?" Harper draws back from the hug and looks over my shoulder, toward my studio corner in the dining room.

I follow her gaze and then her steps as she walks over to the painting still drying on my easel.

"It's beautiful," Harper says, glancing between the canvas and me. "What is it?"

"Thanks. It's, um…" A little bit of pride and embarrassment mingles within my chest in equal measures as she stares at my work.

The painting looks like an abstract blur of colors with shaky thin lines of onyx trailing down the wide canvas, but it's so much more than that. It's a memory—a tribute to the girls and women of Whitewood who didn't make it home with us. There's the icy blue of Sam's eyes and all the layers tucked within them. There are various shades of crimson for Quinn sitting next to buttery and pale yellows for Page and shadow-stained greens for Ms. Evans. Soft lilac and lavenders fade together for Reagan, and blazing oranges burn for Ms. Peterson. The canvas is a riot of colors that complement each other rather than compete. The acrylic paints bleed together, almost like watercolor across the fabric.

"Hold on," I say, standing behind Harper and resting my hands on her shoulders before guiding her to move slightly to the left.

I adjust the angle she's looking from—until the painting morphs away from the abstract, and with a small shift in perception, those thin lines that looked like disjointed scribbles turn into silhouetted outlines of each person: Sam, Quinn, and Page. Ms. Evans, Reagan, and Ms. Peterson. Their likenesses are immortalized on the canvas to remember them by.

Harper gasps at the change, staring at it before turning to me as I let my hands slip off her shoulders.

"You made that?" she asks.

I look at Harper, at a girl who survived literal monsters while her own history is steeped in sorrow. A girl so much like myself. Who is still persevering, trying, and continuing the work on her mental health. A girl so much stronger than she ever knew.

"Yeah," I say, slipping my hand into Harper's as our gazes turn back to the painting I created—something that seemed impossible to do only months ago—and tell her, "I made it."

ACKNOWLEDGMENTS

People talk about writing being a solitary endeavor, but books don't actually get made by one person alone. I'm so grateful for the community I've built over the years, for the amazing people I've been lucky enough to work with, and so thankful to those I get to call my friends too.

To Gabbi Calabrese, my spectacular editor, thank you for finding my stories, advocating for them, and loving them as much as I do. Thank you for your notes that only made this book so much better and for the comments that made me laugh. Thank you for seeing my girls and wanting to share their stories.

To my team at Sourcebooks, thank you so much for the work you've all put into this book! Thank you to my publisher, Dominique Raccah, and my children's publisher, Jenn Gonzalez. Thank you so much to my production editor, Thea Voutiritsas, and my managing editor, Jessica Thelander, as well. And thank you to my art director, Sarah Brody, and my manufacturing lead, Erin LaPointe. Many thanks to my copy editor, Aimee Alker, and I'm sorry for all the missing commas. And thank you to my proofreader, Marinda Valenti. To my cover design team, Lisa Marie Pompilio, Sarah Brody, and Jackie Cummings, and my internal designer, Tara Jaggers, thank you so much for giving me such a gorgeous cover and such beautiful pages inside. I'm so grateful for all the people who put time and effort into this book with me.

Thank you to my amazing agent, Cole Lanahan, who plucked me from the slush and who encouraged me to continue writing horror. Thank you for guiding me with this story and making it stronger than it ever could have been without you. And thank you for being a continued source of encouragement and support in my writing career. I couldn't have gotten here without you.

Many, many thanks to Sarah Marie Page and Caitlin Foley. I'm so grateful to call you guys friends and critique partners. You found me during one of my lonelier writing times, and I couldn't be more thankful to know you both. Thank you for the constant support and encouragement, the help with brainstorming and reading, for being there when I cried over rejections and when I screamed about happy news too. I truly appreciate your friendship and support, and I'm so very grateful to know you both.

To Chrystal Schleyer, my twin and fellow author. We've had our ups and downs, but I'm grateful for the different ways you've supported me over the years and I'm glad to share a love of writing with you. Thank you for reading those first—truly crappy—books when I was starting out.

Thank you to Melissa Hurst, one of my first writer friends so long ago. Your friendship and critiques in those early years helped me get here. Thank you, friend. To Rae Harding and Kate Brecht, thank you for all your support, for those monthly Skype meetings, and for reading my messy drafts. To Jenny Adams, thank you for letting me bother you anytime I needed to vent and for encouraging me during my writing journey. And to Lola Sharp, thank you for your friendship and for celebrating the wins with me.

And thank you to my discord groups! To the Submission Slogs and the 2026 Debut group. You guys have been an invaluable source of friendship, encouragement, information, and help. Thank you all so very much.

To my family, thank you for cheering me on and/or reading my stories. Helena and Angela, thanks for always being eager to read my books. Analisa (told you I'd put your name in my book!), thank you for catching all those typos and errors in those earlier drafts. Nikkie and Aspen, thank you for all the ways you guys have shared about and supported my books. Aunt Danalee, thank you for always asking about my books and for all the ways you've supported me too. And to my parents, thanks for always encouraging your twins to keep writing our stories (and sorry for the cussing in mine).

To the Ferko and Perdew clans, I don't think you guys realize how touching it was to see your excitement and support for my books being published. You guys made me cry (happy tears) more than once, and I'm so blessed to be able to call you all family.

To my children, Corinne and Judah, thank you for making my life richer than I could have ever imagined. The best stories are the ones we make together every day. I love you always and unconditionally.

And Greg, this book wouldn't exist without you. Thank you for always listening to me talk about plots and characters and every weird story idea I've ever had. Thank you for the thousand ways you support me and my writing and for always encouraging me to be my own person and to pursue my interests. I couldn't be happier to have you as my friend and partner in this life. I love you always and forever.

And finally, to my readers, thank you for spending time with my characters and their stories and for trusting me with your time. I hope you enjoyed Penny's story.

ABOUT THE AUTHOR

Christina Ferko grew up in a family of seven girls, including her identical twin sister—who is also an author. Before writing, she dreamed of running away and joining a circus. She even learned how to eat and breathe fire but now spends her time happily writing at home instead. Christina lives in Maryland with her husband and two kids, along with her ever-growing number of animals. You can find her on Instagram @christina_ferko or check out her website at authorchristinaferko.com

sourcebooks fire

Home of the hottest trends in YA!

Visit us online and
sign up for our newsletter at
FIREreads.com

· ·

Follow
@sourcebooksfire
online